PAINTED BLACK

PAINTED BLACK

A NOVEL

GREG KIHN

INTEGRATED MEDIA
NEW YORK

978-1-62467-269-9

Published in 2015 by Open Road Integrated Media, Inc.
345 Hudson Street
New York, NY 10014
www.openroadmedia.com

In loving memory of Christy Harris.
We will miss her immensely.

We also lost Sean Hartter,
brilliant cover artist for *Rubber Soul.*
Rest in peace, Sean.

AUTHOR'S NOTE

This is a work of fiction. None of it actually happened. I took all the facts about Brian Jones and fit my story on top of it. So, technically, you might call it historical fiction. My point is: some of it happened; most of it didn't. Dust Bin Bob, Clovis, and their wives are obviously fictional. Skully and Renee never existed.

At the end of my last novel, *Rubber Soul*, I didn't want to let these characters go, I loved them all so much, so I just kept on writing. What you hold in your hands is the sequel: *Painted Black*.

Much has been written about the mysterious death of Brian Jones. Did Frank Thorogood murder him on the very day he was sacked? Was it because of the treasure rumored to have been hidden in the house? Was it Frank's thuggish day laborers? Was it the Stones? Was it the Mafia? Was there a conspiracy? There are so many unanswered questions. Without a time machine, I doubt we'll ever know.

Once again, I hope you enjoy reading this as much as I did writing it.

PAINTED BLACK

INTRODUCTION

The 1965 European tour by the Rolling Stones had been a nightmare. They'd played most of the cities before but now something new was in the air, like the smell of gasoline and burning tires. Things had become volatile.

Riots ensued wherever they played. Even in such seemingly peaceful places as Zurich, the crowd used the wooden chairs to set fire to the stage. Their rage still dissatisfied, they smashed all the equipment, too.

Every show ended in chaos. The Stones were the champion band for the disenfranchised and rebellious youth of the world. These kids thought rioting and smashing the stage was normal behavior at rock concerts. It was their unstated mission and was demonstrated in their clothes, drugs, and attitudes. None of them would ever get satisfaction. Life was cruel and unfair. *No satisfaction!*

And of course the Stones brought out the absolute worst in their audiences.

Brian Jones was miserable. His chronic asthma made breathing difficult. He suffered through every show. Depression dogged him. He'd never felt so alone on the road as he had on this tour. Detached from London, from his family, from his French girlfriend the Parisian actress/singer Zouzou, Brian was flying solo dangerously low to the ground.

A few weeks earlier, he'd watched while a wild-eyed audience member repeatedly spit on Keith Richards. Again and again, the vile-looking gobs would come arching up from the audience and hit Keith in the chest, hand, and finally the face. Brian could see the revulsion in Keith's eyes when he backed up a few steps. He knew what was coming next. Brian stayed well out of the way, not even pretending to sing into the microphone in front of him. Keith took a two-step running start and kicked the guy square in the face like a penalty kick in soccer. His head snapped back. He went flying head over heels into the crowd, and suddenly a full-scale riot broke out. It was hard to tell if Keith's kick had spurred them on, but suddenly everybody wanted a piece of the Rolling Stones. People began to climb on the stage with blood in their eyes.

Keyboard player Ian Stewart stepped away from his piano and dispensed with another interloper who was running directly at Brian. Stewie stuck his foot out and tripped the attacker who fell face first in front of Brian. A swift kick to the face as he reached for Brian's feet knocked him out. Ian knew if Brian went down, he wouldn't get up again. *Not at this gig.* Brian ducked as the guy's tooth sailed past his head.

The Stones knew when to cut and run. They were practiced at it. They'd seen it all before.

What did all this have to do with the blues? Brian asked himself. This was not why he had created the Rolling Stones. He used to love those minutes on stage with the band. They were the best minutes of the day. It made the rest of the day bearable. It was a reason to get up in the morning. He lived for it. But now, those feelings had soured. There was no relief on stage, either. The tension that accompanied the Stones everywhere they went made Brian uneasy.

Touring together had become a real chore. None of the band seemed to like one another or enjoy traveling. They stayed alone in their hotel rooms most of the time.

Munich had been another typical show, halted several times by the cops while the audience roared its disapproval. The feeling of impending violence was strong in the air like the drop in pressure before a big storm.

During the show, Brian watched scores of young girls carried out unconscious, bruised, and bleeding, yet he still kept playing.

What else could he do? The Rolling Stones onstage were a hurricane of energy. They brought out the passion in people.

They always had their escape routes planned out. The Germans were smart, though, and surrounded the building so that the only thing the Stones could do after the show was wait them out. They were under siege. Outside, the cops used tear gas to break up the crowd.

An argument had erupted backstage as angry voices echoed in the halls. Mick and Keith shouted at Brian about mistakes he made during the show.

Brian just took it. He never fought back. Whenever he felt defensive, he thought, *I started the Rolling Stones. It's my band.*

Suddenly, a lissome blond twenty-one-year-old Italian-born model named Anita Pallenberg walked up to Brian boldly with the idea of introducing herself. She tapped him on the shoulder and when he turned around, she could see tears in his eyes and knew that he'd been crying. Anita was instantly smitten. She reached out and touched his face as one of the tears freed itself from his eye and ran down his cheek.

Their eyes met and time froze.

Brian said, "I don't know who you are, but I need you. Let's spend the night together. I don't want to be alone."

That was how it started with Brian and Anita. Anita was cultured, connected, and spoke four languages. She'd been a professional model from Rome to Paris by the time she was a teenager and had a vast amount of knowledge about the scene. She seemed to know everybody.

She was statuesque; nearly a full head taller than Brian, but she knew how to be small when she had to. Her beauty was feline, mysterious, and she had a touch of madness in her eyes.

The other members of the Stones, namely Mick and Keith, said publicly, "How the fuck does Brian rate a girl like that?"

Brian didn't care. In his mind, he was prince of all he surveyed, including Anita. He believed it was his birthright.

He took her back to swinging London and they became the quintessential hip young professional couple.

This is where our story begins.

CHAPTER ONE

THE RETURN OF DUST BIN BOB

Blam! Blam! Blam!

"What the hell was that?" asked Bobby Dingle, owner and proprietor of Dingles of Newburgh Antique Shop, Soho, London.

It sounded like somebody desperately banging on a glass door with his bare palms. When Bobby went to investigate, he saw a crowd of young mods, at least twenty of them, mostly females, sprinting past the shop. They headed up the street.

The remnants of Bobby's Liverpool accent shone through in moments like this. "'Ang on. What's all this then?"

Patti, Bobby's pretty twenty-one-year-old assistant, looked over his shoulder.

"Looks like they're chasing somebody."

The crowd rounded the corner and disappeared.

"I wonder what's going on?"

They resumed their task of closing up the shop.

Outside, Brian Jones was running for his life. He had his driver park his Rolls-Royce Silver Cloud a few blocks away. He got out and walked quickly through the streets, confident that he could make his destination before being recognized. The problem was that Brian Jones, founder of the Rolling Stones and one of the most recognizable rock icons of swinging London, could not possibly walk down the street without drawing a crowd.

He slowed to say hello to a couple of young dollies outside a trendy boutique. They giggled and followed him when he continued on his way. Then he passed a hair salon that virtually emptied out when they saw him, all the patrons and employees following Brian like the Pied Piper. Two of the hairstylists snipped their scissors as if to say, "I want a lock of his golden hair."

Brian walked faster. A pair of tall girls in miniskirts tried to block him, their long legs moving slightly akimbo as he deftly avoided contact by sidestepping. Their miniskirts rode up pink tights to youthful thighs as they both teetered on their high heels. They stumbled and grabbed at Brian.

Brian broke into a run. Two guys who had been pacing him were talking incessantly to him, but he didn't hear them. They began to run, too. Their chatter became more desperate as they realized Brian was escaping.

Brian picked up the pace. He managed to distance himself when the stumbling girls created a diversion and now he was half a block ahead and still running. By the time they realized he was getting away, they accelerated, too. It was like the opening scene of *A Hard Day's Night* as the fans pressed in on him, except these weren't smiling happy Beatles fans, these were frustrated, pissed-off Stones fans. They all had something to say to Brian.

Brian circled the block and was now approaching Dingles again. Gasping for breath, Brian banged on the glass door a second time. The crowd was closing in. Brian was trapped. He could hear the snipping scissors getting closer.

Brian looked over his shoulder at the onrushing mob. Some had already produced Stones album covers and were now waving them to be autographed.

Suddenly, the glass door opened inward, and a pair or friendly arms reached out and pulled him inside. The door clicked shut and the lock engaged. Bobby flipped the sign in the window from open to closed.

"Hey!" Brian said. "What are you doing?"

"It's okay, I think we just saved you from certain mayhem."

The mob ran past Dingles, unaware that Brian had escaped.

"I don't think they saw you."

"Thank God for that."

Brian straightened. "Dust Bin Bob?"

Bobby shook Brian's hand. "Nobody calls me that anymore except the Beatles."

"If it's good enough for the Beatles, it's good enough for the Stones."

Dingles of Newburgh attracted an interesting clientele. As an antique shop in the middle of the trendy Carnaby Street neighborhood, it seemed out of place wedged between posh boutiques with kitschy names like I Was Lord Kitchener's Valet, Granny Takes a Trip, and Kleptomania.

Swinging London swirled around Dingles; girls in colorful miniskirts and neon leggings and guys dressed in the latest mod gear stopped and looked in the shop window at the myriad of curious items displayed.

Bobby Dingle started at the bottom, growing up poor on the hardscrabble streets of Liverpool with his friends, the young, unknown Beatles. He ran a stall for his father's secondhand shop at the flea market in Penny Lane. It was because of his love for American R&B records that the raw young Beatles sought him out as their friend. John renamed him Dust Bin Bob and the nickname stuck, although Bobby had come to dislike it. He was far from the dustbin now and was proud of his achievements. He'd come a very long way. Bobby Dingle was a successful businessman with profitable antique stores in London and Baltimore. What's more, he was the trusted friend of the Beatles.

The fact that the Fab Four shopped there assured Dingles of Newburgh a fair share of notoriety and a steady stream of scene makers. All four Beatles had been spotted at Dingles on different occasions. It often made the gossip column and did wonders for Bobby's business. He'd been staying open late, attracting club goers and students.

The store itself was an old chemist shop with two large front windows and a beautiful art deco glass display case. Bobby had done some renovations, but the old-time feel of the chemist shop shone through.

The shadows of late afternoon slanted through the narrow street giving everything a golden hue.

Patti gasped. "That's Brian Jones!" she said. "From the Rolling Stones!"

Brian flashed a bemused smile and strolled around the shop dressed in an eye-bending red-and-gold Edwardian outfit with elaborate ruffles and lace.

He was shorter than he appeared on TV; five foot seven or eight, Bobby reckoned. His hair was longer, too. It shimmered with precious highlights in the late afternoon sun. He'd heard that Brian was fastidious about his hair and washed it every day. His mutton-chop sideburns were slowly encroaching down the sides of his face, giving him an out-of-time look.

"Would you care for a cup of tea?" Dust Bin Bob offered. "We were just closing up."

"That sounds wonderful." Brian's voice was soft, nearly effeminate, and he spoke perfect "Cheltenham School for Boys" English.

"Do you mind if I call you 'Dust My Broom' instead of 'Dust Bin Bob'?"

"You mean like the Elmore James song?"

Brian grinned. His face lit up. "I knew I could trust you, Dustman."

"Just because I know about Elmore James?"

Brian nodded slowly. "Exactly. There was a time when we were living in poverty with Mick and Keith at this horrible flat in Edith Grove and we judged *everybody* on their knowledge of the blues. Back then, nobody knew shit. There were just a few of us. We were the keepers of the flame."

Bobby raised an eyebrow. "Well then, I guess I pass the Elmore James test."

"I used to play a good version of 'Dust My Broom.' I did all the Elmore James stuff. I swear, his guitar used to make me cry. It was so beautiful. At the time, I was the only guy in London playing slide."

Bobby respected Brian's roots. They came from the same musical turf. As a youth, the legendary Dust Bin Bob had influenced the nascent Beatles by selecting rare American R&B singles from his collection to play for the band that subtly altered their direction. The memory of those innocent days came flooding back to Bobby.

He remembered John's penchant for singing R&B girl group songs like "Please Mr. Postman," by the Marvelettes and "Baby, It's You," by the Shirelles. John convincingly changed the gender of the song so it always sounded natural. Bobby loved turning them on to songs that no other male Merseyside group would touch with a barge pole. Of course, the Beatles were fearless. The passion in John's voice could make any song his own. Whether he sang the Dust Bin Bob–recommended "Money" by Barrett Strong or "Twist and Shout" by the Isley Brothers, John had no problem moving from one side of the musical spectrum to the other without batting an eye. He could belt them out or sing them straight.

Brian Jones fulfilled a similar role for the early Rolling Stones. He put the band together, gave them their name, carefully chose the material, did the arrangements, and generally assumed command of the musical direction the Stones would continue on for decades.

The Rolling Stones were Brian's band. That was a well-known fact.

Brian created the Stones to do straight blues. At first, it was strictly the purist stuff, but soon they were injecting high-powered Chicago R&B into their live shows: Chuck Berry, Muddy Waters, Bo Diddley, Howlin' Wolf, and the like. The Stones set their roots firmly in black American music. Brian had exquisite taste in R&B and handpicked the songs the band would cover. Musically, it was the same thing musically that Bobby had done for the Beatles.

One of their first singles was "Little Red Rooster," a song written by Willie Dixon and recorded by Howlin' Wolf. Brian's haunting slide guitar gave the song its commercial hook. After it was a hit, he was proud to say, "It's a song about a chicken, man! I'd like to see another group do that!"

It wasn't until Ronnie Bennett of the Ronnettes took the band to see James Brown at the Apollo Theater during their first visit to New York that they realized the true potential of what they were doing. Later, they had to follow James Brown in the feature-length concert film *The T.A.M.I. Show.* James jolted the band into a new reality.

That was right around the time that their manager, Andrew Loog Oldham, cajoled Mick and Keith into writing original material and the reigns of the band slipped out of Brian's hands permanently.

Dust Bin Bob knew the story. John Lennon had told him most of it. Contrary to published reports, the Stones and the Beatles were not rivals. The two bands knew each other and liked each other. Indeed, it was John and Paul's contribution to the Stones of the song "I Want to Be Your Man" that became one of their early hits.

The Stones frenzied R&B–flavored version contrasted greatly with the Beatles version, sung by Ringo on the *With the Beatles* album. The Stones supercharged version was like Elmore James on speed. Once again, Brian's slide guitar provided the hook.

"What brings you to my humble shop?"

Brian lit a cigarette. "You mean besides running for my life? You saved me."

Bobby looked out the window. The coast was clear now.

Patti pointed to a nick on Brian's neck. "You're bleeding?"

Brian wiped it away and looked at the blood on his finger. One of the girls had jabbed him with her sharp fingernails.

"You want a Band-Aid?"

Brian shook his head. "Nah. Let it bleed."

Dust Bin Bob bowed. "As you wish. Anything you care to look at while you're here?"

"Yes, I'd like to look at that antique snuff box again."

"Of course, let me get it for you."

Patti tried not to stare at Brian, but she had been reduced to a giggling schoolgirl. Brian hardly noticed. He was so used to that type of behavior it barely registered with him.

Bobby returned with the snuffbox. He noticed that Brian's

eyes were red and he smelled like he'd been smoking hashish in his limo.

"Here it is. It's really quite exquisite."

He carefully handed the small oval gold-and-enamel snuffbox to Brian. It was absolutely beautiful. Brian turned it over in his hands and opened it.

Dust Bin Bob filled in the history.

"It was created by Pierre-Claude Pottier of Paris in 1789 for Louis XVI. As you know, Louis XVI snuffboxes are extremely rare, and this is a particularly nice one. Notice the engravings of naked women around the sides."

Brian scratched his finger inside and sniffed it.

Bobby nodded. "It's been cleaned, of course."

Brian examined the box again.

"It doesn't hold very much."

"Excuse me?"

"It's not very big. It would probably only hold a couple of grams."

Bobby nodded. "Yes, I see what you mean. This was a standard size for the era. It was designed for snuff."

"It wouldn't hold very much . . . er . . . snuff, would it?"

Bobby raised an eyebrow.

"Whatever snortable material you place in the box would be dry and secure and I'm sure it would fit your needs. It's bigger than it looks."

Brian pointed across the room at something in the window.

"I'd like to see that antique recorder."

Bobby fetched the recorder from the window.

"It's German-made, over a hundred years old. You'll notice it's the classic baroque design, and it's made from pearwood, the preferred fruitwood for superior tone in recorders. It plays beautifully."

Brian took the exquisite wooden flutelike instrument from Bobby's hand and played the famous riff from "Ruby Tuesday." The ageless sound of the recorder cut the air like a sword. It had an innocent, unpretentious sound, with just a hint of melancholy. Brian played the hypnotic refrain. For a moment, time in the shop stood still.

Several people from the crowd that had been chasing Brian were now milling about the front of the shop looking in.

Bobby Dingle was no fool. He realized that a gaggle of curious onlookers would ruin the moment and send Brian on his way. One of the girls tried the door, found it locked, and cupped her hands on the window to peer inside. Bobby surreptitiously slipped over to the side and pulled the shades.

Brian was in his own world playing the recorder.

"Nice mellow tone," he said.

"The fruitwood ages and gives it that rich sound. That's a really nice one. It's in perfect condition."

"Where did you find it?"

Bobby smiled; acquisitions were his pride and joy. He knew just where to look and just what to buy. That was his talent.

"At an estate sale for Lord something or other. The family had fallen on hard times, owed a fortune in taxes, so they had a big sale and auctioned everything off. Finding out about the sale, that's the key."

"It's beautiful," Brian said.

He started playing another tune. This one Bobby recognized as the second chorale from Beethoven's Symphony no. 9 in D Minor. He had heard about Brian's uncanny ability to pick up any instrument and master it in just one sitting. In fact, according to John Lennon that's what kept him in the Stones. He'd played dulcimer on "Lady Jane," marimbas on "Under My Thumb," sitar on "Paint It Black," and a myriad of other instruments to keep him relevant within the band. Brian's multi-instrumentalism became his signature.

"Would you like to buy it?" Bobby asked.

Brian looked surprised. "Yes, of course. Didn't you put it there just so I would find it?"

Bobby laughed. "How did you know?"

Brian tapped his forehead. "ESP, my dear Dustman."

"And the price, did you know that, too?"

"Ahh, the price. Well, to tell you the truth I don't much care about the price."

"Really? Because the Louis XVI snuff box is around six thousand pounds."

Brian shrugged. "One of the reasons I come here is that you always know the discrete way to bill the Stones business office."

Bobby smiled. "I learned that from Brian Epstein."

"It makes life so much easier. Besides, I almost never carry cash."

"I'll make you a great deal on the recorder so it balances out with the snuff box."

"I'll take them both. It's a pleasure doing business with the legendary Dust Bin Bob."

They stepped away from the window into the interior of the shop, away from the gathering crowd. There were at least a dozen people outside now, talking excitedly.

As Bobby went to write the receipt, Brian went into a sneezing jag.

"Allergies: asthma, dust, pollen, you name it," Brian sniffed. "I'm never right."

Bobby finished his paperwork and put it away. He knew better than to give it to Brian. He would send it to Andrew Loog Oldham's office in Ivor Court, Gloucester Place. He knew the address because Kit Lambert and The Who had their offices there and Keith Moon was a regular customer.

Brian played with his new toy, the antique recorder. He seemed to be unaware of the rapidly growing crowd outside the front door. The shades were drawn, but there were plenty of cracks to look through. Bobby realized if Brian stopped to sign autographs he could be there for hours. He knew from his experiences growing up with the Beatles how quickly a crowd could form.

Bobby said, "I suggest you leave by the back door."

Brian seemed surprised.

"The back door? Why?"

Bobby nodded in the direction of the front window of the shop, now full of onlookers pressing their faces against the glass.

"Oh, I see what you mean."

"We have a delivery door that opens into the alley behind the shop. You can avoid the autograph hunters by going that way."

Brian sighed. "Another potential disaster averted. You've done this before, Dust Bin Bob?"

Bobby wanted to correct Brian. His name was Robert Dingle, not Dust Bin Bob. It had taken the Beatles years to get over that nickname, and except for John Lennon, they'd all dropped it. Now here he was building a new myth with Brian. Bobby almost said something, but held his tongue. Things were going so well with Brian, why change the dynamic? Besides, it didn't bother him nearly as much as it used to.

Bobby wrapped up the snuffbox and the recorder in heavy brown paper and slipped the two packages in a bag.

"Thank you, Sir Dust-My-Broom."

"You are most welcome, Prince Elmore."

The delivery door was in the back of the shop, so no one could see them leave. Brian stepped out into the alley and stood next to some garbage cans.

"Where's your car?" Bobby asked.

"A few blocks over. What are you doing tonight?"

Bobby looked back at the shop.

"Well, my wife is leaving town tomorrow, so I'll be staying with her on her last night."

"Anita and I are having a few people over tonight for a late dinner, and I thought you might want to join us."

Bobby blinked. Have dinner with legendary Brian Jones and Anita Pallenberg at Brian's rock-star mansion?

"John Lennon might show up. I know you two go way back. I invited him, but he's so flaky you never know."

"That sounds like fun."

"Where is your wife going?"

Bobby cleared his throat. "She's going back to Baltimore

to see her father who's in the hospital. She's taking my three-year-old son, Winston, with her. I'm afraid we won't be able to make it."

Brian pushed his blond bangs back from his forehead and peered at Bobby.

"Baltimore? Isn't that in America?"

Bobby nodded.

"Well, if you change your mind . . ."

He heard a movement behind him, coming from the trash cans.

Brian and Bobby turned around to see a beautiful twenty-one-year-old groupie emerge from behind a garbage dumpster. She had blond hair cut exactly like Anita Pallenberg's. She was dressed in a black leather micro-mini skirt with lacy black tights and a black silk blouse. She was lithe, with perky breasts and long legs. She wore dark eye makeup.

This girl had obviously studied Anita and had reproduced her look down to the tiniest detail. She appeared out of nowhere.

"I'll come to your party," she said in an American accent. "And I'll do whatever you want."

Brian squinted at her.

"How did you know we would be using the back door?" Bobby asked. "Everyone else is in the front."

"I checked it out when I first got here. I knew these old shops had alleys and that usually means delivery doors. I just put two and two together."

"But how did you know I'd be here?" Brian said.

She had an overly dramatic breathless Marilyn Monroe voice.

"I've been following you. My name is Renee. I'm from New York. I saw you at Carnegie Hall. I think you've seen me around."

"Following me?" Brian looked concerned.

"Lots of girls follow you, so don't act so surprised. I know most of them. Every once in a while you'll take one home. I'm just waiting my turn. It's my destiny."

"Yes, I believe I've seen you."

"I'm ready whenever you are."

Brian was amused.

"You're not lacking in the confidence department, are you?"

Renee smiled her sweetest smile.

"I know what kind of women you like, and I can be any of them."

Bobby blushed. "You look like Anita."

Renee said, "Of course I do. I can look like anything Brian wants."

Brian suddenly became uncomfortable. "It's time for me to leave."

Renee reached out and touched Brian's face.

"You are my destiny, Brian Jones. Don't fight it. If you want, I can come over tonight and do you and Anita, too. We can have a ménage à trois. I know you like that."

Brian looked her over again, reconsidering the proposition. A flicker of interest flashed in his eyes. He did like two or more women in bed. But not tonight.

"No, I don't think so," he said.

"Anyway, think about it. I'll be around."

Brian looked at Bobby and shook his head.

"I'm leaving."

Renee said, "Walk you to your car?"

Brian shook his head. "Not today."

Bobby strolled with Brian back to his limo. Renee stayed a block behind.

"That chick gives me the creeps," Bobby said.

Brian chuckled. "She's just a groupie, what do you expect? There are lots of chicks like that hovering around the Stones."

"She seemed obsessed."

Brian said, "Women and rock and roll, man. Chicks. Chicks are everywhere. They make the world go 'round. I've heard it said that most bands are pulled apart by women. Can you believe that? A band breaking up because of women? That's the difference with the Stones and every other band in the world. If the Stones have women problems, the Stones get new women."

Bobby wanted to comment on what he'd heard about the disruptive effect that Brian's current girlfriend, Anita Pallenberg, had on the Stones but let it pass. It was not his place to judge. Brian was a complex and sensitive individual. Besides, Bobby had heard that same exact quote come out of Keith Richards's mouth, so he figured it must have come from the Stones publicist.

Brian said, "Are you sure you and your wife can't join us?"

Bobby shook his head. "No. Sorry. It's our last night together."

Bobby loved his wife, Cricket. She was an American, a Baltimore girl, and she had recently soured on life in London. She started out loving it, but that was several years ago when it was all exciting and new. She had become increasingly homesick over time. After a long, miserable winter cooped up in their apartment with Winston, she had developed a chronic respiratory infection that wouldn't go away. She coughed all the time and felt miserable. She longed to go home to Baltimore where, she was convinced, she would finally get well.

When her mother called to tell her that her father was in the hospital suffering from diverticulitis, she didn't think twice. She bought her ticket the same day. She wanted to be by his side. Maybe they would help heal each other.

Her bags were packed, her tickets paid for, and she was leaving tomorrow. They hadn't discussed when she'd be coming back.

Bobby smiled and graciously declined the invitation again.

"Thanks, it sounds wonderful, but I'm afraid it's impossible tonight."

Brian slipped a card into Bobby's palm.

"Here's the address in case you change your mind."

Just then, Renee walked up to the limo. Bobby put the card in his pocket. Brian shook his head and chuckled.

"No need for secrecy with that bird. She already knows where I live. She's been to my house."

"What?"

"She camps out in front." He turned to Renee. "Don't you, love?"

Renee expertly reapplied her lipstick, staring into a tiny mirror.

"Of course I do, darling. I'm just waiting for you to let me in."

* * *

Bobby arrived home feeling anxious. Cricket avoided talking about her return, knowing it would upset Bobby, but he knew she would bring it up tonight. They had always split their time between Baltimore and London, with Bobby operating stores in both locations. But now that the London location had become the hip shop of choice for the new royalty of rich rock stars, it was difficult for Bobby to leave. Business had exploded, and he found himself too busy to go back. This didn't sit well with Cricket. On top of being homesick, she had recently become annoyed that their son was developing an English accent. Bobby knew she really wanted him to come with her and wanted to avoid the subject.

"Brian Jones came in the shop today," Bobby said, changing the direction the conversation might take. "He bought an expensive antique snuff box and a beautiful pearwood recorder."

Cricket frowned. "That's nice, but when are you coming to Baltimore?"

"A week or two. At the most."

"A week? I'll bet it's more like a month." Cricket sighed. "I'm going to miss you and so is Winston. It's the first time we've been apart since you traveled with the Beatles in '66."

Bobby put his arms around her.

"I'm going to miss you, too. But you and Winston will be in Baltimore soon, and that will perk your dad right up. He'll get better in no time."

Cricket coughed the chest-rattling chronic cough that she'd had all winter.

"And I can finally get rid of this congestion. This London

weather is horrible. How these Brits cope with it without becoming suicidal is beyond me. What did you say about Brian Jones?"

Bobby paused a moment.

"Brian came into the shop today. He invited us over to his house tonight for a late dinner."

"Brian Jones?"

"Yes, Brian Jones of the Rolling Stones invited us to his house tonight. Late dinner he calls it. I wonder what time they eat."

"Brian Jones? What is he having, some sort of orgy?"

Bobby laughed. "Oh, don't believe what you read in the newspapers. He's a very charming chap."

Cricket looked at Bobby suspiciously.

"What did you tell him?"

"I said my beautiful, precious wife was flying to the States in the morning, and we couldn't possibly go."

Cricket smiled. "Good boy."

Then she kissed him on the cheek.

The doorbell and rang and broke the mood. Bobby answered it quickly. He opened the door to see two old friends from Baltimore, Clovis Hicks and his wife, Erlene. They were the first two people Bobby met when he came to America as a merchant marine. He had walked off the cargo ship *Pilgrim's Progress* and wandered into the infamous red-light district of East Baltimore Street known as "The Block," where Clovis was a guitar player and Erlene was a stripper. All in their mid-twenties now, the group's friendship had been steadfast. Clovis followed Bobby to London to seek his fortune in music. After all, everybody knew that Dust Bin Bob was a personal friend of the Beatles. That couldn't hurt.

The genuinely talented Clovis had landed a job as assistant engineer at Olympic Recording Studios in London and found himself working with the Rolling Stones. Everybody liked Clovis. His good-natured manner was a breath of fresh air in a business where narcissistic, egocentric behavior was the norm. Clovis was not only a gifted musician; he was an excellent technician as well. But it was his easygoing manner and ability to deal with all kinds of people that made him invaluable. He'd enhanced his résumé a little to get the job—and because he was American, nobody seemed to notice.

Erlene and Clovis stood in the doorway, backlit by the sunset streets of London.

"Sorry to barge in on y'all. We dropped by to wish Cricket bon voyage."

Erlene held up a bottle of champagne. She blew into a plastic party horn, and it quacked like sick duck.

Bobby grinned and invited them in. Cricket and Winston ran over and hugged Erlene.

Erlene's Baltimore accent hadn't dimmed in the slightest; in fact, it seemed sharper than ever. Like the Old Bay Seasoning she brought with her for cooking, she never lost the flavor of the Chesapeake Bay.

"I wish I was going back with you, honey. A little shot of the Big B would be just what the doc ordered. Some crab cakes and a nice cold National Bohemian beer. I'd love a Polish sausage from Pollock Johnny's right about now."

"A Natty Bo and a Pollock?" Clovis said. "*Hmm-hmm*, good. Yep, no doubt about it, Charm City has her virtues. Throw in a hot dog at an Orioles game in Memorial Stadium, and I'm in heaven."

Erlene said, "You'll be doing all that by tomorrow, hon. Are you nervous?"

Cricket nodded. "I hate flying, but it's worth it to go home. I was just trying to get my husband here to commit to when he's coming over."

Erlene clucked. "You better get him to make a date or you'll never see him again."

Which city Bobby and Cricket would eventually make their primary residence was a constant bone of contention between the two of them lately. Cricket wanted to live in her hometown of Baltimore, and Bobby was very comfortable in London. They split their time. Knowing he'd eventually lose that battle, Bobby procrastinated.

"Don't say that," Bobby said. "Business is booming. I can't just drop everything and go."

Clovis, whose legendary blond hair had been styled and restyled from Elvis to Wayne Cochran to John Lennon, was currently wearing his hair in a modified Brian Jones cut without the mutton-chop sideburns. His slim guitar player's body sported a few jailhouse tattoos. Clovis had the look of a working musician.

"*Who-wee*, Bobby! Once Cricket leaves town, you and me are gonna have some fun! The mice will play while the cat's away!"

"Clovis, please!" Bobby snapped. "She'll get the wrong idea."

"I've already got the wrong idea," she said, partially joking.

Three-year-old Winston ran around their legs. Erlene picked him up and threw him up in the air.

"Come give Auntie Erlene a nice big hug, hon!"

Winston laughed. "Awn-tie Erlene!"

Cricket said, "See? I told you he was developing a British accent. He calls her 'awn-tie.' We better get out of town before he turns into Little Lord Fauntleroy."

Bobby went into the kitchen and got some unmatching glass champagne flutes.

They all sat around the living room, and Bobby poured the bubbly. He raised his glass to offer a toast, but before he could, Erlene interrupted him.

"To the Big B! May Cricket have a safe trip!"

"To Baltimore!" said Clovis and Cricket. Bobby tapped their glasses.

They drank together. The champagne was dry and the conversation spicy.

Bobby said, "Brian Jones came in the shop today. I was just telling Cricket he invited us over for a late dinner."

"He invited us, too!" Clovis said. "I've been working with the Stones at Olympic. Jonesy left the studio early today and invited me on the way out. Told me to bring Erlene. I wonder what he has in mind?"

"What's a late dinner?" Cricket asked.

Erlene answered. "I think it's around ten o'clock. Are you going?"

"Of course not. This is our last night together," Bobby interjected.

Cricket crossed her arms. Bobby knew that was a sign.

"He's probably going to have drugs and groupies there."

"He better not!" Erlene exclaimed. "I'll rip him a new one!"

"Actually, he lives with Anita Pallenberg, the German movie star. There won't be any groupies there. It's just a dinner party," Clovis said. "He said John Lennon was coming. I'd love to see John."

"How about the drugs?"

Clovis became defensive.

"I'll just smoke a little weed to be sociable."

Erlene went on a Brian Jones jag.

"Isn't he always getting busted? How do you know the cops won't raid the place while we're there?"

Clovis sighed. "Okay, if you don't want to go, we won't go. I'll make up some excuse."

A period of silence followed. Then Clovis flipped to the opposite point of view with a big grin.

"Wait a minute! Are we crazy? Brian Jones from the Rolling Fucking Stones invites us *and* John Lennon to his house for dinner and we're not going? What's wrong with this picture?" Clovis's voice was loud and brassy. "We're goin'. That's it. You too, Bobby-Boy."

"Wait a sec—"

"No, honey, let him speak," Cricket said softly. "He's right, you know."

"What are you saying?"

Cricket put her tiny hand on his shoulder.

"I'm saying maybe you should go with Erlene and Clovis. It's too important to miss. He's about as big a client as they come."

"But . . ."

"I know what I said. I've changed my mind. Just be home before I leave so I can kiss you good-bye."

Erlene said, "We'll keep an eye on him, hon. He's safe with us."

Cricket said, "I trust him."

Clovis said, "I'm bringing my guitar. We're gonna jam. You wanna know something else? It's supposed to be a secret, but I heard that Mick and Keith are gonna drop by. Mick and Keith! That's three fifths of the Stones. If John comes, that's one quarter of the Beatles. If you miss this, you are out of your fuckin' mind."

Bobby looked at Cricket and squeezed her hand.

"Are you sure you don't mind?"

Cricket tried to act cool.

"Go, have your fun. Leave before I change my mind."

CHAPTER TWO

NINETEENTH NERVOUS BREAKDOWN

Brian Jones's address at 1 Courtfield Road, South Kensington was a beautiful mansion townhouse with twenty-foot ceilings. The stately brick building had a balcony over the grand entrance from which Brian could address the people on the street below like the pontiff on Easter morn.

Bobby arrived with Clovis and Erlene. Brian welcomed them like old friends. There were several guests already there that Bobby didn't recognize. Brian introduced Christopher Gibbs, an antique dealer, and Robert Fraser, an art gallery owner. Anita had invited one of her strikingly beautiful model friends. Bobby thought he'd seen her face on billboards around London. Blond, thin, and aloof, she had the same Anita Pallenberg–look that was so popular in London at the time. Anita introduced her as Claudine Jillian.

Brian acted the ultimate host and flittered about refilling

wineglasses and making conversation. Bobby declined all offers of beverages, mindful of Brian's fondness for dosing people with drugs at his parties. At one point, Bobby snuck back to the kitchen and filled his water glass from the tap thinking at least that would be safe.

Anita spoke German, French, Italian, and English, often at the same time. Brian filled a big hookah with hash and fired it up until billowing blue smoke filled the room. Bobby wondered what would happen if the cops happened by just now. Brian didn't seem to care.

Clovis sat on the floor and rifled through Brian's impressive collection of blues records. Bobby sat next to him, intrigued by what they might find. After all, this was the man who created the Rolling Stones. Clovis pulled out the album *Bo Diddley's Sixteen All-Time Greatest Hits* and held it up for everyone to see.

"My favorite album cover of all time!" Clovis gushed. "Just look at this thing!"

Brian took it from him and examined the front as he had done a hundred times before.

"It's just big block letters on a white background. That's it. No artwork, no nothing."

"That's the joke, Brian," Clovis said.

Bobby said, "Marshall Chess didn't budget much for the cover art on that one, eh? What do you think? Thirty-five cents?"

Bobby and Clovis broke up laughing. They thought they were hilarious. Brian just stared at them. He had every album Bo had ever made. It was not a collection he took lightly. Brian Jones had actually recorded in the same room that Bo recorded in at 2120 South Michigan Avenue in Chicago. When the band first walked into Chess Records, Brian got the shock of his young life to find his idol, Muddy Waters, wearing overalls and painting the studio ceiling. Muddy had actually helped carry their amps that day, his face and hair flecked with white paint.

Bobby knew Bo's album covers were always mind-bending. Brian had them all: *Bo Diddley Is a Gun Slinger*, *Have Guitar, Will Travel*, *Surfin' With Bo Diddley*, and *Bo Diddley's Beach Party*.

"Hey, how come all the people at *Bo Diddley's Beach Party* are white?" Clovis joked.

"Because white kids are the only ones who can afford him," Bobby replied with a smile.

Clovis put the record on the record player and with the first song, Bo Diddley leaped from the speakers. The song rocketed past them like a musical missile in the most frantic two minutes and thirty seconds Bobby had heard in a long time. Fueled by the frenzied maracas of Jerome Green, Bo Diddley's music was jet-propelled. It traveled at supersonic speed. Bobby and Clovis could both appreciate the effect it had on the Stones.

Clovis pointed to the album cover for *Have Guitar, Will Travel*. It featured Bo on a red-and-white 1957 Vespa Cushman Eagle motor scooter with his unique rectangular Gretsch guitar hanging off his shoulder.

"Do you know what this means?" he asked.

"Have guitar, will travel?"

"Yeah, there was an American TV show, a western, starring Rickard Boone as a gunfighter for hire named Paladin and his card said 'Have gun, will travel.' See?"

Brian examined the cover.

"Oh, I get it! So it's a take-off on the TV show? Bloody brilliant!"

Brian vacillated between being a blues snob and a giggly kid who just loved the music. Clovis pointed out to Brian that it was the vibrato on Bo Diddley's Fender Super Reverb guitar amp that pushed the music along as much as the maracas. Brian pointed out Bo's finesse with the flat pick had a lot to do about it, too.

The three men talked, shouted, and argued about Chicago blues. They stayed in their private world for more than an hour, ignoring the rest of the party until dinner was served.

"We're having beef with Yorkshire pudding," Brian announced. "I hope no one's a vegetarian."

There were a few laughs around the room. It turned out that Claudine actually was a vegetarian, but rarely ate. She decided to skip dinner entirely and disappeared into one of the upstairs rooms. *What was she doing up there?* Bobby wondered.

The food smelled wonderful. They all ate the beef without delay. Conversation was temporally replaced by the satisfied sounds of eating.

During dinner, there came a knock on the door. Brian got up to answer. He returned a minute later with Marianne Faithfull, the beautiful pop singer and Mick Jagger's girlfriend.

She was apologizing profusely as she entered the room.

"Mick says he's terribly sorry, but he and Keith got a last-minute song idea, and they told me to tell you that they're busy working on the next big hit."

Brian frowned. "They told you to tell me that? Those bastards! It's not enough that they stole the band away from me, now they have to control the songwriting and publishing, too! Rub it in, boys, rub it in. The next Stones hit? Fuck them."

"Well now, perhaps we shouldn't judge them too harshly. They said they might be along later. You know how they are."

Brian snorted. "Yeah, I know how they are. John's not here, either."

His voice took on an ugly edge.

"Right. So why are you here?"

Marianne smiled and lit up the room. She waved her hands around like a dancer.

"Brian, you invited me. I've been looking forward to it. Just because those two are rude is no reason for me to miss out on one of your fabulous dinner parties. That is, if I'm still invited."

Brian softened a little.

"That's nice of you, Marianne. I appreciate it. But Mick and Keith can go fuck themselves as far as I'm concerned."

"I know you planned this evening as a way to bring the boys together, and I admire you for it. Mick can be a bit of an asshole at times. The way they treat you is deplorable."

Bobby watched as Brian's mood swung back and forth. The more he got to know Brian Jones, the more confused he became. Which one was the real Brian? Was it the sullen, depressed Brian brooding over minutia or was it the happy, charming Brian, the one considered the most recognizable of the Rolling Stones and voted sexiest rock star of the year?

Brian instantly became petulant.

"I've been working with Keith behind Mick's back, you know."

Marianne smiled sweetly.

"Mick knows Keith has been hanging here. It's no big secret. He's all for it."

Brian pouted.

"I was hoping we could jam, maybe kick around some musical ideas. I was a fool. Those two don't want me in the band anymore. I can feel it."

Marianne shook her head. She was like an angel. Brian looked into her eyes.

"Don't talk that way, Brian. We all love you. It wouldn't be the Rolling Stones without you, everybody knows that."

Brian's face twitched.

"Really? They could go on without me for another fifty years for all we know."

Marianne laughed.

"Fifty years? That's ridiculous."

"Is it? Keith told me they want to go psychedelic on the next album. I heard some of the songs. If the Stones start doing that crap, they won't last another year. Can you imagine the Rolling Stones going psychedelic? It's a bloody joke."

Brian sat back down at the table and began to eat his steak, chewing it slowly and deliberately. His sullen mood hovered over the room like a dark cloud. No one spoke for a few moments until Marianne suddenly turned to Bobby, Clovis, and Erlene. Erlene quickly introduced herself. The tension broke. Erlene waved at her.

"Why don't you sit over here with us, hon? We don't bite."

Marianne joined them. Normal conversation resumed around the table. Brian ate in brooding silence.

Anita offered a toast. Her German accent colored the words that were already slightly slurred from the wine.

"To Brian Jones and the Stones!"

As they raised their glasses, Bobby hoisted his untouched wineglass. Anita stood like an apparition. The light behind her made her dress look translucent. Her thin fashion model body was perfectly silhouetted. She wore no underwear of any kind. Brian looked up from his plate and snorted.

"Sit down, bitch! How dare you say that?"

Anita reacted as if she'd been slapped.

"I'll say whatever I want!"

"This is my house!"

"Fuck your house!"

Brian raised his hand and rose out of his chair in a threatening manner as if he were about hit Anita. Anita slowly sat down. She took a big swallow of wine and looked around for her cigarettes. She found one, lit it with great finality, and blew the smoke in Brian's face.

Brian sounded like he was on the verge of tears. His voice trembled slightly as he spoke.

"It's not enough that Mick and Keith stood me up for dinner . . . they've taken everything from me. The band is my life, and now they've taken that away from me. . . . The Rolling Stones have always been *my band*. I started it. I can't go on like this anymore."

Bobby, Clovis, and Erlene had been watching the drama unfold with Marianne from their side of the big table. Erlene leaned over to Marianne and whispered in her Baltimore accent.

"Pretty lively dinner conversation, hon, but my steak is tougher 'n shoe leather."

Marianne giggled.

"All English steaks are tough to chew and even harder to swallow. Only the French can cook steak properly."

"I can bar-be-cue the hell out of a T-bone," Erlene opined.

"The English like to boil their meat until it's tasteless, just like they leach the color out of life."

"Hey!" Brian shouted. "Shut up!"

Erlene and Marianne looked up, surprised. Clovis looked at Bobby and shook his head.

"Let it go. It's the wine talkin'," he said in a stage whisper.

Erlene acted as though she was about to say something but suddenly changed her mind.

"How about a song?" Clovis said. He pushed away from the table and picked up his acoustic guitar.

Brian's eyes shifted. The thunder seemed to flow out of him not in one great bone-jarring clap, but slowly like a steam valve opened all the way to relieve pressure.

Clovis played "Mystery Train" by Elvis from the King's Sun Studio sessions. It was hard to resist. Clovis fingerpicked with the precision of Scotty Moore, Elvis's original guitar player.

Brian began slapping the table in time with the beat. The mood in the room had changed entirely by the second verse. Brian sang along with Clovis. The negative energy seemed to flow out of him.

Instead of the traditional guitar solo, Brian picked up the recorder he bought at Bobby's shop and blew a baroque melody that somehow, miraculously fit with the song. It was magical.

They played several more tunes, Clovis showing his monumental range by playing Memphis rockabilly riffs, then shifting to a classical version of "Greensleeves," followed by a Howlin' Wolf blues song. Brian demonstrated the breadth of his musical talent by playing a variety of unusual instruments. He played recorder on "Mystery Train," Appalachian dulcimer on "Greensleeves," and blues harp on Howlin' Wolf's "Smokestack Lightnin'." Brian relaxed visibly as the session continued. Clovis had his number.

Just as the plates were being cleared from the table, the doorbell rang again.

"Maybe it's Mick and Keith," Marianne said.

Brian, suddenly energized, went to answer it personally, a tactic Bobby thought was dangerous considering all the crazy people and police around the area.

There were two freaky-looking people with long hair standing in the doorway. One of them spoke in an American accent.

"Hey Brian, it's me, Skully."

"Who?"

"Skully! I'm Jimi's roadie. I've met you a bunch of times at gigs."

Brian squinted at him.

"Are you talking about Jimi Hendrix?"

"Yeah, man. Jimi. He sent me over here with somebody he thought you ought to meet."

Bobby and Clovis stood behind Brian, listening to the conversation. Brian was still a little wary and kept the door open only a crack. Skully continued.

"This is Acid King Leon from California."

The taller of the two pushed the door open and put out his hand for Brian to shake.

"Hey, man. I'm Acid King. They sent me out here from Monterey to give you the benediction, Brother."

He opened a brown leather briefcase to reveal plastic bags containing hundreds of purple and yellow pills. Brian's eyes got big.

"Is that all acid?" Brian asked.

Leon grinned.

"Sure is. Pure Owsley. Made by the man himself in San Francisco. This is purple haze, my man. It's a new formula that eliminates the bad trips. Think of it. No bummers, brother. Every trip is mellow."

"Come on in," Brian said.

He swung the door all the open and bade them welcome.

"You say you came from Monterey?"

"Yeah, man. The promoters for the Monterey Pop Festival sent me here to ask you to be their guest for a weekend of great music. They want you to introduce Jimi Hendrix onstage. It's his American debut. That's why Jimi sent me here. He asked me to ask you if you'd do it. It's gonna be big. D. A. Pennebaker is shooting the whole thing for a movie and Wally Heider's recording the sound."

Brian seemed interested.

"I've heard of Monterey. When is it?"

"It's during the summer solstice."

Brian shrugged. "When's that?"

"June. Derek Taylor has already contacted the Stones office."

"Derek Taylor, the Beatles publicist?"

Leon said, "He's involved, too. Jimi was hoping you'd introduce him at the gig."

"Are the Beatles playing?"

"No. They won't be there."

They walked slowly back into the dining room. Brian introduced the two newcomers to the group.

"This is Skully. He works for Jimi Hendrix, and this other bloke is Acid King Leon."

They said their hellos and Brian apologized about having just finished dinner.

"Can I offer you anything?"

"Maybe just dessert."

They brought two extra seats to the table and joined the party.

Brian said, "Leon is from the Monterey Pop Festival in California."

"Yeah, man. This is going to be the best festival ever. All the San Francisco groups are going to be there: Big Brother, the Grateful Dead, Jefferson Airplane, Steve Miller, Quicksilver,

Moby Grape, Country Joe, the Electric Flag, Butterfield, plus The Byrds, Booker T, the 'Big O' Otis Redding, and to top it all off, The Who and Hendrix."

"And don't forget Ravi Shankar," said Skully.

Brian clapped his hands. "A sitar recital! Brilliant!"

"Wow," Bobby said, "that's quite a lineup."

"It's going to be a fantastic event. Lou Adler and John Phillips are putting it together. Paul McCartney's on the board of directors."

"What would I have to do?"

"Nothing. Just hang around. Introduce Jimi on the last night."

"That's it?"

"Yep, and the Stones office has probably already cleared it if you want to go."

Brian grinned. He relished the idea of going to California. It meant sunshine and adulation. He didn't have any pressure on him to play. All he had to do was hang out and introduce Jimi. Why not? It would be great to get out of London anyway.

"Damn right I want to go."

Small dishes of vanilla ice cream were served. There were multicolored sprinkles on top of hot fudge. Bobby had a sweet tooth and dug in. It was cold and delicious and refreshed his body and soul.

It wasn't until later when he began to look around Brian's townhouse that he began to feel strange. He noticed a lot of occult objects lying around the room: A painted pentagram on the floor, a glass skull, candles, a strange little altar with herbs, human hair, and books on black magic and demonology. He'd heard that satanist Kenneth Anger had been here to visit. He also knew Brian was fascinated with turn-of-the-century occultist Aleister Crowley. As he looked further, he realized that there was something dark and sinister about the place that made him feel uneasy. Bobby swallowed the lump in his throat.

On a table was a copy of the German glossy picture magazine *Stern*. On the cover, in shocking detail, was a photo of Brian dressed in a full Nazi SS uniform with Anita kneeling at his feet holding a baby doll. The picture was disturbing in many ways, but Brian's face was the worst. He seemed to relish the Nazi attitude. Someone had written the word *rejected* across the cover in red ink. Bobby automatically flipped the magazine over so the photo wouldn't stare back at him.

Were Brian and Anita just interested in black magic, or did they actually practice it? The thought troubled Bobby.

Clovis found Bobby and grabbed him by the arm.

"Are you okay?"

Bobby said, "What do you mean? Of course I'm okay."

"I mean . . . Do you feel anything strange?"

"No."

"Erlene said she could feel her tits growing, and when I looked at her, they were as big as watermelons."

Bobby looked across the room at Erlene.

"She's fine, she looks completely normal."

"Are her tits proportionate to the rest of her body?"

"Yes, they are the same glorious size as always."

"They're not bursting out of her shirt?"

Bobby shook his head.

"Nope."

Clovis nodded as if he'd just had a big revelation.

"Oh . . ."

Brian suddenly appeared and pulled Clovis away from the party into the kitchen. Brian's voice sounded like a French horn to Clovis.

"Hey, man. You want to swap?"

"Swap what?" Clovis said. "Guitars?"

"Women."

Clovis tried to wipe the look of incredulity off his face, but he wasn't much of a poker player. The idea seemed ludicrous to him. He started to laugh.

"Did you say you wanted to swap? Erlene for Anita?"

Brian nodded eagerly. "Just for a little while. We'd all just go upstairs together in the big bedroom. That way, you can watch me do Erlene and Anita together, then I can watch you."

Clovis whistled. "I don't know, pardner. That sounds kinda kinky."

Brian smiled. "Yeah . . . Well, that's the whole point, isn't it?"

Clovis shook his head.

"No offense, but your old lady ain't got much meat on her bones. I mean, Erlene's got a real woman's body, big bazoombas and a hallelujah ass. Plus she's a professional exotic dancer and she knows how to move. Anita's way too skinny and . . . well, don't take this the wrong way, but my tits are bigger than hers. You'd be getting the better end of that deal."

Brian thought it over. "Would Erlene be up for it?"

Clovis lowered his voice and tried to sound sincere. "Truth is, she'd probably slap you across the face if you asked. She's kinda sensitive about stuff like that. She's a stripper, not a whore. Besides, that's my woman we're talkin' about. I won her fair and square. I ain't about to share her with anybody, even for a few minutes."

Brian considered Clovis's words, then asked again. "So the answer is no?"

"What the fuck do you think, Brian? Jeez, you got some nerve. I'm flattered that Erlene turns you on, and I'm real proud of her and all, but shit, man, don't ask me stuff like that. It's out of my league. I'm just a poor guitar player. You're a superstar."

Brian had a strange look in his eye. "Maybe you'll change your mind," he said cryptically.

"I don't think so. You're barkin' up the wrong tree, pardner. I'm warnin' ya, don't piss Erlene off or she'll kick your ass."

Brian whispered, "Sounds provocative."

"What are you, some kinda sex freak? I'll hang out and smoke dope with you and drink your wine, but I ain't gonna let you fuck my woman."

"Very well, my good man. Just a thought. Let's rejoin the others for drinks."

They reentered the living room. Clovis seemed a little unsteady on his feet.

"What's happening?"

Brian grinned. "Oh, it's probably the LSD kicking in."

"The what?"

"I dosed you all! It was in the ice cream." Brian laughed like a lunatic.

CHAPTER THREE

HEART OF STONE

Bobby's heart sank. He'd broken his promise to Cricket and ingested LSD. He'd made a serious mistake. He hadn't been as careful as he thought, and now he could feel the acid surging through his system. It was powerful stuff.

"We dosed the ice cream!" Brian shouted. "Everybody's tripping together tonight, thanks to Acid King Leon!"

Erlene groaned. "Goddammit! You mean to say you spiked our ice cream and didn't tell us, you little son of a bitch?"

"If I would have told you, you wouldn't have done it." Brian smirked.

"Goddamn right I wouldn't! I don't like LSD!" she said, and folded her arms. "That just ain't right."

Bobby spoke up. "I told my wife you were having a dinner party and there wouldn't be any drugs."

Anita laughed. "What a silly bitch! How could she be so provincial? What is she, a Mormon?"

Bobby blushed. "She's a Baltimore girl," he heard himself say. The words left an unpleasant taste in his mouth. He didn't like defending his wife to the likes of Anita Pallenberg.

"Ha!" Anita threw her blond hair back with an air of defiance. Her voice dripped with sarcasm. "You broke your little promise. Big fuckin' deal!"

Bobby was tongue-tied talking to Anita. When he replied to her, each new sentence made him sound more ridiculous. He was tripping now; he could feel it. His mind raced. He knew he shouldn't be matching wits with Anita Pallenberg, but he was already in too deep.

His voice sounded like Donald Duck. Some kind of audio distortion had set in. The more he tried not to sound like Donald Duck, the more he sounded like him.

It was evident now that the vibes in the room had shifted, and everybody seemed to feel the first euphoric effects of the acid as a group.

"Don't be such a wimp," Anita said.

"It's just that I . . . I love my wife . . . And I promised her I wouldn't take anything tonight. And . . ."

Anita and Brian roared with laughter. "Stupid girl! Stupid girl!"

"He loves his wife!" Brian shouted. "The man loves his wife! Oh, that's rich!"

"What's wrong with that?" Bobby said.

Anita's German accent had a surreal Nazi twinge.

"So you promised her that you wouldn't take drugs tonight. Tell us, Mr. Dust Bin Bob, on what night of the week does she allow you to take LSD?"

"Never. I mean, as a rule, I don't take drugs. John dosed me with acid at Weybridge once, and I didn't enjoy it."

"I hate that word," Anita snapped. "People say they enjoy this and they didn't enjoy that. Fuck enjoyment! I want to learn. I want to grow. I want to experience new things. Acid is not for fools. You have to be in tune."

The more Anita lectured him, the more surreal things became. Bobby reacted to her psychic pressure with more increasingly bizarre audio distortions. He began to hallucinate. He thought he saw bugs fly out of her mouth when she spoke. At one point, her face started to melt and then rearranged itself. She became Brian, she became Marianne Faithfull, she morphed into a dozen people, then back to herself. Bobby found it frightening and hard to follow.

He thought he heard dogs barking in the distance. He looked at Anita, and she became an Afghan hound. He thought he heard strange music. He thought he heard whispered voices talking about him. Bobby shook his head, trying to clear it.

To Bobby's ears, his transformation into Donald Duck was complete. He couldn't understand anything he said. His mouth wouldn't work. His tongue and lips seemed oversize and unresponsive. When others spoke to him, he heard the same gibberish as if their voices were running backward.

Bobby leaned back in his chair and closed his eyes. He felt

like he was underwater. When he opened them again everything shimmered.

Brian put on a Muddy Waters record, and they were all transfixed by the gravelly voice of the legendary R&B singer. There was something soothing about the timeless music of the blues. Bobby could see the dramatic effect it had on Brian. He immediately became engaged with the music. It calmed him down, and he lost himself in the three chords of the blues. Bobby had realized a long time ago that they were also the three chords of life.

The acid took Bobby far beyond anyplace he'd ever been before. When he was with John Lennon at John's country house in Weybridge, he'd been dosed against his will then, too. *Was it always like that? Is that how the psychedelic experience worked?* He didn't actually enjoy the experience and would never have voluntarily taken it again. But now it was too late.

Bobby had no idea how long he'd stayed like that, sitting on the floor lost in his thoughts listening to Muddy Waters. It felt like hours. He was vaguely aware of people moving around him. He looked around. People were standing up and putting on their coats.

"What's going on?" Bobby asked. His voiced seemed miles away.

"Get up," a voice said. "We're going out."

Bobby couldn't believe it.

"Going out? But, I can barely walk."

"Brian's driving."

"Brian's driving? How is that possible?"

"You got me, pardner." Bobby realized he was talking to

Clovis. "But the man has a Rolls-Royce Silver Cloud the size of Cleveland, and he's driving us all down to The Scotch of Saint James for a nightcap. Personally, my night's already been capped, but we might as well go. It's sure to be an adventure. Besides, we can't stay here."

"Where is it?"

"I have no idea, but the car's out front."

"What should I do?"

Bobby tried to focus his eyes but they were blurry and dry. He had a huge irresolute smile on his face, but he didn't know why. Clovis peered into Bobby's face and whistled.

"You really look fucked up, pardner. Stick with me and Erlene. We'll take care of you."

"What about you guys?"

"Erlene's as solid as a rock. I doubt if the acid affects her all that much. And me? Well, let's just say we're all bozos on this bus."

Bobby muttered something in his Donald Duck voice.

Clovis continued, "It's Brian and Anita I'm worried about. He's as fragile as an eggshell, and she's liable to say or do anything. They're totally fuckin' crazy. They can argue about anything. Brian's the one who suddenly wanted to go out. It's his show. I guess we gotta go."

Bobby stared at Clovis with wide, fevered eyes.

"Brian? Oh yeah, Brian. The Stone who stoned us."

"Come on, get up. We're leaving."

Marianne didn't eat the ice cream and was straight as an arrow. She left at some point, although time distortion had set in and Bobby had no idea if it was two hours ago or ten minutes ago. Claudine came downstairs and called for a cab. Christopher Gibb and Fraser joined her, and they disappeared into the night. Skully and Acid King Leon said they'd meet everyone at the club and walked off down Courtfield Road.

That left Brian and Anita in the Rolls with Erlene, Clovis, and Bobby in the backseat.

Bobby marveled at Brian's ability to drive while tripping his ass off. But he seemed supremely confident behind the wheel. Brian was so short and the car was so huge that he had to sit on a cushion to see over the dashboard.

The Scotch of Saint James was *the* hangout for rock stars in London after dark. Bobby had been there before with George and Pattie Harrison. It was an unassuming brick storefront with tall glass doors leading to a two-level nightclub. Bobby glided through the room behind Brian, watching people's reaction as they passed by. Brian was royalty here.

Anita strutted like a peacock. Everybody turned to stare. You could hear the conversation stop then start again.

"That's Brian Jones."

They hadn't been there more than five minutes when Brian spotted a dear friend, Ronni Money, wife of musician Zoot Money. Ronni had taken care of Brian several times during times of crisis. She was indeed a true friend who cared for Brian. When he felt depressed or suicidal, he always called Ronni.

Ronni was on the second floor, and Brian could see her on the balcony. She was talking to Jimi Hendrix and Eric Burdon.

"Ronni! Ronni, darling!"

Brian rushed up the stairs and hugged her, making a grand show of it.

"Brian. It's so good to see you out and about! I've missed you! Are you well?"

"Yes! Yes! Fantastic!"

Brian hugged Ronni again. Like all of Brian's female friends, Ronni was beautiful and stylish, but she was not a groupie nor an ex-girlfriend. She was just somebody who loved Brian for the sensitive and tortured soul he was.

Anita watched. Her anger mounted. She stood with her hands on her hips and sneered.

"So who's this slag, Brian?" Anita spat. "Another one of your one-nighters? I thought I'd met them all by now."

Brian spun around on his heel and slapped Anita in the face. He hit her hard enough to knock her off her feet. She fell back into a chair and sat down hard. The blow was so ferocious and sudden it took everyone by surprise. Some people saw it and gasped. Others missed it entirely in the noisy nightclub. It happened so fast.

Brian shouted, "Don't you ever dare talk to her like that, you fuckin' bitch!"

Blood began to seep out of Anita's nose. People in the immediate circle stared at Brian, shocked at what they'd witnessed. Perhaps more shocking was the fact that Brian did it in public, in complete view of everyone, without hesitation. As the blood dripped down her face and onto her dress, several waiters rushed forward with white linen napkins to staunch the flow.

Anita pressed the napkins against her nose and tried to act

as if nothing had happened. Jimi chivalrously offered her one of his lace handkerchiefs. She pushed Jimi's hand away.

Clovis and Erlene looked at each other and shook their heads in unison. Brian was clearly out of control.

Bobby watched it all like a movie. The sight of Anita's blood made him nauseous. It was bright red and alive and seemed to move on its own. He found he couldn't look at it while he was tripping. He turned to Clovis and grabbed his arm.

"I gotta get out of here!" Bobby gushed. "The walls are closing in and Anita's blood is moving."

Erlene looked around the room.

"He's right. Let's go."

"We don't have a car," Bobby said.

"We'll walk through the park," Erlene replied.

Bobby nodded. The park would be quiet and soothing after the throbbing intensity of The Scotch of Saint James.

"The park. Yeah, that sounds good."

"What about Brian?"

Clovis shrugged. "He probably won't notice we're gone."

"Wait a second," Erlene said. "I'll be right back."

She walked over to Brian, unsnapping the front of her pink cowboy blouse as she went. She wasn't wearing a bra, and Brian had been ogling her nipples all night. She tapped him on the shoulder. When he turned around, she pulled open her blouse and exposed her breathtaking breasts to him. They were stripper's breasts, meant to be flaunted and admired. Brian's eyes went to her nipples and locked on.

"Men pay good money to see these!"

Her magnificent breasts displayed, she smiled.

"Now that I got your attention . . ."

She punched him in the gut with her left fist, hitting him hard just below his ribs. He exhaled sharply and doubled over in pain.

"That's for hitting Anita, even if she is a witchy little bitch."

While Brian was hunched over, she landed a straight, hard right jab that made contact with his chin, knocking him sideways. Brian teetered on his high-heeled boots for a moment then fell back onto his ass, landing hard on the dance floor. He looked confused.

"And that's for dosing us at dinner, asshole!"

She stepped over Brian and walked away.

"Okay, let's go," she said cheerfully.

Clovis just shook his head.

"Damn! What a woman! And she's all mine, pardner, all mine!"

They walked through the park. It was a wondrous place on acid. The trees moved. The forest spoke to them. The grass was soft and thick beneath their feet. Clovis took off his shoes and ran through the moist lawn. Then he took off his pants.

Erlene giggled and ran after him. When she caught him, they stripped their clothes off and made love behind some bushes.

Bobby wandered through the trees listening to the forest whisper to him. The acid peaked at some time around three in the morning. The effect was overwhelming. Bobby hung on to his sanity like a drunk hugging the floor as the room spun around him.

He lay on his back, watching the stars until the sun came up. At some point, he too had shed his clothes, but unlike Clovis, he had managed to put them back on again when he got cold. Except he'd lost his socks, shoes, and underwear, and his shirt was buttoned wrong. His knees and feet were muddy, and there were leaves in his hair.

Clovis appeared next to him with a handful of wild blackberries he had picked.

"Try one. They are the best blackberries you'll ever eat."

Bobby put one in his mouth and chewed. The sweet berry burst with flavor like an explosion. It completely rejuvenated him and hydrated his parched mouth. Bobby sat on the lawn eating berries with Clovis, grinning like a maniac.

"Where's Erlene?"

"She went to find out where we are."

"Maybe she'd be better off finding out who we are."

Clovis laughed. "Oh, I know who I am. I'm Clovis Hicks and I play the guitar. Sometimes I play the fool. Who are you?"

Bobby thought for a moment. *Who was he?*

"I don't know. I don't remember."

"When you finally figure out who you are and what you're doing, you can turn the corner on this thing."

"On what thing? Why is everything so strange?"

Clovis put his hand on Bobby's shoulder.

"You're Dust Bin Bob, aka Bobby Dingle from Liverpool. You took a drug called LSD at Brian Jones's house and you're on a trip."

"I am?" Bobby blinked. He couldn't stop smiling.

"That's about the gist of it, pardner."

"Am I always going to be like this?" Bobby said.

Clovis's voice was reassuring.

"Nah, it's already starting to wear off. You'll be fine in a couple of hours."

"Thank God."

Erlene returned. She looked surprisingly clean and fresh.

"I found a gas station and washed up in the restroom."

Clovis looked at Bobby. Bobby translated.

"She means she found a petrol pump and washed up in the loo."

Erlene held up a greasy white bag of food.

"I found an all-night fish and chips shop and I had some money in my pocket, so I bought you guys some breakfast."

She handed the food to Clovis and Bobby, and they ate ravenously.

Erlene looked around. The sun was up now.

"We're gonna have to walk home. We better get started."

"Home? Oh my God! Cricket! I promised I'd be home."

The unlikely trio trudged through early morning traffic. Bobby and Clovis were barefoot. After a few minutes, Bobby developed several large blisters on the bottom of his feet and walking became difficult. He wound up hobbling through the streets of London.

It took most of the day to find their way back to Bobby's apartment. He opened the front door and shouted Cricket's name even though he knew she was gone. His clothes were disheveled and filthy, his feet were black with dirt. He had a wild look in his eye, and his hair looked like he'd slept on the ground.

There was a note tacked to the inside of the door. Bobby snatched it and read.

> *I hope you're all right and nothing bad happened to you, so I can kill you later. How could you? You promised you'd be home to say good-bye.*
>
> *—C*
>
> *PS Here's a dime. Call me when you grow up!*

A shiny American dime was taped to the paper. Bobby looked down at his dirty clothes and black feet like he was discovering them for the first time. He rubbed the shiny new dime between his fingers and felt bleak. It would cost a lot more than a dime to call her now. He looked at the clock and saw that Cricket and Winston wouldn't arrive in Baltimore for several more hours. He couldn't call and explain yet.

CHAPTER FOUR

SWEET SCHADENFREUDE

Bobby didn't remember going into his apartment. He didn't remember taking a shower and lying down on the bed. He didn't remember falling asleep. He didn't remember anything.

But when the phone next to his bed rang, it all came screaming back like the sooty shockwave of some terrible memory. He looked at the ringing phone, and for some reason he began to cry. It sounded so sad and mournful. He couldn't make his hand reach out and pick it up. He realized he was still tripping.

"Who is it?" he shouted at the ringing phone. "Who's inside of you?"

The absurdity of the statement made Bobby laugh. *Who's inside of you?* Indeed, who was inside that black plastic box? *What did they want?* Bobby doubted he could carry on much of a conversation anyway, so maybe it was a good thing to just shout at it. As if in response, the phone stopped ringing.

He watched it cautiously, afraid it would come alive and bite him.

What if it was Cricket?

Could he talk to her in his present condition? *No problem*, he thought, *I'll just tell her the truth. It's a crazy story, but Clovis and Erlene will back me up.*

Then he thought, *No, maybe I shouldn't tell her. She'd only get mad at me. I broke a promise.* Bobby realized with a jolt that for the first time in his life, he was contemplating lying to his wife.

He watched the phone.

Cricket would understand, wouldn't she? Bobby wasn't too sure anymore. Once upon a time, she would have. But now, it seemed unlikely.

The phone didn't move. It stopped ringing. The silence was deafening.

Guilt, perhaps fueled by the residual effect of the psychedelics, ate away at Bobby's mind. The overall effect left him feeling drained.

The phone suddenly rang again and made Bobby jump. It sounded as loud as a fire alarm. Bobby snatched it up, expecting to hear Cricket's accusing voice. His face felt sore from smiling for the last twelve hours while tripping. His upper cheeks must have been locked in a rictus grin for hours because now they hurt. Also, his mouth and throat were as dry as cotton.

"Cricket?" he rasped.

It was Brian Jones's voice. "What? Buddy Holly and the Crickets? No, I want to talk to Dust Bin Bob!"

Bobby was confused.

"Who?"

"It's Brian! Brian Jones! You were at my house last night."

Brian! The asshole! Was he calling to apologize? It was all his fault.

Bobby's voice was hoarse and throaty.

"What is it?"

A tsunami of emotions unexpectedly swelled up in front of Bobby. Suddenly, he couldn't control himself and he began to tremble. He thought he might cry again. Bobby hoped his tremors weren't audible on the telephone. He took a deep breath.

Fighting back his own spontaneous tears, he suddenly realized that the sobbing he heard was coming from Brian.

"It's Anita! She's gone!"

Bobby looked at the phone as if it were alive in his hands, twisting like a snake.

"I can't help you. I've got my own problems."

"What do you mean?" Brian couldn't conceive of anyone else's problems being more important that his.

"My woman is gone, too," Bobby said, shaking. "She left after you made me break my promise. Remember? You and Anita laughed at me? Well, now she's gone back to America, thanks to you."

"Sorry, don't remember a thing."

"Well, because of you my wife has left me and taken my son."

"Because of me?"

"Then you beat up Anita at The Scotch of Saint James. Do you remember that?"

"Oh God!" Brian gasped. "That was it! I didn't see her after that."

"You mean to tell me you don't remember a thing?"

"Nothing. Was I a complete bugger?"

Bobby sat up.

"Yes! Yes you were! You really fucked up."

He must not even remember being punched out by Erlene, Bobby thought. *Score one for Clovis, it could have cost him his job at Olympic.*

"Sorry. But will you come over and help me find Anita?"

Bobby laughed.

"You gotta be kidding me. Can you go to America and help me get Cricket back?"

"Yes!" Brian shouted. "For God's sake, help me get Anita back. I'll do anything!"

"You beat her up in a packed nightclub, Brian. You bloodied her nose in front of all her friends. I would think she'd be half-way back to Munich by now."

"No!" Brian sounded like a petulant child. "Look, if I take you to America and help you patch up with Cricket, will you help me get Anita back?"

Bobby sighed. Brian Jones was a piece of work. He sincerely believed that being a rock star and a member of the Rolling Stones gave him license for anything.

"What can I do?" Bobby sighed.

"You helped the Beatles. I know. John told me the whole story. You saved their lives. You have the magic. Now I need you to save mine."

Bobby still felt mildly psychedelic. It was hard to separate fantasy from reality. *Was this conversation really happening? Was it a dream?*

"Are you there?" Brian asked after a long pause.

"Huh? I can't talk now. Let me wake up a little," Bobby croaked.

"Take your time. Have some tea."

Bobby couldn't think straight yet. His mind was still scrambled from the LSD. He compared his earlier peaceful trip with John to the chaotic trip with Brian and his friends. With John, it had all been quiet contemplation and peace. Just the two of them.

With Brian, it was a roller coaster ride. He loved to surround himself with people. Faces came and went looming out of the shadows. The background conversation at The Scotch of Saint James became white noise. It all swirled out of control and all Bobby could do was watch and listen. The gravitational field generated by Brian's own personality guided the chaos, pulling along his dinner guests just for the fun of it.

He realized the extraordinary differences between John and Brian. *Maybe that's why they're such good friends*, Bobby thought. *Opposites attract.*

Music propelled both men through life but with very different engines. John was all about creating new songs, new opportunities, new vistas. He was a dedicated revolutionary. He exploded with creative energy, which extended from writing to artwork to music. To John, it was all about the next song, the next challenge.

Brian, on the other hand, felt that every great song had already been written and that the musician's role in life was to reinterpret the music through his own eyes. Brian strove to make old songs sound new. For the first three albums, the Stones followed that same path. It was all about the blues then. What could be more perfect than the blues? Three chords were all you ever needed.

"Bo Diddley" came back to him. In his mind, he replayed every second of that song. The maracas sizzled, the guitars throbbed, the vocal echoed. Bobby couldn't get it out of his head. He made a mental note to purchase *Bo's Greatest Hits* as soon as possible.

Bobby realized that he had been dosed by two of the greatest musicians of his generation. Instead of feeling special, he felt nauseous. He made the same promise to himself that he'd made after his first trip with John: *Never, never again.*

Bobby looked at the clock on the wall and realized he hadn't called Cricket.

Oh my God, I missed my window of opportunity! They're already there. How many hours ahead are they? Or is it behind? She's gonna hate me!

His mouth was as dry as the Sahara and he could hardly talk, but he was determined. He dialed the number with shaky hands. The aftereffect of the LSD made him clumsy.

The transatlantic telephone connection was horrible. There seemed to be a half-second delay, and at times the static overwhelmed the signal.

"Hello? Hello?"

"Bobby? Is that you?"

"Cricket? Honey?"

"Don't 'honey' me! It's three o'clock in the morning here. You probably woke up Winston. I guess you didn't think about that."

"Honey, look, I'm sorry. I can explain—"

Cricket cut him off.

"I don't want to hear it! Call back at a decent hour if you want to discuss it!"

She hung up.

Bobby tried to call back but got a busy tone. She'd obviously taken the receiver off the cradle.

It's off the hook, he thought. *I've been taken off the hook.*

Guilt swept over Bobby like a sheen of perspiration.

He had to go to Baltimore. He had to be with Cricket. Even though he still felt woozy from the purple haze, he reached for the telephone to call the airlines. He made up his mind that he would make arrangements to travel to Baltimore as soon as possible.

But unbeknownst to Bobby, all the airline companies were on strike. In fact, the entire country seemed to be hobbled by a general strike. Bobby wasn't sure why, but the airline workers, baggage handlers, food handlers, ticketing agents, and maintenance workers were all out. It would be impossible to leave the country for at least the length of the work stoppage.

"Shit!" shouted Bobby at the telephone.

There was nothing he could do. He considered calling Cricket back and telling her, but that would only make matters worse. He'd tell her on the next call. Maybe the strike would be over by then.

Bobby wasn't going anywhere soon.

"Are you crazy?" Clovis Hicks asked Bobby.

He was standing in the doorway of Bobby's apartment.

"After the shit that guy pulled? You wanna help him?"

Bobby nodded.

Clovis said, "So, let me get this straight. You totally fucked up with Cricket and when you tried to call her and explain, she hung up on you?"

Bobby nodded.

"Aw, man, you are in for the shits. She ain't coming back anytime soon, I can tell you that. You're gonna have to go over there and beg her to come back. You made a promise to your woman and you broke it? There's gonna be hell to pay."

"I was avoiding all fluids all night long, but he got me with the ice cream."

"Who'da thunk it? He's a devious little motherfucker, I'll give him that."

"He was actually proud that he'd managed to dose us."

"Yeah, these fuckin' rock stars! Ain't they a bunch?"

"Maybe Erlene could call Cricket and explain my side of the story."

Clovis let out a long and suffering sigh. "Let's let a little water pass under the bridge first, pardner. Give it some time. Erlene's still pissed off, too."

They stood in silence for a minute or two.

"Could you drive me to Brian's?"

"Are you sure?"

"Yes, I don't know what else to do. Maybe if I help find Anita, Brian's karma will help me get Cricket back. Who knows?"

Clovis chuckled. "Jonesy can barely tie his own shoes, man. He's a mess. His karma stinks."

Bobby put a hand on Clovis's shoulder.

"You want to know the truth? I don't know why I should go over there. It just seems like something I should do. I got this feeling of inevitability, like it's part of my fate."

"That's the acid talkin', pardner. All that fate and inevitability shit. Sounds pretty trippy to me. Look, I'm your friend. I'll take you. That's that. No magical mystery tour, okay?"

"You're a good man, Clovis Hicks."

"I know. Erlene tells me that all the time."

Bobby snapped his fingers.

"It's hard to believe that Erlene punched out Brian Jones at that fancy nightclub last night and he doesn't even remember."

Clovis laughed.

"She don't take no shit, man. She told me she thought Anita was a witch and Brian was a warlock."

"She might be right."

Number One Courtfield Road was dark in the afternoon. The windows were drawn and the house appeared closed.

When Bobby rang the doorbell, he felt a slight electric shock and pulled his hand away from the button quickly.

"Did you get a shock?" Clovis asked.

"Yeah, as soon as I touched it."

Clovis rang the doorbell, too. He received no shock.

"Nothing."

Bobby touched it again and got another shock.

Just then, Brian opened the great door and peered at them through red squinty eyes. He'd been crying.

"Come in, come in," he said. "Hurry, before they see you!"

"Before who sees us?"

"Them . . ."

"What the fuck?" Clovis said. "There's nobody out here, Brian. You're just paranoid."

He pulled Clovis and Bobby inside and shut and locked the door with multiple locks.

He led them into the living room where they had been getting high the night before. The remains of the merriment were still there.

Bobby was surprised to see Skully and Acid King Leon sitting on the couch. They must have returned to Brian's sometime during the night. Clovis saw them at the same time Bobby did, and they shared a frown.

"What are they doing here?" Clovis asked, nodding toward the couch.

Clovis made no attempt to hide his distrust of the two Californians. They knew hardly anything about them other than the unofficial connection to the Monterey Pop Festival, but something about them made Bobby uneasy.

Brian was apologetic.

"I'm sorry. I was lonely. Anita's gone. She took her things."

Clovis put his hands on his hips.

"Well, somehow that doesn't surprise me."

"Oh, shit. . . . I must've been crazy."

"No argument there." Bobby looked around. *Yep. Crazy as a shit-house rat, as old friend and R&B philosopher Preston Washington used to say.* The place was a mess. It looked like the lair of a madman.

He asked, "Do you have a cleaning lady?"

Brian, distracted by thoughts of Anita, mumbled something to the affirmative.

"Then I suggest you call her. Let's get both you and this place cleaned up. Take a shower and I'll make some tea."

"I don't have time for that. I have to find Anita."

Bobby said, "You don't want her to see you like this. You have to wash your hair."

That comment struck a nerve. Brian was incredibly vain about his hair and washed it meticulously every day.

"Yes," Brian muttered. "You're right."

Bobby led Brian back to the shower, turned it on, and made sure the temperature was right. He left the room and heard Brian enter.

Clovis looked at Skully and Leon.

"What are you guys here for? Planning some kind of a party?"

They looked at each other.

"We're here for Brian."

Clovis, a Baltimore boy from the wrong side of the tracks, pulled no punches. He spoke his mind in every situation. He put his hands on his hips in a cocky, defiant stance.

"You're here for Brian? That's a laugh. What the fuck have you guys ever done for Brian? The best thing you can do right now is leave."

"But Brian invited us!" Skully protested.

"He doesn't need you anymore, man. Why don't you take a hike?"

Leon shook his head. "Why don't you let Brian decide that for himself?"

Clovis bristled.

"Why don't you fuck yourself? You heard me. Take your acid and get out! That shit is scrambling Brian's brain and making him unable to work."

Acid King Leon looked incredulous. His mouth hung open as if to reply but no words came. Clovis blunt statement caught him by surprise. After all, Acid King was welcome everywhere he went, wasn't he? Clovis paused a moment to let his words sink it. Then he punctuated the statement with one more remark.

"Now!"

They looked to Bobby for sympathy. "Are you gonna let him treat us like that?"

Bobby said, "You heard the man."

Leon took his briefcase, and Skully took a brown leather shoulder bag. Bobby didn't see them come in and didn't know to whom the shoulder bag belonged. He said nothing, though, and watched them leave.

Thirty minutes later, Brian sat at the kitchen table and sipped a cup of tea. Bobby made some buttered toast with strawberry jam that smelled so heavenly they all gulped it down like starving men.

"Did you know those two before last night?"

"Skully works for Jimi," Brian said. "At least that's what he told me."

"Hold on a second, pardner."

Clovis held out a hand making the universal stop sign.

"I haven't seen that guy around and I just worked with Jimi at Olympic. I know most of Jimi's roadies. There's Neville Chesters, who shares an apartment with Noel Redding; a long-haired kid named Lemmy who's always crashing there; and Tappy Wright, who was hired by the management team."

Brian shrugged. "Are you saying Skully lied?"

"Well, he sure ain't tellin' the truth," Clovis said. "I just a got a funny feelin'. I'm gonna call Noel Redding."

"Of course," Bobby said, "Jimi's bass player ought to know."

Clovis looked in his address book and called the bushy-haired bassist for the Jimi Hendrix Experience.

"Noel? How are ya, pardner?"

"Clovis?"

"Of course it's Clovis. Who else you know talks like this? Hey, I'm checking somebody out and they claimed they worked for you."

Noel listened.

"A guy named Skully and another guy named Acid King Leon? I don't know if Skully is the first name or last."

On the other end of the line, Noel tapped the mouthpiece rhythmically as he thought. His sense of humor was as dry as Vermouth. He delivered his punch lines like Noel Coward with a martini glass and a smoldering joint in a cigarette holder.

"Did you say Acid King Leon? Jimi has several freaks who follow him around and give him acid. We've got an Acid Queen Marcy; we've got a Captain Trips; we got Tony Baloney, the King of Pepperoni; and Rasheesh, the Sheik of Hashish. Jimi draws royalty wherever he goes. No Acid King Leon that I can remember, though. I'm not really part of that scene. Acid is not really my thing."

"How about Skully?"

"First name or last?"

"I don't know."

"Doesn't ring a bell."

"No Skully? You're sure of that?"

"Hold on a sec."

Noel cupped the phone and shouted into another room. Bobby could hear it.

"You ever heard of a roadie named Skully?"

A moment later, Noel was back on the line.

"No Skully . . . Although there was a guy named Skull working for The Pretty Things briefly a couple of years ago."

"Could it be the same guy?"

"I doubt it. Somebody told me that other guy was a junky, and we never hire junkies."

"Thanks, bro." Clovis signed off.

Clovis looked at Brian and Bobby.

"Noel says he never heard of either one of them."

* * *

When Bobby returned to his apartment, he was beginning to feel human again. The LSD had taken over a day and a half to wear off, and he still had occasional flashes of wild disorientation. He bought a newspaper on the way and read about the airline strike. There was no resolution in sight, according to the *Times*. He'd been waiting for a chance to collect his thoughts and call Cricket. It was nine o'clock at night in London, and Bobby's calculations made it four in the afternoon in Baltimore. A good time to call. Bobby had no idea what he was going to say when he finally got Cricket on the phone. He just knew he had to say something.

He dialed the overly long international number to their place in Baltimore and waited. It rang and rang. There was no answer. Was she ignoring him? Maybe she was out. Maybe she was with her father in the hospital. That made sense. It was visiting time at the hospital. Bobby briefly considered calling the hospital and asking for her father's room in the hopes that she'd be there. Then he realized she wouldn't talk in front of her family. Bobby wondered what she had told them.

Bobby hung up the phone after a few minutes of listening to the ringing tone. He was reluctant to cut the connection even though he knew there would be no answer. His thoughts swirled around Cricket. *Had he blown it?*

Bobby decided to send Cricket a telegram explaining the airline strike. He wrote out the message to her and called Western Union.

My Dear Sweet Wife—

Can't fly out due to airline strike. Stop. Will arrive ASAP. Stop. Miss you. Stop. Can explain everything. Stop.

Your Loyal Husband, Bobby.

Everybody liked Claudine Jillian. She was a sassy blonde from Sheffield, raised just far enough away from London to be untouched by its pretense and close enough to know what to watch out for. For a while, she had been the girlfriend of several major rock stars. Lately, she'd been floating around between boyfriends and having a ball as one of London's most beautiful faces. Her modeling career had made her a substantial independent living before her rock star liaisons, so Claudine could pick and choose her way through life.

Of course she knew Renee. Renee was part of the same scene but lacked the class of Claudine. Claudine had a modeling career. Renee did not. Claudine knew Anita Pallenberg and had been inside Brian's house several times. Renee had not. Renee was very jealous but never showed it. As part of the infamous London club scene, Renee and Claudine were sisters in arms. They drank and danced together at a mod place called The Speakeasy Club at 48 Margaret Street. That's where they were the night after Brian slapped Anita at The Scotch of Saint James. Brian hitting Anita was the talk of the town. Both girls were obsessed with Brian Jones and had trouble believing he had actually struck Anita. No one they knew had actually witnessed it.

And if he did, so what? The crazy bitch drove him to it, that much you could see. To Claudine and Renee, Brian Jones was a saint, incapable of such savagery.

Claudine knew most of the same people Renee knew; they were all familiar faces on the nightclub scene. After a few hours of nursing drinks and hanging out at The Speakeasy Club, Renee had given up and gone home. It was around one in the morning. Claudine stayed for one last drink when Brian walked in. He walked right up to Claudine and touched her cheek.

"Hi," he said.

"Hi," she replied.

"Let's spend the night together."

Claudine blushed. She was speechless for a moment. Was Brian quoting a Stones song or propositioning her? The lustful look in Brian's eye gave him away. This is what she'd always wanted, a whole evening with Brian Jones. Her heart raced and she tried not to look too thrilled.

"I don't want to be alone," Brian whispered.

"Okay," said Claudine.

Brian's intoxicating presence made her bolder.

"Your place or mine?"

"Better make it yours. I'm afraid I'm being watched."

Claudine scanned the room to see who was looking. She shouldn't have bothered. Every eye in the place was on them. It would be hard to walk out of The Speakeasy Club with Prince Jones without half the world knowing it, including snooping Fleet Street reporters who hung around the clubs looking for a story. Claudine picked up her vodka tonic and smiled.

"Just let me finish my drink."

Brian gently took it out of her hand and drank it down in one swig. Then he ordered four more. By the time they actually left the club, Claudine was well lubricated and had forgotten all about who might be watching.

They wound up back at her Belgravia apartment. Claudine showed him her black silk sheets and her collection of lingerie. Brian forgot all about Anita. Conversation ceased. Claudine and Brian made mad, desperate love all night. Brian clung to her like a drowning man clings to a life preserver. He craved constant affection in order to feel alive.

In the morning, with the sun peeking through the windows, Claudine tried to make Brian stay, but he was a restless, troubled man.

"Why don't you relax and stay awhile and I can make some breakfast?"

Brian got out of bed and paced the room.

"I've got things to do."

Claudine pouted.

"Like what? Find Anita? I'd appreciate it if you stopped thinking about her. Here we are, and we've been making hot, passionate love all night. It's a beautiful morning, and all you can think about is her? I should be insulted. What's so special about Anita? Why are you so obsessed?"

Brian shook his head. It was clear he'd been asked this question before and had no answer then or now. That was the mystery of Anita. Maybe she'd used black magic to capture Brian's heart and caught his soul instead.

"I've never known a woman like Anita. She's completely unique."

"If you ask me, she's making you crazy."

Brian paced like a caged animal.

"There's no denying that. But something deep and unforgiving has got its hooks into me. Maybe we were lovers in a past life."

Conflicting emotions tore Brian apart. Part of him felt wracked with guilt for spending a night of unbridled passion with another woman. Not that it would make a difference. Brian and Anita had a more or less open relationship. But she would find out anyway. She always did. And when she did, she would punish him. Anita could play high-stakes sexual politics with the best of them.

Claudine said, "I shouldn't say this because Anita is a friend of mine, but she's making your life miserable. There's something about Anita that's affecting you in a very bad way, Brian. She has a natural sense of schadenfreude that gives her that nasty edge."

"What's *schadenfreude*?" Brian asked.

"It's a German word. It means taking pleasure out of other people's misfortunes. Schadenfreude. Remember that."

"The Germans actually have a word for that?"

Claudine ignored the question and spoke frankly.

"Brian, I've been worried about you since you met her. You're too fragile for Anita. Get rid of her. Let her go. She'll break your heart."

Brian listened to Claudine. She was a sensible girl and her

words had weight and value. It's just that everything she said went against Brian's heart.

"I have to go," Brian said suddenly. "I'll call you."

Their night of lovemaking had been magnificent. Brian needed to decompress. Afraid he might find Anita waiting at home and unwilling to confront her in his current state, Brian checked into a hotel instead of going back to Courtfield Road. He wanted to be where people couldn't find him. He needed to be alone to sort things out.

He felt tremendous guilt and at the same time he felt he needed to punish Anita, the ungrateful bitch. The yin and yang of these conflicting emotions ran through his head like a psychic speedball, pulling him apart. It gave Brian a headache.

He took a sleeping pill, fell asleep, and slept for hours.

Claudine met some friends for lunch and then intended to explore some new boutiques that had sprung up around Carnaby Street. She shopped alone, taking her time. Claudine enjoyed shopping this way. She hated other people making her rush.

She spent the afternoon zigzagging around Regent Street, checking out the little shops that seemed to spring up like mushrooms on the damp side streets.

Halfway through the afternoon, she noticed someone following her. At first she wasn't sure, but after she'd seen the same strange person several times, there could be no doubt. There was something both bizarre and familiar about the stalking figure. It was female, she thought, about her same size and weight. She wore a long seedy overcoat. The stranger had long stringy black hair that hung in her face. She wore huge Audrey Hepburn-style *Breakfast at Tiffany's* sunglasses. She also wore a black silk scarf around her head. What the sunglasses didn't cover was obscured by the scarf, making her unrecognizable.

Claudine felt a sense of wrongness. Why would this person be wearing a long overcoat on such a warm sunny day? And why so anti-fashion, wearing a ratty overcoat on Carnaby Street? The peculiar appearance of the stranger disturbed her. She was obviously in disguise. *Why?*

Claudine stepped up her pace, trying to lose the stranger. But no matter how she tried, she couldn't shake the mystery figure. At one point, she actually ran across the street and tried to disappear behind some taxicabs, but the stranger hung tight.

Alarmed now, Claudine began hurrying, looking for a policeman and trying to stay ahead of the frightening stranger. She wanted to cry out for somebody to help but she realized how ridiculous it would have sounded in broad daylight.

After Claudine thought she had finally lost her, she ventured a look behind only to be shocked to see the stranger was back, looking as determined as ever. Claudine panicked. She cut across streets and alleys, frantically trying to lose the stranger, but no matter what she did, there she was, like a phantom.

She hurried down Shaftsbury Avenue bumping into people and stumbling forward. She wanted to scream, but she didn't. She couldn't. She just kept running in little steps in her high heels. Saint Patrick's Cathedral was ahead.

She dodged a group of tourists and sprinted toward the back door to Saint Patrick's. There would be priests there, someone who could help her. It would be a safe haven. She was sure.

Claudine ran up the steps to the old church, taking them two at a time, and launched herself through the unlocked oversize wooden doors. She expected worshippers, but the church was barren. Blind from going from bright afternoon sunlight into the darkness of the church, she stumbled past one of the pews. She nearly ran into one of the priests.

"Oh, thank God!" Claudine said. "Somebody's following me! I need help!"

Claudine stopped. As her eyes adjusted to the semi-darkness of the cathedral, she noticed some alarming things about the priest she had just bumped into. He wasn't really a priest. He wore a black hooded robe that kept his face in dark shadow. The cross around his neck was upside down. It was made of some kind of polished black stone.

Claudine's terrified heart nearly leaped out of her chest. She tried to scream when the powerful arms of the counterfeit priest grabbed her by the shoulders, spun her around, and pulled her back against the wall. One of the evil priest's hands clamped over her mouth, and the other applied a chokehold around her neck. Claudine couldn't move or make a noise.

Like a ghost, the female stranger entered the church. She silently withdrew an elaborate WWII Nazi SS dagger from an inside pocket of her overcoat. The blade gleamed menacingly. It looked razor sharp. Claudine got a good look at the stranger. She saw her own terrified reflection in the stranger's sunglasses. She couldn't help thinking, *I know this person.*

Claudine tried to scream, but it was too late. The knife plunged into her heart. The blade shoved deep enough into her chest to cover the German inscription *Meine Ehre Heißt Treue* (My Honor Is Loyalty).

Claudine slid to the floor.

CHAPTER FIVE

MIDNIGHT RAMBLER

Brian woke late the next day and ordered a room service breakfast and a newspaper. When he saw the headlines, he nearly choked. He was struck numb to read about the murder of Claudine Jillian. It took several disbelieving moments for the truth to sink in. Brian turned a whiter shade of pale.

His ears rang and his heart raced. *No! Not Claudine!* For a moment, his hands shook so hard he couldn't read the words. He put the newspaper down and spread it on the bed. He read the article three times. The lurid headlines shouted at him: TOP MODEL KILLED BY NAZI RIPPER!

Brian's paranoia agitated his fear. *It had to be a dream. It had to.*

But it wasn't.

There was no mention of Brian being with Claudine in her apartment the night before, thank God. Was Brian a suspect?

And who would kill Claudine? Why? It didn't make sense. She was such a sweet girl with no known enemies. The papers called it a ritualistic killing with a German WWII SS knife. The knife was left in her chest, shoved in to the hilt, the German inscription, *Meine Ehre Heißt Treue*, covered in blood.

The thought of it pushed Brian's already fragile paranoia over the top.

Nazis, thought Brian, *we've brought out the bloody Nazis. It must have been that damn photo. Thank God* Stern *magazine refused to run it, but the tabloids have had it for weeks. Everybody's seen it now. They think I'm a Nazi! It was Anita's idea. The crazy bitch. She loved the controversy. She said, "Who cares? If they don't like it, fuck them. Besides, you look good in a Nazi SS uniform."*

Brian didn't know what to do. He didn't want to call the Stones office, and besides, there didn't seem to be anything to keep out of the papers as of yet. Brian and Claudine were the only ones who knew they were together that night. Brian's heart sank as he remembered making love to the beautiful, vibrant Claudine. And now she was dead. Was it in some strange way his fault? Did that night of passion have anything to do with her murder? Could the killer have been after Brian?

What did the inscription on the knife mean? "My Honor Is Loyalty." Loyalty? Whose loyalty? The Stones? The fans? A spurned lover from the past? Brian let his mind stumble over all these thoughts like a blind man on an obstacle course.

He had to tell somebody. Brian called Bobby.

"Dust Bin Bob?"

"Yes?"

"Something terrible happened last night. Claudine Jillian was murdered."

"I just saw the newspaper. It's shocking. They're calling it the Nazi Ripper. She was stabbed through the heart with a WWII Nazi SS dagger in Saint Patrick's Church. How bizarre."

"Who would kill Claudine? She was a threat to no one. Everybody adored her. This is all rather upsetting. I somehow feel responsible. Can you come over? I need to talk with you privately. I'm afraid the phones may be tapped."

Bobby sighed.

"Why don't we meet in my shop? We're closed now. It's one hundred percent private, and I guarantee you no one's eavesdropping."

"Yes, excellent! I'll see you there in one hour."

Bobby hung up the telephone. John Lennon stood behind him. His hair longer and starting to creep over his shoulders. He'd grown a beard and mustache, too, like all of the Beatles. John's charisma glowed in the half-light.

"Did you tell him I was here?"

Dust Bin Bob shook his head.

"He has no idea John Lennon will be waiting for him."

John rubbed his hands together.

"Good! Suddenly, the worm is on the other foot!"

"The worm?"

"The worm of truth!"

"Are you sure you want to surprise him? The guy is as jumpy as a chicken on a hot plate."

John Lennon smiled soulfully.

"When we met Elvis, he told us an outrageous story about his manager, Colonel Tom Parker. Seems the Colonel used to promote a dancing chicken on the county fair circuit. He used an actual hot plate to burn the chicken's feet until the unfortunate bird couldn't help but dance. Elvis told me sometimes he felt like that dancing chicken."

"Looks like Brian has a case of dancing chicken hot foot himself."

John said, "He's my friend. He needs help. I think he deserves a good turn. You know I appreciate acid as much as the next freak, but there comes a point when you have to step back."

Bobby spoke softly. "The problem is, he's expecting some kind of magic from me, like in the Philippines."

John nodded his head.

"Manila was a nightmare for sure. And he's right. You did have magic that day. Maybe you can summon that same mojo again. You foiled an assassination attempt by your own brother. No one else could have done it. It was karma. God knows what would have happened had you not been there. The way I see it, you saved my life and the lives of all the Beatles."

Bobby said, "Clive was certifiably insane."

"Is he still alive?" John asked.

"Yes, he's still alive, rotting away in a Filipino prison. He'll never walk again. Let's hope he stays there."

John said, "If one of those bullets would have even so much as grazed one of us, it would have been an international incident.

It was your fate to be there, just like it's your fate to save Brian now."

Bobby raised his hand. "Now hold on. Save Brian? I hardly know him. It's not like you and me. We were like brothers in the beginning. It's not the same with Brian."

"He's *my* brother," said John. "And that makes him your brother, too."

Bobby's voice sounded whiny. "How can you expect me to save him? I can't save him from himself. The man's a bloody basket case."

"It has to be you," John said firmly.

"Why?"

John grinned, breaking the tension. "Because you're legendary Dust Bin Bob! Savior of rock stars!"

"Must you call me that? Now Brian's using it, too."

"Because it has something to do with your mojo. As Bobby Dingle, you're just another guy, but as Dust Bin Bob, you're king of vinyl, friend of the Beatles, you have magic. You're a lifesaver."

"Why don't you just help him yourself?" Bobby posed the logical question.

John shook his head.

"Can't do it. I'm a Beatle first and foremost. And Beatles can't get involved in another band's business, especially the Rolling Stones. No, I'm afraid it's up to you, Dusty."

Bobby said, "I'm leaving for Baltimore as soon as the strike is over."

"From what I read in the newspapers, it might be more than a couple of days."

Bobby waved his hands as if directing traffic on Mars. "The minute that strike is over, I'm leaving. My wife is expecting me."

John put his hand on Bobby's shoulder.

"I know, but can't you help just a little bit while you're here?"

Bobby couldn't say no to John Lennon.

"Why are you so concerned about Brian?"

John lit a cigarette and blew the smoke into the air.

"Let me tell you a little story. Do you remember when Andrew Loog Oldham asked me and Paul to write a song for the Stones because they didn't have any original material? They desperately needed an original song and they were not songwriters at the time. We were flattered that he would ask us; after all we were beginners ourselves. It was a big deal. We went over to watch them rehearse. I had a little idea and Paul had a little idea so we stuck 'em together. Well, we worked hard on the song and it turned out to be a good one—'I Want to Be Your Man'—Ringo sang it for the Beatles. When it was all over and we handed the song to Mick and Keith, they didn't even thank us for it. Maybe they forgot, I don't know. The only one who acted like he really appreciated it was Brian. We became friends after that. I never forgot that. I remember Mick and Keith were aloof about the whole thing. I think they were a little put off by the fact that we could write songs and they couldn't at the time. They probably resented Andrew going over their heads and asking us directly."

Bobby listened to John. He hadn't heard that story before.

An hour later, Dust Bin Bob, Clovis, and John Lennon sat around the closed shop waiting for Brian and drinking tea that John had thoughtfully brewed on the office hotplate. Bobby knew John made the world's best cup of tea. He had special way of doing it that brought out the full flavor. Always started with the dry teabag, then poured the hot water over it. He added the milk and sugar to the hot water immediately thereafter as the tea was steeping.

John and Clovis were deep in conversation.

John said, "You're with them in the studio every day, why do the rest of the Stones treat him so shabbily?"

Clovis looked John Lennon in the eye.

"I'll tell you the truth, pardner. They see Jonesy as a big fat liability. He can't be counted on. When they're touring, he misses gigs all the time, claiming one type of illness or another. And when he does show up, he's usually whacked out of his gourd and can't play. Keith resents having to play all the parts. You know the Stones are a two-guitar band. That's their sound. One man can't do it alone."

John said, "But Brian plays all the instruments that give the Stones their exotic sound. He even showed up last week at Abbey Road Studios and blew some sax on a Beatles tune. He's multitalented. Everybody in the Beatles loves him."

Clovis replied, "That's true, but you can always get a session cat to play those parts, and you don't have to give them a full share of the band's money. It doesn't replace being onstage every night and delivering a simple twelve-bar blues. John, you know it's a marathon, not a sprint."

John nodded.

"Ringo missed a portion of the Australian tour when he had his tonsils out. We replaced him with a session drummer named

Jimmy Nicol. Nice bloke. The guy was an excellent drummer, but it wasn't the same."

Clovis paused, deep in thought.

"To my knowledge, the only time Keith ever missed a gig was when he was electrocuted in Sacramento during the 1965 tour. If he hadn't been wearing rubber-soled Hush Puppies that day, he probably would have died. His strings brushed a live microphone, and the electric shock knocked him right off his feet. He was out cold for an hour and woke up in the hospital. But he bounced right back and played the next show."

"How do you know that?" Bobby asked.

"He told me."

Bobby grunted.

John knew a thing or two about touring and hanging out with the same guys day after day. The Beatles had managed to live through it. Their camaraderie held them together. Music was the glue. Professionalism was their badge of honor. It was all for one and one for all. Most bands are strongest during their "us against the world" period of development.

John said, "Fame does not sit lightly on anyone's shoulders. And on some people's shoulders, like Brian's, it doesn't fit at all. It's like a gorilla."

Bobby nodded.

"What do you know about this American bloke, this Acid King Leon?" John asked. "He's been spreading this new purple haze around. It's pretty good shit. Does anybody know his last name?"

Bobby held up a hand.

"Silverman, his name is Leon Silverman. I did a little snooping."

"Silverman?" John said. "Why does that name sound familiar to me?"

Somebody rapped lightly on the glass door of the shop. Bobby went to answer it. It was Brian. He looked nervous and pale. He was sweating profusely even though the weather was cool. The bags under his eyes seemed heavier than usual. They twitched involuntarily every few moments.

Bobby let Brian in, locked the door behind him, and then led him back though the shop to his office.

Brian was surprised to see John Lennon standing next to Clovis.

Bobby said, "I brought a friend of yours."

"John . . ." Brian coughed and held back a tear. "It's so good to see you, man."

John hugged Brian. They were two veterans of the rock 'n' roll wars.

"I heard you were having some problems."

"John, John . . . thank you so much. Nobody else could possibly understand."

John patted Brian's back.

"It's okay, mate. I'm here. Dust Bin Bob is here. Clovis is here. We're here to help."

Brian shivered. "Things are strange."

John pulled out a joint from his pocket and lit it with one of Bobby's silver WWII-era Zippo lighters. The smoke filled the room like a velvet fog. No one said a word, and they smoked in silence for a few minutes.

Finally, Brian said, "Did you hear about Claudine Jillian?"

"Yes," they all said. "It's front-page news."

Bobby said, "Didn't I meet her at your house the night of the dinner party? She's one of Anita's modeling friends, right?"

"Yes. A really beautiful girl. I was with her the night before she died."

Bobby's jaw dropped.

"You were . . . what?"

Brian told them the whole story.

"We met up after hours at The Speakeasy Club. I was looking for Anita and I ran into Claudine. She was alone. She looked good. And I was so depressed, I didn't want to be alone. We went back to her place and humped like rabbits all night long. She was incredible. Now she's dead."

"Do the police know?"

Brian shook his head.

"Nobody knows."

"The cops are sure to search her apartment. Did you leave any evidence?"

"Maybe some pubic hairs. I arrived and left with the clothes I was wearing."

"Think carefully," Clovis said. "Did you leave anything behind? Some matches, a guitar pick, cigarettes, things like that?"

Brian stammered. "I may have left a roach in the ashtray."

"Did it have lipstick on it?"

"Yes, I think it did."

Clovis looked at John and Bobby.

"The cops will probably assume that the roach belonged to Claudine."

John's voice dropped.

"Brian, do you know anything about this you're not telling us?"

"You mean about Claudine? God, no! I was just as shocked as you were when I heard about it! Claudine was incredible. I made love to her all night long, and now she's stone cold. You know what that's like? Christ, I feel somehow responsible for this, but I don't know why. I just have a bad feeling. It feels like I've been kicked in the chest."

John put his hand on Brian's shoulder.

"Maybe it's time you took a little vacation and got some perspective."

Brian managed a wan smile.

"With you?"

John said, "No, I can't leave now, but Bobby and Clovis are two of the most capable people I know. Maybe they can take you for a little trip somewhere."

The phone rang and Bobby didn't answer. After too many rings to ignore, Bobby picked it up.

"Hello? Brian? No, he's not here at the moment. Can I take a message?" Bobby recognized Keith's voice. "Keith?"

"What are doing at your shop at this time of night?"

"Just hanging out."

Keith's voice was tobacco rough and Tennessee whiskey smooth. He slurred his words a little and laughed at his own private jokes. He was hard to understand in person, much less over the phone.

"Listen, mate. I'm tryin' to bring this fuckin' band back together again. I'm inviting everyone up to my place at Redlands for a nice quiet weekend away from London. Tell Brian I want him to come and bring Anita, too. I'll send a driver out to pick him up. You're invited to join us, too, Dusty."

Dust Bin Bob smiled.

"I'll have Brian call you back if he shows up."

Bobby hung up.

"Keith is inviting everybody to Redlands for the weekend. He wants to bring the band back together again."

Brian's mood had flipped. Suddenly, he was as happy as a puppy.

"Bring the band back together? That's wonderful! Good old Keith."

"He said he'd send a car."

"What about Anita?" Brian said. "I can't go without her."

John thought long and hard and said, "I can contact some Beatles fans and Apple scruffs. They'll know where to find a posh bird like Anita. Don't worry."

John made several telephone calls and managed to locate her through mutual friend Robert Fraser. She had been staying at Fraser's art gallery in a small apartment behind his office. There was no sexual tension between Anita and Robert because Robert was gay, which assuaged Brian's jealous nature.

Before John had to leave, he spent several minutes talking with Brian alone. They were deep in conversation in the corner of the room. Bobby realized that they were the only two people in the world who could have that conversation. John Lennon talked of fame and keeping his sanity and had a lot to say while Brian listened intently. When John said good-bye, Bobby saw a tear in Brian's eye.

Bobby and Clovis quickly organized an expedition to find Anita and put Brian in the backseat of the Mini. When they arrived at Fraser's gallery, they found Anita sipping champagne and looking gorgeous in a new dress. The minute she saw Brian, she rushed into his arms. They held on to each other, hugging and kissing. All their past animosity evaporated instantly. It was as if it never happened. Bobby noticed Anita's black eye was nearly healed, and with makeup it had almost disappeared. Bobby knew the ugly truth though. It was still there and nothing could erase it.

"Keith invited us to Redlands for the weekend!" Brian shouted.

"Keith did that? What a wonderful idea!" Anita sang. "Let's go."

Bobby added, "Keith said that George and Pattie Harrison are coming down and so is Robert. It's going to be a great weekend."

Brian swept Anita off her feet and out of the building. Later, as Anita packed her suitcase, she asked about Claudine Jillian. Brian said nothing about being with her the night before her death. Mutually, they decided not to go to the funeral because it would be too much of a bummer. Besides Mick and Marianne had already left for Redlands, and Keith was right behind them.

Clovis and Bobby decided to take Keith up on his offer, plus

John suggested they keep an eye on Brian to make sure he didn't get too whacked out and embarrass himself. Brian insisted on having dinner in London that night, so the foursome would make the drive the next morning.

When Clovis got home and told Erlene about the party at Redlands, she steadfastly refused to go. She didn't like Brian anymore. She didn't want to have to act like she didn't punch him at The Scotch of Saint James.

"Fuck that little weasel," she said. "You better be careful honey, or they'll dose you with that LSD again. That's some nasty shit."

"I will."

"And for God sake, watch what you put in your mouth."

"Okay."

"You can't trust those damn rock stars."

Bobby walked through the silent apartment, remembering all the gleeful noises Winston made, and he felt empty. He still hadn't been able to have a real conversation with Cricket and apologize. Had she been avoiding him? Every time he called, it was the wrong time. Tonight, he was determined to finally get through and resolve their differences. He dialed her number in Baltimore.

The overseas operator connected him. The static and crackle on the phone lines made ordinary conversation difficult.

A female voice answered.

"Hello?"

"Cricket? It's Bobby."

He waited a second for some type of response. When there was none, he plunged ahead.

“Honey, we’ve got to talk.”

“Okay, I’m listening.”

Bobby told Cricket the whole story, about how Brian dosed them and how he wandered through the park all night. He left nothing out. When he finished, Cricket sighed.

“I already know,” she said.

“What do you mean?”

“Erlene called. She told me everything. She managed to get through on the telephone, even though you couldn’t. She even called at a decent hour. Unlike you.”

“Did you get my telegram?”

“Yes, I got your silly telegram. What’s wrong with you, Bobby Dingle?”

“So much has happened since you left. A girl was murdered and Brian’s a mess.”

Her voice was cool.

“Brian’s state of mind doesn’t surprise me, but a girl was murdered? What happened? Did he kill her?”

“No, of course he didn’t! She was a model friend of Anita’s. She was stabbed in public.”

Bobby could hear sobbing in the background. He realized that Cricket was crying and holding the receiver away from her face.

“Honey? Are you crying?”

Cricket sniffed into a tissue.

“Why don’t you come home? You’re getting sucked deeper

and deeper into Brian's sordid little soap opera. Get out. Get out now before it's too late. I miss you. Winston misses you. We're waiting for you."

"It's tough right now. I've been trying to get a flight, but there's an airline strike."

"It's about Brian Jones, isn't it?"

"Yes, but . . ."

Bobby thought he could hear Winston in the background playing. It made his heart ache.

Cricket's voice was firm.

"I don't want you hanging around with Brian. He has really bad karma. I can feel it. It'll rub off on you. He's a disaster waiting to happen. Your place is with your family, not hanging around with decadent, narcissistic rock stars."

Bobby sighed.

"I can't leave yet. Brian needs me."

"What's more important, your family or Brian Jones?"

"I just can't walk out on him now. I promised John."

"Choose, Bobby Dingle. A month ago, you didn't even know this guy; now you're babysitting him. How much of this is you being starstruck? You, Bobby Dingle, are hanging out with one of the Rolling Stones, the big bad Stones, the anti-Beatles. Isn't your relationship with John enough? Do you really need this?"

Bobby contemplated his answer, but before he could say anything, she spoke again.

"Winston and I want you to come home."

"You know I love you and I miss you and Winston more than

I can say. As soon as the planes are flying again, I'll come right back."

"How long will that be?"

"As soon as the strike is over. It's already been a couple of days, so hopefully it will be resolved soon."

"And you promise you'll come right home?"

"As soon as I can get a flight."

Cricket sighed again. "All right. But be careful."

The weekend retreat at Redlands was turning into quite a party. The list of friends grew to include Robert Fraser and his Moroccan servant, Mohammed Ajaj, and Christopher Gibbs. Someone had invited a King's Road flower child named Nicky Cramer, and he drove up with Robert. Nicky was a space cadet and why anybody would have invited him was a mystery. Tony Bramwell, an associate of the Beatles and friend of Mick Jagger's, plus photographer Michael Cooper also made the trip.

Redlands was Keith's country estate with plenty of bedrooms, a huge dining hall, and grand living room.

Keith's usual driver, Tom Keylock, was ill, and somehow Skully got the job to drive down to Redlands. He'd been hanging around the Stones office lately, looking for a way to ingratiate himself and put him next to the Stones.

"Drive Keith? No problem," he said cheerfully.

Keith's entire entourage stopped at Abbey Road Studios before they left London to witness the Beatles recording a brilliant new song called "A Day in the Life." Buzzed from the genius of the song and several joints, Keith led the throng into the night feeling creative and exultant.

Skully invited Acid King Leon Silverman to ride with them, which pissed Keith off. However, once he saw the contents of Leon's briefcase, he changed his mind. It was an apothecary of recreational drugs, including huge amounts of purple haze.

They arrived at Redlands around midnight on Saturday. After building a roaring fire in the huge Tudor fireplace, they set about exploring the contents of Acid King Leon's briefcase. Keith was particularly keen to try the purple haze.

They sat around the cozy fire and rolled joints. Keith pulled out his guitar and played. He strummed his vintage Gibson Hummingbird acoustic. The same chords that would eventually become the song "No Expectations." The chords were sad, yet beautiful. Keith's guitar playing could hover on the edge between feelings. He had the ability to make you hear what he *didn't* play, along with what he did. Everyone in the group was mesmerized by his playing. He played far into the night.

The next day, Keith woke up around noon and found Acid King Leon already up. Leon suggested a magical mystery tour of Sussex in his minivan, including a trip to the beach. Most of the guests went along, happily tripping through the countryside. Leon dispensed the purple haze freely. Before long, the entire group was flying.

They returned to the house after dark. Everyone was tired and feeling mellow after a long acid trip. Robert Fraser's servant, Mohammed, made dinner. George and Pattie Harrison left to return to their house in Surrey. Marianne went upstairs to take a bath. She was the only one who hadn't brought a change of clothes, so after the bath she wrapped herself in a large fur rug and came downstairs just as Keith put on Bob Dylan's latest album—the masterpiece double album *Blonde on Blonde*. Someone noticed a face peering through the window.

"It's probably just a fan," Keith said. The doorbell rang.

"Let's be quiet and maybe they'll go away."

Shortly after George and Pattie left, Keith heard knocking at the door. He looked through the peephole and saw a group of twenty uniformed dwarves dressed in blue with shiny metallic bits and helmets. Keith swung open the big front door and invited them in with open arms.

Flying on acid, Keith said, "Wonderful attire! Am I expecting you? Come on in, it's chilly outside."

In stepped Chief Inspector Gordon Dimely.

"I have a warrant to search this premises," he said curtly.

Keith was so high, he didn't realize it was a bust.

"Yes, yes," he said, "Come on in and we'll read it by the fire."

The police searched everyone. Policewomen searched the ladies. Marianne ran upstairs wrapped in her fur rug and let it drop just as she got to the top step.

"Search me first!" she squealed.

Acid King Leon Silverman's briefcase was sitting on the table in plain view. One of the cops asked about the contents of the briefcase.

Silverman quickly explained it contained sensitive film for an American TV show that would be exposed if the briefcase were opened. Miraculously, the cops believed him. There was enough LSD in the briefcase to send him to prison for a long time, but apparently not today.

The phone rang and Keith picked it up. It was Brian and Anita saying that they were about to leave Courtfield Road to come to Redlands. They'd been shopping, and it had taken extra time to leave the house, but now Brian was anxious to get rolling.

"Don't bother," Keith deadpanned. "The cops are here. We've just been busted."

CHAPTER SIX

YESTERDAY'S PAPERS

Brian ran around his townhouse like a maniac, throwing things into two suitcases open on the bed. Anita had caught a full dose of Brian's paranoia and was frantically doing the same.

"Hurry!" he shouted. "They could bust in any second!"

Bobby tried to calm him.

"Be cool. Nothing's going to happen."

Clovis had turned on the TV in Brian's bedroom and was watching BBC News. The Redlands bust was the lead story, the biggest story of the year so far. The video of Mick and Keith being led away in handcuffs, surrounded by cops, was disconcerting. Every tabloid, including *News of the World*, screamed the headlines, fanning the flames.

"That's what they want to do to me!"

Brian pointed at the screen.

"As soon as they get their hands on me, I'm finished!"

The picture shifted to the Chichester, West Sussex, police station where a large crowd had gathered. The reporter breathlessly read the copy, accentuating the well-known rock star names. Clovis watched with intense interest.

"Skully and Silverman. I'll bet they had something to do with this. There was something not right about those guys," Clovis said.

Bobby sat down next to Clovis to watch the TV screen. A press conference had just begun. A gaggle of cops and dignitaries was gathered in front of a bank of microphones. Reporters didn't wait for instruction. They began to shout questions over the din. These weren't the civilized Fleet Street reporters who worked for the well-known news sources; these were sleazy tabloid reporters who tried to spin the news to make everything seem more salacious. They were the bottom-feeders. Their questions were rude, pointed, and dripping with sarcasm. They seemed to have professional disdain for the Rolling Stones and took great comfort in their troubles. It was the very definition of schadenfreude. The bad karma seemed to swirl around the Stones endlessly.

Clovis pointed at the screen and shouted, "Wait a second! I know that guy!"

"What guy?" Bobby asked.

Clovis pointed at a man in the background wearing a black suit with a gray fedora pulled low over his eyes. He was nervously smoking a cigarette.

"That guy," Clovis said, pointing.

"Who is he?"

"He's a Baltimore narc I used to know on The Block. His name is Bruce Spangler. He was the biggest, baddest narc in town and eventually rose to be the top man in drug enforcement in Baltimore. Everybody knew him. He was a deal maker. He used to come in and watch the late show when I played at the Two O'Clock Club. He liked one of the strippers there. He busted me once for smoking a joint. What an asshole."

Bobby scratched his head.

"Why would a Baltimore narcotics cop be in West Sussex?"

Clovis continued. "He eventually got promoted and went to work for the feds. Remember, Washington is right down the street from Baltimore, and he had a lot of friends. The Baltimore City Police Narcotics Enforcement Division was one of the most corrupt in the country when he was there, so he fit right in with Washington."

"Are you sure that's him?"

Clovis squinted at the screen.

"Yep. See the way he holds his cigarette? The way he stands? That's him for sure. That son of a bitch busted me between shows! I was out in the alley and I had just lit a joint, and here comes this big asshole with his stripper chick. He sees me and wants to impress her. Next thing I know, I'm in handcuffs and spending the night in jail."

Spangler pushed his hat back, and Clovis got a better look.

"See? That's him! He's got a tattoo on the back of his hand."

"What's his name again?"

"His name is Bruce Spangler. I'd know that face anywhere. If an American narc is involved in the Redlands bust, you know something is rotten somewhere."

Brian had been watching over their shoulders.

"Wouldn't you know it? That's Nobby Pilcher standing next to him."

They all crowded around the TV.

Anita said, "The *News of the World*'s favorite detective sergeant."

"The bastard," Brian mumbled.

Brian seemed on the verge of a nervous fit. His breathing had become rapid and shallow. His asthma flared. Sweat bloomed on his forehead. He twitched.

Clovis said, "If those two have joined forces, it's gonna be a very bad scene, man."

Brian rasped, "I must be next. We've got to get out of here."

Bobby tried to be the voice of reason.

"But where can you go?"

The telephone rang, jarring them back to reality. When Brian and Anita made no move to pick it up, Bobby acted as valet.

"Hello?"

The voice on the other end was instantly recognizable with its thick Scouse accent.

"Dust Bin Bob? What are you doing at Brian's house answering the phone like a common career girl?"

Bobby recoiled.

"John? Is that you?"

John Lennon's voice could be incredibly funny at times, especially when he delivered his deadpan punch lines.

"No, it's the Duke of Prunes, Dusty. I'm just checking to see if Brian's getting enough fiber."

"I just happened to be standing here next to the phone. Brian and Anita are packing."

John cleared his throat.

"Good, because it's you I want to talk to. Thanks for hanging out with Brian. He hates to be alone and he's too trusting of people. The cops are on the warpath lately. It's a recipe for disaster. If he should get busted and go to jail, he'll freak out. I believe he's actually capable of suicide."

Bobby interrupted. "John, I understand, but really, I can't be his minder twenty-four hours a day. I have my own life. Remember, as soon as the strike is over, I'm flying to Baltimore to be with my wife and son."

John waited a beat. "Please keep an eye on Brian while you're still here. I sense something terrible is coming. Do it as favor to me."

Bobby let the words sink in.

"I will. But I won't be around much longer."

"Maybe Clovis could keep an eye on Brian after you're gone. Everybody loves Clovis."

"Why don't you ask him? He's standing right next to me."

"Jolly good! Let me talk to him."

Bobby handed Clovis the phone.

"It's John Lennon."

Clovis smiled and took the phone, half expecting it to be a joke. "There's three words I thought I'd never hear."

He brought the phone to his mouth and pressed the earpiece against his head. "What's up, Johnny?"

John's accent left no doubt.

"When Dust Bin Bob goes back to Baltimore, would you keep an eye on Brian for me?"

"Sure, man. No problemo."

"You saw what happened at Redlands. Let's make sure it doesn't happen to Brian."

"Will do."

"Considerate it a personal favor to me."

"You got it, pardner."

Clovis hung up and looked at Bobby.

"Easy as pie, see?"

"I hope you didn't bite off more than you can chew just now. This stuff has a way of wearing you down."

Driving back through London traffic in Clovis's Mini, BBC News played on the radio.

Bobby said, "I hope you did the right thing."

Clovis became indignant.

"Hey, man. I don't know about you, but when John Lennon asks me to do him a personal favor, I do it."

"I've known you a hell of a lot longer than I've known Brian. I care more about you getting in over your head."

"I don't care. I just gave a Beatle my word. My word means something. If it's a nightmare, it's a nightmare. I'm still doing what I said I would do."

"Just be careful, okay?"

Bobby and Clovis were alone with their thoughts when BBC News interrupted through the speakers. The strike was over.

Bobby said, "Take me home. I have to pack."

* * *

"Morocco," Brian said. "We're going to Morocco. Brion Gysin invited me to come over and see the Master Musicians of Joujouka. He's been trying to get me to come over and hear these guys. He says it's the world's only four-thousand-year-old rock band. He wants me to record them."

Brian didn't have to explain to Anita that Brion Gysin was a beat-generation expatriate living in Morocco; she already knew that. She knew William Boroughs hung out with Gysin at the legendary Beat Hotel. She knew he invented the "cut up" technique of writing used by Burroughs in his landmark novel *Naked Lunch*. She also knew Gysin was a friend of Brian's.

Clovis whistled low.

"Morocco? Man, that's far away."

Brian said, "Everything's legal there. We can smoke and relax without fear of the cops kicking in the door. We should all go together. Christopher Gibbs goes there on buying trips all the time for his antique shop. Why can't Dust Bin Bob do the same? Moroccan stuff is very popular these days."

"Because he's on a plane bound for Baltimore as we speak."

"Oh . . ."

No one had asked Clovis to go on the trip, and he was grateful. He had lots of work at Olympic Studio, more than he could handle. Still, he stood by dutifully and waited for Brian.

Brian would be surrounded by the Stones and their entourage. What could go wrong?

Indeed. Brian's problems never seemed to end. The gravitational pull of the black hole at the center of Brian's bad karma sucked Clovis ever closer to the abyss. Clovis felt sorry for Brian. For a man who had everything, he never seemed happy.

Bobby checked the time and called Cricket again.

The phone rang several times before it was answered. A series of clicks that preceded every transatlantic phone call ensued. Bobby waited until he was sure whoever had answered was listening clearly.

"Cricket? This is Bobby. Are you there?"

Bobby heard someone breathing on the other end of the line, but no words were spoken. After a few moments the phone hung up, breaking the connection.

What the fuck was that? Was that Cricket and she just hung up on me? Was it someone else in the house? Bobby's heart raced.

He redialed the number quickly. This time, there was no answer. His mind began to weave strange scenarios.

He dialed one more time with the same result. Bobby felt a wave of Brian Jones–style paranoia pass over him.

The Stones office approved Brian's trip to Morocco. They were anxious to get Brian away from London, away from the newspaper headlines, and most of all, away from the cops. At least in Morocco, there was no chance of getting busted.

Keith decided to come along, too. Mick and Marianne were already there. The plan was simple. Tom Keylock would meet Brian, Anita, and Keith at the Hôtel George V in Paris. He would bring Keith's car, nicknamed "Blue Lena." It was a huge blue 1965 Bentley S3 Continental Flying Spur, one of a limited edition of eighty-seven. Keith described it as, "Three tons of machinery, made to be driven fast at night." It was six inches wider in the back than the front and required an experienced driver.

Tom Keylock's duties weren't spelled out. He was what they called a fixer. Tom Keylock was a hard man with a shady past. He seemed capable of violence, but no one had actually ever witnessed it. He acted as enforcer, bodyguard, concierge, and, of course, driver. From the Stones management's view, he was the perfect man for the job. His number one job was keeping the Stones out of trouble and off the front pages. He worked along side the Stones respected publicist, Les Perrin.

Bobby's flight touched down at Friendship International Airport in Baltimore on Saturday morning. Bobby took a cab to the duplex that he had purchased after his marriage to Cricket on Southway, just a few blocks from Memorial Stadium.

He considered knocking on the door. He had a key, but he didn't know what to expect on the other side of the door. In the end, he just let himself in.

"Hi, honey! I'm home!" he shouted cheerfully as he dropped his bags inside the front door.

He walked through the house to the kitchen. Cricket's mother was feeding Winston a grilled cheese sandwich. As soon as Winston saw Bobby, he jumped into his arms.

"Daddy!" he squealed. "You're home!"

Bobby hugged Winston and stole a glance at Cricket's

mother, Mrs. Samansky. She looked concerned.

"Where have you been?" she asked.

"Didn't you hear? The airlines were on strike. I got back as soon as I could."

Mrs. Samansky eyed Bobby suspiciously.

"It certainly took you long enough."

"Couldn't be helped. Where's Cricket?"

Mrs. Samansky cleared her throat and spoke clearly and precisely.

"She's gone with her friends to the Read Street Festival."

"What's that?"

"It's a street fair on Read Street. They block the street from traffic, set up a stage, and have bands. All the kids go. It's become quite the thing to do."

"Are we open through all this?"

"What do you mean?"

"Is Dingles of Read open during the festival?"

Mrs. Samansky stood there and gaped at Bobby.

"I don't know what you mean."

"Oh, for God's sake!" Bobby rummaged through a drawer and came up with a well-worn set of keys. He dashed out the door.

"I'll be right back, Winston! I gotta go find Mommy!"

Bobby found his old pickup truck parked in the alley behind the house. He doubted it would have enough juice in the battery to start. It had been sitting for months.

He got in, said a quick prayer, and twisted the keys in the ignition. To his surprise, it started right up, belching a great cloud of black smoke out the tailpipe. Bobby gunned the engine. More black smoke billowed out. After a few minutes, Bobby put the truck in reverse and rumbled out of the crumbling concrete carport. The tires crunched the uneven surface of the alley, which was full of gravel, broken glass, and garbage. He drove south to Read Street. Several blocks of the western end of the street were closed off and full of people. He parked his car several blocks away and walked to his antique shop, Dingles of Read.

Bobby walked down Read Street. The sleepy old street had changed. Now it was hippie central. Everyone was dressed in bright colors. Beads, feathers, and fringe were everywhere.

Unlike the fashion cool of London where the hipness was more sophisticated and the people expertly coiffed, these people had long unkempt hair, headbands, and wore crazy Indian clothes. They shuffled around as if they hadn't a care.

Up toward the end of the street, near the Bum Steer leather store, a spattering of head shops had opened with Zap Comix and water pipes in the display cases. You could buy a poster of Albert Einstein and a pack of Zig-Zags at the same time.

A large stage had been erected at the western end of the street. Bobby could hear rock and roll blasting out the speakers. It wasn't the gentle, upbeat rock and roll of the Beatles, it was much more aggressive. The group on stage was called the Uncertain Things, a Jefferson Airplane–style band with a female lead singer named Kathy. They were tight and loud. Bobby was transfixed. This was more like what he'd read about San Francisco than Baltimore.

He walked down the block and found the doors of Dingles of Read locked. He used his key to open the shop. He phoned his assistant manager, Graham. Graham's mother said that Graham was at the Read Street Festival along with just about everyone else in Baltimore under the age of thirty. Bobby put the phone down hard, a little miffed that Graham had missed the retail opportunity of the year. He closed the shop and walked west on Read toward the stage.

He passed some familiar faces, Read Street regulars. He searched for Cricket's face among the crowd. She was nowhere to be found.

The Uncertain Things had finished their set and Baltimore's most popular band, the Urch Perch, were setting up their equipment. The female lead singer for the Uncertain Things approached Bobby.

"Aren't you Robby the Limey?"

Bobby laughed. No one had called him that in years. Clovis had given him that nickname on his first night in town.

"You must know Clovis Hicks," Bobby replied.

"Clovis is a good friend of mine. He helped me write some songs once. I'm Kathy."

Bobby shook her hand. "Your band sounded great."

"Thanks."

Kathy noticed Bobby constantly scanning the crowd.

"Are you looking for somebody?"

"Yes, I'm looking for my wife, Cricket."

"I know her! She was at the Maryland Institute, right?"

"Have you seen her?"

Kathy shrugged. “This place is crawling with art school people. I’m sure you’ll find her.”

Bobby said, “Have you noticed if my store has been open much lately? I’ve been out of town and I’m a little concerned. It’s called Dingles of Read. It’s right down there.”

Bobby pointed down the crowded street.

“I know that place. I couldn’t tell you when it’s open. The street has got lots of new businesses on it. It’s become a hot spot. I only come down here on weekends.”

Just then Bobby caught a glimpse of Graham on the periphery of the crowd. He was standing next to a girl his age with his hands in his pockets, looking in the general direction of the stage. Graham looked as though he didn’t have a care in the world.

“Excuse me,” he said to Kathy, and dashed after Graham.

The crowd was thick and it took a few moments to get next to him.

Bobby shouted. “Hey, Graham!”

Graham looked up, surprised to see Bobby.

“Mr. Dingle?”

“How come the store is closed?”

“You’re here?”

Bobby nodded. His voice took on an exasperated tone. “Yes, I’m here. And you obviously didn’t think I’d find out about this. Why is the shop empty on a Saturday?”

“I couldn’t get anybody to work today.”

“Well, how about you? You’re supposed to be in charge when I’m gone.”

"I wanted to go to the festival," he mumbled.

"On the potentially biggest retail event of the year? With a street fair going on right outside our door? What were you thinking?"

Graham shrugged. "I figured most of the stuff we sell is too old for these people."

"That's what an antique store sells. Old stuff."

Graham gave Bobby a long, hard look. "Graham, I hate to do this. You're a nice kid, but you're fired."

Graham's mouth dropped open. He clearly wasn't ready to be fired. Reprimanded yes, but not fired. He needed this job. He was in school and jobs were scarce.

"Please, Mr. Dingle, don't fire me. My parents will kill me. I need the money for school."

Bobby studied Graham for a moment, looking him over. He was an honest kid, a little young for an antiques salesman, but he'd done a passable job. Teenagers and old ladies liked him, but he stunk as a salesman.

Bobby sighed. "All right. Maybe I was a little hasty. You promise not to do anything irresponsible like this again?"

Graham perked up. "I promise!"

The Urch Perch were running a line check, and it was very loud.

"Test! Test one! Test two!"

Bobby led Graham away from the speakers so they could talk.

"Get down there and open the store right now. Give everybody that comes in a free lollipop."

"A lollipop?"

"There's a box of them in my desk, bottom drawer. Put them on the counter."

"Okay. What else?"

"Fifteen percent discount all day! No! Let's say twenty! Twenty percent off everything during the Read Street Festival Sale. Make a sign, put it in the window."

"Yes, sir, Mr. Dingle."

"And give everybody a free button. There's a box of assorted buttons behind the counter."

"Those old ones? Like I LIKE IKE?"

"I bought that whole collection and nobody wants to buy them, so maybe we should give them away. Put the box on the counter marked FREE. Those old buttons are cool."

"Okay."

"And where's my wife?"

Graham grinned. At last, he had an answer.

"Oh, Mrs. Dingle was with some of her friends, and they hung around for a while then they left. I heard one of them say they were going over to the Bluesette tonight after the festival."

"What's the Bluesette?"

"It's a teenage nightclub on Charles Street. The Urch Perch live upstairs. They're the house band there."

"Why would Cricket go there?"

Graham's crooked smile amused Bobby.

"For fun?"

"Cricket doesn't go in much for nightclubs and drinking."

"Oh, it's a non-alcoholic club. They just have Cokes."

Bobby was immediately reminded of the early days of the Beatles at the Cavern Club in Liverpool.

"Why do people go there?"

"For the music. It's a scene. They get good bands. Grin is playing there tonight."

"Grin?"

"Yeah, they're from DC. and they have a great guitar player named Nils Lofgren. I predict big things for that guy. They are really, really good."

"Sounds like you hang out there a lot."

Graham said, "There aren't too many places to go."

Bobby spent the rest of the afternoon looking for Cricket. He hung around the stage, walked up and down Read Street, browsed the new head shops, but Cricket was nowhere to be found.

Bobby walked to places downtown that she liked to go. He visited Abe Sherman's Bookstore and browsed the magazines and the black light posters. He walked to the main branch of the Enoch Pratt Public Library on Cathedral Street and strolled through the stacks. He loved the quiet elegance of the old building, the smell of leather chairs, books, and paper. Built in 1931, it reminded Bobby of Liverpool. He checked out the Washington Monument and the park around it. He even stopped in at the Peabody Book Shop. No Cricket.

Where could she be?

Bobby remembered walking these same streets with Clovis, trying to explain the Beatles. Try as he could, he could never make Clovis understand the way he felt about the band, the way they were like brothers. It wasn't until Ed Sullivan that Clovis got it. Everyone got it then. They'd gone from rags to riches in less than a year and a half.

Now it had all changed. John Lennon was a millionaire, and George Harrison lived on a country estate. Their friendship had changed, too. Bobby knew it was predicated on respecting their privacy. If they needed him, they knew exactly how to find him. The phone rang when it rang. Just like elderly Mrs. Swithins used to say in the old days at the flea market, "A watched pot never boils, La."

Mrs. Swithins was a true philosopher. Whenever Bobby asked her how she was, the old lady would say she was "flat as piss on a plate." You can't get much flatter than that.

He remembered taking the Beatles to the Hi-Dee-Ho Soul Shack and introducing them to proprietor Preston Washington, greatest record salesman in the world. He smiled when he remembered John and Preston's conversation. The boys loaded up on records that night. It was still something they all remembered.

Bobby walked up Charles Street, lost in thought.

Where was Cricket?

Bobby became concerned. He decided to go to the Bluesette that night if he couldn't find her. Maybe showing up unannounced in Baltimore wasn't such a great idea after all. He expected to be welcomed with open arms, but the reception thus far had been disconcerting.

Eventually, he made his way back to Read Street where the

Urch Perch had just finished their set. The crowd loved every note. Bobby was used to the Liverpool beat groups and the loose, jammy San Francisco hippie bands sounded strange to him. He liked it though.

The show was over, and the crowd began to dissipate. Bobby's feet hurt. He was depressed and tired. But he still hadn't found Cricket.

Walking back to his truck, he remembered the night he met Cricket and how she used her black belt judo skills to vanquish two muggers on the street. He remembered how shocked he was and how taken aback. Cricket was no ordinary woman. He found that out the first night.

But where was she?

He drove home hoping to find her there, but she was still out. Her mother, babysitting Winston, sent disapproving looks his way when he suggested she go home. She refused, citing the Grandmother's Babysitting Creed. Winston was still her responsibility until his mother returned, she explained. Period.

CHAPTER SEVEN

2,000 LIGHT-YEARS FROM HOME

Keith Richard's Bentley, Blue Lena, rolled south outside of Paris with Tom Keylock at the wheel. Keith stayed in the front seat smoking joints and playing 45 rpm singles on Lena's front-seat record player. The American R&B music blasted out of the car as they rolled through the French countryside.

Somewhere near Toulouse, Brian suffered an asthma attack. He heaved and gasped for breath. On the surface, Anita and Keith acted concerned, but they were nearly fed up with Brian and all they really wanted was to get to Morocco as soon as possible. They planned to drive through France and Spain, then cross over to Morocco at Gibraltar.

On the second day, Brian became too sick to continue. He developed a respiratory infection and had to be hospitalized. He told Anita, Keith, and Tom to continue without him and that he would catch up in a day or two in Tangier.

As soon as Brian was gone, Keith and Anita's sexual tensions began to rise. They'd been eyeing each other for some time now, and Brian's unpleasant personality only made Keith seem all the more desirable. After being careful not to become too friendly while Brian was around, they let their inhibitions go as soon as he was out of the car.

As the Blue Lena rolled through the night, Keith and Anita attacked each other like oversexed tigers. Tom Keylock—sworn to secrecy by Keith—could hardly keep his eyes on the road as Anita gave Keith a major blowjob. Shortly thereafter, they made passionate, penetrating love in the backseat. All three of them knew it was playing with fire. Brian's reaction would be impossible to gauge, but he was sure to become violent eventually. Keith and Anita didn't care.

They arrived in Morocco and registered at the beautiful El Minzah Hotel in Marrakech. Although they booked separate rooms, Anita slept with Keith. They smoked hash and drank wine. They strolled the storybook Kasbah shopping area for whatever pleased them. They bought colorful scarves and jewelry and paused for mint tea and pastries at the outdoor restaurants. The two love exiles seemed supremely happy.

For once, Anita was free of Brian's terrible temper, but Keith warned Anita again and again not to take their liaison seriously. It was temporary, he insisted. And when Brian returned, they would have to return to their previous relationship. Clearly, Keith didn't want to destroy what he had going with Brian.

Two days later, a demanding telegram from Brian arrived. Reluctantly, Anita agreed to return to Toulouse and escort her boyfriend either back to London, where he could fully recover, or on to Tangier, if he felt better.

Anita returned to France dutifully. Brian was now insisting on flying to Morocco to meet his friend Brion Gysin as well as Mick, Keith, Marianne, and driver Tom Keylock.

The minute Brian saw Anita, he could see deceit and betrayal in her eyes. He immediately accused her of what he was convinced had happened and which indeed was the sordid truth. Keith and Anita had been playing house the whole time he was gone.

Screaming at Anita, Brian described the scenario.

"As soon as I was gone, Keith made his move, didn't he? And he had his way with you, didn't he? You cheap little German slut! You had sex with him! Admit it! You sucked his dick! You spent every moment together, didn't you? Didn't you?"

Of course, Anita denied everything. Her ability to lie was quite sophisticated, and she could stick like glue to the flimsiest of plausibilities.

The fight came to blows as most of their big arguments did. In the end, Brian relented and they drove on to Marrakech.

That first night, the Mount Vesuvius of Brian's paranoia erupted again and the Pompeii of his ego was buried under tons of ash. He was devastated by the idea that Anita would cheat on him. And with Keith! That made it ten times worse. He thought Keith was his friend, his band mate. Didn't he know something like that would destroy Brian? How could they be so callous?

The thought ate away at Brian. He became even more enraged. He attacked Anita and she fought back, throwing things and destroying most of the hotel room. Brian beat Anita to the verge of unconsciousness. The sounds of the physical abuse echoed through the ancient hotel, making Keith wince. He spent an unpleasant night listening to the woman he had just been making love to a few days before being beaten senseless. Eventually, the hotel management knocked on the door and threatened to throw them out if they didn't quiet down.

In the morning, sitting around the pool with Keith, Mick, and Marianne, Brian and Anita were coldly silent. They both bore a few cuts and bruises. The tension was terrible.

That night, Brian and Anita had another row. This one was even louder and nastier than the night before. Anita locked herself in the hotel room and wouldn't let Brian in. He became completely unhinged and pounded on the door until the concierge threw him out. He stormed out, cursing and slamming doors.

Brian returned a few hours later with two tattooed Berber prostitutes. He demanded that Anita participate in an orgy. Anita refused. Brian overturned a platter of food and began throwing things. He grabbed Anita and beat her. The two prostitutes fled in terror, and Anita stood her ground. Brian was a disgusting pig, and she had had enough.

Brian chased her around the hotel suite, beating her mercilessly. Fearing for her life, Anita fled to Keith's room.

Keith looked at Anita and said, "Fuck this. I can't watch Brian do this shit to you anymore. I'm taking you back to London."

As the sun rose the next day, Tom Keylock knocked on Keith's door. He opened it a crack and squinted out.

"What now?" Keith rasped.

"There's a plane-load of reporters that just landed at the airport. They're digging around for more Stones stories."

"Oh, shit."

"We gotta get Brian away from here for the afternoon. I got Brion Gysin to take him to the central square of Jemaa el Fna to record some local musicians on the portable tape recorder."

Keith rubbed his unshaven chin. His hair was standing up as if he'd seen a cartoon ghost. He looked like hell, but at the same time he looked elegant. There was a gypsy quality to Keith that Tom Keylock admired.

Keith said, "This is our chance! I want you to drive me and Anita back to Tangier today so we can catch a ferry back to Málaga."

Tom Keylock, who answered to the Stone management team, was hesitant.

"Ahh, Keith . . . we just can't leave him here."

Keith said, "Yes, we can! Don't give me a hard time about it! We're doing it and that's that. Fuck Brian. He's out of control."

Tom Keylock waited for Keith to say something more, but the conversation was finished and Keith closed the door.

"Get packing, Anita. We're leaving just as soon as Brian is out the hotel."

"But . . ."

"Are you having second thoughts? After the way he beat you last night?"

Anita sighed. "This is going to kill him."

Keith sneered. "Ha! It'll probably kill you first."

"I don't want to hurt him."

"Are you daft? Get packin'. It's time for Brian to face the truth."

When Brian returned to the hotel after a carefree day listening to and recording the local musicians, he was shocked to find everyone gone and the rooms empty.

All the color drained from his face. His worst dreams had come true. They had all checked out.

He phoned Brion Gysin in a panic. His voice trembled, and Brion could barely understand him.

"They're all gone! They've abandoned me! I don't know where they went! The hotel won't tell me! There's no message! I'm here all alone! Please help me!"

The Bluesette was a tiny Baltimore nightclub built into a row house on Charles Street. They didn't serve alcohol so teenagers could go there. It was the center of the rock and roll scene in Baltimore. It was very small, like the Cavern Club, but lacked the moist WWII bomb shelter ambience.

As Bobby looked around, he visualized the savage, young Hamburg Beatles blowing these people away with great songs and tight harmonies. There were no long guitar solos for the Fab Four, just straight rock and roll. Anything rock and roll reminded Bobby of his time with the Beatles in one way or another. Bobby suddenly wondered what Brian was doing. He hadn't thought of him now for one full day. A pang of guilt quickly flashed through his mind. He'd skipped town and left

Clovis in charge. Clovis was used to the structured world of the recording studio. Brian was an enigma. He lived in the age of rock and roll wildmen like Keith Moon, yet he was a gentle soul and wouldn't dream of driving a Cadillac into a swimming pool. But when Dr. Jekyll turned into Mr. Hyde, he would get incredibly violent. He became a woman beater. Anita usually paid the price. Brian Jones had a number of different demons, to be sure.

To Bobby, the Beatles differed from every other band on the planet. In the early days, they were closer than brothers. No one had ever gone through what they were experiencing and it drew them closer than words could tell. Like explorers, they were constantly in unknown waters, navigating by the stars like ancient mariners. Bobby watched the transformation himself. If you listened to their music, you could hear the magic between the notes. There had never been a band like the Beatles. Never would there be the likes of them again. Bobby was convinced of that.

The Rolling Stones were made from completely different DNA. As individuals, the band didn't seem to like one another very much. In fact, the overall impression Bobby got was that they tolerated one another as coworkers—no more, no less. Bassist Bill Wyman and drummer Charlie Watts seldom hung out with the others. They had nothing in common with the rest of the band. They kept their distance from the glimmer twins, Mick and Keith, who were as close, in their own way, as John and Paul. But the two bands had different atomic structures and were driven by different powers.

And then there was Brian, the ultimate outsider. He orbited

around the double stars of Mick and Keith in a wobbly figure eight. The Stones and the Beatles seemed forever opposites, yet balanced somehow within the musical universe.

The Bluesette reminded Bobby of countless Merseyside and Reeperbahn rock and roll joints. He could smell the energy. He could sense the excitement. His feet stuck to the floor, making gentle sucking sounds as he walked up the steps. It felt good to touch base with such an old and dear friend as live rock and roll.

The cigarette smoke stung his eyes and brought back memories of the Cavern. The Bluesette had its own roxy toxic atmosphere. It fit twenty-five people, fifty if you squeezed them in like sardines. But on summer weekends, it was not unusual for a hundred kids to show up and just hang around the building listening to the bands from outside.

Art Peyton ran the place with his wife, Sharon. They presented local bands and sold overpriced Cokes. The club was popular with rock fans from all over the city. All the Baltimore bands played there.

The band known as the Urch Perch, also managed by Art, lived upstairs in cramped apartments above the club.

Cigarette smoke swirled through the lights. The band onstage was loud and surprisingly good. Bobby Dingle walked in and edged his way around the tiny dance floor to the bar and ordered a Coke. The band hit the chorus like a sledgehammer. The lead guitarist also sang lead vocals. His voice was high and edgy.

"Hey, baby!" he screamed. "See what love can do!"

The band finished their first set and took a break. Bobby scanned the crowd. He didn't see Cricket.

"First time here?" a voice asked.

Bobby looked around to see a guy in a cranberry shirt and white Levis smoking a cigarette. His hair was a little long, but nothing like the shaggy musicians. He was no teenager but had the excitement of youth in his eye.

Bobby's ears were still ringing from the loud music.

"What?"

"I said first time here?"

"Yeah . . ."

"I'm Art. I own this place. I can tell a first-timer, they always have big eyes."

"I'm English. I just got in."

"Hey, are you in a famous band?"

"No, actually, I'm an antique dealer."

"Are you looking for somebody? You have that look."

Bobby waved cigarette smoke away from his face.

"Yeah . . . a girl named Cricket."

Art Peyton laughed.

"Funny name."

"Funny girl," replied Bobby. "What's the name of that band?"

"You don't know? These guys are the most popular band in the Baltimore-Washington area. I thought that's why you came in here. They're called Grin. The lead guitarist is amazing. His name is Nils Lofgren. He plays piano, accordion, guitar, everything—and he writes great songs."

Just then, Bobby saw Cricket coming in the door with four of her art school friends, including Dirk, a former boyfriend, who still made Bobby jealous.

He pretended not to notice her at first. As soon as she came into the club, that became impossible. The intimate dance floor pressed everybody up against everybody else.

"Bobby!" she squealed. "You came!"

She rushed into his arms, and he hugged her tight.

"When did you get here?"

"Just today. I went by the house, and your mother told me you were at the Read Street Festival, and then Graham said you might be here . . . so I came."

Cricket hugged him again.

"Oh, Bobby!"

Bobby noticed the band had returned to the stage. The drummer was already testing his drums. Nils Lofgren plugged in and hit an E chord, which reverberated in Bobby's teeth.

Bobby shouted over the noise.

"Let's get out of here. It's gonna get loud."

As they left the club, they noticed dozens of teenagers hanging around the door. Some were dancing to Grin right there on the sidewalk. Bobby and Cricket walked up Charles Street arm in arm. Bobby had a million things to say, but didn't. It wasn't the right time.

"How's your father?"

"Oh, he's just about out of the woods. They say he'll be home in a day or two."

Bobby stopped walking and turned to Cricket. He put two hands gently on her shoulders and guided her around to face him.

They both looked somewhat lost.

"Do you love me?" he asked.

Cricket blinked.

"Do I love you? Of course I love you! You're my husband and the father of my son."

Bobby stopped. That was the answer he sought.

"Do you love me?" she asked back, challenging him.

"Yes, of course I do!" Bobby answered.

"Then what's the problem?"

Bobby looked around at nothing and slowly shrugged.

Cricket smiled and sniffed. The unbearable notion that Bobby might not return dissipated. She hugged him as tightly as she had ever done.

"Let's go home," she whispered.

The next few days were blissful for Bobby. The soothing influence of Winston and Cricket pushed away all his misgivings about Brian.

He was 3,628 miles away.

As the days passed, Bobby fell into a groove. Cricket's friend Bonnie lived nearby and loved to babysit Winston. One day, she invited them to a party being thrown by some musician friends of hers.

"These people are incredible musicians. They play western-swing-jug-band-blues-ragtime music. They all live in this magical little section of Baltimore that's like a time warp. The houses are pre–Civil War. They have actual dirt roads right down in the middle of the city. A bunch of musicians took over a couple of the houses, and they all live there together. The group is called Bloody Mary and Her Black Plague Trolley Car Museum."

Bobby laughed. "What a great name! I love it!"

"Oh, they have several names, depending on who got the gig and who's singing lead."

"Are they all as good as Bloody Mary?"

"How about Omar St. Groovy and His Snake Stomping Review? Or Orange Juice Jake and the Blind Ethnic Peg-leg Pygmies?"

Bobby's laughter was genuine.

"You've got to be kidding me! Who makes this shit up?"

"These are highly unusual people."

"I can imagine."

"But they're very serious about their music. They dress in old-time clothes and have handlebar mustaches. The only thing is they don't actually have a jug player. Nobody could figure out how to play it and not look like a fool. So, technically, they're jugless."

"A jugless jug band! Brilliant!"

Cricket said, "That's about as far away from the Beatles as you can get."

Bobby said, "Well, no, not actually. The Beatles started as the Quarrymen, a skiffle group in the tradition of Lonnie Donegan. Skiffle is very much like American jug band music except, like your friends, it has no jug. That's a southern-fried American thing. They both use homemade instrumentation—washboard, washtub bass, stuff like that."

"You've got to meet Tom Naylor," Bonnie said, "He's the lead guitarist."

"Sounds like an interesting fellow."

"You'll love him."

The party was crowded. The tiny rooms of those pre–Civil War stone and mortar houses on Mill Race Road seemed to burst. Bloody Mary and Her Black Plague Trolley Car Museum were playing in the backyard. People crowded the makeshift stage and danced. The air was redolent of skunky pot smoke and barbecue. Bobby studied the jugless jug band. Bloody Mary, the supposed leader of the group, was either the bearded guy wearing a WWII leather flight helmet complete with goggles or the flashy kid with a painter's cap and granny glasses playing guitar.

All the bands these days seemed to have long weird names like Country Joe and the Fish or Big Brother and the Holding Company.

The guys in Bloody Mary were excellent musicians. The lead guitarist played a jazzy cowboy blend that sounded part Les Paul and part Bob Wills. The fiddle player played that same gypsy jazz style as the guitarist, and it cooked. The banjo player was the guy in the leather flight helmet. A washboard player with metal thimbles on his fingers scratched out a crazy beat.

A "gut-bucket bass" completed the ensemble, consisting of a washtub turned upside down with a hole in the middle of it through which a bass string was threaded and held by a washer. The bass string was attached to a broom pole at the other end. Ingeniously, the broom pole had a groove notched in its base, and it fit against the rim of the washtub. When you pulled back on the pole, the string became taut and the notes went up, and when you let it go slack, the notes went down. The washtub bass was amazingly loud and sounded like a real bass.

They played a song Bobby vaguely knew called "I'm Satisfied with My Gal."

It bounced along with an infectious ragtime beat. The fiddle player did a jazzy solo, and they finished with a flurry of showy riffs. Bobby studied the washtub bass player.

The band put down their instruments and picked up beers.

"Break time," shouted Tom Naylor, a good-looking man a few years younger than Bobby.

Bonnie introduced Bobby to Tom. They shook hands.

"Watch out, he's English."

"Can you show me how to play that washtub bass?"

"Sure. It's real easy. You're basically playing by ear. There are no frets, no actual notes; you approximate the notes by pulling back on the pole. See?"

Tom showed him.

"I noticed the guy was wearing leather work gloves when he played."

"Yeah, those bass strings can rip up your fingers something fierce. You have to wear the gloves to protect your hands. Spider John uses a real bass string, but to tell you the truth, a clothesline works just as well. Here. Why don't you give it a try?"

He handed the pole to Bobby and showed him how to position himself. Bobby pulled back on the pole and thumped some notes. It sounded surprisingly good.

"Try walking the bass."

Bobby knew that phrase meant a group of notes that climbed

up the scale then walked back down during a single phrase. It was widely used in jump blues and uptown R&B.

He tried it and it worked. Bobby was thrilled.

"Hey, I can do this."

"It's not rocket science."

Bobby continued to fiddle around with the washtub bass. It was truly a homemade treasure. In no time, he was thumping out riffs to Beatles songs.

"Bonnie tells me you own an antique store."

"Yes, Dingles of Read."

"I know that place. I'm a bit of a collector myself."

Bobby perked up.

"Really? What do you collect?"

"I collect old stereographic viewers. I've got a bunch of them."

"Stereographic viewers? Would you consider selling some?"

"Actually, yes. I would actually like to make a trade. I also collect antique instruments for the band."

"Would you be interested in an antique harmonium?"

"Yes, I would."

Bobby handed Tom a business card. "Come by the shop."

"Will do."

"You're from Liverpool, aren't you? You sound like the Beatles."

"Yes, I can't deny it. It's the Scouse in me."

Just then they heard a scream and somebody fell down the steep, narrow stairs. Tom and Bobby went to check and saw Spider John lying at the bottom of the stairs, legs akimbo, yelping in pain. Spider John was as thin as a rail and seemed to be all elbows and knees. When he fell down the stairs, it sounded like a loose cannon in rough seas.

"My wrist! I think I broke my wrist!" Spider John whined. "Shit! It hurts!"

Tom went down the steps and examined John's wrist.

"It's already swelling up. We've got to get this man to the hospital."

Several partygoers offered to take Spider John to the emergency room. They helped him out the door.

"That's what you get from excessive drinking."

"Was he drunk?"

"Well, let me put it this way, he wasn't sober."

"There goes my bass player," Tom said.

The rest of the group gathered around Tom. He introduced them to Bobby.

"This is Donald Slick, fiddle player extraordinaire; Jo Jo Snuggs, washboard, kazoo, and harp; Buck Armacost, banjo." They all shook hands.

Donald said, "What are we going to do for a bass player? We got a gig next Saturday night at the Foghorn."

"Shit!" said Buck. "We need a replacement. Does anybody know any washtub bass players?"

"Are you kidding me? Spider John was the only one in the greater Baltimore area. We're screwed."

Tom looked at Bobby.

"How about you? You were sounding good just now."

"I've only been playing for five minutes!"

"Let's do a song and see how it sounds."

"What do you know?"

Bobby said the first song that popped into his mind.

"'Rock Island Line,' by Lonnie Donegan. It's a skiffle classic."

"We know it. Let's jazz it up."

They picked up their instruments and played the song. Bobby didn't know what he was thinking. He was obviously out of his league, so he just dove in. It took him a few minutes to find his groove. Thumping the washtub bass with the thick leather gloves was awkward, but Bobby eventually got the hang of it. He held his own.

After that they played several more hopped-up blues standards like "Big Boss Man" by Jimmy Reed, "Can't Judge a Book By Lookin' at the Cover" by Bo Diddley, and "That's All Right, Mama" by Arthur "Big Boy" Crudup. Bobby enjoyed every moment of it.

Suddenly, he realized what being in a band was all about. He caught a little of the magic his friends made. For a split second, he felt it. *This must be what it's like for the Beatles*, he thought.

At the end of the jam session, all the members of the group gathered around Bobby.

"Would you fill in for John?"

Bobby grinned. "Sure. I'd be glad to. Sounds like an adventure."

"The gig is at the Foghorn Folklore Center next Saturday night. Can you be there?"

"Don't you think we should rehearse more before the gig?"

"Good idea. Let's shoot for Wednesday night. Right here on Mill Race Road."

Cricket and Bonnie found Bobby playing the washtub bass, thumping out rhythms behind Tom's guitar work. He wore the biggest grin Cricket could remember seeing on him.

"Guess what, honey?" Bobby said. "I'm in a jugless jug band."

"Don't you need a license for that?"

CHAPTER EIGHT

UNDER MY THUMB

Clovis answered on the first ring. The local time in London was 8:00 p.m., and Clovis happened to be standing next to the phone.

"Who is it?" Clovis snapped.

"It's me. Bobby. What the hell are you doing picking up on the first ring? You never do that."

Bobby heard Clovis cough.

"You won't believe it if I told you."

"What's going on, Clovis?"

"I just got a call from Brian. He's in a panic. Anita ran off with Keith, and the whole band just flew the scene without telling him. They just abandoned him in Morocco."

"Keith? Holy shit! That's bad."

Clovis cleared his throat.

"Yeah, and Brian's damn near suicidal. To him, it was

the ultimate betrayal. His friend, his band mate, his musical brother, stealing Anita and running away like a schoolboy. He's a mess."

"What are you going to do?"

"I'm packin'. I'm going to Morocco to collect Brian and bring the pieces back to London. According to Brian, they took the money, credit cards, the stash, and most of his records. Just left him high and dry. He's crushed."

"Why didn't he just call the Stones office?"

"He didn't want to. He's embarrassed. The Anita thing damn near destroyed him."

"It's hard to believe that Keith would do that to him."

"He's absolutely devastated about it."

Bobby whistled. "I'm lucky I'm not there or he'd make me go to Morocco, too."

"Ha! He wants you to come. He told me to track you down and insist that you come with me."

Bobby's voice was firm.

"I can't leave right now. It's out of the question."

"Well . . . That's what he wants."

"Tell him you couldn't find me. Tell him you don't have my address in Baltimore. Tell him anything."

"Hey, man. I really don't care. All I know is that I, Clovis Hicks, have to fly to North Africa and bring back the world's most famous basket case. I don't know what Brian was up to the night before Anita flew the coop, but it must have been some nasty business for her to run off with Keith like that. She can take a lot. She's tough. But he must have pushed her over the edge. When he gets physical with her, she fights back. They fight like cats and dogs."

"You think this will break up the Stones?"

Bobby had genuine concerns. "I remember Brian telling me, 'If the Stones have woman problems, the Stones get new women.' Little did he know . . ."

"I thought Keith said that."

"Who knows? It's ironic either way, no matter who said it."

Clovis paused. "I think that goes for guitar players, too. If the Stones have guitar player problems, the Stones get new guitar players."

"You think so? It's hard to imagine the Rolling Stones without Brian Jones."

"Somehow, the Stones will survive. I wouldn't give you two shits for Brian's future with the band, though. He's not going to be able to stand up there every night and act like nothing's wrong with the guy who betrayed him and stole his woman. I know Brian. It will kill him. Mark my words. He's going to let this thing eat away at him until he winds up dead, crazy, fired, or all three."

Bobby sighed.

"So, you're going to Morocco?"

"Yep. Check this out. I'm taking the Marrakech Express down from Tangier to Casablanca to Marrakech."

"Those names sound so romantic and adventurous. I've never been to any of them."

Clovis snorted. "Well, it's a pain in the ass as far as I'm concerned."

"Is Brian so fucked up he can't even make a plane reservation?"

"That's about the size of it, pardner."

"How did we get here?" Bobby said.

Clovis chuckled.

"You promised John Lennon you'd take care of Brian Jones, that's how we got here. Don't you remember? Then you left town and told John good ole Clovis would babysit."

"You're the one who promised John, not me."

"I should've never opened my mouth."

The transatlantic phone call crackled with static for a moment. It reminded Bobby how far away he was from London, Clovis, and the rest of his friends. He honestly wondered if he could make the transition to an uneventful life in Baltimore running an antique store.

Bobby sighed. He felt guilty leaving Clovis alone to carry the load.

"We can't let John down."

"Yeah, that's easy for you to say. You're over there. I'm the one who's going to North Africa."

"When I said we'd help Brian, I meant in the most general way. We didn't sign on for a twenty-four-hour personal care."

"I think what John meant was that if something super bad comes down, you'll know. It will be spontaneous."

Spontaneous. That was the word. Bobby's mind flashed back to the moment in 1966 when he flipped his brother, Clive, over the edge of the roof at Manila Airport. He'd done it spontaneously. There was no thought, no decision making; it was pure gut reaction. He acted to save the lives of his friends, the Beatles.

He'd relived that moment a thousand times, and each time it turned out the same with Bobby looking over the roof at his brother's broken body fifteen stories below. He was still alive, but he'd never walk or talk again.

Bobby suddenly remembered the reason he'd called.

"Hey, I just joined a jug band. Actually, we're a jugless jug band. I'm playing washtub bass. Our first gig is Saturday night."

"Well, whoop-dee-do! I'm going to Morocco and you're playing in a fuckin' jug band? What's wrong with this picture?"

"I saw Bruce Spangler in the news the other day. You were right. They sent him over to work with the London police as a consultant, and according to the *Baltimore Sun*, he says he's going to bust more rock stars."

"Another great moment in law enforcement history," Clovis deadpanned.

Bobby paused.

"I wish I knew what was going on with that asshole."

"Seek the wisdom of Preston Washington. He knows everything."

"Preston Washington? You mean at the Hi-Dee-Ho Soul Shack?"

Clovis said. "He knows more about what's going on in Baltimore than anybody."

Bobby hadn't thought about Preston in over a year. The large black man ran one of the greatest record stores in the known universe. Bobby never left Baltimore for London without a buying trip to the Hi-Dee-Ho Soul Shack. Preston was an affable shopkeeper with an encyclopedic knowledge of R&B music. He knew everybody. Bobby had taken the Beatles there after their concert at the Baltimore Civic Center. Preston had opened the store for a private shopping adventure for the Fabs. The Beatles loved it.

"What can Preston tell me?" Bobby asked.

Clovis chuckled. "He can probably tell you everything you want to know about Bruce Spangler."

"You mean they know each other?"

"He busted Preston once. Cost him a lot of money. He almost lost the store. You could say that Preston Washington has more than a passing interest in Bruce Spangler. Once you've been busted by a guy, you follow his law enforcement career forever."

"I had no idea."

"Well, now you do. Go talk to Preston. And while you're at it, drop in on Manny Brillstein at Livingston's Loans on Baltimore Street where we first met."

"The pawnbroker?"

"Manny's got connections. He has to trust you first, but if he likes you, he'll fill your ear. If you mention my name, he might even remember you were a customer."

"He would know about Spangler?"

"Manny's an old-timer. You can't run a pawnshop on The Block without having underworld ties. The mob owns half the real estate down there. As the top narc in town, Spangler made all kinds of deals. He's in it up to his eyeballs. Then he went to Washington where the shit is really deep."

Bobby said, "Why would they bring in a guy like that to Scotland Yard? He's a thug."

"There are mobs on both sides of the Atlantic. Maybe they figured busting rock stars takes the heat off of them and they made a deal with the Americans. Who knows?"

There was a pause in the conversation while both parties considered what had been said.

Bobby said, "You realize the cops will be on Brian like flies on fecal matter the minute he steps off the plane from Morocco."

"I know, man. I know. I'm not looking forward to this. I need a place to hide him."

"Hide him at your place."

"Erlene would bust my balls for that. Hey, how about your place? It's empty."

Bobby waited a beat. He didn't want to volunteer his apartment. The thought of Brian Jones in his apartment where his wife and son lived made him nervous.

"Come on, man! 'Fess up. Your place is perfect."

"I don't want Brian in my place. God knows what kind of damage he could do, not just to me and my stuff, but to my reputation. I don't need to get evicted."

"Think about it."

"I did, and the answer is no."

Clovis's voice changed. "You forget I've got a key, and you're on the other side of the world."

"You wouldn't!"

"I would."

"Clovis! Goddammit!"

"I'll call you when I get to Morocco. I gotta go."

* * *

Clovis perspired profusely in the hot shade of the midday Moroccan sun. He'd been traveling alone for two days and had just arrived at Brian's hotel.

He sat across from Brian at a tiny table in a tiny café on a tiny street walking distance from the hotel. The table was strewn with pastries, teacups, and finger sandwiches. Dominating the table, a large hookah sat billowing great clouds of blue hash smoke. Brian stoked the bowl and took another hit.

He handed the long stem to Clovis, who took a much smaller hit and put it down. His head was already spinning. Brian had been smoking dope since Clovis got there. Clovis couldn't blame him; he was self-medicating to dull the pain of losing Anita to Keith, the only friend he'd had left in the band.

Clovis took a sip of room-temperature sweet tea to lubricate his parched throat.

"How soon do you want to leave?"

Brian looked up. His eyes were fiery red, and he looked as if he hadn't slept for several days. He had bags under his eyes, and his complexion was sallow.

"Leave?"

"Yeah, don't you want to hightail it back to London?"

Brian grunted. "Yes, yes, of course, except . . ."

Clovis said, "You want to see if this old hound dog can pick up the scent of Keith and Anita and track 'em down? So you can confront them once and for all? Is that what you're thinkin'?"

Brian smiled awkwardly, as if the muscles in his face had

atrophied from chronic depression. No one else talked to him like Clovis, and it was an upbeat change of pace.

"Yeah . . ." Brian drawled.

"You devil! Looking for some revenge, are we? Who said it was best served cold? Well, my best bet is that they all went back to London. So let's catch the next plane out of Dodge."

Brian looked confused. "Dodge?"

Clovis seldom explained his cowboy references. They were all steeped in American culture, and if English guys couldn't follow, well, tough shit.

"We can catch a flight from Menara Airport tonight if we start now."

Brian remained silent for a few moments. He seemed deep in thought.

"Let's go tomorrow. We can have one last night in Morocco before we go back to London."

Clovis shrugged.

"Sure, pardner. If that's what you want."

Cricket and Bobby had been inseparable since the Bluesette. Bobby's mind worked overtime trying to separate his feelings for Cricket and Winston and the endlessly unfolding saga of Brian Jones. His mind bounced from one thought to another.

"You look distracted," Cricket said.

"I am."

"Want to tell me about it?"

"It's Brian. Anita dumped him and ran off with Keith. They ditched him in Morocco."

Cricket frowned.

"And how is this your problem?"

"I promised John I'd look after Brian."

Bobby was surprised to see anger in Cricket's face.

"What about us? What about your wife and son? If you want my opinion, I'd forget about Brian before he drags you down with him."

Bobby gazed at Cricket. Her temper had always been a controlled quiet storm. This flare-up bewildered him.

"But I promised John I'd look after Brian . . ."

"Oh, come on! I'm sick of hearing about Brian! What's more important? Brian, or me and Winston?"

Bobby stammered. "Y-you are! Of course!"

"Then what's the problem? Don't you want to live here with your wife and child?"

"Of course I do!" he shouted.

"Well?"

"I'm going for a walk!"

Bobby stood and stormed out of the house.

Bobby walked up Southway and turned right at Greenmount Avenue. He walked by Mr. Hacks Shoe Repair Shop on the corner and across the street, past the barbershop and the Stadium Pub.

He wandered aimlessly down toward Read's Drug Store. The big newsstand on the corner offered everything under the sun, even *Melody Maker* and *New Musical Express*. He bought a copy of each from the toothless vendor. He crossed the street to Pete's Tavern and went inside. He ordered a cup of tea and scanned the front page.

The tavern door flew open, and Cricket marched in. Bobby, surprised that Cricket had followed him, remained motionless with the English music press in front of him. He looked at her face and for the second time today saw something he hadn't expected—shock.

"Bobby!" she cried. Her voice sounded desperate. "Bobby!"

She swooped toward him and practically landed on his lap. She threw her arms around him and buried her face in his neck.

"Oh, Bobby! Daddy's dead!"

Bobby heard the words, but their meaning seemed to fail him. He stared at her for a moment, blinking in disbelief.

"Oh, no."

"Arthur just called from the hospital."

"I thought he was doing better."

"He took an unexpected turn for the worse. I can't believe it!"

The tears, which she had valiantly fought all the way from Southway, broke through.

"My daddy is dead!" she wailed.

The people in the restaurant watched the drama unfold. Bobby gently lifted her out of his lap and stood hugging her.

"He's gone . . ." she sniffed. "I feel numb."

Bobby felt tears welling up. He knew how much pain Cricket was experiencing. He remembered when his father died. It created a hole inside him that never went away.

He hugged her tightly, felt the tears of grief flowing from her face to his shoulder.

"I'm so sorry."

He walked Cricket back to Southway as quickly as possible and called Arthur, who was still at the hospital.

"He was doing fine," said Arthur. "We thought he'd be coming home in the next day or two . . . then this infection set it. It didn't take long. . . ."

"It doesn't seem real."

"I was speaking to him last night and he sounded fine."

"What should we do?"

Arthur paused. "Nothing. I'll make all the funeral arrangements. Just take care of Cricket. Let her grieve."

On the other side of the world, Renee sat at the hotel bar and sipped a martini. She wore a black vinyl miniskirt, high heels, and a lace blouse. It was an eye-grabbing ensemble to say the least, especially in North Africa, where most of the women covered up. Renee looked sexy and alluring.

Men had been flirting with her all night, but she brushed them off. She would not be distracted. She had a mission.

Brian walked in with Clovis and sat down at a table in the corner. Renee noticed them as soon as they walked into the bar. She'd been waiting for him. With her breasts thrust out, she checked her makeup.

Satisfied she looked her best, she slipped off the barstool and walked back to Brian's table. As she approached, Brian noticed her and looked up with bloodshot eyes.

Renee's voice was smoky.

"Well, imagine running into you here."

Brian didn't say anything for a moment. He just blinked and stared. Then he stood and kissed her. Renee kissed him back.

Without saying a word, he led her back though the door and out into the lobby.

Clovis watched them go, alarms going off in his head. He had seen Renee hanging around with a gaggle of groupies outside the recording studio.

There is something odd about her, something not quite right, he thought. *Why would she be here in Morocco? How did she find out what hotel Brian was in? How did she know he'd be alone and vulnerable tonight?* Clovis concluded that Renee had inside information. That made him feel even more apprehensive.

Not that Brian cared; he didn't. All he wanted was a smooth young body to make love to. Maybe he believed having sex with another woman would somehow dull the pain of Anita and Keith. Renee was here, she was now, and she looked good.

Brian treated Renee's arrival in Morocco as divine intervention. God had sent her to soothe his pain. There could be no other explanation. Brian led Renee back to his hotel suite and pushed her down on the bed.

"Did you come here to make love to me?" he asked.

She nodded.

"I know what you like," she said.

Brian's tight mouth curled into a wicked grin.

"You know what I like?"

"I want you to dominate me, tie me up, subjugate me."

"Then get your clothes off."

The sex was rough and desperate. Brian ravaged Renee all

night. His erection never flagged. Then at last, he fell asleep in her arms, holding her urgently close.

While Brian slept, Renee slipped out of bed and took a pair of scissors out of her purse. She held the cold silver blades against his throat for a moment. After a few moments, she moved away and carefully snipped a lock of his blond hair and folded it into a tissue. Then she went around the room collecting small trophies. She stole a scarf, some jewelry, a brush, and a hash pipe. Placing all the items in her purse, Renee slipped back into bed with Brian. As soon as he felt her press against him, he rolled over and hugged her tightly.

Downstairs, Clovis stayed in the bar and had several more drinks. He tried not to imagine what was going on upstairs between Brian and Renee. He told himself she seemed harmless enough. She was just another crazy groupie, but something about her gave him an uneasy feeling. He couldn't put his finger on it, but there was a troubling gleam in her eye. Brian was extremely vulnerable now. *Not a good time to be humping strange women in a foreign country.*

Clovis finished his drink and tried to get some sleep, but jet lag haunted him and he tossed and turned all night. He thought of Erlene. He didn't want to be in Morocco. Nothing was familiar here. Clovis counted the hours until he could leave.

In the morning, Brian woke up in a dreadful mood. His dark side had control of him. All the ugliness about Keith and Anita came flooding back. He felt dirty and hungover. He took a long, hot shower and washed himself thoroughly, spending extra time with his hair. He didn't notice the small snippet missing from the back of his head.

He walked out of the shower with a towel wrapped around him. He looked at Renee and frowned.

"You're gonna have to leave."

Renee looked at Brian. "What?"

"I need to pack. I'm leaving."

"What do you mean? I thought we—"

"Look, I really appreciated last night. The sex was great, but now I need to get back to London and deal with things."

"But, Brian, it was such a beautiful night last night. Couldn't we have just one more? Didn't I fulfill all your wildest desires?"

"Yeah."

"So? Stay here with me and I'll make you forget all about Anita."

Brian looked at her. His voice was soft but firm. "Nothing could make me forget Anita."

The crestfallen look on Renee's face forecast an emotional hurricane on the horizon.

"I'm sorry, but I'm leaving for the airport. You can stay in the hotel suite for a few hours, but you'll have to leave this afternoon."

Renee's eyes narrowed. "Leave? You can't treat me like this."

"Like what?"

"You can't just use me and toss me away. It's not right."

"You're the one who came up here last night. I didn't force you."

"Well, can I at least fly back to London with you?"

Brian shook his head. “I can’t be seen with another woman. Not right now. The place will be crawling with reporters.”

“Oh, for God’s sake!”

Renee gathered her things in a snit and left just as Clovis came to Brian’s door. She stomped past Clovis and slammed the door.

“What’s wrong with her?”

“Forget about her. Let’s get back to London.”

CHAPTER NINE

PRODIGAL SON

Mr. Samansky's funeral was dignified, but Bobby felt uncomfortable among Cricket's extended family. He felt their pain, having lost his own father, but the Americans grieved differently. Bobby's funk continued for days.

Even as the rest of the family got back to normal, Bobby continued to mope around. He didn't have much interest in the shop lately. In fact, the only thing that brought him joy was playing in the jugless jug band. To be able to feel even a microscopic amount of what it must be like for his old friends the Beatles filled him with a kind of energy he'd never experienced before.

Cricket could see the difference in Bobby. She herself had changed. After her father died, she stayed home a lot, preferring to watch the three local Baltimore channels of fuzzy black-and-white TV than to socialize. She read incessantly and spent a lot of time with her nose in her sketchbook, drawing.

Cricket liked Tom Naylor and the rest of the musicians in Bloody Mary. She viewed them as a positive influence for Bobby, and a distraction from Brian Jones, John Lennon, and all his other English rock-star friends. She encouraged him to play.

Bobby learned that Tom had booked the gig at the Foghorn, which meant that Tom would be fronting the band that night instead of Buck. That meant that, for the night, they would be known as Omar St. Groovy and His Snake Stompin' Review. Omar St. Groovy was Tom Naylor, of course, and Tom's jug-band repertoire differed slightly from that of Bloody Mary and Her Black Plague Trolley Car Museum or Orange Juice Jake and His Blind Ethnic Peg-leg Pygmies. Tom threw in a couple of originals, which Bobby thought were quite good, and rounded out his set with some Bob Wills and Hank Williams numbers. It gave the boys a chance to play. Everyone soloed, even Bobby on the primitive washtub bass. He began to feel like a member of the band.

The Wednesday-night rehearsal went long into the night. Bobby enjoyed it immensely. Jug-band music is good-time music. His fingers became full with blisters after the first hour, so Bobby wrapped some Band-Aids around them under the gloves. It took some getting used to, but he was on his way to becoming a decent washtub bass player.

Bobby noticed that while he was playing, he forgot about all his other problems. The positive power of music sustained him. It was a revelation. *This is what the Beatles have been feeling for years.*

Clovis called in the middle of the night with an update from the airport. He and Brian were about to board a plane back to London. He filled Bobby in on what had happened with Brian. He told Bobby about Renee.

Bobby said, "Jeez, I wish he'd stay away from her. She gives me the creeps."

Clovis snorted. "Hey, man, I still can't believe what Keith and Anita did to Brian. Who does that kinda shit to his own band mate?"

"It creates some really bad vibes."

"When are you coming back?"

"Not any time soon. Unless there's an emergency."

Clovis chuckled. "Define 'emergency.' To Brian, that's losing his sunglasses."

"You realize there will be reporters everywhere as soon as you step off the plane. You'll need to keep Brian under wraps."

Clovis didn't answer right away. "Ahh . . . about that . . ."

"Oh, shit!" Bobby said, suddenly realizing that Clovis was going to stash Brian in his apartment while he was out of town.

It was a good idea; that was true. No one would think of looking there. Bobby shuddered when he thought about the debauchery Brian would visit upon his quiet little flat. He made a mental note to have the place cleaned and the sheets washed before he returned.

"You're not taking him to my place, are you?"

"Yes, I am. It's the price you pay for skipping town and leaving me in charge."

Bobby sighed. "I guess you're right. I just won't tell Cricket."

"You won't have to. Erlene will. That woman holds nothing back."

Brian sat in Clovis's Mini and pointed down the street.

"I just want to pop in at Courtfield Road and pack a few things. A friend of mine is meeting me. Why don't you drop me off there and pick me up later?"

"Sure," Clovis said.

He was dead tired. He hadn't slept much in Morocco, and he couldn't sleep on the plane. Brian just seemed to keep going.

When he arrived at Courtfield Road, his friend Prince Stanislas Klossowski de Rola, better known as Stash, was sitting on the front step waiting for him.

Clovis was about to ask Brian in what country Stash was a prince, when Brian jumped from the car and ran up to his entrance.

"Stash!" Brian cried. "So good to see you, mate! You won't believe what I've just gone through."

Clovis drove off, leaving Brian in front of his townhouse. Brian waved as Clovis tapped the horn.

Clovis drove home like a zombie and hugged Erlene.

"Honey, I missed you."

"So how was Morocco?"

Erlene's buttery smooth Baltimore accent sounded like home to Clovis.

"Hot. Dusty. Lonely. I couldn't sleep."

"How's Brian?"

"That is one messed-up cowboy. You know, the guy has all

the money he could ever spend, he's in one of the biggest bands of all time, he's on the cover of magazines, he can have any woman he wants . . . yet he's just a miserable son of a bitch."

"Some people are like that, hon."

Clovis kissed Erlene.

"I wouldn't trade with Brian for all the gold records in England. As long as I got you, I'm the richest man in town."

Erlene smiled. Clovis was a silver-tongued devil, that was for sure, but he had the soul of a poet and Erlene never got tired of him. "You're sweet, hon."

"You know, it's funny. When I first hooked up with Brian, I thought it was so cool. He was my idol. I looked up to him. But, now that I've got to know him, I kinda feel sorry for him, you know?"

Erlene pressed her bodacious stripper's body against Clovis. "Oh, baby. I have something to tell you."

Clovis looked into her eyes. He wasn't sure what he read there. "What is it?"

Erlene paused. There was a twinkle in her eye. "I'm pregnant!"

Brian phoned around midnight and told a groggy Clovis to just forget about picking him up. The coast was clear. He had decided to spend the night at Courtfield Road and leave the next day.

"What could happen in twenty-four hours?" he asked.

"Plenty," Clovis wisecracked. "I'm going back to sleep now. Remember, tomorrow Keith and Mick go in front of the judge for the Redlands bust, so be on your toes. There are bound to be reporters around."

"Stash is here. We'll be fine."

"Don't open the door for anyone."

Brian and Stash stayed up all night drinking brandy, smoking copious amounts of weed, and listening to John Lee Hooker records. The blues always seemed to soothe Brian whenever he was upset or distracted.

Brian loved to talk music when he was high. Stash was a good listener and a fellow student of the blues.

"If you notice, John Lee Hooker never changes chords. The other guys in the band do. It's implied of course, but he stays on the root chord the whole time. His mind doesn't work like yours and mine, he cuts right to the essence of the blues."

Stash considered Brian's words. Light filled the eastern skies. Dawn was approaching. The room was full of smoke.

Stash said, "But I've heard you speak of three chords, the universal three chords of life."

"Yes, three chords for you and me and everyone else in the world. But only one chord for John Lee Hooker. He only needs one. It's not about the music with John Lee, it's about the pain."

The morning passed without incident. Brian made tea and toast. John Lee Hooker gave way to Muddy Waters and Little Walter.

There came an insistent knocking on the door. Brian, immediately paranoid, jumped up and looked around.

"Who is it?"

"It's probably the milkman."

"The milkman never knocks twice."

"Isn't that the name of a Hitchcock movie?"

Brian looked through the peephole and saw an officious-looking gentleman in a brown suit. He foolishly opened the door.

"Yes?"

"Brian Jones?"

Brian's heart sank. He looked past the suit and saw Detective Sergeant Norman Pilcher looking smug standing behind him.

"Pilcher!" Brian gasped. "Why do you keep hassling me?"

"You know the game, Jones. We have a warrant to search these premises."

They stepped past Brian. He saw twelve uniformed officers standing outside waiting to come in and toss everything he had upside down.

Brian stood there stunned as the police swept in. They searched for forty-five minutes, and the only thing they came up with were a few joints. Brian stood by, tears streaming down his face.

"Leave me alone! Why can't you just leave me alone?"

Sergeant Pilcher showed Brian a vial containing white powder.

"Is this your cocaine?"

Brian held up his hands, visibly shaken.

"Whoa no! That's not mine. We smoke weed and hash, it's true, but I stay away from the hard stuff. Somebody must have planted it. One of your blokes, perhaps?"

As they left for the police station, a crowd of reporters gathered outside. They had obviously been tipped off. TV cameras lit the morning like a movie set. They were waiting for this moment.

The cops handcuffed a trembling Brian. It was completely unnecessary, of course, Brian was zero-risk flight threat. It was all for show.

They led Brian and Stash directly in front of the throng of shouting reporters. They drove them to the Kensington police station. A mysterious purple leather bag containing some grass turned up. Neither Brian nor Stash had ever seen it before. It was clearly a plant by the cops, and Brian complained bitterly. *It was all a setup.*

At the police station, there were more cameras and reporters. The circuslike atmosphere was all captured on TV and broadcast around the world. Brian was convinced the tabloid *News of the World* had engineered the whole thing to boost circulation.

The message was clear. First Mick and Keith and now Brian. The Stones were under attack from every quarter. *The establishment had declared war on the Rolling Stones.*

Unlike the Beatles, who spread goodwill from the British Empire throughout the world, the Stones were dirty. They took drugs and spread dissent. Finally, they were going to get what was coming, according to the papers. The line had been drawn.

A week later, Brian called Clovis. He was afraid to go home, convinced the cops were out to get him at that address. He'd been staying in hotels around London.

"John invited me to come over to Olympic and record a sax solo for their new single. All the studios at Abbey Road are booked so they decided to visit Olympic for a change. I need you to pick up my sax and dulcimer at Courtfield Road and take me over there."

"You want me to bring you to a Beatles session?"

"Yes, exactly."

Clovis was stunned. "Do I get to hang out?"

Brian chuckled. "I don't see why not, as long as George Martin doesn't throw you out."

"But . . . I work for Olympic, not you. I can't just drop everything and go."

Brian paused. "Why don't you come and work for me?"

Clovis shook his head. "I can't quit my job at Olympic. I need the money."

"I'll pay you twice what you're getting now."

"Now hold on there, pardner." Clovis banged the phone on the table, then brought it back up to his ear. "There's something wrong with the phone. It sounded like you said double the pay. You don't even know what I make."

"I can guess. It's a pittance, correct?"

"Well, it ain't chicken feed."

"I'll pay you twice what Olympic is paying you to be my personal assistant."

Clovis scratched his chin thoughtfully. "I don't know, man. . . . No offense, but you're no day at the beach."

Brian laughed. "Come on, think about it. Do you know how to restring a dulcimer?"

"Sure."

"Tune a sitar?"

"It would take a while, but yeah . . ."

"Fix a hundred-watt Marshall stack?"

"I got my own soldering iron. No problem."

"Then you're well worth the money."

Clovis began to grasp the enormity of the situation. He immediately thought of Erlene. She didn't like Brian. That would cause problems. But to work with a Rolling Stone . . . *for double the pay*. It was too good an offer to refuse.

"I'll have to talk to my wife first," Clovis mumbled.

"Sure, sure, take all the time you want. But the session is tomorrow, and if you want to go, you gotta make a decision."

Back in Baltimore, Bobby read about Brian's bust in the newspapers. He felt terrible. If he'd been there, maybe he could've prevented it. He'd been trying to call Clovis all day but all he got was Erlene.

"He ain't here, hon. He's out workin' for a livin'."

"Well could you tell him to call me the minute he comes in?"

"Sure, but what's so all-fired important?"

"Well, it's Brian, he—"

When Erlene turned up the heat, her voice got husky. When she got mad, she barked.

"Brian, Brian, Brian! That's all I hear around here. I'm so sick of that man. He's got Clovis jumpin' like a goddamn horny toad. I wish he'd keep his nose out of our business."

Bobby sighed. "Brian's just going through a tough time right now."

"Tough time, my ass. He's wicked. I swear. He put the evil eye on Clovis. Him and that German witch of his, Anita."

"They've broken up."

The sarcasm in her voice was evident.

"Oh yeah, I forgot. She's with Keith now, hopping from bed to bed like a randy little rabbit. That was a real classy move on her part." The sarcasm gave bite to her words. "They're all depraved if you ask me."

"I was shocked when I heard about Anita and Keith."

"I wasn't. Their karma is terrible. It only makes you wonder what Brian did earlier in his life to have such misfortune now."

"Tell Clovis I called."

Something in Erlene's voice sounded uncharacteristically shy and uncomfortable.

"Bobby?"

"Yes?"

"I've been having dreams."

"What kind of dreams?"

"Bad dreams. Like we're all in danger. Like something terrible is going to happen."

"Relax, Erlene. Nothing's going to happen."

"That's what Clovis said. But I have a premonition."

"Have you had these dreams before?"

Erlene was clearly embarrassed. Her voice dropped to a whisper.

"Uh-huh, I'm psychic. I get 'em all the time."

"How many of them come true?"

Bobby expected a low number, like zero or one. He waited for her answer.

"All of them."

Clovis came home late. He waited for an opportune moment to bring up Brian's job offer, but it never came. Clovis decided to try another tack.

"We sure could use some extra money around here with the baby comin' and all."

Erlene hugged Clovis. "As long as we have each other, we'll be fine, hon."

"Well, I'm talkin' about some real money."

Erlene stepped back. "What do you mean?"

"I had a job offer today for twice the money I'm makin' now."

"Oh, honey, that's wonderful. Who with? EMI Abbey Road?"

When Clovis didn't answer right away, the smile on Erlene's face dropped.

"Oh, no . . . Not him!"

Clovis nodded. "Brian Jones asked me to be his personal assistant."

Erlene's sarcastic tone couldn't squelch her Baltimore accent.

"What do you have to do, score drugs for him and get chicks?"

"No! Of course not. I'm a professional. I'll be tuning guitars and changing strings and assisting him in the recording studio."

"Goin' on tour, too?"

"I guess so."

"You're gonna need that extra money for a psychiatrist."

"I told him I had to talk to you first."

"At least you did one thing right."

Erlene rubbed her belly. "You know what would be nice, hon?"

Clovis shrugged.

"A trip to Baltimore after I have the baby."

Clovis paused.

"Yeah?"

"Do you really want to take this job?"

A flicker of doubt flashed past Clovis's eyes, like the shadow of an unseen predator.

"I do . . . and I don't. I mean I love Brian and all, but it's hard to watch him destroy himself."

"Maybe you can make a difference. It's the Christian thing to do, I guess. I just have a bad feeling about Brian."

"Do you have a bad feeling about me?"

"No, not directly. I just fear that Brian could drag you down. You promise to never sleep with other women or take drugs?"

"Come on, hon. You know me. I just smoke a little weed now and then. That's all. I got you. Why would I want any of these skinny stuck-up English groupies?"

Erlene looked out the window at the streets of London.

"If you promise to take me back to Baltimore and raise the baby there, I'll let you work for Brian for one year. We can put the extra money in the bank."

Clovis exhaled. "So, you'll have the baby in London and then we move back."

Erlene nodded. "Back to the Big B."

Clovis swept Erlene up in his arms. "Honey, you're the absolute best!"

"Can you handle this?"

"If he gets too crazy I can always quit."

"Then it's agreed?"

John Lennon made himself comfortable in the control room at Olympic Recording Studios. He showed Paul McCartney what he had so far for the song that would later become the flipside of "All You Need Is Love." They strummed acoustic guitars and composed the song on the spot.

"It's great being out of Abbey Road for a session," John mused. "Gives us a chance to see what else is going on outside."

George walked in at that moment, and with incredible deadpan comedic timing, said, "Yeah, but I miss the white lab coats."

The Beatles broke up laughing.

George explained to Clovis, "All the employees of EMI Abbey Road wear coats and ties, and the engineers have to wear white lab coats."

Paul bounced around several ideas, finally combining the chorus from another song with John's verses. "Baby, You're A Rich Man" came together in the studio in one six-hour session.

They went from song inception to finished mix in one long pass. Clovis had never seen the Beatles work in the studio. He was amazed at how quickly they moved. It seemed effortless. The Beatles were at the height of their creative powers during this period. They ruled the recording studio like young lords. The band recorded several takes of the basic track before deciding which one to use. They laid down the vocal in two takes.

Brian was impressed. After the Stones laid-back work

ethic, watching the Beatles fly through their session was refreshing.

Clovis kept out of the way, standing with Brian. During the playbacks, Brian experimented with different instruments lying around from the last orchestral session. Among them was a rare electric instrument known as a Clavioline. It made a spacey keyboard sound and had been used on the Tornados' classic "Telstar" and Del Shannon's "Runaway."

John wandered into the studio and saw it.

"Oy, what's this?"

"It's a Clavioline."

Engineer Eddie Kramer plugged it into an amp and John began fooling around.

George Harrison encouraged Brian to try some of the instruments. Brian had originally considered playing sax, and he was an excellent sax player, but somehow it didn't sound exotic enough. He picked up an oboe and began to play what sounded like an Arabic riff in the intro.

"That's it!" John said. "That's the sound!"

He began to play the same type of Middle Eastern melody on the Clavioline. John created a weird sound with the Clavioline, and with Brian playing the oboe, it melded and sounded otherworldly. Sometimes dissonant, sometimes strangely in sync, the combined sound was compelling.

They quickly recorded a track of Brian improvising on the oboe. It was uncanny what Brian could do. The weird Arabic oboe part combined with the Clavioline sounded a little like a backward guitar.

A few minutes later, John changed his mind and the oboe was dropped. He played all the Arabic parts himself on the Clavioline. It sounded less cluttered that way.

The Beatles ran through the track while the engineers set up their microphones and got their levels. Ringo was in a soundproof cubicle, smiling and playing his Ludwig drum set. He could see the others and they could see him, but there would be no sound leakage onto the other mics. The Beatles liked to record live with the full band playing on the basic track, then they overdubbed the other parts.

The vibe was good as the Beatles carried out their magic. Clovis was in awe of them. *This is why they are the number-one band in the world*, he thought. *Nobody else can do it like they do.* They were light-years ahead of everyone else.

Brian pulled John aside. He was disappointed he couldn't contribute to the song.

"Sorry about the oboe, John."

"That's okay. I got the sound I wanted on the Clavioline. We were hoping to get something different like the sax solo you did on 'You Know My Name (Look Up the Number).'"

"I brought the sax."

"Don't worry about it, I'm happy with the Clavioline. How is Clovis?"

"He's working for me now as my personal assistant."

"Good. People don't understand. We don't play by the same rules. You need a guy like Clovis."

"He just started today."

"Let me know if you want anything from me."

The Beatles finished recording and mixed "Baby, You're A Rich Man" by three a.m.

Clovis drove Brian to Bobby's apartment. He was afraid to go back to Courtfield Road, thinking the cops had been watching him, tapping his phone, and bugging his rooms. But Clovis brought Brian to Bobby's place with great trepidation. He knew Bobby would be against it. He warned Brian to be on his best behavior. "Remember, this is Dust Bin Bob's apartment. Nobody knows you're here."

"Thanks, Clovis. I appreciate it."

"I'll keep you hidden for the time being."

"I gotta get out of London. Things are getting worse and worse. Pilcher is out to get me."

"Where can you go?"

Brian thought for a moment, then drew a breath and said, "Monterey. It's the biggest gig ever. The Stones office has already bought the tickets. We can look up Dust Bin Bob. I want to go to that incredible record store he's always talking about. You know, the place he took the Beatles to."

"The Hi-Dee-Ho Soul Shack?"

"That's it! We can invite Dust Bin Bob to go to Monterey with us. I really feel guilty about how I treated him. He fled back to Baltimore to get away from me."

"Dust Bin Bob wanted a little time off with his family."

Brian said, "Monterey would be perfect. I hear it's beautiful there on the shores of the Pacific Ocean. We can kick back and hear some great music. Otis Redding, Ravi Shankar, Hugh Masekela, plus all the San Francisco bands like Big Brother with

Janis Joplin, Jefferson Airplane, the Grateful Dead, Country Joe, plus the Who and Hendrix. I'll be introducing Hendrix. It's going to be huge."

"He'll really love that."

"We can stop in Baltimore and surprise him."

"I'll take my wife, Erlene, and she can visit Cricket while we're in Monterey. She's been homesick."

"Excellent idea!" Brian said. "Let's arrange it straightaway."

CHAPTER TEN

SYMPATHY FOR THE DEVIL

Bloody Mary and Her Black Plague Trolley Car Museum headquarters was at Mill Race Road. The ancient stone and mortar houses were cramped and primitive, but somehow the music sounded great there. They reminded Bobby of the Liverpool two-up, two-down row houses he grew up in. Like Liverpool, these tiny houses had two rooms up and two rooms down. Squeeze in a bathroom and that was it.

This obscure neighborhood of unpaved roads in the middle of Baltimore had somehow missed the passage of time. Even with the addition of indoor plumbing and electricity, these houses had always stood apart from the rest of the city.

The basement of Spider John's house was full of rocks, dirt, and junk. Tom got the idea to clean it out and make a proper rehearsal space. He recruited some friends and began excavating the basement.

They uncovered many Civil War–era items—pieces of pottery; bottles; bric-a-brac; a shoe; a rusted handgun, its barrel packed with mud; and several large rusty pieces of metal no one could identify. Once they cleaned out the top half, they took to the bottom half with shovels. Digging the dirt out was a grimy job. It was several feet deep. The smell was fetid. The dirt was moist.

Digging in the southwest corner, Tom made a shocking discovery. He found a human skull buried in the dirt floor. It looked pretty old, although no one there had any experience in dating skulls. Tom asked Bobby to take pictures of it, then he carefully reburied it in the corner of the basement.

Bobby didn't want to handle it. He used a shovel to move it. He photographed the skull from every angle. He couldn't wait to give it back to Tom.

"That was creepy, man. I wonder who it was."

Tom shook his head. "That's it. I'm giving up on the whole basement project. I don't want to dig up any more surprises. God knows what else is down there."

They decided to keep the discovery among themselves and not call the authorities. Whoever's skull it was had been buried a long time, probably more than a hundred years. The case was no doubt as cold as a dead fish. Besides, no one wanted cops crawling around the neighborhood. That was asking for trouble.

A few nights later, while rehearsing in the living room, the jugless jug band had worked their way through a case of beer. The music was extra hot that night, and the rehearsal had turned into a real party. A couple of friends of friends dropped in, then a couple more, and then the chicks that lived at the end of block stopped by after hearing the music. They showed up with more beer. And some wine. Whenever you gave them an audience, the jugless jug band responded by playing even louder. Pretty soon the house was rockin'.

After an hour of hot skiffle licks, Memphis blues, and Texas swing, Bloody Mary and Her Black Plague Trolley Car Museum took a break. The only restroom in the house was a tiny little cubicle on the second floor at the top of the stairs. There were bedrooms on either side. To the right was Spider John's room and to the left was his friend George's. George was a successful musician in his own right and had actually cut an album. Everyone respected George. Lately, he spent most of his time in New York.

One by one, each man trudged up the narrow stairs and relieved himself with the appropriate sighs and grunts until it was Bobby's turn. His bladder was as full as the others, and he was anxious to stand before the porcelain basin and "bleed the lizard" as John Lennon would say.

Bobby took the steps two at a time. When he got to the top, curiosity got the best of him, and he couldn't resist peeking into George's bedroom.

Sitting on the edge of the bed was a pale young woman in a long white dress. Her black hair flowed down her back. Her head was bent as if in prayer, and Bobby could hear her weeping softly. A cool breeze drifted through the house as if someone had opened a window and caused a rush of cross-ventilation. Bobby caught a whiff of the same moist earthy smell of the cellar.

Bobby thought nothing of it. He assumed that the girl was George's girlfriend.

"Oh, hi . . ." Bobby said. "I didn't know anybody was in here."

The girl didn't react at first. She just bowed her head and cried.

"Are you okay?"

She turned toward him. He saw her face. It was the face of infinite sadness. Her eyes looked like they had shed a thousand tears and looking at them made Bobby catch his breath. She seemed to look right through him.

Bobby stood there for a minute frozen in time, then his bladder reminded him of the reason he came upstairs.

"I gotta go," he said, and ducked into the bathroom. While he finished his business and washed his hands, he thought of the girl in George's room. How striking she was and how incredibly sad she looked. When he returned to the party, he made a point of not looking in as he passed George's door.

He returned to the party in the living room.

"Who's that girl?"

"What girl?" Tom replied.

"The one in George's room. Is that his girlfriend?"

Tom looked around at the others. Spider John had taken over on harmonica and kazoo since he broke his wrist. He tapped his Hohner Marine Band harmonica against his thigh.

"Did she have a long white dress on?"

"Yeah," Bobby said. "What about it?"

"Was she crying?"

"Yes. So why don't you tell me what's going on?"

Spider John took a deep breath. Suddenly, the room got very, very quiet. Something creaked on the steps.

"We think she's a ghost."

Bobby felt the hairs on his neck stand on end. He felt a shiver.

"What do you know about her?"

"We don't know anything. George told me about her. He's seen her many times. I've heard her crying. He calls her Eleanor Rigby, you know, like the girl in the Beatles song?" Spider John sang the melody to "Eleanor Rigby."

"I know the song."

"You think that was her skull we found?" Bobby asked.

Spider John rolled his eyes.

"God, I hope so. I don't want to live in a multiple skull home."

Bobby still felt goose bumps.

"Have you ever seen her?"

"No. She has chosen not to reveal herself to me. She must like you."

"Are you sure it's not George's girlfriend?"

"George doesn't have a girlfriend."

Tom, Bobby, and Spider John all spontaneously looked at one another.

"She's probably still there. You want to go see?"

They ran up the steps, turned the corner, and peered into George's room.

It was empty.

Bobby felt strange for the next few days. He had to convince himself of what he had seen. Had he literally seen a ghost? Or was it just a neighborhood chick? He kept replaying the incident in his mind, trying to remember every detail. She didn't seem overly ghostly, unless you looked into the face of infinite sadness. Bobby wondered where that phrase had come from. It had popped into his head when he saw her face.

For some reason, he thought of that song by the Monkees written by Neil Diamond. It began to play in his mind.

He told Cricket about it and it frightened her. From that day forward, she refused to step foot in the house on Mill Race Road. Cricket believed in ghosts and apparitions, and they scared her.

Bobby couldn't get the experience out of his head. He'd always been a pragmatic man. He never believed in the supernatural. Not until now. His faith in an orderly, easy-to-explain universe was shaken. He couldn't sleep. His appetite waned. He had trouble concentrating.

What was happening?

The next day at the shop on Read Street, he found himself staring off into space most of the day. People asked him questions but he couldn't respond.

If she really was a ghost, why did she reveal herself to me?

Bobby closed up the shop early and went home in a daze. He lay down on the couch and took a nap.

Who was she? When did she live?

The doorbell rang. He thought he was dreaming, but when it persisted, he sat up. Cricket was in the kitchen. He could hear her scuttling about as Winston helped her make tuna salad sandwiches.

"Can you get it, hon?" Cricket called.

Bobby sat up and collected his thoughts.

The doorbell rang again. Bobby got up and walked to the door in his bare feet. He opened it and was flabbergasted.

Standing before him were Clovis, Erlene, and Brian Jones. Bobby blinked. *Am I dreaming?*

"Surprise!" Clovis shouted. He lunged forward and hugged Bobby.

"Clovis? What are you doing here?"

"We're going to Monterey! You want to go? Brian's got a ticket for you."

"Monterey?"

"Yeah, man! The Monterey Pop Festival."

Bobby sputtered. "Well, come on in." He called back to the kitchen to Cricket, "Honey, you won't believe who just walked in!"

Cricket came out wiping her hands on a towel with Winston at her side.

"Oh my God!"

Cricket hugged Erlene. "You came back."

They entered the house. Bobby hugged Brian like a long-lost brother.

"How are you doing, man?"

"I'm over Anita if that's what you mean." One look into Brian's eyes and Bobby knew that was a lie. But Brian put up a brave front. After all, he'd recently had to endure a tour of Europe standing next to Keith onstage. He was the man who not only stole the love of his life, he was also the man who had taken the reigns of his beloved blues band so they could record garbage like *Their Satanic Majesties Request*. That must have been painful.

"The cops are clamping down," Brian said. "I had to get out of London."

"The Stones office had already arranged for the tickets," Clovis explained. "Our man Brian is the guest of honor, and he's going to introduce Jimi Hendrix."

"What about Acid King Leon Silverman? Wasn't he the official envoy?"

Clovis said, "He wasn't the official anything, the stinkin' little weasel. He was a plant by the *News of the World* to get us busted at Redlands. He disappeared right after. People think he was working for the cops, and that's why they didn't open his briefcase."

Brian grunted, "The bloody snitch! I'm gonna find that guy one day, and when I do, I'm going to teach him a lesson."

Clovis said, "You'll have to stand in line because I want a piece of him, too."

They talked for several hours before Brian went back to his hotel room. Erlene and Clovis stayed in the guest room at Bobby and Cricket's house on Southway.

They talked far into the night. Bobby told the tale of the beautiful ghost in George's room at Mill Race Road. They all got goose bumps. Erlene said she could feel the presence of the ghost on Bobby, like dusty fingerprints after he'd touched a room that had been empty for years.

Erlene said, "Her aura is still with you. I can tell that it made quite an impression."

"You can?"

Clovis said, "Erlene's psychic. Lately she's been extra sensitive, I don't know why."

"I do," Erlene replied.

Erlene let a mischievous smile slide across her face. Clovis winked at her.

Bobby said, "A few weeks ago, I'd have dismissed the idea of ghosts as silly superstitions. But now, after what I've seen, I'm not so sure anymore. If ghosts exist, what else is out there? If Erlene says she's psychic, I'm inclined to believe her."

"Do you mean psychic or psycho?" Clovis joked.

No one laughed.

Erlene hit Clovis on the head with a rolled-up newspaper. "Don't you make fun of me."

"I'm sorry, hon. I was just foolin'."

Now that she was back in Baltimore, Erlene's accent flared in all its glory. Her attitude was back, too. Yet, she sounded sincere.

"I ain't kiddin' about being psychic. Lately, my inner senses have been lightin' up like a pinball machine. Up until now, it's all been about Brian, but now . . . well, I think this girl is somehow connected."

Clovis shook his head. "Don't get all goofy on me, you guys. I'm still a skeptic, and I don't believe in any of this crap. How could a girl who probably died over a hundred years ago possibly be connected to Brian Jones?"

Erlene rubbed her chin.

"I don't know. But I aim to find out. Can you take me there?"

"What? To Mill Race Road?"

Erlene nodded.

"I want to meet her."

"I don't know . . ."

Clovis looked at Bobby with an exasperated "this has gone far enough" look. Clovis shrugged.

"She's my wife. If that's what she wants . . ."

Bobby sounded tired.

"All right. I'll take you in the morning."

Cricket said, "How can you go over to those creepy little houses, Erlene? I'm never going inside there again."

Erlene looked around the room. "It's important. I don't know how or why. It just is."

Clovis said to Bobby, "How do we even know you saw a ghost? It could've been some girl from the party. Lots of hippie chicks wear granny dresses. Maybe she used the bathroom and slipped into George's room to be alone and then she left. You said she was crying. Maybe she was sick."

"Should we take Brian with us to Mill Race Road? Afterward, we can go to the Hi-Dee-Ho Soul Shack?" Clovis asked.

"Why not? He might like Mill Race Road. He's into the supernatural, and that's a part of old Baltimore that most people never get to see."

Erlene said, "I think I know why I'm so psychically sensitive these past days."

Cricket looked concerned. "Why is that, hon?"

"It must be because I'm pregnant."

Cricket let out a war whoop and hugged Erlene again. "You?"

Erlene nodded.

"Congratulations! You're pregnant! How wonderful!"

Erlene said, "We're coming back to Baltimore right after I have the baby."

"That's wonderful! Are you going to Monterey?"

"No, I'm staying here in Baltimore while the boys are at the festival."

"That's perfect. You can stay here with me. I could use the company."

When the tires of Bobby's pickup crunched onto the rutted gravel path that was Mill Race Road, Brian took note. It was a tight squeeze in the front seat, and four across was the absolute maximum. They pulled up to the house.

"Looks charming," Brian said. "Why are we here?"

"We're here to meet a ghost," Erlene said.

"A ghost? A real one?"

"Yes. As real as a ghost can be."

Brian slapped his hands together. "Excellent!"

"You're a big believer in the occult, Brian. Have you ever seen the real thing?"

Brian shook his head. "But I'd like to."

They walked into the house. The front door was not only unlocked, it was wide open. Spider John was lying on the sagging couch in his jockey shorts and T-shirt, blowing blues riffs on a harmonica. When he looked up and saw Bobby, Clovis, Erlene and . . . *Who was that?* Brian Jones! He jumped to his feet.

"Holy shit! You're Brian Jones!"

"That is correct, my good man," Brian said, "no need to dress for us. We're only here for a minute, so be cool."

"We want to go to the room where Bobby saw the ghost," Erlene said.

"Sure . . ." Spider John replied. "You know where it is. Go right up the stairs. George is out of town."

Erlene put a hand on Clovis's shoulder.

"Just me and Bobby go up first. I don't want to spook her."

Bobby led Erlene quietly up the stairs to George's room. They looked in. It was empty. Tentatively, they walked into the room.

Bobby was about to speak when Erlene shushed him.

They stood in absolute silence. The birds stopped singing outside and the cicadas in the trees stopped humming. Suddenly, it was as quiet as a snowy night. Erlene closed her eyes. They remained that way for five minutes, Erlene listening and breathing softly. Someone started up the stairs. The *clomp, clomp, clomp* of the boot steps drew nearer.

Brian got to the top of the stairs and peered in.

"Is this where it is?" he said.

Suddenly, Erlene felt dizzy. She wavered for a moment, then crumpled to the floor.

"Clovis!" Bobby shouted. He knelt beside her and felt her pulse.

Clovis came up the stairs quickly. He saw Erlene on the floor, scooped her up, and carried her downstairs. He went right through the house, past Spider John, out to Bobby's truck. He sat her in the cab and rolled down the windows.

"Breathe some air, hon."

"I'm sorry," she said, "I felt faint for a second."

Clovis was concerned.

"You're pregnant. You went up those steep stairs and got all emotional and had a bad reaction, that's all. Nothing supernatural about it."

"But I felt her presence."

"The girl?" Bobby said.

He had followed them out and now stood near the passenger side window.

Erlene nodded. "At first, I got the feeling she was trying to . . . to tell me something. Then Brian came in. And she reacted so strongly to his presence, it was incredible. She got all excited, and I could feel her trying to send a message inside my brain. I don't know what it was, but Brian was definitely the one that triggered it."

Clovis shook his head.

"You were faint. Low blood sugar, whatever, that's all it was."

Erlene looked at Clovis. "I love you, honey, but that was more than morning sickness."

Clovis looked at Bobby for a long unhappy moment.

"Dust Bin Bob, can I talk to you in private for a moment?"

"Sure."

Bobby and Clovis stepped away from the car, out of Erlene's earshot.

Clovis put his hand on Bobby's shoulder. "Hey, man, would you do me a favor? Don't encourage Erlene with all this ghost talk. The truth is your mind has been working overtime since Tom found that skull in the basement."

"I know what I saw, Clovis."

Clovis looked around to make sure no one was listening. "You know what you saw? You saw a chick from the party with a long dress on. You saw a chick who probably smoked too much weed and drank too much wine and got a little sick and came up here to go to the bathroom. You saw a chick who wandered into George's bedroom and sat down on the bed, and that's all. She split right after that. That's why you didn't see her at the party. She wasn't a ghost. That part was all in your mind."

"But I saw her!"

"I know you saw her. That's not the question. Was she transparent? Could you see right through her? Did she disappear into thin air in front of you? Did she exhibit any ghostlike characteristics? Did she float around the room? No! So how can you be so damn sure she was a ghost?"

Bobby stammered. "But . . ."

"All I'm saying is be cool around Erlene. God bless her, she means well, and she's convinced that girl was a ghost. She's pregnant. I don't need any extra pressure on her. Can you understand that?"

Bobby hung his head. "Yeah."

"So you promise to cool it?"

"Yeah."

"You've got no proof either way, right?

Bobby shrugged.

"No proof . . ."

Brian came out of the house like aristocracy visiting the peasant village at the foot of his castle.

"Our work here is done. I didn't see a thing. Let's go buy some records."

Despite what Clovis said, Bobby couldn't get Eleanor Rigby out of his mind. That was as good a name as any other to call her. And it seemed to fit. She haunted his waking hours.

Bobby drove through the streets of Baltimore. Brian was fascinated by all he could see through the windows. This was the gritty soul of a city, something a visiting Englishman would never know. Brian took it all in.

They parked the car and walked half a block to the world famous Hi-Dee-Ho Soul Shack in East Baltimore. The shop was on a corner in a distressed neighborhood. It had accordion folding bars to cover the windows at night. Several businesses along the block were boarded up. Trash blew in the streets and children grew up amid the debris.

To say that Brian stood out would be an understatement. The Golden Stone was dressed like the Prince of Strange in a flowing gold robe over purple velvet pants and white ruffled shirt.

As they approached the shop, Preston Washington, the three-hundred-pound black goliath of a man who owned and operated the store, looked up. He sat in a wooden chair in front of the shop, balancing a plate of pork ribs on his knees. He had barbecue sauce on his chin, and he held a bone in his meaty fingers.

Preston wore a three-piece pimp-master pinstripe suit with a black silk shirt and a silver tie that looked like it had been knotted by Eskimos pulling hard with their teeth after chewing on whale blubber.

When Preston saw three white men and a drop-dead beautiful white woman heading his way, he dropped the bone and quickly wiped his hands and face.

When they got close enough for Preston to put on his glasses and squint at them, he recognized Bobby and Clovis.

"Robby the Limey! Clovis, my man! What brings you to my humble soul shack . . . with all these beautiful people?"

Bobby and Clovis hugged Preston Washington. Preston knew that Bobby always brought him great customers, including an after-hours buying spree with the world-famous Beatles.

"This is a very important person," Bobby said, waving his hand at Brian.

"Yes, I can see that." Preston looked Brian up and down, then cracked a huge smile and laughed. "I'd like to meet his tailor."

"Preston Washington, this is Brian Jones of the Rolling Stones."

"You don't say?"

They shook hands.

"I've heard of you boys. You play a lot of blues and R&B."

"Used to," Brian said. "The rest of the band wants to play psychedelic shit."

"Oh, well that's too bad."

Bobby said, "Brian wants to buy some records."

Preston's baritone voice filled the room.

"Oh, I get the picture. You want the Hi-Dee-Ho Man's recommendations. Save you some time, right? The crème de la crème of the R&B scene."

Preston led them into the amazing Hi-Dee-Ho Soul Shack,

where every inch of wall and ceiling space was covered with posters, picture sleeve singles, album covers, and signed photos. Preston pointed at a picture sleeve single of "Get Off My Cloud" by the Rolling Stones. Sure enough, there was a young Brian on the far right, looking out from one of the most famous haircuts in rock and roll.

"I knew I had one of yours."

Brian was overwhelmed. He stared at the walls in amazement.

"Where do I begin?"

Preston wasted no time putting on the first record.

"Check this out, a cat named Toussaint McCall, out of New Orleans on the Ronn label. The song is called 'Nothing Takes the Place of You.'" The song was slow, like gospel, and featured a Hammond B3 organ. The vocal sounded downright painful to sing, and Toussaint McCall sang his guts out.

Brian had never heard anything like it. "I'll take it!"

"How about something new by Little Milton on Checker? J. J. Barnes on the Groovesville Label? 'Pata Pata' by Miriam Makeba? Unbelievable! 'Shout Bamalama' by Mickey Murray! I loves my chicken, honey! Slim Harpo! Robert Parker's 'Barefootin.'"

They spent the next forty-five minutes building a massive pile of records on the checkout counter for Brian to purchase. The experience of the Hi-Dee-Ho Soul Shack was Mecca to an English audiophile like Brian. He chose so many records that he had to arrange for shipping back to London.

Preston loved showing the English kids what was real. He had an encyclopedic knowledge of R&B music. They spent a blissful hour going through Preston's recommendations.

"One last thing," Brian said. "I want a copy of that unbelievable song by Harvey. The one that John keeps raving about."

Preston laughed like Santa Claus, his massive belly jiggling in his loose silk pants.

"You English boys! I love you guys! What is it about Harvey that drives you nuts?

"It's like nothing we've ever heard before," said Brian truthfully.

Preston spun around with practiced speed and whipped out a 45 rpm copy of "Any Way You Wanta" by Harvey on Tri-Phi Records with its distinct blue-and-turquoise label. He handed it to Brian.

"I keep 'em handy. Always have some in stock. One of the great R&B finds of the decade. A minor hit, but a huge turntable favorite. Harvey is Harvey Fuqua of the Moonglows. Every person I play it for buys a copy."

Brian examined the label. He saw that Harvey was indeed "Formally of the Moonglows" on the credits. He also noted that the song was written by Fuqua and Fuqua. He wondered who the other Fuqua might be.

Preston said, "This song has magic. I never get tired of it."

Preston snatched the record out of Brian's hand and put it on the turntable behind the counter. He dropped the needle, and the song filled the room with a bouncy irresistible rockin' cha-cha beat.

The nonsensical lyrics made perfect sense. Harvey did his monkey cries, and when he got to the "sucky, sucky, sucky" parts, Brian was dancing in the aisles.

"Sucky, sucky, sucky, suck-kay! Any way ya wanta! Anywayawant, anywayawant, anywayawant, a-nong-nong-nong ANY-WAYYYYY! Koo-koo-koo-choo!"

"No wonder John loves it so much!" Brian shouted. "This is genius!"

The song wound through, pulling Brian along like a man being dragged by sheer force of will.

"Give me two copies of that one!" Brian said.

After Preston tallied up the sale and gave Brian a hefty discount, he smiled. He'd made a tidy profit. It constituted the biggest sale he'd made since the Beatles were there.

"Can we have a word?" Bobby asked Preston.

"Of course."

After Bobby, Clovis, and Brian went into the other room, Preston closed the store and locked the door. "Now, what is it I can do for you?"

"Our friend Brian here just got busted for drugs in London. Bruce Spangler was there. Seems like he's working for the English cops, too."

Preston smiled. "Well, that's something we've got in common. I've been busted by Spangler, too. He tried to shut me down. What an asshole."

"What's he doing in London?"

"He loves to bust celebrities. Especially rock stars." Preston lowered his voice. "I know a few things about Bruce Spangler. When he came after me, I had to get nasty to get him off my case."

"What do you mean?"

"I mean, Spangler's got an Achilles' heel that no one knows about . . . 'cept maybe me."

Bobby said, "Well, what is it?"

"I can't tell a nonbeliever. This stuff is too powerful to trust outside the church."

"The church?" Clovis groaned. "Are you nuts?"

"You mean he won't tell us?" Bobby asked.

"Not until we all get confirmed in the eyes of the Lord," Clovis said.

"Are you putting me on?"

Preston was adamant. He wagged a finger. "You got to fix it up with Jesus before I can tell you a word."

"How do we do it?" Bobby asked.

"Tomorrow's Sunday, you all come with me to see Reverend Julius Cheeks. Then we'll talk."

Bobby said, "You can't be serious."

"But I am. You all come to church with me tomorrow and get infused with the power of the Gospel, and I'll consider you trustworthy enough to share my secret."

"Ah, we're not really churchgoers, Mr. Washington," Brian said.

"Well, you are tomorrow."

"Who is this Reverend Julius?"

Preston had been waiting for that question. He paused, cracked a big friendly smile as if he finally got to tell the punch line to his joke. "Who's Julius Cheeks? Only the greatest singer in the world, and he's preachin' the Gospel right here in Baltimore at noon at the First Pentecostal Church of God. Would you expect me, Preston Washington, the Hi-Dee-Ho Man, to take you to some second-rate gospel show?"

Bobby blushed. "No, of course not."

Preston's voice boomed. "Hell no! I'm telling you, this man has the voice of the ages. He taught James Brown and Wilson Pickett how to sing. He was in the Soul Stirrers with Sam Cooke. He was in the Sensational Nightingales. This man wrote the book on soul shouting. Every time you hear a great R&B singer get down and scream, you're hearing Julius Cheeks. When I say he is the greatest, I don't mean one of the greatest. I mean *the greatest of all.* Got that? Guys like Wilson Pickett would have to stand on a chair just to kiss Julius Cheeks's ass. Someday, all you'll remember about tomorrow will be *that was the day you got to see Julius Cheeks in person.* I have given you a rare opportunity, my friends. Grab it while you can."

Preston walked over to a bin of gospel music and checked the Julius Cheeks section. He pulled out several rare Julius Cheeks records on the legendary Peacock Label

"How come I don't know about this?" Clovis asked.

"White people don't know shit about gospel. You never got religion, so where would you hear it? I grew up in church."

Brian's voice was soft. "Everything else this man has shown us has been absolutely brilliant. I have no reason to think it would end here. I say we go and hear the greatest singer of all time."

Bobby said, "Then you'll tell us about Bruce Spangler's Achilles' heel?"

Preston Washington's eyes were big and watery. "Get right with Jesus, and I'll get right with you."

CHAPTER ELEVEN

PLAY WITH FIRE

Clovis and Bobby walked down East Baltimore Street on the infamous "Block." It brought back memories for both of them. Clovis got his start by playing guitar in the strip clubs that lined the Block.

Most of the old places were still open, but with different management. Blaze Starr no longer headlined the 2:00 Club, she owned the place now. It was the place where Clovis had fallen in love with Erlene, watching her strip for the fat, bald men smoking cigars and stuffing twenties into her G-string from the front rows. They walked past the famous Gayety Theatre, past the peep-show sex shops, past countless bars, to the end of the block where Livingston's Loans pawnshop stood on the corner.

"Everything looks different," Clovis said.

"Everything looks the same," Bobby replied, "just dirtier." They went inside the shop.

The walls were filled with instruments and the display cases were full of jewelry. Manny Brillstein was sitting in the same place he was the first time Bobby walked in years ago. He was eating a corned beef sandwich, just like he was the first time they met.

He eyed Clovis suspiciously. "I know you. You're that drunken guitar player who always got fired."

"Yep."

"Clovis Hicks! I never forget a face! Where have you been? I assumed you were in prison or dead."

"Thanks for the vote of confidence, Manny. Actually, I've been in England, working in a recording studio."

"You mean you got a steady job? Hey, you ever seen Erlene anymore? She disappeared around the same time you did."

"I married her."

"Well, I'll be damned. And I remember your friend here, Robby the Limey, right? You bought the Gibson."

"Yep."

"What can I do for you?"

They explained about Brian and asked if he had any information about a certain well-known Baltimore narc.

Manny got real quiet. "Let's step out for a cup of coffee. What do you say?"

"Sure, Manny." Clovis could tell that Manny didn't want to talk in the store. The place was probably bugged.

They stepped around the corner to a rundown luncheonette. Manny ordered coffee and a piece of cherry pie. Clovis had a Coke. Bobby had a cup of tea. Manny made small talk until the waitress walked away.

Once she was gone, he wrote something on a napkin with a disposable ballpoint pen. He looked at it for a moment, as if weighing whether to give it to them or not. He seemed torn. Then, after a few moments, he slid it across the counter to Bobby. There were just two words on the paper: *Angelo Arnello.*

Bobby folded the napkin and put it in his pocket.

"Is that it?" he asked

Manny nodded. "You can take it from there."

Bobby and Clovis got up and left.

The church was a storefront with whitewashed windows. Painted by hand in block letters at eye level on the door was the simple notice FIRST PENTACOSTAL CHURCH OF GOD along with a handpainted cross. Inside, the room was sparse and warm. There was a coffee urn at one end and some pastries on a table. Bobby began to sweat immediately. Rows of metal folding chairs filled most of the room. A single podium sat on a six-inch riser. On the riser were a set of pink champagne Ludwig drums, an upright piano, and a Fender Super Reverb amp with a beautiful sunburst Gibson ES semi-hollow body guitar leaning against it. It was the same model guitar Chuck Berry used.

"Check out that guitar," whispered Brian to no one in particular. "I wonder if he'd sell it."

"That would be in bad taste," Bobby pointed out. "It's an instrument of God."

"Don't you already own a Gibson ES?" Clovis asked.

"No, I have a Thunderbird."

Clovis nodded. Brian loved the way Gibsons played. The

neck felt very comfortable in his hand. It wasn't too thin like a Rickenbacker or too wide like the Vox Phantom series. Gibsons were just right.

Dust Bin Bob, Clovis, and Brian Jones were the only white faces in the crowd. Preston had insisted that Erlene stay home because, with her stripper's body, "she might start a damn riot" among the brethren.

To say that they stood out would have been an understatement. Everyone stared. Especially at Brian. He appeared to them like a visitor from Mars.

A few people approached Preston Washington and greeted him warmly. He hugged all of them, his bulk swinging freely around the room.

Preston introduced his white English friends. Just before the service, the great Reverend Julius Cheeks came out in all his glory, surrounded by his entourage, and personally worked the room. He had a handshake and a good word for everybody there. He made a special point of welcoming Preston Washington and his white guests.

"Well, well, what have we here?" Julius said. He nodded at Brian and the outlandish way he was dressed.

"This man looks like the King of Something."

Julius Cheeks was dressed like an R&B singer in a shiny silver sharkskin suit, baby blue tab shirt, and crisply tied black silk tie. He sported a processed pompadour haircut and a Clark Gable-style mustache, trimmed to a tight line just above his lip.

You wouldn't know to look at him now, but Julius had lived an incredibly hard life. His childhood was spent in deep poverty, and he suffered every indignity of an uneducated black in the segregated South. He'd left school in the second grade to pick cotton in the fields. Singing his heart out in church was his only release.

Julius's smile was incredibly soulful.

Preston did the introductions. "This is Brian Jones of the Rolling Stones."

Julius looked Brian up and down. "You don't say."

Brian shook his hand manfully. "It's a pleasure to meet you, Mr. Cheeks."

"That's Reverend Cheeks, son."

"Yes, of course. Reverend Cheeks."

"They tell me you're a famous rock star. That's the devil's music. Are you ready to accept the Gospel of Jesus?"

"I am."

"Have you ever been to a gospel program like this?"

"No, never."

"Get ready to be sanctified in the eyes of the Lord."

Preston said, "We don't get too many white Englishmen here. In fact, you're the first. I hope you dig it."

Julius went backstage and the band warmed up the crowd with some instrumentals. Every seat was packed. The anticipation mounted. Reverend Julius Cheeks was a holy man, and he was bringing his gift from God into this place.

When Reverend Julius Cheeks entered the church this time, it was as the one true voice of God. His background group, the Sensational Nightingales, struck up an a capella call-and-response chorus. Everyone clapped on the beat.

"*Wellllll, you know I'm all right now, I said I'm all right now . . .*" they sang. "*I'm all right now, I said I'm all right now!*"

Julius Cheeks's voice exploded behind them.

"*Since I fixed it up with Jesus . . . I'm all right now!*"

The foundation of that old church began to rumble. Julius Cheeks's voice was beyond anything Bobby, Clovis, and Brian had ever heard. It was a revelation. And the band hadn't even come in yet!

Julius Cheeks was in his own personal gospel tent, talking and shouting at his own God. His gravelly voice pushed past James Brown, Wilson Picket, Ray Charles, and every other singer in the world. He made those R&B shouters sound as smooth as Mel Tormé. His voice was like forty miles of bad road. He shouted the lyrics until they ceased to be musical tones. They became pure energy. He screamed, but he screamed on key. Julius raised his voice by increments. Each phrase a little higher, a little more insistent, a little more intense than the last.

Julius sang with astonishing conviction.

"*He taught me how to walk, and he taught me how to talk . . .*" Julius's voice rose again. "*SINCE I FIXED IT UP WITH JESUS, I SAID I'M ALL RIGHT NOW!*"

The three white men, two of whom were English, had trouble making out the words, but the overall message was solid as a rock. They were transfixed. Julius never let it fade. Reverend Julius Cheeks was the master.

"*Since I . . . since I . . . since I . . . since I . . . SINCE I FIXED IT UP WITH JESUS, I'M ALL RIGHT NOW!*"

As Brian and Bobby watched, Julius came down the aisle and into the audience. People were singing and wailing and crying out "Amen!"

Julius Cheeks touched people on their heads and on their shoulders as he went. He looked into their eyes and shouted the words of the Lord directly into their faces.

After Reverend Julius Cheeks worked his way down to the first and second aisles of seats, he stopped and looked into Brian's incredulous white face and cupped his hands around Brian's jaw.

"Do you feel it, son?"

"Y-yes," Brian sputtered.

"Do you *FEEL IT*?"

"Yes!"

"Can I get a witness?"

"Yes! I'll be your witness!"

Julius had started the a capella song "All Right Now," strong and compelling, and then moved effortlessly into his sermon as part of the song, which he sang with incredible fervor.

Then, suddenly, he dropped down on his knees and balled his hand into a fist and pretended to pound the music home. The room reacted as if they'd been shocked in their seats. It reminded Clovis of when he saw *The Tingler* at the Boulevard Theater in Baltimore and everyone jumped when William Castle's seat buzzers went off. They jumped up as one, raising their hands in the air, and started singing along.

Brian looked around him. He couldn't believe it. Here he was in a storefront church in East Baltimore singing along with the great Julius Cheeks. Nothing else mattered anymore. Brian had been transported to another world, one that few Englishmen would ever see.

He looked over at Preston Washington, who had his eyes closed and was shouting out vocals like Solomon Burke.

Several female members of the congregation were singing professional harmony, adding more layers of soul to the already heady gumbo Julius cooked up.

Reverend Julius Cheeks had some athletic moves. He jumped to his feet and began to wave his hands above his head.

Julius belted his sermon between the background vocals.

"*When I was in trouble, I didn't have no God on my side, Jesus came unto me, said I am the truth and the light!*"

Brian was mesmerized. Julius Cheeks was a giant, and he couldn't believe he'd never even heard of the guy.

"*I been to the water, been baptized, soul been converted, I feel all right, I said FATHER! FATHER!*" Julius's voice was on the verge of a supernova.

"*Father, Oh Father!*"

Brian felt the hair on the back of his neck stand up. Julius Cheeks took it even higher with an octave jump that made time stand still.

"*Yeeeeeaah!*"

The energy level had doubled. The song ended and everyone fell back, exhausted. The old ladies fanned themselves with the printed program, and Julius Cheeks took his place behind the podium.

Julius was breathing heavily, having given the opening song all he had. Rivulets of sweat traced down the sides of his face.

Brian and Bobby exchanged glances. *Where did this guy come from?* They were astonished. This was better than James Brown at the Apollo!

Preston Washington patted Brian's knee.

"See? What did I tell you? This man is the greatest singer of all time."

Julius wiped his face with a white handkerchief. He paused and smiled at the congregation.

"Praise Jesus!"

"Praise Jesus," they replied.

The piano started playing.

"You know, I went home the other day . . . and an oooold lady was a-sittin' on the porch. She had a son . . . he and I were raised together . . . and she asked me if I'd seen him . . . and I said no . . . I COULD SEE THE TEARS IN HER EYES!"

Julius second sermon had already begun in the guise of another song. The band vamped behind Julius, shouts of "Amen!" and "Praise the Lord!" erupted spontaneously from the people in the pews. His backup singers sang a chorus of "Ahhs" behind him, reminiscent of doo-wop harmonies.

Bobby got a good look at the patrons as the program unfolded. The congregation was made up of families, couples, old ladies, and well-dressed and polite children. Julius went out and laid hands on his flock. He sang and shouted and hugged and whispered and prayed. Every single moment of it was riveting in a way Brian Jones had never imagined. He'd seen greatness, he'd been part of greatness, and he'd found greatness thrown out with the trash, but he never dreamed of finding greatness here in East Baltimore. God bless Preston Washington.

Reverend Julius Cheeks worked his way through a program of gospel music and sermons, mixing the message just right. His charisma was tremendous. He dominated the room preaching and pontificating from the ceiling to the floor. When he rocked, it was with such force that the whole building shook. These people had come to receive the word! To them, Julius Cheeks was as close to the voice of God as they were going to get in their lifetime.

Julius fell on his knees, cried out to the Lord, and beseeched the crowd to join him. He crawled around on the floor. Bobby could see the root elements of R&B; going from a whisper to a scream, getting down on the stage, even the famous cape routine. Julius invented it all and was content to do it for small groups of people in churches for a fraction of the money a guy like James Brown would get. In fact, if Julius Cheeks ever decided to go secular and leave the gospel scene, he could be one of the greatest entertainers of all time. All this was going through Bobby's head as he watched the master create his magic. It was a whole new world. It was the world where the R&B that he loved was born. Little by little, Bobby heard the staples of R&B plucked directly from what Julius Cheeks was doing.

Julius was the missing link.

According to Preston, Julius did all his big hits, "Waiting for My Child to Come Home," "How Far Is Heaven?" and finished with a rousing version of "Morning Train."

During his encore, "Almost Persuaded to Turn My Back on God," he told a rambling story about how they were trying to get to California back in the 1950s where they would be "backgroundin'" Sister Rosetta Thorpe. They ran out of money in Tucson, and a man with a nightclub offered to give them enough money to get all the way to California if the group would just sing for the crowd.

Julius's voice was ravaged from singing his heart out. He shouted out the message.

"You mean sing the devil's music? I was almost persuaded! I thought about it! But, what a mistake I would've made!" According to Julius, God led them to California. The program was timeless. Bobby had no idea how long they had been in the church. When Julius Cheeks opened his mouth, the most amazing sounds came out. Nobody wanted it to end.

Walking out of the church, Dust Bin Bob, Clovis, and Brian Jones were in a daze. The galvanizing performance by Julius Cheeks had blown their minds. Now that Brian had felt the presence of the Holy Ghost, he wondered what other ghosts were out there. Something in Julius Cheeks's sermon had struck a chord with him. A spiritual seed had germinated somewhere in his heart. He felt as though he were walking a foot off the ground.

"That was amazing," Brian said.

"Amen," Clovis muttered.

"I told you you'd get sanctified, didn't I?" Preston said. "Now, who's got the spirit of the Lord in them?"

They all replied at once.

"I had no idea places like this existed," Brian said. "That was life-changing. We've gone beyond blues, beyond R&B, beyond everything . . ."

"Now you know where the music comes from."

Preston took them back to the Hi-Dee-Ho Soul Shack and reached behind his desk. He pulled out a quart jar full of clear liquid and poured four shots.

"Here's to your health," Preston said, and threw it back in his throat.

The others did the same.

"Who-eee! What is that shit?" Clovis howled.

"That's genuine White Lightning. Here, have another slash."

Preston poured another four shots and threw it back even quicker than the first set.

Dust Bin Bob's eyes watered.

"That's some strong hooch."

"Damn right it is. Now, are you ready to hear old Preston's story?"

"Yes," said Bobby. "I really want to know."

Preston nodded slowly.

"Well, now that you been sanctified, I can tell you."

He took his time, making himself comfortable in his office chair and loosening his tie.

"Bruce Spangler has a thing for young black women. It's gotten him into trouble more than once. As Baltimore's number-one narc, he had a chance to make many deals with the city's biggest players. Believe me, these aren't the kinds of guys you fuck with."

Preston paused and sent the quart jar of White Lightning around the room again.

"Are you with me so far?"

They all nodded. Preston's voice lowered to a very un-Preston-like whisper. "Listen up."

They all moved in a little closer.

"The Gambino family runs this town from New York, and they've been affiliated with Angelo Arnello for many years.

"Doing business in Baltimore requires a certain . . . shall we say . . . *relationship* with Angelo, which I have. I knew his father."

Preston swallowed another sip of the powerful fluid and cleared his throat.

"Bruce Spangler became involved with a sixteen-year-old street pusher named Anita. He got her an apartment, gave her money, jewelry, dope, kept her hidden from his wife and family, and for a while everything was all right."

"What happened?"

"Driving home about three in the morning, he rolled his car into the black waters of the inner harbor with Anita in it. He got out; she didn't. It looked like his career was over. It was a huge scandal. Do you know what Anita's last name was? It was Washington. She was my niece. Now she's my dead niece."

Brian's eyes got big.

"So when he swept it under the carpet, I kept quiet. I knew the score. Later on when he busted me, I called Angelo. He told Spangler to back off. When he didn't do it fast enough, Angelo sent him a message. He threatened to expose the whole thing.

Then he kidnapped one of his kids and sent him one of the boy's fingers."

"Holy shit . . ."

"He threatened to blow the lid off the whole thing."

Preston paused, letting the story sink in.

"Needless to say, Bruce Spangler got right in line before further surgery was required."

Brian, Bobby, and Clovis were spellbound by the story. They hung on every word.

"So, if you have any problems with Bruce Spangler, I can always give Angelo another call. He knows where all the bodies are buried. Believe me, Spangler's got no friends among those guys. Now that he's a fed, they hate him even more."

Brian said, "Can we get him to leave me alone?"

Preston looked at Brian long and hard.

"Yes, I believe we can."

CHAPTER TWELVE

MONTEREY POP

Baltimore's Friendship Airport was sparsely populated as Dust Bin Bob, Clovis, and Brian Jones made their way to the gate. Erlene, Cricket, and Winston were there to wish them bon voyage. They hugged in the jetway.

"Take care of yourself, hon," Erlene said. "And watch out for Brian."

"We will," Clovis said.

Brian's clothes always drew stares. He never wore anything normal anymore. His wardrobe was as colorful and exotic as a Moroccan prince. He walked through the airport like an emissary from outer space.

They flew from Baltimore to San Francisco, rented a station wagon and drove south to Monterey with Clovis behind the wheel. Bobby rode shotgun, and Brian sat in the back. As they neared the fairgrounds, they began to see groups of long-haired rock fans streaming into the venue.

"I've never seen so many freaks in one place," Clovis said.

"This is going to be great," Brian said.

They drove slowly through the crowd to the VIP parking area. Californian sunshine poured down from the sky. The smell of food cooking drifted through the air. Marijuana smoke wafted freely across the grounds.

It was a glorious afternoon in every sense of the word. Clovis had believed the trip would be good for Brian, and so far they had already witnessed a life-changing performance by the Reverend Julius Cheeks thanks to Preston Washington. They couldn't wait to see Ravi Shankar, Janis Joplin, Jefferson Airplane, The Who, Hendrix, and of course, the great Otis Redding.

As soon as Brian got out of the car, he was inundated with fans. Most of the musicians at the festival admired and respected Brian. Here, at Monterey, he was a conquering hero. His problems were behind him here.

Brian wasted no time. He wanted to walk through the crowd and soak up the atmosphere. Bobby realized he'd left his camera in the car. And while he and Clovis went to fetch it, Brian wandered away.

Bobby retrieved the camera. As he did so, Clovis grabbed his arm.

"Look!" he whispered, and pointed across the parking lot to a white van. Getting out of the van were none other than Bruce Spangler and Acid King Leon Silverman. Leon had his brown leather briefcase, the same one the cops didn't search at

Redlands. It was generally believed by Mick and Keith that Silverman was the snitch and had been working for *News of the World*.

His disappearance after the Redlands bust was suspicious enough, as was the fact the cops had not charged him with anything. To see him here at Monterey was a shock.

Bobby raised his camera and took half a dozen pictures of the group.

"Holy shit! What are those two doing here?"

Fascination turned to consternation when Renee got out of the van behind them. Bobby took a few more pictures of her alone and with the group.

Clovis gasped.

"It's that chick that Brian had in Morocco. Something's going on here."

"I know who she is. I've met her. She's obsessed with Brian."

She walked briskly away from the van and the three men.

"They're working together. We better warn Brian."

They had only been gone five minutes, but when they returned, Brian had already left the backstage area to wander free among the hippies.

Clovis and Bobby searched for Brian. What they didn't know was that Brian had his own agenda, and her name was Nico, the exotic blond German chanteuse of The Velvet Underground, one of the hippest New York bands. Nico was part of Andy Warhol's Factory scene and Brian had met her briefly the last time he was in New York. She was just his type; tall, blond, German, and bitchy. Her high cheekbones and aristocratic German accent more than reminded him of Anita. They made plans to get together at the festival. Nico hadn't forgotten.

Nico found Brian before he could find her. Brian had been on her radar screen since they first met. To be seen and photographed with Brian Jones at Monterey would only make her a bigger star. Brian was only too happy to oblige. He couldn't wait to get her naked back in the hotel at night's end.

A small crowd of people gathered around Brian. They moved through the fairgrounds as one. People offered Brian joints, hash pipes, and pills of every type, and he accepted them all without reservation.

Renee came out of nowhere and slid close to Brian. He looked up, surprised to see her. Her hand snaked its way around his waist and caressed his butt.

"You're here?"

"I'm here for you, Brian."

Brian spoke softly. "Well, I hate to disappoint you. But, I'm with Nico for the weekend."

Renee spat. "Nico? She's just another one of your playthings. I came all the way here to be with you. I'm the one you really want; you just don't realize it yet."

"I don't think so, darling."

Renee walked away, clearly upset. Brian and Nico found it all amusing, another muse for their common schadenfreude.

Clovis and Bobby found the crowd that followed Brian.

"Dust Bin Bob! Clovis! You must meet Nico."

He introduced them, and she promptly ignored them.

"Have you seen Jimi?"

"He's backstage looking for you."

"Oh, I'd better go."

Brian and Nico walked away like royalty. The backstage scene was lively. All the San Francisco bands hung out together. The Grateful Dead and Big Brother hung out with their Berkeley counterparts Country Joe and the Fish, smoking joints. The Southern California groups stuck to themselves: The Byrds, Buffalo Springfield, the Association, the Mamas and the Papas. They didn't fraternize much with their NorCal cousins. The San Francisco bands loved smoking dope and dropping acid. There developed a subtle rift between the two camps. Then there were the English bands that had nothing to say to the Californians.

Organized by John Philips of the Mamas and the Papas and producer Lou Adler, the event looked incredible on paper. Rumors about who might perform continued to swirl right up until show time—which no doubt fueled the ticket sales. In truth, the lineup kept changing as more groups dropped in and out.

The Beatles were coming! The Stones were on their way! The Doors! Cream! No-shows included Donovan and the Kinks, who had been refused visas, and the Beach Boys, who were battling the government trying to keep Carl Wilson out of the army. Everybody was talking about Jimi Hendrix and The Who. Excitement was in the air.

Monterey was the first major rock event of its kind, and it generated tons of interest all over the country. Modeled on the Newport Folk Festival, it featured three days of concerts, a virtual who's who of rock and pop. In addition to the rock acts, several interesting additions piqued the crowd's curiosity, like Indian sitar master Ravi Shankar, folk duo Simon and Garfunkel, funk masters Booker T. and the MG's, African jazz trumpeter Hugh Masekela, and R&B legend Otis Redding.

Indeed, the three-day concert featured everyone Bobby and Clovis had ever wanted to see in one place: Lou Rawls, Eric Burdon and the Animals, Big Brother, Canned Heat, Quicksilver, the Electric Flag, Moby Grape, Steve Miller, Butterfield, Booker T., The Big "O", the Grateful Dead, Jefferson Airplane, and of course, The Who and Hendrix.

"Brian, can we talk to you privately for a minute?" Bobby asked.

Brian looked surprised.

"What is it?"

They led Brian away to a quiet part of the hospitality tent and gave him a Budweiser.

"Drink this."

He did.

"We just saw Bruce Spangler."

Brian drank the beer too fast, and it foamed up and wet his front. He coughed. "Spangler? He's here? In the fairgrounds?"

Dust Bin Bob whispered, "*Shhh!* Keep it down. It was Spangler all right. He got out of a white van with Silverman and Renee. Somehow, those three are connected. I think there's a conspiracy going on."

Brian's face went white. "I saw Renee just a little while ago. She said she came all this way to be with me. When I told her

I was with Nico for the weekend, she got pissed off and walked away."

"And what about Spangler? How could they possibly know each other?"

"I'll tell you what I think," said Clovis. "I think Spangler hired Silverman and Renee to infiltrate the rock world to set people up and bust them . . . or worse."

"What do you mean 'or worse'?" Brian asked.

"You know what I mean," Clovis snarled. "*Or worse.* They don't want people like Brian Jones becoming heroes to their kids."

Bobby said, "They obviously don't want these dope-smokin' hippies ruining the youth of the world. The government is against it. They'd love to put all the rock stars in jail and throw away the key."

"So, it's a conspiracy, then?"

Clovis nodded.

"Sure looks that way. I tell you one thing. We better keep an eye on Brian at all times. Spangler obviously knows he's here and he's looking to bust him."

"Not necessarily. Brian's not listed on the official program. He won't know for sure until just before Hendrix plays. Until then, it's just a rumor."

"Except Renee knows. Shit! She's liable to tell Spangler that Brian's here. And I was looking for a mellow time in sunny California."

"As long as Spangler, Silverman, and Renee are around, we have to be on our toes. Better change hotel rooms too."

Just then a black man dressed in a Sergeant Pepper–inspired faux military jacket with a rainbow of colored scarves and a wildly teased afro hairdo ambled up. He reached out for Brian.

"Hey, man! It's good to see you!"

Brian Jones hugged Jimi Hendrix. The two men circled each other for a moment like two dogs.

"I'm introducing you on Sunday night."

"Yeah, man. Oh, wow. I'm gonna do some STP for the show. I got some special stuff from Owsley."

"STP?"

"It's a new form of LSD with a little speed mixed it. It's powerful stuff, man. I'm tripping for the show. You want to join me on the other side?"

"The other side of what?'

"The other side of reality."

"You're going to trip onstage in front of all those people?"

Jimi grinned. "Yeah, why not?"

"I never knew anybody who could play a concert while tripping their brains out. You might forget how to play."

"I never forget how to play, man. Besides, the San Francisco bands do it all the time. It's no big deal."

"We'll either catch lightning in a bottle or melt down like a short candle."

"Hey, that's a great lyric, man. Can I use that?"

Brian shrugged. "Be my guest."

"You know, I'm in the 'Lightning in a Bottle' business," said Hendrix. "Just keep the jar screwed tight so it won't get away."

Noel Redding, bass player for the Jimi Hendrix Experience, passed by. He saw Clovis and shouted a greeting.

"Clovis!"

Clovis hugged him like a long-lost brother.

"Good to see you, man."

"We're gonna tear this place down."

"I don't doubt it."

"Jimi said Brian's supposed to introduce us. Is that true?"

"Yeah, we're here with Brian, as a matter of fact."

"Are you staying at the same hotel? We have to party together tonight."

He handed Clovis a slip of paper with *Leon Gnidder* written on it.

"Who's Leon Gnidder?"

"I am. Look, see? It's Noel Redding spelled backward. That's the name I'm registered under. Call Leon Gnidder on the house phone."

Clovis laughed.

"What a great name, Leon Gnidder!"

"Just call me Lucky Gnid. Come on over to my room around midnight. We got some incredible chicks dropping in. I think you'll enjoy it."

"Hey, I'm a married man. If it involves chicks, I gotta beg off."

"Jimi draws chicks like you wouldn't believe."

A gaggle of wild West Coast peacock-plumed groupies walked by slowly enough for Noel to notice them. He watched them pass.

"I gotta go. See ya tonight."

Brian drew a crowd wherever he went. He visited Big Brother and the Holding Company's tent to meet Janis Joplin. He was welcomed like a hero. Even his drug bust and bad boy persona gave him additional celebrity status among this crowd.

He met Steve Miller, Paul Butterfield, and two guys from Booker T. and the MG's that he had always admired, Steve Cropper and Donald "Duck" Dunn, who, along with drummer Al Jackson, comprised one of the greatest rhythm sections of all time.

Brian remained chipper and carefree all afternoon. He stayed for parts of the evening concert. He caught Steve Miller, Hugh Masekela, Booker T., and the grand finale—the great Otis Redding—the "Big O" closing out the night.

Brian watched Otis Redding closely while Otis gave the show of his life at Monterey. His performance caught the hippie audience ("The Love Crowd," he called them) by surprise. They had never seen a seasoned R&B legend like the Big O before. Otis had been doing this on the chitlin' circuit for years. These young white kids were a lot easier to impress than the drunken two a.m. crowd at a sweaty Georgia roadhouse.

Otis was absolutely brilliant. He paced his set like a pro, from ballads to shouters to rockin' sing-alongs and timeless riffs. He opened with "I Can't Turn You Loose" and it brought the house down.

Brian, zonked out of his brain on a cocktail of recreational drugs, watched every moment through the lens of his American experience.

He saw Reverend Julius Cheeks. In fact, he saw Julius

Cheeks in everything Otis did. He wanted to kiss Preston Washington for that connection. Julius Cheeks *was* soul music. And nobody outside of the gospel world knew who he was. It blew Brian's mind that absolutely nobody knew about Julius Cheeks in London. His friends would freak out. His blues purist buddies would flip out. This man was *the source*, and he was unknown.

Once people had seen Julius, they could understand his place in rock and roll history. They could see how he influenced Otis and every other great R&B shouter from James Brown to Wilson Picket. Otis proved it all at Monterey. Brian was astonished.

The Rolling Stones were great, and they knew how to rock a crowd, but Otis Redding was in orbit. As Hendrix said, he was in the "Lightning in a Bottle" business, too. They all were.

Brian Jones walked into the Jimi Hendrix's Monterey hotel room just past midnight. Renee was in bed with Jimi, naked and smoking a joint. Her breasts were fully exposed, drawing his attention. Brian was surprised to see her. He didn't know she knew Jimi. But whether she did or didn't really was of no consequence since the talented Renee knew how to seduce men of any stripe. She curled around Jimi like a python, stretching her legs like a sleeping cat.

"Hello, Brian," she cooed. "Imagine seeing you here."

Hendrix laughed.

"Do you two know each other?"

"Yes, we do."

"She's got the sweetest little pussy in town."

If Renee was faking it, she sure knew how to blush. Maybe she did have a shred of modesty left, who knew?

"You're the one with her boobs hanging out," Brian said.

Brian wanted to pull Jimi outside the room and talk to him privately. But he didn't want to be an alarmist to one of his rock friends.

"Where's Nico?" she said sweetly.

Brian looked at her with thinly veiled disgust.

"None of your business."

"Hey, man, be nice," Jimi said. "I just made love to this woman."

"Yeah, Brian, be nice," Renee repeated sarcastically. "Where do you think Anita is tonight? With Keith?"

Brian lost it. He lunged at the bed and at Renee's throat.

"Fuck you, you bitch!"

Renee retreated behind Hendrix.

"Hey, man! Cool it!"

Hendrix held Brian back.

"She's a narc!" Brian screamed. "She's working with a federal drug guy named Spangler who just busted me!"

"I'm not working for anybody. You're crazy."

"How do you explain you, Spangler, and *News of the World* sleaze bucket Acid King Leon Silverman getting out of a white van together?"

"Those guys? I was hitchin' a ride, and they picked me up. I never saw them before in my life."

"The cops are here and they're looking to set us up!"

Jimi looked at Brian. "Don't be so paranoid. You're creating bad vibes, man."

Renee spent five minutes denying involvement in anything. She swore that she had no idea those guys were narcs when she got in the van. Jimi and Brian listened to her, but it was clear, Renee's trust had expired.

Jimi was famous for his devil-may-care attitude about women, and he resented being held down or told what to do. He never got too involved. He loved sex, but Jimi was a free soul, incapable of being monogamous.

It was true. It was all true. Jimi was a gypsy. And if you didn't like it, tough shit. He dealt with women like he dealt with men, roadies, and dogs.

"I can't trust you anymore, Renee," Jimi said.

"You don't believe him, do you?" she whined. "He just doesn't like me for some reason."

Jimi paused and looked at Brian.

"Yes, yes, I do believe him," Jimi said softly.

"But what about . . ." She waved at the bed. She was close to tears.

"There are plenty of other chicks around."

"But . . ."

She stood up completely naked and slipped her panties on. She picked up the rest of her clothes and made a step toward the bathroom.

Jimi looked at Brian mischievously.

"Don't get dressed in here. You might be wired for sound. Just leave the way you are."

CHAPTER THIRTEEN

SPIDER AND THE FLY

Sunday's concert was the apex of the festival. All the big acts came out. Brian got to the fairgrounds early to see Indian sitar master Ravi Shankar give an afternoon solo concert that opened his eyes to a whole new world. Brian had been playing sitar for almost a year, but he was a beginner compared to Ravi Shankar. Like the Master Musicians of Joujouka, Ravi's music was thousands of years old, using scales and time signatures foreign to the Western ear. Brian sat transfixed in his front-row seat with Nico.

Dust Bin Bob and Clovis hadn't been able to keep up with Brian. He didn't like to stay in one place too long. Noel Redding, who had been with Brian off and on for the entire festival, swore he wasn't taking acid. Although he was obviously stoned on copious amounts of weed and hash, he didn't appear to be tripping. Bobby and Clovis took it as a good sign. Brian seemed happy with Nico, the sun was shining, and Renee was nowhere to be found.

The music was incredible. After Ravi Shankar, Brian stopped for a snack at the hospitality tent. The problem was that once Brian had been recognized in a public place he got no peace at all. It was an unending stream of well-wishers and autograph seekers. They all idolized Brian. He was the baddest boy in the definitive bad boy band—stoned like they were, a rebel against society.

Clovis told Brian about Big Brother and the Holding Company and their amazing lead singer, Janis Joplin. They were coming up next with an encore show due to popular demand (and the fact that Janis wanted their performance to be filmed and included in the movie D. A. Pennebaker was making called *Monterey Pop*). They were making a triumphant return to the stage. It was just one of the little dramas that played out under the magnificent skies of Monterey. Many people had missed their first show when Janis absolutely electrified the audience with her performance. She was the talk of the festival at that point, and her second performance was even better than the first.

The great American musical adventure continued. Three pilgrims—Dust Bin Bob, Clovis, and Brian Jones—were on a musical odyssey across America to worship at the altar of rock and roll. And here they were, among the gods on Mount Olympus.

Brian would remember every note. Reverend Julius Cheeks, Ravi Shankar, Otis Redding, Janis Joplin, and Jimi Hendrix were all an unending train of inspiration.

His mantra never changed.

It was the same three chords of life. All music was the same. They were all branches of the same tree.

Brian and Nico sat just in front of Micky Dolenz and Peter Tork of the Monkees and Mama Cass and Michelle Phillips from the Mamas and the Papas. The other stars drew energy from Brian's charisma. They seemed to shine brighter when next to him.

But Brian outshone them all. His outrageous clothes, his legend, his celebrity. He was true rock-and-roll royalty in a way none of these other acts, no matter high they rose, could ever be. Dust Bin Bob and Clovis got a good strong dose of Brian's notoriety just hanging out with him at the festival and watching the way other musicians acted around him.

Bobby recalled the insane days of Beatlemania, but this wasn't like that at all. Everybody here was a freak. They were all like one big family. The attitude was peace and love. No one screamed; no one charged the stage; there were no fights or riots. Even the cops seemed resigned to turn the other way when they smelled pot smoke.

It was incredibly therapeutic for Brian. He needed to see and be seen. His fragile ego got a huge boost. His quest to soak up as much music as possible couldn't have gone better. Here he was among his peers being treated like a prince, with Nico on his arm and a joint in every pocket. For the first time in months, he didn't feel paranoid.

He wandered into Big Brother's tent to meet Janis. He almost didn't notice Renee, who was styling Janis's hair. She whispered in her ear, and for a moment the two seemed as close as sisters.

Renee leaned forward and kissed Janis on the lips. It was a playful kiss, but one packed with portent. Brian's first reaction was to warn Janis, but the tension in the Big Brother dressing room was too thick. The band had just had a major confrontation with their manager about not appearing in the film. They wanted to be in it, Janis most of all, especially in light of their response the day before. They brought the house down, and it was not captured in film. Janis turned to Bob Dylan's legendary manager, Albert Grossman, who just happened to be hanging around the festival with other bigwigs like Clive Davis, for advice. Of course he told her the film would make her a star. That's all she needed to hear.

So Big Brother and the Holding Company were brought back for a second time on the following afternoon, and Janis knocked them dead. But in the tension-filled minutes just before that second show, Janis was nervous. She knew what she had to do. That seemed so easy on stage at the Fillmore in front of her fans, but here in the bright sunshine in front of people she didn't know, it was daunting.

To see her now with Renee buzzing around her like a honeybee made Brian apprehensive.

He was ready to leave without saying a word when the rest of the band spotted him.

"Brian! Hey, man! Wanna smoke a joint?"

Janis looked up. "Brian Jones? I heard he was around. I want to meet him."

"I'll introduce you," said Renee.

"Do you know him?"

"Yeah."

Renee pulled Janis Joplin over to Brian Jones and Janis blushed like a schoolgirl.

"Janis Joplin, meet Brian Jones. Brian Jones, meet Janis Joplin."

Brian hugged Janis.

"I'm such a Stones fan," she said. "I love you guys."

"I'm flattered," said Brian. "Good luck on your show. I'll be watching."

"Thanks. That means a lot."

Brian looked at Renee and frowned.

"Renee, what are you doing here bothering Janis right before her show?"

"Oh, she's not bothering me, she's doing my hair and makeup," Janis said innocently.

"She's trouble."

Janis giggled. "Trouble, eh? They said I was trouble, too."

"Just watch out for this one," Brian said.

He didn't want to bring up the fact that he thought Renee was a narc right before the show. It was sure to distract Janis.

Backstage and up close, Janis was not what the show biz types would call a knockout, but when she sang, she became beautiful.

When Brian and Nico made it back to their seats, Big Brother and the Holding Company were just finishing their first song "Down on Me" with Janis belting out the vocals like her life depended on it. By the time she got to the final song, "Ball and Chain," the audience was wrecked. She blew the lid off the place. In fact, "Ball and Chain" had so much impact that the film crew asked them to perform it a second time to make sure they had a complete version.

Janis happily complied and the audience felt like they were in on the moviemaking. Janis just kept getting better.

Brian was enchanted.

Bobby and Clovis followed Brian past security into the performer's area just in time to witness a backstage argument between Jimi Hendrix and Pete Townsend of The Who. The Who were known for destroying their instruments at the end of the set, and Hendrix had been doing much the same lately, but taking it one step further by setting his guitar on fire. The Who were scheduled to perform after Jimi Hendrix on Sunday, the final night of the festival. Pete was beseeching Jimi to let The Who go on first. A showdown was brewing.

Dust Bin Bob, Clovis, and Brian happened along at just the right time.

Pete grabbed his idol, the famous Rolling Stone.

"Brian! Who should go on first, The Who or Jimi? We can't follow Jimi, you know that, nobody can. I'd rather not look like a fool."

Jimi said, "That's not what you really mean. What you really mean is you don't want me to go on first. You want to be first up there with the guitar smashing."

Pete took exception. "Jimi, I swear, that's not what this is about."

"Oh yeah? Then why are you so sensitive about it?"

The two musicians were used to getting their own way. Both were tenacious, some would say ruthless. Neither one would back down.

Chas Chandler, Jimi's manager and former member of the original Animals, spoke up.

"Are The Who saying they won't go on unless they go on before Jimi Hendrix?"

"No, that's not what I'm saying at all," Pete said. "If anybody should go on last it should be Jimi, he leaves the audience completely drained."

"But the fact remains, The Who will be the first to smash their guitars and that's what you're asking."

Clovis laughed and broke the tension. "It's like that old Abbott and Costello bit 'Who's On First?'"

Brian and Pete looked at Clovis.

"Who are Abbott and Costello?"

Dust Bin Bob spoke up. "Hey, I've got an idea that's completely fair. Why don't we flip a coin? One coin toss, winner takes all."

Both parties agreed.

"Pete, you call it in the air, okay?"

Bobby got a quarter out of his pocket and showed it around.

"George Washington is heads, and the eagle is tails. Gentlemen, here we go."

Bobby expertly flipped the quarter and caught it in midair and slapped it on his wrist.

As soon as it left his hand, Pete called, "Heads!"

Bobby withdrew his hand to show the quarter heads-up.

"Heads, it is. The Who go on first. That's that."

Clovis, still wisecracking, said, "It really doesn't matter does it? Years from now, all people will remember about this night is the Association."

"The Association? You mean 'Along Comes Mary'?" They all cracked up. Clovis had managed to defuse the situation. Jimi Hendrix and The Who couldn't be farther from the light pop of the Association.

As showtime got closer for The Who, they seemed to be more than a little nervous. They had performed their equipment-smashing routine many times in the UK, but never in America. Pete Townsend wasn't sure what kind of reaction they would get. The faces of the other musicians seemed to say "guitars are sacred; you don't destroy them." It takes most guitarists years to save up for their first professional model. And now The Who wanted to destroy them over and over? What kind of madness was that?

Who were The Who? And what was the message?

Jimi, on the other hand, couldn't care less. He would do anything he pleased.

Filmmaker Dennis Hopper showed up backstage. Clovis and Bobby had been watching Brian like a hawk all day, but even then they couldn't stop the secret exchange of STP that had taken place a few minutes earlier. More powerful than acid, it had the ability to seriously scramble your brains.

Clovis said, "You didn't drop acid, did you, Brian?"

Brian grinned. "Nope. I dropped STP!"

"Well, do me a favor, pardner. Don't wander away from the wagon train, okay?"

The Who stood ready on the side of the stage. They were introduced and ran out. They looked clean and stylish. Singer Roger Daltrey wore a silk cape and moved with professional vigor. He spun and dipped and strutted across the stage. The whole group dressed foppishly mod. Musically, they were interesting, yet somewhat tame among the shaggy hippie bands. Tunefully, somewhere between the Kinks and the Faces, their set was derived from their successful London shows. They started with "Substitute," then Pete's mini rock opera *A Quick One While He's Away*. They followed quickly with "Happy Jack," their current single. By the time they got to the last song, "My Generation," the tension that had been building all night broke.

Looking off to his left, Pete could see Hendrix watching him from the side of the stage with his arms crossed. Everyone was waiting to see what would happen next.

Pete approached the microphone and said, "This is where it all"—he paused for a moment for dramatic effect—"ends."

They started "My Generation," its two-chord intro as snotty an anthem as any teenage Frankenstein could dream. Pete windmilled his arms and struck upward on the strings, causing seismic ripples way out on Monterey Bay.

Roger twirled the microphone like a lariat. He stuttered the lyrics on purpose, like a London mod on pills. Drummer Keith Moon never stopped soloing. It was one long drum fill from top to bottom. John Entwistle's bass playing snarled against the high end of the guitar. He wasn't actually playing bass lines, he was filling in the sound for half the band. The lower half.

Pete's windmilling grew more violent by the minute. At last, frustrated by just playing the guitar, he took the new Fender Stratocaster that he'd been using all set off his shoulder and started tossing it into the air. The first few times he caught it and spun it ever higher, then, shockingly, he let it crash to the stage, body first. The shock of watching a beautiful guitar being deliberately destroyed had incredible impact. Some people shouted, "No!" Others stood, ready to charge forward and save the guitar.

Then, in the blink of an eye, it became chaos. The guitar's neck broke, leaving the guitar strings hanging. Pete still swung it over his head and pounded it down like he was chopping wood. Smoke bombs went off. Pete rammed the splintered neck of the guitar through his amplifier. The speakers howled and shrieked. Keith Moon kicked over his drums. Explosions went off.

Many people in the audience, unable to make heads or tails of The Who's destruction act, thought they'd gone insane. They stood and backed away from the stage, lest they be hit by flying shrapnel.

Stagehands appeared and tried to save some of the microphones from certain destruction, but The Who were fanatical. John Entwistle stood stone-still through the whole thing, calmly playing his bass, providing a fitting accompaniment to the shrieks and howls coming from Pete's amplifier. Pete pushed over his 100-watt Marshall stack. It toppled like the walls of Jericho. Feedback began to double and triple and soon became earsplittingly loud. Pete and Roger wandered off the stage. Keith gave his drums a final kick and then he, too, was gone. Finally, John was the only one. He riffed for another minute, calmly removed his bass and gently handed it to a roadie.

To say the members of the audience were in shock would have been an understatement. As soon as John Entwistle stopped playing and the feedback ended, people looked at one another in various stages of denial. *What just happened here?* The LA groups didn't understand it; in fact, they reacted with hostility. The San Francisco groups were freaked out by the violence. For the English groups, it was just another day at the office.

Brian and Bobby had heard about The Who and had witnessed their smash-up "no encore possible" performances around London. Brian was knocked out. How many times had he been tempted to do the same thing with the Stones? Except with his frustrations it wouldn't have been an act, it would have been real mayhem.

The stage was cleared and the next band, the Grateful Dead, began loading their equipment. Their roadies swarmed the stage.

The Dead were the exact opposite of The Who. Laid back and laconic, they exuded a stoned confidence that seemed to say, *Don't worry about The Who, follow us into the musical unknown.*

Clovis and Bobby watched the Dead set up. One of the roadies looked damn familiar. Clovis got closer so he could get a better look. It was Skully, who once claimed to have worked for Hendrix. Skully, who brought Silverman to Brian's house. Skully, who just happened to be at Redlands when Keith got busted. He'd grown a beard and his hair was longer, but there was no doubt about it. Clovis slid up next to Dead guitarist Jerry Garcia and pointed to Skully.

"Do you know that guy?"

Jerry looked surprised.

"Nope. Many of roadies are volunteers. Except for our core of equipment guys who go to every show."

One of the people walking past handed Jerry a beautifully rolled joint. Jerry accepted it and took a huge toke.

"Look at this," Jerry said. He held up the joint. "Did you ever see a more beautifully rolled nimrod?"

Clovis smiled. "You've got yourself a good one there, pardner."

"We got a guy. That's all he does. His job is rolling joints for the band. He keeps 'em coming, and we do our best to smoke 'em all."

Clovis realized he was talking to one very high musician. Jerry Garcia was a happy camper. He loved to get high and play music, and Monterey was his backyard.

"So, you've never seen him before?"

"Seen who?"

Clovis pointed to Skully who was moving some equipment across the stage. "That guy. His name is Skully."

"Nope."

"Did a guy named Acid King Leon Silverman visit you backstage?"

"How come you're asking so many questions? Are you a cop?"

"No, I'm with Brian Jones and Brian wanted me to check these guys out. He's looking for the snitch that set the Stones up in London."

Jerry took another toke.

"Oh, yeah, Brian Jones from the Stones. Yeah, okay . . . You're looking for a snitch, eh? I hate snitches. I did see that guy Silverman, Acid King Leon, a little while ago. He had purple haze tabs. He offered them around. Nobody trusted him so we didn't take any.

Besides, my guys all have their own special blend: one-hundred-percent pure Owsley acid. We don't mess with unknown acid."

"Did you know Silverman?"

"Never saw him before in my life."

"Where would he get the purple haze if not from Owsley?"

Jerry lowered his voice.

"There was a bust a few months ago, and the cops raided one of his labs. They carted away several thousand hits of Owsley acid. Could've been from there."

"Thanks, Jerry. I thank you and Brian thanks you. Have a great show."

"Should I smash my guitar?"

Clovis laughed. "Then what would you use tomorrow?"

The Dead played a laid-back San Francisco set similar to what they'd been doing at the ballrooms like the Avalon and the Fillmore. The band had absolutely no pretensions. They were one-hundred-percent pure San Francisco. Loose and jammy, they let songs go on forever.

It was right in the middle of the Dead's set when Monkee Peter Tork walked out onstage and crashed their performance. He grabbed a microphone and started making announcements over the music. Jerry looked at Phil Lesh and rolled his eyes.

Peter Tork shouted into Jerry's microphone.

"People! It's me again! Hey, I hate to be dumb like this, but there's a crowd of kids, and this is to whom I'm talking. They're trying to break down walls and kick down doors because they think the Beatles are here! And they're not!"

Phil Lesh looked Peter Tork in the eye and said, "Well, why don't you let 'em in?"

Peter Tork stuttered. He wasn't ready for that response.

He started again, saying the same thing and Phil shouted over him, "The Beatles aren't here, but come in anyway!"

With that, the Dead had made their statement. Peter Tork left the stage, never to return again that weekend. Some of the San Francisco bands thought it was incredibly rude of the Monkees, who weren't really even a band but just a bunch of actors pretending to be a band, to interrupt a set by the Grateful Dead, a real San Francisco band. It was bad ballroom etiquette. But having never played the ballroom circuit, how would they know?

The excitement backstage built in anticipation of Hendrix. Nobody in the country had seen the Jimi Hendrix Experience.

Pete Townsend knew. Relieved that he didn't have to follow Hendrix, and thankful for the opportunity to be the first to do the guitar-smashing bit, he'd fulfilled his dream. He watched the Grateful Dead with mild interest as backstage in Jimi's tent, Hendrix dropped STP with Dennis Hopper and Brian Jones.

By the time the Grateful Dead were finished, the acid was coming on. The way the other members of Jimi's band looked, and with Jimi's LSD experience mushrooming, you could tell that something extraordinary was about to happen. Jimi looked like a Martian warrior with his sonic weapon around his neck. He was draped with scarves and lace. His hair was teased into a thick black tumbleweed.

As Jimi and Noel Redding plugged into their monolithic amps and Mitch Mitchell took his place behind the drums, a low-intensity feedback hum began somewhere in the monitors. It created an air of trepidation. Rather than try to kill the hum, Jimi played with it. It was all part of Jimi's sound. He used every sound a guitar could possibly make.

Brian Jones was introduced and emerged from the dark to stage center. His flowing robes and electric clothes lit up the stage. As soon as people heard his name, they sat up and took notice. The great Brian Jones was here!

They stood and applauded. Brian absorbed it all, his badly bruised ego healing nicely in the Mediterranean climate of Monterey Bay.

A professional voice made the announcement.

"And now . . . the next act . . . is one of the hottest bands from England . . . led by an American . . . Jimi Hendrix. Here to introduce him, all the way over from London, is Brian Jones of the Rolling Stones!"

Brian grinned.

"Ladies and gentlemen, all the way from England, Brian Jones!"

The crowd gave Brian a standing ovation. They cheered and clapped. Brian waited for it to pass.

Brian stepped up to the microphone. He wasted no time at all.

"I'd like to introduce you to a very good friend of mine. He's a brilliant performer and has the most exciting sound I've ever heard. The Jimi Hendrix Experience!"

A smattering of applause, more for Brian than for Jimi, trickled around the venue. No one had any idea who Jimi Hendrix was or what they were supposed to experience when he hit that stage.

And then the intro was over, and Jimi rolled his guitar's volume control from zero to ten in one easy motion, letting the feedback begin the introduction to the Muddy Waters classic "Killin' Floor Blues."

Hendrix's set was short and sweet—nine songs in total. At first, people didn't know what to make of it. They did notice the guitar playing, though; that was hard to miss. The manic energy of Jimi's performance made the air crackle. Jimi chewed gum to work off excess energy, and his jaw moved so fast at times it looked like he was grinding his teeth. His patter between songs was nearly unintelligible, delivered in short bursts of hipster jive, like a psychedelic Lord Buckley.

"Hey, baby, what's happenin'? Dig, you know what? Let's get down to business. Yeah, I tell you, brother, it's outta sight here, didn't even rain, no buttons to push . . . I'd like to dedicate this song to everybody here with hearts, any kind of hearts, and ears . . ."

He slid into "Like a Rolling Stone" by Bob Dylan like a thief, starting up a riff that couldn't possibly be it, but then it was. He ran through the set list like a maniac, devouring each song, milking every minute. His guitar work was revolutionary. No one had ever heard anything like it before. Like Charlie Parker or Louis Armstrong, Hendrix was an American original, a true genius. Everyone at the fairgrounds realized it at the same time. Suddenly, it was all okay. They got it.

He won the audience over in one song and took them on

a journey they would never forget. He played the Stratocaster behind his back, with his teeth, with his tongue, over his head, and every conceivable way to make a noise.

He blasted through his first single, "Hey Joe." Then it was three Hendrix originals in row. "Can You See Me?" "The Wind Cries Mary." "Purple Haze."

There comes a time in every show when you know something is coming, but you don't know what it is. But you know it's out there, coming fast, and it's gonna hit you like a mystery asteroid. Clovis, Brian, and Dust Bin Bob felt that moment approaching. The hair on their arms stood up.

Their ears were ringing from the volume. A constant hum vibrated somewhere in the sound system. Jimi kept everything turned all the way up, all the faders and dials, the amp, treble, bass, and middle, master volume, distortion, all up to ten. His guitar ceased to be a guitar. It became a theremin, a foghorn, a freight train, a chorus of heavenly angels, a train wreck, and a garbage truck.

He's still chewing that same piece of gum, Clovis thought. *That's remarkable staying power, I wonder if there's any flavor left?*

Jimi began to talk. He rambled on in a stoned monologue.

"You know, I could sit up here and say thank you, thank you, thank you . . . But, I wish I could just grab you, man. . . . But dig, man, I just can't do that. So what I'm gonna do is sacrifice something that I really love."

Just then Noel Redding thumped his bass to check the tuning. Jimi paused and looked at him.

"Thank you very much from Bob Dylan's grandmother."

Noel stopped.

"So, anyway, I'm gonna sacrifice something that I really love, and don't think I'm silly, because I don't think I'm losing my mind, although last night . . . Ooh God . . . Wait! Wait! Anyway, I'm not losing my mind, but this is for everybody here, this is the only way I can do it. This is the English and American anthem combined. Don't get mad. I want everybody to join in, too."

An extended free-form feedback solo the likes of which no one had ever heard before began. Jimi coaxed sounds out of the guitar that were almost human.

Now Hendrix was pointing to his ears. What did that mean? Was he signaling the monitor man to turn up his monitor? The monitor man had given up and had gone over to the beer concession long ago. Was he signaling to turn up the main house system? Who knew anymore?

Hendrix went through a simulation of sex with his guitar. He humped it, stroked it, pulled the most nasty sounds out of it. The night took on a strangeness that made it all seem overly psychedelic. It certainly was for Jimi, who was tripping like mad the entire time he was onstage.

How was that possible?

Then the moment came that swept them all away, the one that would be remembered as one of those defining moments in rock and roll history where time stands still and you're sucked into the black hole of genius.

Jimi humped his guitar into his amp. He violently smashed it into the speaker cabinet while wild shrieks of feedback howled. It was much more sexual than when Pete Townsend did it. Jimi made love to his guitar. Finally, he got on top of it and grabbed the whammy bar and rode the guitar like he'd ridden Renee the night before. The feedback squealed like it was having an orgasm. The bump and grind of Jimi's hips were hard to misinterpret. For the first time onstage or anywhere, this was shrieking guitar sex.

Jimi fell to his knees. His guitar lay in front of him, and he bent over and kissed it. The lighter fluid came out of nowhere. He just seemed to have it in his hands all of a sudden. He squirted lighter fluid all over the guitar. Then he took an ordinary book of cardboard matches and struck one. It flared yellow and bright. Jimi held it for a moment, then tossed it onto the guitar.

The guitar went up like a signal fire. The body of the guitar burst into flames. The finish of the guitar began to crack and bubble. Jimi tossed the guitar high in the air and let it fall. The Stratocaster's neck snapped off. The guitar kept burning. He picked it up and swung it over his head, bashing it into the ground. The burning pickups in the guitar body were still sending out a signal, and the guitar cried for mercy.

Bobby and Clovis took a look at Brian. He was rapt. His eyes were as big as saucers. He was completely sucked into the performance.

As Jimi's guitar died its final death, he tossed the severed neck to Clovis who was sitting in the front row. Brian was transfixed. His life had changed yet again. Julius Cheeks, Janis Joplin, Ravi Shankar, Otis Redding, The Who, and now Jimi Hendrix, it had been quite a ride. He would never be the same musically again. He had seen too much.

He looked at Bobby as Jimi left the stage. Tears were streaming down his face.

"That was amazing . . ."

The Mamas and the Papas were about go on next and close out the festival. But it had already been closed out. And, like Pete Townsend said, nobody could follow Hendrix. Not now, not ever.

Brian was numb.

Their ears were ringing as they left the venue.

CHAPTER FOURTEEN

STRAY CAT BLUES

Brian had a fit of paranoia after Jimi's show. He saw Hendrix swept away by a crowd of well-wishers as soon as the smoke cleared from his burning guitar. Clovis still held Jimi's splintered guitar neck, expecting to hand it back to Hendrix, but Jimi showed no interest in it at all. Clovis looked down at his hand. *Was he holding a historical artifact of rock and roll, or just a piece of wood?*

Brian said, "Let's get out of here before we get busted. Spangler saw me introduce Jimi; he knows I'm here."

They wasted no time. Clovis drove the rented station wagon. They returned to the hotel to pick up a few items before heading for the airport. As Clovis drove into the parking lot, he saw three cop cars parked there, lights flashing. They were in the general vicinity of their rooms.

Brian's eyes were wide and he gaped at the cops. Residual

effects of the STP flooded his senses. Their flashing red and blue lights were hypnotic. Brian sat low in the seat, trying not to be noticed.

"Somebody's getting busted. I sincerely hope it's not us."

Clovis pulled right back out of the parking lot and parked on the street, away from the entrance.

"You guys stay here. I'll be right back."

He got out of the car and circled around the lot to get a better view. He walked along the periphery, staying low; trying to see whose room the cops were interested in.

He saw one of the cops holding Brian's gold cape. No doubt about that, there wasn't another one of those within two thousand light-years. Clovis backtracked the way he'd come. He still had the guitar neck in his hand as if it were a magic talisman that would protect him. He wondered why he still had it. He hadn't let go of it since Jimi handed it to him at the end of his performance.

As he retraced his steps behind the cars, he saw somebody else standing in the shadows.

He could see a shadowy figure. Coming closer, by the light of the streetlamp, he could now see the mystery figure. It was unmistakably Acid King Leon Silverman.

"You!" Clovis said in surprise. "You got another bust set up? You fuckin' narc!"

Silverman lunged at Clovis.

"You lose, asshole!"

Clovis parried and danced away.

"He's here!" Silverman shouted to the cops. "He's—"

Clovis swung the Fender Stratocaster neck like a baseball bat. He whacked Silverman on the side of the head. The last word hung in his mouth as he went down.

Silverman dropped like a sandbag. He crumpled to the blacktop, instantly unconscious.

"That was for Redlands . . . asshole."

Clovis walked briskly back to the car. He got behind the wheel and started the engine. He drove casually out of the area and got onto State Route 1, the Pacific Coast Highway, along the ocean. He put as much distance as he could between them and Monterey.

"That was a close one," Clovis said.

"Were they waiting for us to go back to the room?"

"Yep, with a bag of weed to plant on us, no doubt."

"We got out in the nick of time."

"It's about a hundred miles to San Francisco International Airport. We can make it in an hour and a half. I don't want to speed and risk getting pulled over."

"You think they know our vehicle?"

"I think we're one step ahead of them. They're still waiting for us to show up at the hotel after the show. Unless they found Silverman."

"What did you do to Silverman?" Brian asked.

"I cleaned his clock with Jimi's guitar neck."

"What does that mean?"

"It means I whacked him on the head and knocked him out cold before he could yell for the cops."

"That's assault," Bobby said.

"So what? We're gettin' the hell out of here and we ain't comin' back!"

Bobby looked around. "Don't look now, but there's a cop on your ass."

"Oh, shit!"

California Highway Patrol Officer Mike Kwan wasn't looking for anything in particular, and Clovis was within the speed limit. He drove past them without so much as a passing glance. Clovis shivered involuntarily.

"*Phew!* That's a relief. They must not have us in their system yet."

"Let's just get to the airport, man," Brian said.

The CHP car disappeared in traffic up ahead. Clovis drove like a pro.

"I think we're gonna make it," Clovis said.

Bobby kept looking behind them. They took Route 101 right up the peninsula. They passed Menlo Park, Redwood City, San Mateo, and finally Burlingame.

Bobby noticed a white van sneaking up behind them. Alarms went off in his head. It looked like the same white van they had seen at Monterey.

"We got company," Bobby said.

Everybody looked back just in time to see the white van swerve in front of another car so it could be directly behind Clovis. They got a good look at the driver. It was Spangler, and he looked mad. His hair was messed up and hanging in his sweaty face. He was shouting something but they couldn't hear.

The white van inched up on the bumper of their rented 1967

Chevy Caprice station wagon. Clovis gunned the engine and the Caprice leaped ahead just as the white van tried to rear-end the wagon.

"Look out! He's nuts!"

"Here he comes again!"

Clovis put his foot into the 454 Turbo Jet V-8 Big Block Chevy engine, and the Caprice pulled away. Spangler caught up again and tried to run Clovis off the road. Clovis knew how to drive. He'd stolen cars as a youth and knew how to elude capture.

"Hang on!" Clovis shouted.

The station wagon accelerated like a speedboat. The huge land yacht fishtailed across multiple lanes of traffic to get away from the van. The big engine snarled. Clovis pushed it past eighty, past ninety, past one hundred miles per hour. The white van couldn't keep up. Whatever it had under the hood was no match for the Big Block Chevy.

The airport exit was coming up. Clovis kept to the inside lane until the last second, then cut across four lanes of traffic to make the exit by inches. The white van tried to repeat the maneuver but it didn't have the power and it was out of position.

California Highway Patrol Officer Mike Kwan looked up just in time to see the white van cut cross four lanes of traffic to make the airport exit at about ninety miles per hour. Officer Mosey had missed the Clovis move a moment before when he was distracted by his radio. Tires squealed and rubber burned. He flicked his siren and lights on and took off after the van.

Spangler cursed and pounded his steering wheel. There was no way he could catch Brian now. The CHP car would run him down and pull him over, so resistance would be futile. He knew he'd have to do a lot of explaining, and Brian would be long gone by the time it was over.

Clovis could see the cop's lights flashing and heard the siren, but he didn't stop or slow down. Soon it receded in his rearview mirror. He took the airport exit and drove directly to the departure level.

"Let's go!"

"What about the car?"

"Just leave it here with the keys. They'll find it."

Clovis, Bobby, and Brian took off on the dead run into the airport. It was late and the place was nearly deserted. They ran down the concourse, toward the gates.

"What plane are we looking for?"

"Any plane."

"Going where?"

"Anywhere."

They passed a United Airlines red-eye flight to Pittsburgh that was just boarding.

"Here we go. Perfect."

Clovis bought three tickets at the gate with his credit card and they boarded the flight without further delay.

They arrived in Pittsburgh in the early morning hours and caught a connecting flight to Baltimore.

As soon as they landed, Cricket picked them up at the airport. She whisked them away back to Southway.

Erlene had a heartfelt reunion with Clovis. She missed him terribly when he was gone.

Brian said, "I think it's time to see the Hi-Dee-Ho Man to make a deal with his friends to keep Spangler off my back."

"You got the money?"

"I can get it."

Preston Washington was just opening the store when Clovis, Dust Bin Bob, and Brian Jones walked in.

"Well, well, what brings you white rock and rollers back to see the Hi-Dee-Ho Man?"

"I want to make a deal," Brian said. "I have to get Spangler off my back."

Preston nodded.

"It's gonna cost you ten grand in cash, plus a slight carrying charge for me, because whenever you deal with the Arnellos, there's always a risk."

"What's the total?"

"Fifteen grand."

"Done. I'll need to contact the Stones office in London for an advance."

"Well, you better do that right away because you're gonna need cash."

"Then what?" Brian asked.

"Then you leave it all up to me, Preston Washington. I'll set up a meeting in a public place; you let me do the talkin'. Arnello hates Spangler, and it's just about time for some payback as far as he's concerned. Plus he's got teenage kids who love you."

Brian chuckled. "Always the kids . . ."

The place Angelo Arnello chose to meet was Salvatore's, a restaurant he owned in Baltimore's Little Italy. Brian caused quite a stir as he entered the tiny Italian eatery. The fact that he was with a big black guy only heightened the effect. The diminutive Golden Stone and the Nubian giant.

Angelo Arnello sat with his three teenage sons in a private dining room. As soon as Brian arrived and was introduced to the kids, they disappeared.

Some antipasti magically appeared at the snap of Angelo's fingers. He folded a thinly sliced piece of salami between his fingers and popped it in his mouth.

Brian felt like he was in a movie. Angelo Arnello looked like a real gangster. He was big and intimidating, dressed in what could best be described as Sicilian casual. His silk pants were high-wasted and shiny. He had a neatly trimmed mustache and slicked-back dark hair.

"So, let's get down to business. I hear you've been having some trouble with Bruce Spangler, correct?"

Brian nodded.

"Well, we've dealt with Spangler before, haven't we Mr. Washington?"

"That is true."

"And we found a way to . . . shall we say, *influence him*. I'd be willing to bet that that same strategy would work again."

Brian swallowed hard. Being in the presence of guys like Arnello was disconcerting, even for regular people, but for rock stars like Brian, it was even worse. It was like being in a movie. He squirmed in his seat.

"You say you've been busted?"

"Yes, in London. Spangler worked with Scotland Yard! How did he get to London?"

Angelo shrugged.

"All cops are the same. Their job is to bust people like you."

"Then, in Monterey, we just got away in the nick of time. They always plant something on me."

"That's the way it is, my friend."

"Can you get him to stop?"

Angelo sipped a glass of red table wine. He smiled at Brian.

"I forget, you're not from around here, you're an Englishman. Maybe you don't understand how it is. But to answer your question, yes, I can most assuredly make him stop. Nothing would bring me greater pleasure. Spangler's been a thorn in my side long enough."

Brian looked at Preston, not sure how to proceed.

Preston said, "Ahh, I think the boy wants to know the tag."

Angelo leaned back in his chair.

"To influence his behavior a second time will require ten thousand in cash to me and five thousand for our mutual friend and trusted benefactor, Mr. Preston Washington."

"That was the agreed-upon price."

What Brian didn't know is that Washington would kick back half of his five grand to Arnello.

Brian stepped to the door and waved to Clovis, who was in the car with the motor running. Clovis cut the engine, went to the trunk, and retrieved a parcel wrapped in brown paper. He brought it in and handed it to Brian. Brian peeked. It was a brick of hundred-dollar bills.

"You want to count it?"

Angelo snorted.

"Who would cheat me? You'd have to be crazy."

"Yeah, I guess you would."

"Now here are the rules. You give me the money, and that's it. No questions. You don't tell me how to run my business, and I don't tell you how to run yours. *Capisce?* In a short while, your problems will go away. At that time, consider all debts between us settled."

"You're not going to kill him, are you?" Brian asked.

"*Tut-tut!* I said no questions!"

"I don't want his blood on my hands."

Angelo put a fatherly hand on Brian's bony shoulder. "I really don't think it will come to that. We're both reasonable men. I'm sure we can come to some agreement."

"But no killing?"

"I'll try to avoid it."

Erlene was anxious to talk to Bobby and Brian. Clovis, still a skeptic, listened to her story.

She'd been spending more time at Mill Race Road while Bobby's jugless jug band rehearsed.

Omar St. Groovy and His Snake Stomping Review had a gig coming up over the weekend, and Bobby was excited about it. Tom Naylor had secured the gig at a coffeehouse in Timonium, Maryland, just past Towson, called Patches 15 Below. Patches was a local TV personality and he and his wife, Liz, ran a wonderful basement coffeehouse, fifteen steps below the parking lot of a modest strip mall. The name Patches 15 Below referred to the amount of steps you had to descend to get in. It was fifteen steps below the parking lot.

Patches was a nice guy. When Tom approached him about playing a weekend slot at the coffeehouse, he smiled and said, "Sure, why not?" He knew Tom from the Sunday night hootenanny, where anybody could sign up and play three songs.

Timonium was a long drive from Southway up Greenmount Avenue until it became York Road.

By rule, since Tom got the gig, the name of the jug band that night would be Omar St. Groovy and His Snake Stomping Review.

"We need to talk," Erlene said to Bobby and Brian.

"What is it?"

"It's Eleanor Rigby. She's trying to communicate with me."

Brian said, "Is she still trying to say something about me?"

Erlene nodded.

"I have to show you. I can't explain it. But I think you and Brian should see this before you leave."

Bobby drove Erlene and Brian to Spider John's house on Mill Race Road. The house was just the way they left it.

Erlene told her story.

"I had the strongest urge to come back here. I got the distinct feeling Eleanor Rigby was trying to get a message through. I came over here with Tom Naylor one night when the jugless jug band was rehearsing. I went up and sat in George's room."

"What happened?"

"Nothing. I was about to leave when I got the idea to look in the bathroom. I don't know why, it just came to me. I was checking my makeup in the mirror when I noticed something strange."

They walked into the living room and found Spider John fully clothed and listening to the first American Rolling Stones release, *England's Newest Hit Makers*. Like most American Stones fans, he loved the album and played it nonstop when it first came out. He jumped up when he saw Brian Jones.

"Brian! You came back!"

Brian grinned. "Couldn't stay away, mate."

Erlene cut to the chase. "We came back to see the ghost of Eleanor Rigby again."

Spider John snapped his fingers. "That dead chick gets more visitors than I do."

Bobby led them upstairs. George's room was still deserted. He hadn't been home in more than a month. They entered quietly.

Erlene whispered. "Notice the cold spot? Right next to the bed?"

Bobby put his hand out and felt the air.

"It doesn't register on any thermometer. I tried several."

Bobby got goose bumps.

"Jeez, that's freaky."

"But that's not what I wanted to show you. Brian, I want you to see this."

She led them into the tiny second-floor bathroom.

"I was standing right here, looking in the mirror. The light was about the same as it is now. And I noticed this."

She pointed at the mirror.

"Look at it in the sidelight."

A faint impression of a handprint, so light it was barely noticeable, had disturbed the dust on the glass. It was a small print, delicate and feminine.

"That wasn't there before."

"Somebody could've touched it."

"Look here," Erlene pointed at the glass.

Brian and Bobby leaned in and squinted. There, written in a dusty fingertip, so light as to be barely discernable was one word: "Jones."

"Jones?" Brian said. "Bloody hell, that's me."

Erlene's voice was down to a whisper.

"Now, I want you to look very closely, and tell me what you see. Just study it for a while."

Brian and Bobby stared at the dusty message.

"She's definitely trying to get to Brian. But why?"

Bobby suddenly noticed what Erlene meant.

"Wait! I see it! Holy crap. This message is written on the *other side of the mirror*."

"You mean the side that doesn't exist?"

Brian shivered.

"And she mentions my name. Why? What's going on here?"

Bobby examined the mirror. He opened the medicine cabinet and looked at the backside. It had been painted over at least a dozen times over the years and showed no evidence of being tampered with recently. It would have been impossible to take down the mirror and write on the reverse side. It was merely a reflection of reality. As Gerty Stein would say, there was no *there* there. The surface of Brian's side of the mirror had its own patterned layer of dust. You could see if someone had disturbed it. No one had.

This message was on the other side of the looking glass.

Bobby said, "How is this possible?"

Erlene said, "That's just it. It isn't."

Brian returned to London the next day. He tried to sneak into the country but, of course, there were reporters crowding the terminal. Once again, word had leaked out and the circus that followed Brian wherever he went was back in force.

His new girlfriend, model Suki Poitier, former girlfriend of Guinness heir Tara Browne, who died when he wrapped his Lotus Elan around a South Kensington tree, was there to greet him. Instead of going back to Courtfield Road, they stayed in various hotels around London, living like gypsies, trying to stay one step ahead of the reporters. Brian was terrified of being busted again. He was convinced Courtfield Road had been bugged.

The trial of Keith Richards and Mick Jagger began at Chichester Crown Court. It became instant front-page news around the world. They were both found guilty and remanded to prison for sentencing. Keith got a hero's welcome at Wormwood Scrubs, the well-named medieval dungeon of a prison in West London.

As Brian's trial neared, his anxieties increased. He tried to hide it from the public, but people were starting to notice. Suki convinced Brian to enter Priory Nursing Home together to be treated for severe emotional distress. They were both completely drained.

Two weeks later, Brian was part of the superstar chorus at the Beatles International TV broadcast of "All You Need Is Love" on the BBC. He joined Mick and Keith in the big production and enjoyed himself. John took a few moments to speak with him in a secluded corner.

Shortly after the TV broadcast, the Rolling Stones announced they were splitting with their longtime producer-manager, Andrew Loog Oldham. From now on, Mick and Keith, the Glimmer Twins, would produce the Stones.

A few weeks after that, the Stones solicitors Joynson-Hicks summoned Brian to their offices.

"Look here, what's all this rubbish about Claudine Jillian?"

Brian's jaw dropped. His mouth became dry. He couldn't speak for a moment.

"Who?"

"Claudine Jillian. The police want to question you in her murder investigation. What's all this about?"

Brian's heart pounded.

"I don't know."

"Well, they will be here in a few minutes. I had to lobby for the interrogation here in our offices rather than downtown at the police station."

"Interrogation?"

"Yes, and it's very important that we know, truthfully once and for all, did you have any knowledge of this girl's death?"

"No . . ."

"Several witnesses have placed you at a nightclub with her the night before she died; that would make you one of the last people to see her alive."

"Oh God . . ."

A door opened.

"Sergeant Pilcher is here!"

"Norman Pilcher? He's going to interrogate me? You've got to be kidding! He hates me! He's busted me before. He's just looking for anything he can get on me."

Joynson kept his cool.

"Just tell the truth, son. That's all I can say."

Pilcher entered the room with several other detectives. He nodded at Brian.

"Good day, Brian."

"What's so good about it?"

The Stones lawyers spread out around the room, placing themselves between the cops and Brian.

Joynson took charge.

"Let's get started, shall we? I understand you have some questions you would like to ask my client. I will allow a reasonable number of questions at this time."

"Very well, sir."

"But not from him!" Brian pointed to Sergeant Norman Pilcher. "He makes a living out of busting me!"

"Has Sergeant Pilcher been the arresting officer in any case regarding Brian Jones?"

"Yes," Pilcher said meekly.

Sir Alec made a face as if he'd just smelled an unpleasant odor.

"You have the gall to bring in someone with a history against my client, someone prejudicial to his standing?"

The cops looked at each other.

"Sergeant Pilcher, you will leave the conference room."

Sergeant Pilcher got up and walked out. Brian watched him go feeling somewhat satisfied. For the record, Joynson made a point of exposing a pattern of unprofessional behavior by the police.

"We would like to ask a series of simple questions."

"Proceed." Joynson's voice was already slightly agitated.

"Mr. Jones, did you know Miss Claudine Jillian."

"Yes."

"Were you in her company on the night before her death?"

"Yes."

"You were seen together at a nightclub known as The Speakeasy Club. Is that accurate?"

"Yes."

"Several witnesses said that they saw you leave the nightclub with Miss Jillian. Is that an accurate statement?"

"Yes."

"So you must have been one of the last people to see Claudine Jillian alive, would you say?"

"Yes."

The interrogator paused and looked at Brian's eyes. Bloodshot though they were, he stared right back at his interrogator defiantly.

"Mr. Jones, where did you go with Claudine Jillian after you left The Speakeasy Club?"

Brian waited before answering. He knew that his answer would be scrutinized from every angle. Everyone waited for his response.

He glanced at his solicitor, who nodded sagely and said, "The truth, Mr. Jones."

Brian looked around the room. Even without Pilcher, he didn't have any friends here, and he knew it. He decided to tell the truth.

"We went back to her place."

"What did you do there?"

"We had wild sex all night long."

The interrogator stopped.

"You had sex?"

"Yeah, we were lovers. I ran into her at The Speakeasy Club."

"So . . . you picked up Miss Jillian in a bar . . ."

Brian shouted, "That's right! You want all the sordid details? I picked her up in a bar and I took her back to her place and had my way with her! And I must say she was a magnificent lover, and this world is a lesser place . . . a colder, darker place without her in it."

"Did you see her the next day, the day of her death?"

"I left in the morning. Said good-bye. I didn't see her after that."

"Do you know anything about the circumstances of her murder?"

"No."

"Do you know who killed Claudine Jillian?"

"No."

"Did you, or anyone that you know of, have anything to do with the murder of Claudine Jillian?"

"No."

Joynson looked around the room at his defense team and the cops.

"Well? You gentlemen asked the questions, my client answered them. This constitutes the end of this interview. If you have any further questions, contact my office. Thank you all for coming."

The cops filed out one by one, each one with his mouth hanging open with twenty more questions ready to go, but the truth had been told. There was nothing more to learn. Brian testified that even though he was with her the morning of the day she died, he had nothing to do with the murder of Claudine Jillian.

CHAPTER FIFTEEN

NO EXPECTATIONS

Brian watched the progress of Mick and Keith's drug bust trial with great interest. The war against the Rolling Stones raged on in the front pages of England's press. The newspapers banged away continuously at the Stones drug-taking, narcissistic lifestyle. Daily tittle-tattle from this ex-housekeeper or that mechanic always painted a crazed, decadent picture of the band. They were arrested for public urination. They sneered at authority. Since the Redland's bust, they were held in contempt by every major law enforcement entity in the world. It was open season. They had targets on their backs. The game was on. Barely a day went by without some snide reference to Marianne, the girl in the fur rug, or the outrageous and untrue candy bar rumor. Somehow the outrageous story that Marianne was caught with a Mars bar in her pussy circulated around London. There was a Mars bar on the table when they were busted, but how it made its way into her pussy was never explained. It was typical of the nasty rumors swirling around the band.

In this atmosphere, it was impossible to get a fair shake from anybody, much less the press. They were selling papers like never before. There was nothing like a scandal to bring in the cash, and the Stones were scandal central.

As the sentencing came down for Mick and Keith, it went from a bad dream to a nightmare. Mick was sentenced to three months in jail at Brixton Prison, and Keith drew an astonishing one year behind bars. He was carted off to the infamous, ancient Wormwood Scrubs. Brian's apprehension grew.

Would he be going to jail, too? The future of the Rolling Stones was in jeopardy.

Bobby and Clovis flew to England to be with Brian in his darkest hour. Cricket had a change of heart about Brian and insisted that Bobby go. After spending some time with Brian, she now felt sorry for him and shared his concern. Brian seemed to take pleasure in being a tragic figure. It was a role he was born to play.

Clovis needed help keeping Brian's head above water. Between the Stones and his personal life, Brian had a busy schedule but could barely get out of bed. Besides, Erlene was going off about protecting Brian. Eleanor Rigby had ignited a sense of urgency in her. She felt strongly that having Clovis and Bobby with him would thwart whatever disaster was going to happen.

Brian's trial was a typical public circus. The Rolling Stones solicitors convinced Brian to dress in appropriate clothes, and he responded by wearing a gray suit. Entering the courthouse through a gaggle of fans, Brian appeared dazed. Bobby and Clovis kept him moving through the crowd. Brian resented being paraded before the cameras like a circus monkey. He shielded his eyes and kept an expressionless face. In truth, he was scared, afraid of what could happen to him in this building. He was going in a free man, but how would he come out?

Inside, the courtroom was packed. Everyone came to see Brian Jones crucified.

He pleaded guilty to possession of cannabis and using his home for the consumption of illegal substances. He pleaded not guilty to possession of cocaine and Methedrine.

Brian stood nervously in front of the judge, an anxious, beaten man, waiting to hear his fate.

"Guilty!" the judge said with a whack of his gavel.

Brian felt faint.

"I sentence you to nine months in prison."

Whack went the gavel again. Brian felt his heart break. He looked at his solicitors with panic in his eyes.

"Take him away!" the judge boomed.

They handcuffed a sobbing Brian. Shaking, with tears streaming down his face, they took him to Wormwood Scrubs, the same place Keith had been incarcerated.

Appeals flew in the winds of the legal hurricane that followed. The *Times* published a scathing editorial "Who Breaks a Butterfly on a Wheel?" in defense of the Stones' prison sentences, making reference to Alexander Pope.

Brian could be heard pleading with the solicitors as they led him away.

"Please, I can't go to jail, I'm not well, please . . ."

His pleas were ignored and he was stuffed into a van and taken to prison. Built in 1891 with convict labor, Wormwood Scrubs was as gloomy a place as can be imagined. It was the last stop for many a law-breaking reprobate. Hardly a place for the great Brian Jones. He sat in his cell quietly brooding. Brian spent a harrowing night in the ancient prison and never slept a wink. Several times, he was harassed by the guards, who threatened to cut his hair off to comply with prison standards. When they got rough with Brian, the other prisoners shouted encouragement.

"Don't worry, Brian! We're with you! They can't get away with this!"

The next morning, he was released on bail awaiting appeal. The experience at Wormwood Scrubs had left Brian Jones a traumatized man on the verge of a nervous breakdown. His hands trembled, and he smoked one cigarette after another.

Bobby and Clovis did their best to encourage him. They drove him to his doctor visits, his psychiatrist, his solicitor's meetings, but it seemed that Brian's life had become one long court case, followed by an endless cycle of rehabs.

When his psychiatrist testified that Brian should not be incarcerated because he would suffer a complete mental collapse, Bobby and Clovis believed it. When he testified that Brian was borderline suicidal, they nodded in agreement.

All Brian wanted to do was get back to playing music. But even that was threatening to collapse.

The Rolling Stones' most recent album, *Their Satanic Majesties Request*, had been received poorly. Sales sagged, and it appeared that Brian had been right after all. The fans rejected their effort to become something they were not. The psychedelic Stones were no more. Now it was back to their R&B roots, a place Brian knew well. He saw it as his chance to prove himself to the band musically.

Brian had been showing up for Stones sessions whacked on an increasingly bizarre array of drugs. Even with Bobby and Clovis watching him like a hawk, he still managed to sneak things past them. He spent his days trying to escape reality. Brian hit rock bottom. His nickname became "Liability" Jones.

Clovis threw up his hands and shouted, "Brian! Get your shit together! You've got a session tonight and you're drooling like a spastic leper."

"That's how they treat me. Like a leper."

"Well, of course they treat you that way. Look at yourself. Don't you have any self-respect? Shit, man! Sober up and start playing the kind of music I know you can play. Quit being such a pathetic loser."

"How dare you talk to me like that!" Brian snapped. "You work for me."

Clovis shook his head.

"Not anymore. I quit. You've changed, Brian. I used to be thrilled working for you, a real live Rolling Stone, a living legend. I was proud. Now look at you. You're a fuckin' joke. How long are Mick and Keith gonna put up with your shit? I give up. You wore me out."

Brian watched him walk out and said nothing. What could he say? The man was right.

The next day, Brian appeared at Clovis's apartment door in London. He was contrite and apologetic. He begged Clovis to come back.

"I can't trust anybody else," he whined. "Please don't leave me. You and Dust Bin Bob are my last two real friends."

Clovis kept a poker face. "If you want me to come back and work for you again, you're gonna have to get your act together."

"I promise I will. I've been going to the court-ordered psychiatrist, and he says I'm making genuine progress."

Clovis voice was stern. "There's a session tonight at Olympic Studios. I expect you to be there, be sober, and be ready to play. It's up to you, Brian. The Stones are lost. It's up to you to lead the band back to their R&B roots and get this psychedelic shit off the table. That's your mission."

Brian clapped his hands. "Let's do it!"

Sometimes, when musicians are at their lowest point, and you think there can't possibly be anything left in the tank, they do their best work. Does genius love madness? Does the lowest point signal the highest creative peak? Bobby didn't know. He'd seen the Beatles create, but that was usually a group effort. The Stones were harder to read.

Who knows what goes on in the minds of musicians?

Clovis and Bobby had never seen it before, but the exact moment when shit turns to gold was at hand. From fecal matter to twenty-four-carat gold ingots in a few short seconds.

That's exactly what happened with Brian on the night they recorded a new song by Mick and Keith called "No Expectations."

Not expecting much, Mick and Keith had been vague in their instructions to Brian.

"Just play some bottleneck guitar . . . see how it sounds."

Unknown to Brian, they already had another bottleneck slide track by American virtuoso Ry Cooder in the can in case it didn't work out. Such was their faith in Brian.

A crew had been filming the Stones in the recording studio for a documentary by French filmmaker Jean-Luc Godard. Having the lights and cameras there created new problems. It was hot and crowded in the studio. The Stones hired Bobby as their photographer to shoot the session. He was also another set of hands.

Only a few days before, one of the lights had overheated and started a fire that halted recording. Bobby did his best to stay out of the way. Clovis stayed next to Brian, ready to spring into action. When he told Clovis to change the strings on the Gibson Hummingbird and tune it to a D chord, Clovis did as he was told and handed the guitar right back.

The Rolling Stones sat around a circle on the floor with open mics and messed around. Keith played in the same lonely guitar tuning he would later use on "You Can't Always Get What You Want." It had a melancholy sound.

Brian tried not to sulk, but his mood couldn't have been bleaker as he sat down to listen to the track he was supposed to overdub. Brian had been smoking like a chimney all night. He lit another cigarette and closed his eyes.

Something happened behind those eyelids. Brian listened to the whole song without saying a word. It was a beautiful twelve-bar blues, honest and pure, with meaningful lyrics. As Brian listened, he knew the song was about him. *It was a song about being left behind.*

Brian reached deep down into his soul and produced his finest moment as a member of the Rolling Stones since his slide guitar propelled them to number one on the English charts with "Little Red Rooster."

When Brian started playing the bottleneck guitar, time stood still.

All of the magical musical moments he had absorbed in America came out in those tortured notes. It was a cry for help. It was a declaration of love. It was Reverend Julius Cheeks, Ravi Shankar, Otis Redding, Janis, Jimi, and all his brothers and sisters around the world all rolled up together. It was all these things. It was pure music, the universal language of the heart.

Brian had a way of phrasing that was both haunting and familiar. He hunched over his guitar, the glass slide on his finger, and spun a web of beautiful simplicity. He swooped from note to note, the vibrato he created by rubbing the slide up and down the strings adding personality and depth. Plucking lush chords then sliding them up the neck made Bobby's heart ache.

It was such a lonely sound, like someone crying into the darkest night of the soul.

Keith and Mick were transfixed. They looked at each other in astonishment. Brian's slide guitar was brilliant. It was absolute magic. It was exactly what the song needed. Understated and elegant, it bridged all the gaps. Brian poured his heart and soul into that slide guitar. If Mick and Keith would follow, it would surely lead the Stones back to their roots.

How a shattered man like Brian Jones could come up with something of such genius was beyond them. It just happened.

Mick sang the lyrics. The words hit Brian like an arrow in the heart.

"Take me to the station, and put me on a train, I've got no expectations, to pass through here again."

Tears filled Brian's eyes, well hidden by his long bangs. No one could see. Neither could they see the weight of the world on his heart. Brian always kept it all inside, only letting it come out now and then. Except, this solo was different. This solo was the one they'd remember.

"Once I was a rich man, and now I am so poor, but never in my sweet short life have I felt like this before."

Mick's vocal inspired Brian. His lyrics were true. That's exactly how he felt. How could Mick know?

"Your heart is like a diamond, you throw your pearls at swine . . ."

Brian's slide was so in sync with the song that it lifted it to a higher level. *A song about being left behind.* If there was one moment that defined what Brian Jones meant to his band, this was it.

He nailed it in one take, leaving Keith speechless. Mick just stared.

"Brian, that was incredible."

Brian modestly took off his headphones and put down his guitar. He looked at Keith as only two men who were desperately in love with the same woman can look. Something passed between them, something that hadn't been there for a long time.

The song was brilliant and Brian's solo was a triumph.

"Nice song," Brian said with a wry smile, and walked out of the room.

They left the studio after two o'clock in the morning. Clovis acted as chauffer and Brian sat in the backseat of the Rolls. The huge Rolls stood out like a sore thumb on the nearly deserted streets of late-night London.

As soon as the police car saw it leave the parking lot, it began to follow them. The cops knew it was Brian's car. It was hard to miss. They flashed their lights and pulled them over.

A pair of cops strolled up on either side of the vehicle.

They indicated for Clovis to roll down the back windows so they could shine their flashlights inside.

"Good evening, Mr. Jones. How are we doing tonight?"

"Fine."

"Have you ingested any illegal drugs this evening?"

"Just a Cadbury bar."

"Ha! A Cadbury bar! I thought you Stones boys only loved Mars bars!" The cop sprayed the window with spittle as he laughed. "Get it?"

"Very funny."

"Tell me, Mr. Jones, did she really have a candy bar in her pussy?"

"I wouldn't know. I wasn't there, remember?"

"Oh yeah, otherwise they'd have gotten you, too."

"Right. Is this a friendly antidrug warning?"

Sparse late-night traffic swirled around them. The cops smiled at each other.

"You know what it's about. Where's the money?"

"I don't have it on me."

"Well, you better get it. The next time I pull you over, I'm taking you in."

Brian frowned. "Are you blackmailing me?"

"You really have to ask that question? I think it's obvious."

"But I don't even have any drugs on me."

One of the cops reached in his pocket, pulled out a baggie of marijuana, and held it up. "I don't care. I can always plant this on you and take you downtown."

Brian frowned. "That shitty brown dirt weed? I wouldn't be caught dead with that garbage. You know I only smoke the best."

"Get the money, Brian."

"Why do you guys always pick on me?"

"You know the game."

The cops withdrew from Brian's Rolls and faded back into the light in the rearview mirror. Clovis carefully put the car in gear and drove away.

"What was that all about?" Clovis asked.

"It's a shakedown. They want a thousand quid a month."

"That's outrageous! We should turn them in."

"That's what I have to put up with. Now the cop on the beat wants a pay-off or he'll bust me, too."

* * *

"So, now we have this connection between Spangler, Silverman, Renee, and Skully. The un-Fab Four."

Clovis was sipping some iced tea and making notes.

"What do we know about them?"

Bobby said, "We know that they're all Americans. And they all seem to have some connections to the rock and roll underground. I saw Renee with Jimi Hendrix, Janis Joplin, and Brian, of course. What do Hendrix, Joplin, and Brian Jones have in common?"

"They were all at Monterey."

"Good! Yes, they were all at Monterey."

Clovis wrote it all down.

Brian had been so paranoid about getting busted that he was afraid to return to Courtfield Road. He bounced around from place to place trying to stay one step ahead of the cops.

He rented a flat in Belgravia where he could stay in town after recording late. But even that became too hot for Brian. He took to staying in hotels.

He sent Clovis to Courtfield Road to collect some items. While Clovis was inside, Linda Keith, Brian's part-time girlfriend, went into the Belgravia flat and took an overdose of sleeping pills. She stripped off all her clothes, lay down on his bed, and called everybody she knew to tell everyone what she'd done.

Eventually, an ambulance arrived and took her to the hospital. The newspapers went crazy with the story. STONE GIRL NAKED IN DRUG DRAMA! screamed the headlines. Brian was shocked when he found out. Why would Linda do that? It seemed that everywhere Brian turned now was madness and chaos. His life was spinning out of control.

Bobby suggested that Brian get out of town for a while. He knew Brian loved the Moroccan musicians Brion Gysin had introduced him to. He'd already made some rough field recordings. He suggested going to Morocco to record an album with the Master Musicians of Joujouka. It was a project Gysin had started with William Burroughs in the fifties. It seemed like a perfect idea to Brian, and he was anxious to get out of London before something else happened.

He had taken refuge in another hideaway he'd rented in the Royal Avenue House on the King's Road. One morning, he was rudely awakened by a loud and persistent pounding on his door at 7:20 a.m. Brian ignored it for as long as he could. It grew even more insistent. He dragged himself out of bed and looked through the peephole to see several uniformed cops outside his door.

Oh no! This can't be happening again!

Brian sat on the living room floor and called Clovis. "They're coming through the windows, Clovis!"

Clovis knew the drill. He called the Stones office and alerted Les Perrin, the official Stones publicist. Les began damage control even before the solicitors had responded. Brian swore that he had nothing in his flat, that there would be nothing for the cops to find.

But Brian was cursed. The police searched his flat and found a ball of blue yarn in a dresser drawer. He'd been careful to keep all his places clean.

"Is this your yarn?' they asked.

"I don't knit. I don't darn socks. I don't have a girlfriend who does, either."

They unraveled it to find a sizable lump of hashish. Brian's heart sank. His probation was blown. His legal status would collapse like a house of cards now.

Once again, Brian was trundled down to the police station, booked, and fingerprinted. He couldn't help but fall into a deep depression.

Bobby and Clovis arrived within minutes. The TV cameras were already there. It was obvious from the press turnout that they had been alerted ahead of time yet again. Among the cops, Clovis spotted Spangler and pointed him out to Bobby.

Les Perrin showed up to deal with the reporters. The Stones legal team swung into action. This was becoming routine for them.

And Brian continued to sink.

CHAPTER SIXTEEN

THE PIPES OF PAN

Preston Washington picked up the phone at the Hi-Dee-Ho Soul Shack in Baltimore. He could hear the crackle of the transatlantic phone connection before anyone said a word. He knew who it was.

"What the hell happened?" Bobby said. "I thought your guy was supposed to make him back off? Brian just got busted again. This time, it's serious because he's violating his probation. He won't be able to tour in places like the Americas and Japan. He's facing jail time."

"I don't know what to say. If Arnello says he's taking care of it, it's taken care of. Maybe Spangler is a hardhead."

"Nobody's head is that hard. He must have thought he could get away with it."

The door to Preston's shop opened, and Arnello came in with two bodyguards. He didn't look happy.

Preston told Bobby, "Hold on, he just walked in right now."

Arnello took the phone from Preston's hand.

"Who is this?"

"It's Bobby Dingle, sir. I work with Brian Jones of the Rolling Stones."

"Oh, yeah. Robby the Limey. Okay, here's the deal. I don't know what kind of shit Spangler was tryin' to pull, but it ain't gonna work. It makes me look bad. So you tell your boss, the rock star with all the hair, I'm taking care of Spangler personally. Got that? I guarantee it."

"Yes, sir."

"Now hang up while I talk business with Mr. Washington."

"Yes, s—"

Arnello hung up before Bobby could say good-bye. Preston took the phone.

Arnello was unhappy. His face seemed more comfortable scowling than smiling. He never looked happy.

"This asshole Spangler has pushed me too far. It's time for some payback."

Preston said, "Is he so thick that he thinks he can cross you and get away with it? Or is he so dumb he doesn't realize what he's doing?"

"I think he's ahead of his time. He's a new breed of trouble-maker from the future. He's stupid dangerous. Soon it's gonna be like this all over unless we nip it in the bud."

Arnello turned to his bodyguards. "Let's pick him up, Carmine."

"You got it, Boss."

Spangler had just returned from England the day before Arnello intercepted him in front of his house. He was about to go to the grocery store for some hamburger. The barbecue was already smoking. His wife and kids were getting hungry. He stood next to his big red Chevy Bel Air station wagon, not knowing whether to duck, run, or be cool. Since there would be no running from Arnello, he tried to stay cool and kept his jittery hands in view.

Arnello's Lincoln Towncar slid into Spangler's driveway, blocking the way. The window opened and a puff of blue cigar smoke wafted out.

"Hello, Narc."

"Mr. Arnello? What are you doing here?"

"I came to talk to you."

"So . . . talk."

"Not here. I need some privacy. Get in the car."

Spangler got in the car.

"We're going to the airport."

"Why?"

"I got a real estate deal I want to show you, but you can only see it from the air."

"Real estate? But why include me?"

"We feel we owe you one. I'm pulling a couple of people together to throw down a million each to develop a strip of land we just bought. Houses, condos, golf courses, retail space, the works. There's a lot of money to be made. We thought you might be interested."

"But my wife and kids are waiting for their hamburgers. Couldn't we do this some other time?"

"Forget about them. We got things to talk about."

Spangler suddenly became very nervous.

Brian's hands were shaky as he tried to light a cigarette. He sat at the dinner table with Clovis and Dust Bin Bob in Bob's London apartment.

"What else did he say?"

"He said he's taking care of it personally," Bobby said.

"What does that mean?" asked Clovis.

Brian's voice had an emotional edge to it. He sounded whiney and petulant. "It probably means he's going to kill him. Then I'll have blood on my hands."

His face had aged ten years. The bags beneath his eyes quivered. His skin sagged. He had four months of freedom left before his most current bust went to trial, and he was still out on probation with court-ordered regular psychiatric care. In the house of cards that had become Brian's life, the first card had fallen, and soon the entire structure would come tumbling down.

"I have to get out of here," Brian said. "I have to get out of London."

"Where can you go where they won't bug you?"

Brian sighed.

"Morocco. I can go to Morocco and record the Master Musicians of Joujouka."

"The Master Musicians of your hookah?"

Brian was somber.

"No, man. The Master Musicians of Joujouka. I've always wanted to record them."

"Are you serious?"

"Yes," Brian said. "That's the cover story. We're off to make a record, and we'll be gone awhile. It will keep the reporters at bay. We can get some rest and record some great music."

"Won't the reporters follow us?"

"Where we're going, they won't be able to. It's too remote."

Clovis and Bobby stood with their mouths open.

"We can't go to Morocco, we're married. Our wives would worry about us."

"Let's call 'em right now." Brian looked at his watch. "It's not too late over there."

Clovis and Bobby exchanged worried glances. Brian called the international operator and placed a call to Baltimore. A minute later, Cricket answered.

"Oh my God! This is so weird! We were just talking about you guys."

"This is Brian. Bobby and Clovis are right here. I just got busted again, and I have to get out of London as soon as possible. Can Dust Bin Bob and Clovis come with me? We're going to the Rif Mountains to record the Master Musicians of Joujouka."

"Where is that?"

"Morocco, North Africa."

"Um . . . Can I talk to Bobby?"

"Yes, of course."

He handed the phone to Bobby.

"Hello?" he said.

"Hello, honey. Brian wants to take you to Morocco. Is it safe there?"

"Yeah, it's okay."

"He says he wants to record the master magicians of something or other?"

"Yes, I know."

"I really don't want you to go. It seems dangerous. I know nothing about Morocco. Erlene insists as long as you stay with Brian, nothing bad will happen. Erlene says you two are the key. You have to stick together."

"I really don't need this."

"How do you think I feel? I want my husband to come home as soon as possible. You couldn't be any farther away; you're on the other side of the world."

"A few months ago, you would have never let me go on a trip like this. Why the change of heart?"

Cricket's breathing was so full of frustration and anxiety that Bobby could feel it three thousand miles away.

"Erlene says she's been communicating with Eleanor Rigby."

"Oh, shit. I don't want to hear this."

"She's trying to warn Brian about something."

"Maybe we shouldn't go to Morocco at all."

Erlene took the phone from Cricket's hand. "No! You have to go! You have to stay together! That's the key."

"For how long?"

"Until this is over."

"When's that going to be?"

"I don't know."

"Forget it," Bobby said.

Cricket and Erlene began talking at the same time. Cricket had great trepidation about the trip, but Erlene kept trying to reassure her that everything would be all right as long as they stayed together. She was insistent. In a weird way, they canceled each other out. Bobby was in the middle.

Eventually, Cricket came back on the phone alone.

"Bobby? As much as I don't like it, I guess you're going to have to go with Brian and Clovis to Morocco. Oh God. This is such a nightmare. I'm scared for you. Please be careful."

"I will. Brian wants me to photograph the trip. I am going to do some buying for the shop as well. Moroccan stuff is very popular now."

"Don't get into any trouble over there."

"Of course not."

Bruce Spangler was nauseous. Angelo and Carmine had put him in a private plane despite his most fervent protestations, nearly forcing him into the cabin. Carmine's suit jacket came open while they struggled, and his gun flashed momentarily in its shoulder holster. Spangler stopped resisting.

They took off from a small airfield in Maryland with Angelo at the controls and circled the airport. Angelo flew the plane for about twenty minutes until they were over some rugged terrain in a remote region.

"Where's the real estate?" Spangler asked innocently.

He hadn't said a word since they took off.

Carmine said, "There ain't no real estate. We're gonna throw your ass outta the plane, chump."

Carmine frisked Spangler from behind and took a .38 Special snub-nose revolver out of his pocket.

"What?"

Angelo laughed. "He's joking. Relax."

Carmine finished his inspection of Spangler and found a two-shot Derringer in an ankle holster. He held it up. "Cute little gun. I'll just take that." He slipped it his coat pocket.

"You know, you really pissed me off," Angelo said. "You made me look bad. Why?"

"I thought everybody wanted those dirty Rolling Stones behind bars."

"You think I forget this shit? You gotta be crazy. I told you specifically to lay off Brian Jones and the Rolling Stones, and you went ahead and busted him anyway. Why is that?"

"I didn't bust him. Scotland Yard already had it planned. They were hot to trot. I couldn't stop 'em."

"What? You have no influence over these guys? Your fuckin' buddies? That's weak."

Spangler tried to sound convincing. "They have a thing for Brian Jones. They want to bring him down."

"I don't care. When I told you not to bust Brian Jones, I meant it. He's under my protection now. Remember, I got the goods on you twenty times over. Now you're gonna have to pay for your mistake. Open the door, Carmine."

"No! Please! Don't throw me out!"

Carmine unlocked the door to the small aircraft. Wind came howling through the crack. Carmine pushed the door open.

"Stop!" Spangler yelled, "I learned my lesson."

"No, you didn't. Get ready, Carmine."

Carmine unlocked Spangler's seat belt. Spangler held on to anything he could. His fingers gripped the lip of the door like iron clamps.

"When you cross Angelo Arnello, it shows disrespect. I can't let you get away with that. Gotta set an example every once in a while. Besides, my kids like the music."

"That first step is a bitch, so watch it," Carmine joked.

Spangler begged. "Please, Mr. Arnello, just listen to me! I know a lot more about these rock stars than you think!"

"Yeah, like what?"

Spangler began to weep. "They're being set up! The real heat ain't drug busts; it's getting rid of them!"

"That's nuts. They make money for people."

The wind howled through the cockpit. Spangler had to shout to be heard.

"No! I swear! They're gonna start rubbing them out. I got nothing to do with it. It's a secret group. It might even be the government."

"What do you mean?"

"They're gonna get rid of these rock stars. They got some kind of mission. It's in their blood. These men control the world; they own the companies that own the companies."

"You lie!"

"No I don't! They got a hit list! I've seen it!"

Arnello signaled for Carmine to shut the door. Without the wind whipping through the cabin, the atmosphere got a lot less frantic. Spangler had a chance to catch his breath. His heart was hammering.

"All right, who's on the list?"

"Brian Jones, Hendrix, Morrison, Joplin . . ."

"How do you know this shit?"

"I worked with a guy, he was part of the drug bust team, but he didn't work for any known agency. He was just there. He said Brian Jones had a price on his head. He was working for that secret group I told you about."

"What's his name?"

"I think it was Skully."

"Skully what?"

"Just Skully. He had a chick with him."

"Jimi Hendrix? Jim Morrison? Janis Joplin? These people are rebels. I like rebels. I'm a rebel myself. I live outside the law. I take offense if somebody whacks one of my friends."

Spangler looked hopeful.

Arnello paused and let his voice drop to a low and threatening level. Spangler concentrated so he could hear every word.

Arnello said, "Okay, here's what I want you to do. I want you to guarantee Brian's life, got that, asshole? His life! If any harm should befall Mr. Jones, if he should get hit by a truck or fall off a bridge, I would be extremely upset and I would come after you. Do you understand that? He dies; you die."

"But, it's already too late! They're already coming!"

"That's not my problem."

Spangler rubbed his forehead.

"Aw shit . . ."

"Let's get this over with so I can be back in time for dinner. You want to live, Spangler? I'll give you one chance. You just saved your life."

Without warning, Angelo banked the plane sharply to the right, and Spangler's unlocked door flew open and hung down at the ground, slapping back and forth. His seat belt was still unhooked and dangled in the wind. He held on for dear life.

"Gravity is a powerful thing," Angelo said. "It has the ability to make all men speak the truth."

Spangler screamed. He was terrified. He looked down and saw the treetops far below.

Arnello shouted above the din. He pointed down. "If I find out you're lyin' to me, that's where you're gonna end up!"

Arnello righted the plane. The door swung shut again and the handle clicked. Spangler slid the lock in place. He was shaking with gratitude.

"I'll find out who it is, Mr. Arnello, and who put the contract out on Jones."

"Find out more about this secret group that wants to kill rock stars. My kids love that shit. Me? I don't hear it, but if there's a conspiracy I want to know."

"I'll do whatever you want, Mr. Arnello."

"I know you will, Spangler. I know you will. Because you know I'm serious."

The 747 touched down as soft as a kiss on the runway in Tangier–Ibn Batouta Airport. Bobby stared out the window at the foreign world outside. He'd been absorbed in a lengthy article in the onboard magazine. The article described Morocco's legendary racing pigeons. Strong, intelligent, and brave, they'd been bred for generations to do amazing things. During WWII, the pigeons flew with honor through the skies of North Africa. Some historians surmised that the Germans, who resented having "dumb animals" carry their most secret messages back and forth, may have actually won the war in the desert had they embraced Morocco's ancient warfare traditions. The Allies did.

Before they left, Bobby and Cricket agreed to talk on the phone twice a week on Tuesday and Thursday while the men were in Morocco. The only problem was that when they traveled to Joujouka in the Rif Mountains, there would be no phones or electricity. Bobby said he would find a way to keep in touch when they left civilization behind.

Brian, Clovis, and Dust Bin Bob set out for another adventure. Brian stuck to his story that he was going to the Rif Mountains to record the Master Musicians of Joujouka. He needed no special visa to record there.

As the passengers left the plane and walked down the movable steps across the tarmac, Clovis could see a few reporters in the arrival lounge. They were pointing at Brian and talking excitedly.

"Look who's here."

"The tabloids? Big deal. We'll tell them the truth."

Bobby grabbed Brian's arm. "Hold on. These guys don't print the truth. The truth is boring. They want sensationalism."

"Okay, we'll tell them we're recording in the nude!"

"Get serious, Brian," Bobby said. "We're supposed to be looking after you. Let's just avoid the reporters altogether."

The heat in North Africa can be debilitating. It shimmers in the afternoon like ghosts hovering above the stones. Clovis couldn't take it and told Brian so, but he just laughed that soulful laugh of his and pointed at the hookah. "That's what that's for."

"Oh . . ." said Clovis. "In that case . . ."

Brian lit a big wooden match on the side of the table and fired up the bowl of fragrant brown hashish. The smoke billowed across the room. Brian coughed violently.

"Steady there, *kemosabe*. Take it easy."

Brian smiled, his eyes watery and far away. "I shall never take it easy, Clovis. It's not part of my code. Life is too bloody short for that kind of thinking."

Clovis leaned forward, took a short pull on the pipe, and sat back, his head spinning. He let a lazy, blue cloud of smoke drift from his mouth. Nothing tastes quite like hash. Pungent and mysterious, stinking of dreams, it's the very essence of Morocco. A waiter brought more room-temperature tea, and they sipped it to cool their throats. Brian shook his head.

"This is the first place I came after Keith stole Anita from me. The rotten bastard took half the dope and half the records, too."

"It could have been worse. He could have taken it all."

The bags under Brian's eyes quivered. "He must have had a rare attack of conscience. But the fact remains, he might have taken only half the stash, but he took *all* of Anita. And that's what really hurts."

Brian had been an emotional train wreck following the first trip here, and Clovis knew those wounds were still fresh. The complex relationships that swirled around the Stones and their women made for the worst kind of decadent rock-and-roll soap opera.

Bobby returned from the hotel where he'd been taking care of registration for the group and sat down with them.

"Everything's set up. I got a rental car—a Land Rover, rigged for desert driving. This is going to be a hell of an adventure."

"I can't wait," Brian said.

Bobby worried about Brian. Mick and Keith had taken over every aspect of the group, and Brian had become the odd man out. He wasn't driven the way they were. He wasn't as obsessed with keeping up with the Beatles as they were. He reacted to Mick and Keith's musical activism by staying zonked out on drugs most of the time. Bobby could see their point. The Stones were a business, one of the two great bands of their era, and they had to deliver every time out. Brian lived up to his nickname, "Liability" Jones.

So now Brian, Clovis, and Dust Bin Bob sat in a café in Tangier waiting for writer/artist Brion Gysin, a friend of Brian's. They'd only been here two hours and Brian was anxious to get out in the field. Clovis brought a pair of portable battery-powered Uher tape recorders, the best money could buy, and a selection of microphones to make sure they got every note. The machines were only two-tracks, but Brian assured Clovis there would be no overdubs.

"These guys play live, all-in, one take. You gotta be ready, man."

Clovis would be ready, if the equipment worked. They'd have to lug it on their backs across the barren landscape, which was probably the real reason Brian brought Clovis and Bobby in the first place. It was worth it. Clovis had never seen Brian happier.

"This place is magical. You can smoke dope right out in the open. I love it."

"Do you know where we're going?"

Brian shook his head. "Brion Gysin actually knows these Joujouka guys. He hangs out with them in their little village up in the mountains. He'll take us there. Without him, we would never find them."

Brian busied himself with another match, another toke. This time the others shook their heads when the pipe was offered.

"I'm stoned . . ." Clovis said. "That's some strong shit, man."

Brion Gysin entered the café looking like something out of a Hollywood biblical epic. He was dressed in a long white robe and sandals.

"Going native?" Brian said as they shook hands. "You look more Moroccan than the Moroccans."

Gysin was deeply tanned and wore a small fez on the crown of his head. His piercing blue eyes sparkled.

"When in Rome, dear boy . . ."

"These are my colleagues Clovis Hicks, recording engineer, and Bobby Dingle, photographer and antique dealer."

"This is Mahmoud, my house boy."

They shook hands. Gysin and Mahmoud pulled up chairs.

Gysin ordered strong Turkish coffee and sweet Moroccan pastries. The hash pipe came to life again, and the air turned thick and lazy.

Gysin said, "I am prepared to take you to record the Master Musicians of Joujouka. You're in fantastic luck, because the Pipes of Pan Festival starts this weekend."

Brian gave the thumbs-up.

"We've got portable recording equipment. We're ready to rock, man. Now, just exactly where is Joujouka?"

The way Gysin looked directly into your eyes when he spoke was somewhat disconcerting, and Bobby could see Brian squirm under his unblinking gaze.

"Joujouka is in the Rif Mountains, about sixty miles south of here. Deep in the country, my friend. I took William Burroughs there, and it blew his mind. And Bill's mind is hard to blow. It's like going back four thousand years."

"And the music?"

Gysin smiled.

"Trancelike. Passionate. Extraordinary. The pieces rise and fall, reaching crescendo after crescendo. Sometimes one song can last indefinitely."

"I hope we can fit it all on one reel."

The coffee arrived at the table. Gysin spooned in some sugar and stirred. His voice was soft. One got the feeling that he'd given this speech before.

"The Master Musicians of Joujouka all come from one incredibly huge, ancient family. Their music has been handed down for generations, from father to son. It's amazing when you think about it. Bill Burroughs called them the world's only four-thousand-year-old rock band."

Brian sniffed.

"Kinda makes the Stones and the Beatles seem somehow . . . insignificant."

"A man named Hadj Abdessalam Attar is their leader. I know him. He's a good person. I'm sure he will cooperate with the recording. He worked with Ornette Coleman when he came here several years ago."

A disturbance in the streets outside caused them to look out the window. An old man beat a young boy with a cane. Mahmoud thought the kid had stolen a piece of fruit.

"That's a serious crime if both the boy and shopkeeper are Moslem."

By now, a crowd had gathered, and the kid was being dragged away by the wrists. The boy fought violently. Excessive force subdued him.

"What are they gonna do, cut off his hands?" Clovis asked, half-jokingly.

The somber expressions of Gysin and Mahmoud silenced him. Brian turned away from the window and swatted a fly off his cup.

"What kind of place is this?"

Gysin used his hands when he spoke, illustrating the sentences with elaborate gestures.

"Tangier? It's a beautiful anarchy, my friend. There are three official languages; French, Spanish, and Arabic, but most people speak a little English. Two official currencies, the peseta and the franc, but dollars and pounds are welcome, too. Almost everything is legal—drugs, prostitution, homosexuality. Legend has it that Hercules killed the giant Antaeus and buried him here. Apparently, he had the hots for Antaeus's wife and she for him. Antaeus is the god of losers. Tangier has always been an open city. Matisse lived here at one time."

Brian raised an eyebrow.

"I had no idea."

"This is a very old town. The foundation of the building you're sitting in dates back to the time of the Roman Empire."

Clovis looked at the floor.

"Jeez . . ."

Gysin continued. "The music can be traced all the way back to ancient Egypt. These people still worship the great goat-god Pan, whose followers stretch back into the dawn of antiquity, centuries before Christ."

The crowd outside dispersed as the heat pressed down on them.

"That's some mighty old shit."

Gysin laughed. "Yes, some mighty old shit, indeed."

Brian cleared his throat.

"Will we be able to communicate with them? Can we jam? What language do they speak?"

"Slow down. One question at a time. Even though there are three official languages, Morocco actually has eleven languages, two of them nearly extinct. In the section of the Rif Mountains where we're going, they speak Ghomara, one of the almost extinct languages. Luckily, Mahmoud speaks Tarifit, which is quite similar to Ghomara. Hadj speaks a little English, plus some standard Arabic, so we'll get along just fine. Besides, once the music starts, there is only one language."

"I can't wait to get started."

Gysin grinned.

"A Rolling Stone and the Pipes of Pan. This, I'd like to see."

"What are your plans for the rest of the afternoon?" Brian said.

Bobby said, "I've got to see someone about a pigeon."

"What are you talking about?"

"The famous Moroccan racing pigeons. The son of one of our English diplomats raises these racing pigeons right here in Tangier. His name is Kevin Cheswick and he's the son of Sir Alfred Cheswick. They live in the British mission right here in town."

"Why on earth would you want a racing pigeon?"

Bobby smiled.

"That's my secret. Now tell me about that auction."

"A local shaman died, the last of a very long line of shamans. His estate is being auctioned to pay creditors. I think there might be some rather esoteric, one-of-a-kind items available. Care to view the merchandise with me?"

Bobby said, "Absolutely. I'm on a buying trip while I'm here."

"Then you should come along."

Clovis shook his head. "I think I'll skip the auction. You guys go and have your fun. I'll see you when you get back."

One hour later, Brian Jones, Brion Gysin, and Dust Bin Bob were at the auction house—a huge, smoky room full of sweaty men of all nationalities. A large water stain on the ceiling resembled a map of Sri Lanka. Business was conducted in rapid-fire French and moved quickly. Items they had viewed earlier were brought out and placed upon a table where a one-armed auctioneer presided.

Bobby bid on several ornamental boxes, rugs, and tapestries, purchasing all of them. Gysin did the same. Brian, on the other hand, seemed bored. He wasn't really keen on any of the stuff and acted indifferently throughout.

That is, until an odd little mirror went on the auction block. Bobby noticed it at the viewing. It was about the size of a standard eight-by-ten photograph. A frame of black, polished stone, carved with tiny hieroglyphs, surrounded a rectangle of smoky, uneven glass. When Brian looked into it, the reflected image was slightly distorted.

"That's that weird little mirror you were looking at," Bobby said. "Might be a valuable antique."

Gysin gripped Brian's arm.

"That's a very special mirror. Buy it."

Brian raised his hand, and the auctioneer began babbling incomprehensible phrases at warp speed. The veins on his neck stuck out like vermicelli. Brian, with Gysin's help, outbid three other guys and bought the mirror.

"What did you mean, special?"

"Magic," Gysin whispered. "Ancient, beautiful, actual magic. That mirror is for gazing; scrying some call it. It's a form of meditation. It's said to open the third eye and cause the gazer to see amazing things. Some believe that Nostradamus was a mirror gazer and wrote many of his quatrains after gazing into the glass. Mirrors like that have been found in tombs over a thousand years old."

Brian beamed.

"And now it's mine. All the posh birds of London will powder their noses in it. Maybe we'll use it to snort coke off of. It's a trip, man. Dig it, I own a magic mirror."

Gysin's voice modulated down a half-step. "Don't make light of it, my friend. You, of all people, should be receptive."

Brian's eyes were bloodshot. They'd been smoking hash and drinking wine all day, and Bobby knew Brian had to be pretty whacked by now. Bobby became suddenly worried. *Maybe the mirror is fucked up; maybe buying it was a bad idea. Maybe it's evil. Maybe, in the light of day, we'll regret it.*

"That thing gives me the creeps, man." Bobby said. "I think it's evil. I don't want anything to do with it."

Brian seemed genuinely amused. "Dusty, I'm surprised at you. Evil? Afraid of it, are you?"

Bobby tried to laugh but produced only a dry, coughing sound, like low water pressure through turn-of-the-century English plumbing. Brian eyed Bobby.

"You bloody wimp. You're looking at a man who just recorded a song called 'Sympathy for the Devil.' Come on, man. I wrote the book on all that demonic shit. I've been to the edge and looked over the rim, and you're afraid of a fucking mirror?"

"I'm just sayin', if this was a horror movie, you buying that mirror would be act one."

CHAPTER SEVENTEEN

MASTER MUSICIANS OF JOUJOUKA

The next day at dawn, Brian, Clovis, Dust Bin Bob, Brion Gysin, and Mahmoud set out for the Rif Mountains. Brian had the mirror with him. Bobby could feel its unnatural weight when he loaded the bags into the back of the Land Rover. Although Clovis thought the mirror was nothing but a harmless antique, Bobby had begun to believe that the mirror really did harbor some kind of evil magic. He avoided touching it.

Mahmoud drove south through the sunbaked towns and Bedouin camps. Outside Tangier, the road simply vanished beneath their tires, and the desert swallowed them. Off to the south, they could see the blue ridge of foothills to the Rif Mountains. They looked ominous to Bobby. Brian suggested Bobby start taking pictures of the scenery, but every shot he took seemed the same.

"I want you to document everything," he said.

Hours passed, the mountains drew closer, and the land changed from arid desert to rolling hills. Mahmoud proved to be an excellent driver and navigated the Land Rover through the valleys until the terrain became impassable.

"We'll have to go on foot from here. The village is not far, just a few miles."

They climbed a mountain pass with the tape recorders on their backs and cameras swinging from their necks. Mahmoud carried two knapsacks full of blank tape and film canisters.

The mirror was in there, among Brian's toiletries. Bobby felt glad he wasn't carrying it. It occupied his thoughts as they walked. The damned thing had been owned by some very strange people over a very long period of time, and Bobby could only conjecture the peculiar things it had reflected over the centuries. Were those images trapped forever behind the warped and uneven looking glass?

They walked into the village of Joujouka at dusk. The festival was already in full swing. Bobby realized at once how far from Western civilization they had come. All the creature comforts they took for granted were absent: lights, electricity, phone service, plumbing, paved roads, restaurants, hotels. Nothing was familiar here. To Bobby, it was off-putting, and he felt even further removed from his home. Burroughs was right; it was like traveling back four thousand years.

None of it fazed Brian. He was in a state of musical euphoria.

"Oh my God, we're missing all this great music! Quick, Clovis, get the equipment set up as soon as you can."

Gysin calmed him down. "It's okay. The festival goes on for

days, and there will be lots of music to record. This is just the warm-up group. Why don't we secure lodging for the night and have some dinner first?"

"You mean that's the support act?"

"Things happen at their own pace here. Your job is to adjust to it, not fight against it. The real ceremonies get under way tonight. You absolutely don't want to miss that."

Mahmoud had relatives in Joujouka and arranged for them to stay in the house of an uncle. The uncle killed a goat and cooked the meat on skewers over an open fire.

The people of Joujouka were quite taken with Brian's appearance. The man with the long golden hair and colorful clothes drew a crowd wherever he went. They had never seen anything like him. Brian, a mystical shaman in his own right, was one of the Master Musicians of London, a fellow seeker of truth, and he had come all this way to see them. They treated him like royalty. Bobby got the feeling they would still be talking about it years from now; the time the man with the golden hair, the great Brian Jones, came to their village.

As the sun set, Clovis placed his microphones on boom stands around a hilltop, bordered on one side by a high stone wall, which he figured would act as a big resonator. The musicians gathered for their evening performance. Gysin cautioned Bobby and Clovis not to be surprised by some of the aspects of the Pan Festival, namely the dancing, which he said could become quite frenzied.

"Whatever happens, just go along with it. If it gets to be too much for you, duck down and move away."

"What do you mean by that?"

Before Gysin could answer, the first notes of the evening concert began.

Fifteen rhaita players blew a shrill fanfare on their oboelike double-reed horns and a line of drummers pounded a rumbling, complex beat. Clovis listened through the headphones, adjusting the levels to capture all the instruments. The scene was lit by several bonfires, casting eerie shadows into the night.

Just as he arrived at a workable mix, Clovis's attention was distracted by a naked old man, standing between the drummers and the horn players. At first, he just seemed like one of the throng, another pilgrim here to see the festival. As he began to move, Clovis realized he was much more than an onlooker. He had to be part of the ceremony. The naked old man started to dance, and within minutes he was jumping around like a twenty-year-old London mod on speed. His wrinkled, sunbaked skin shook and shivered as he stomped the ground, testicles bouncing like tiny burlap sacks, penis flapping comically, and a set of large dry hemorrhoids quivering like sea anemones. It was not a pretty sight. He had incredible energy for such an old man.

The music seemed to drive him insane. Something gleamed in the firelight. A large knife appeared in his hand. The band played louder and faster; the old man whirled like a dervish.

Clovis looked at Brian and Gysin who were enthralled by the music and didn't seem to notice the old man. How could they not? A naked old man with a Bowie knife is hard to miss. The knife flashed, and, for a fraction of a second, their eyes met.

Clovis had never seen eyes like that. They were completely crazed, without fear, capable of anything. *The eyes of a maniac.* He wanted to look away, to scream, but the old man held Clovis in his gaze. Then he stuck his tongue out at Clovis and spun away.

What the fuck?

Bobby shot pictures of the old man, his shutter going off at intervals. He'd seen the exchange between Clovis and the naked dancer, but he was too busy trying to concentrate on his own job to say anything. Besides, you couldn't talk anyway. The music dominated everything.

Using existing light was damn near impossible, but Bobby was determined to shoot without flash, which he thought would ruin the party. The torches and bonfires provided uneven and constantly flickering light.

All the while, the amazing music pulsed. The band seemed to have doubled in size while Clovis and Bobby weren't looking, because now there were fifty or so musicians going great guns. Clovis remembered Gysin saying that once the music started, everything else stopped. He said it would be hard to concentrate, that the trancelike music sucked you in, that to fight it would make you insane.

Clovis believed him. The horns cried and ululated, like centuries of grieving Arab women, shrieking above the cacophonous wall of sound. Clovis acted as a stone age Phil Spector with the four-thousand-year-old wall of sound mix. He kept checking the levels of the microphones so they wouldn't distort. He was getting a good clean signal.

The lack of anything resembling a standard Western melody was disconcerting. Suddenly, Clovis was uneasy. The old man was on the move now, the knife between his teeth.

The sound of a camera clicking distracted Clovis enough to notice Bobby still shooting pictures. Clovis glanced at Bobby and nodded. Bobby nodded back.

Yeah, you said there would be weird shit. How weird can it get?

What happened next took them all by surprise.

Someone released a terrified goat into the crowd. The people moved back, forming a circle, as the trapped goat ran from side to side, frantic to escape. After much dancing, the old man jumped on the goat and pretended to hump it. He reached around with the knife, and with one practiced motion, slit the belly of the goat open. Blood and entrails spilled out onto the ground. The music hit another crescendo. The goat bucked one last time, then died twitching in the old man's arms.

The music was so loud it was impossible to think, louder than a rock band, louder than the Stones themselves. But it wasn't just volume of sound, it was *psychically loud*, broadcasting into their brains at fifty thousand watts on the astral plane.

The old man laid the goat on the ground and began to remove its internal organs. Bobby and Clovis gagged more than once, but the tapes kept rolling and the band kept playing. While they watched, the old man picked up the freshly skinned goat and got inside the carcass. It draped over his shoulders, the goat's head above his head, the hooves hanging uselessly, dripping blood. He began to dance again.

Gysin looked at Bobby and mouthed the words, "Master of Skins."

The old man in the goatskin danced for hours. When, at last, he threw it off, he was covered in blood mixed with goat fat. At one point during a frenzied moment of particularly intense music, the old man danced over to Brian.

He writhed before Brian like an eel with an arrow in its head. Brian looked on, a bemused expression on his face. The old man keyed on Brian for a while, then moved on. He couldn't spook him. The Golden Stone never flinched.

The music lasted until dawn. Clovis used up most of the tape he had with him. They were exhausted and their heads throbbed. The incessant music had been such a driving force during the night, now its absence was deafening. Clovis took some aspirin with a swallow of brackish water and trudged back to their host's house. Brian, Clovis, and Dust Bin Bob crashed on the floor, too tired to move. Conversation evaporated. The Pipes of Pan had drained them body and soul.

The next day, Brian was up early. "Wake up, Clovis. A new day has begun. There's much to do."

"What the hell time is it? My watch has stopped."

Brian shrugged. "I don't wear a watch, man. Time is a bummer."

Time is a bummer?

"Is there any food around? I'm starving."

"Yeah, Gysin's gone to fetch some breakfast. I suppose it would be too much to ask for some bacon butties."

Bobby sat up. "Did somebody say bacon butties? That sounds wonderful."

Clovis laughed. "I hear the goat's good."

Brian lit a cigarette and squinted at Clovis and Bobby through the smoke.

"Could you believe that old man last night?"

Bobby shook his head. "That was insane."

"Did you take pictures?"

"Hundreds." Bobby sniffed his fingers. The aroma of goat turned his stomach. "I got everything: sight, sound . . . and, unfortunately, smell."

Gysin and Mahmoud entered with bowls of rice and steaming tea.

"Breakfast is served."

Brian said, "What was all that last night about the Master of Skins?"

Gysin settled next to Brian.

"That was the reenactment of the legend of Bou Jeloud. The Master of Skins is supposed to be the god Pan himself, half-man, half-goat. It goes way back to before the time when Saint Sidi Ahmed Sheikh introduced Islam to this region around eight hundred AD. He gave moral authority to the Master Musicians of Joujouka. Since then, they've been venerated. They are a living link to the Holy One. But in fact, they are pre-Christian and pre-Islam. They go all the way back to the time of the pyramids. There's no one else like them in the world."

"I'm sure the goat didn't appreciate it," Bobby said.

Gysin raised an eyebrow. “The goat was chosen. It was a great honor.”

“Tell that to the goat.”

Brian raised his hand, as if in school. “Question? Will there be more music to record today?”

“Oh, absolutely.”

Brian looked at Clovis. “How much tape is left?”

“I used almost half of it last night. My guess is we’ll be able to record another four reels, if we conserve.”

“Good. That’s settled, then.”

Brian clapped his hands together. He turned to Gysin. “All right, man. Let’s talk about mirror gazing.”

Gysin smiled. “Yes, of course. That intrigues you, doesn’t it? The mirror you bought is very powerful. You want to try it out? I can understand that. Today is the last day of music. Why don’t we stay tomorrow, and I’ll show you the technique.”

They spent the day recording music. The old man did not make an appearance. Clovis used every inch of tape he had, filling each with the weird, hypnotic keening of the horns and the raging cadence of the drums. If you listened to it, it drove you crazy; if you didn’t listen to it, it drove you crazy. It was impossible to tune out. When the second night of music was over, Clovis felt relieved. He’d done his job. Brian seemed satisfied.

Gysin acted as tour guide through the ancient stones of Joujouka, answering Brian’s questions and pointing out sacred sights. It seemed that almost everyone in the village was a musician related to the Attar family.

Brian Jones walked through the town like a holy man. People wanted to touch him, to be near him, to gaze upon him. He smiled and waved, blond hair radiating in the sunlight.

During the afternoon, Clovis began to feel sick. Something he'd eaten (possibly the goat) didn't agree with him. His stomach began to gurgle and heave. He developed terrible diarrhea. He went back to the room they had slept in and laid down on the dirt floor in his sleeping bag. He began to shiver.

Bobby, ever prepared, brought some Pepto-Bismol along with aspirin in his toiletries. He gave some to Clovis and told him to rest.

Dust Bin Bob turned to Brian and said, "Clovis is pretty sick. We have to make sure he's hydrated, but the water might be bad. I suppose we could boil it."

"We better keep an eye on him. It would be a bummer to have a medical emergency way out here."

Bobby looked at Brian.

"Could you postpone the mirror gazing? I don't want to do it without Clovis."

Brian made a face. "Are you scared? Come on Bobby, it's just a mirror."

"Don't lie to me, man. It's much more than a mirror."

The mirror gazing began at dusk. After eating a few of Mahmoud's hash cookies, Brian was anxious to try it. In a room lit by dozens of candles, Gysin explained the technique. He sat Brian on some pillows on the floor and placed the mirror in front of him so his face filled the glass.

"Look past the mirror. Concentrate just beyond the plane of the glass. Remember, this is a form of meditation, so complete relaxation is essential. After we leave the room, take a moment to clear your mind. Focus on your breathing. Try not to think any thoughts, just keep your mind blank. The third eye will open only after the conscious mind shuts down."

Bobby rolled his eyes as he listened to Gysin speak. All that third-eye jazz was a little too esoteric for him. Besides, something about the mirror still upset Bobby, and he didn't felt comfortable with the whole experiment.

Gysin said, "Think not so much of it as a mirror, but as a portal."

"A portal to what?" Brian asked.

"Why . . . the other side, of course."

Brian was keen on seeing it through, so after making his feelings known, Bobby remained silent. It was Brian's party now.

Brian pulled Bobby aside. "Hey, man, I found a way to do this." He pointed to an open window behind him. "You'll be out there, using the zoom lens and a tripod. You can shoot over my shoulder and still get the entire mirror in view. No glare because of the distance. If something appears in the glass, get a picture of it. Shoot at an oblique angle with a zoom."

"But, Brian, that's impossible."

The weight of Brian's hand on Bobby's shoulder surprised him. He wasn't a very physical person, but he shook Bobby hard.

"Wake up, Dust Bin Bob! Nothing's impossible! If there's one thing I've learned from being a Rolling Stone, it's that nothing, absolutely nothing, is impossible. It may be difficult, it may be hard as shit, but nothing is impossible. I would only expect you to do your best."

The worried look on Bobby's face must have troubled Brian.

"It's all right, man. Nothing bad will happen. Why are you so spooked by this thing?"

Bobby's voice quivered slightly. "I don't like supernatural stuff. Never have. Gives me the creeps."

"Hey, man. It's all part of nature. Too bad Clovis isn't here to hear you whinin'."

"Nature, my ass. It's evil."

Brian raised his eyebrows. "Anyway, this is just an experiment. Can you do it? Are you capable?"

Bobby sighed. "Aw, shit, Bri. . . . All right, I'll do it."

"Great! Okay! Let's rock!"

"What if nothing appears in the glass? I mean, what if you're the only one that can see it?"

The Golden Stone shrugged. "Then shoot a picture of the blank glass every three to five minutes. We'll examine the film later."

"The frame of the mirror is pretty small. Do you want me to stay well within those parameters?"

"Of course! We're only interested in things that happen *in the mirror*."

"I don't know, man. . . . This whole thing sounds pretty squirrelly to me."

Brian was losing his patience. "It would mean a lot to me, man. Look, I'll pay you extra."

"Money's not the issue."

"Humor me, Dust Bin Bob. Just sneak up and snap off a

picture every few minutes. Easy as pie. If there is something going on inside the mirror, I want to see."

"I wish Clovis was here."

"But he's not, is he? He's conveniently sick. Leaving you alone to face the unknown."

Gysin called Brian to the mirror.

"Stare into your own eyes, until your face dissolves, then look beyond."

Brian glanced at Bobby conspiratorially. Bobby looked away, not wanting to goad him on. Gysin adjusted Brian's position.

"Stay here for as long as you can. It could take many hours. Remember, keep your mind blank."

Gysin exited the room, leaving Brian Jones alone. Surrounded by a dozens of flickering candles, he stared intently into that strange little mirror. Brian glanced back over his shoulder at Bobby and winked.

Brian sat like a child with an expectant, curious look on his face. Candles flickered as the disturbed air rushed past. Bobby could see their reflection in the dark glass of the mirror.

Gysin and Mahmoud went to get something to eat, leaving Bobby skulking around the back window of the house with his camera. Feeling like a voyeur, Bobby watched Brian through the window. He sat very still, his glorious blond hair hanging down around his shoulders. Bobby noticed that his breathing had slowed. It was barely perceptible now by the slight rise and fall of his back. Bobby checked his camera. He had the right film and lens for the job, allowing for the lowest light. All he could do now was wait.

Twenty minutes passed. Bobby decided to take some pictures. As quietly as he could, he snuck up to the window, aimed the camera over Brian's shoulder and focused on the mirror. Its surface seemed as black and liquid as oil. Bobby took three quick exposures. For the next several hours, he took pictures every ten minutes. No change in the mirror.

Bobby felt silly carrying out Brian's request and was about to sod the whole thing, when something happened.

He was preparing to take another set of photos, and he aimed and focused the camera exactly as he had before, but now the mirror looked different. Instead of reflecting Brian's face, it seemed lighter. Bobby thought he could discern a cloudy image coalescing behind the glass. The camera whirred and clicked, and Bobby felt an involuntary chill. *Brian's doin' it, man. He's actually doin' it.* Whatever it was, Bobby got it on film, but it was like photographing smoke.

Slowly, the new image became more defined.

The reflection of a weeping young girl in a long white dress came into focus. Eleanor Rigby put her hand against the glass on the other side of the mirror. It was small and pale.

Her hand seemed to strobe and flicker as it touched the glass. It flashed in and out for a second or two. Bobby was glad he'd chosen to use super high-speed film. He kept his finger on the shutter release button and the camera shot continuously for several seconds. The image faded. He stood ready to photograph the next. But none came. He stayed there for another hour, sweating as if he were in a sauna, waiting for some change. The image had not returned. He took a few pictures anyway, just for the hell of it. Bobby had the camera aimed the same way, about to depress the shutter release, when suddenly Brian's head turned. His face loomed in the camera's viewfinder, red eyes blazing, looking utterly mad. He reminded Bobby of the old naked Master of Skins. He had that same manic look. It startled Bobby and he pressed his finger down, taking another rapid burst of pictures of Brian. Brian's pale face, with bags under his eyes, nostrils flared, upper lip quivering, seemed to glare at him through the lens. Bobby captured it all.

"I'm . . . out of the group," he whispered. "The Stones go on without me. . . ."

Bobby didn't know how to respond. Was Brian hallucinating? He certainly looked like he was tripping. He eyes were dilated and his mouth was dry.

"Brian?"

"Huh?"

"Brian? You okay?"

Brian blinked. "What's going on?"

"You were mirror gazing. Then you turned around said something to me. Do you remember what you said?"

Brian shook his head. "I don't remember." He looked dazed.

"Let's get some sleep, man. We'll talk about it in the morning."

"Did you take the pictures?"

"Yes," Bobby said. "I took lots of pictures."

"Was there something there?"

"Yes," he said. "I think there was something there."

CHAPTER EIGHTEEN

DEAR DOCTOR

"Get me out of here," Clovis rasped. "Please . . . I'm gonna die if I stay here."

"You're not gonna die," Bobby said. "You're just dehydrated. We'll get you to a doctor today. You'll be fine."

"I can't walk anymore. My legs are cramped."

Clovis was unshaven and pale. The dark circles under his sunken, haunted eyes looked like *Night of the Living Dead* zombie makeup. He was alternately glistening with sweat or shaking and feverish. His voice was parched.

"I call upon the power of the great Dust Bin Bob," Clovis whispered, "Please . . . Pull off another of your miracles, pardner. Take me home. Just get me the fuck out of here. I don't care about anything else."

Mahmoud felt Clovis's forehead and shook his head. He left the room after conferring briefly with Gysin.

Bobby put a hand on Clovis's sweat-soaked, greasy hair. "Don't worry, old buddy, I'll get you out of here if I have to carry you on my back. And I might."

"Is that a promise?"

Bobby said, "Damn straight." Clovis managed a weak smile and held his hand out for Bobby to grasp. He squeezed his friend's hand. "I got you covered. We're getting out of here right now."

The two buckets that Clovis had filled during the night, one from his diarrhea and one from his nausea, were reeking in a corner near the sleeping bags. Bobby picked them up and emptied them outside in a shallow pit, which he covered over. He found a towel and cleaned Clovis up as best he could. Clovis trembled uncontrollably. Gysin brewed him some weak mint tea with clean boiled water. Clovis sipped tentatively.

Gysin said, "The mirror gazing went well. According to Dust Bin Bob, he was able to photograph several images in the glass."

Clovis looked at Gysin. "The mirror's a fake. You guys are wasting your time."

"We won't know until the pictures are developed, but there was definitely something there," Bobby said.

"Bullshit." Clovis pulled the blanket in which he was wrapped tighter around his neck. "I've never felt so sick in my entire life. I can't believe you dragged me all the way out here for this dog-and-pony show."

Brian Jones entered the room like a rock star, stretching from his ten-hour sleep resulting from the hash cookies.

"Jesus, those hash cookies kicked my ass," Brian said. "How's Clovis today? Will he be able to travel?"

"He's not good," Bobby said.

Brian went over to get a closer look at Clovis. He looked rough. "Yeah, you're right. We're definitely not shooting the album cover today."

Presuming what Brian said was a joke, Bobby didn't laugh.

Bobby said, "I'm worried about Clovis. We can't waste any time getting him to a clinic."

Gysin explained his plan. "We may have to carry him out. I sent Mahmoud to rent a camel, and he can ride on the camel until we get back to the Land Rover."

Brian said, "How do we get rid of the camel when we get to the car?"

Gysin said, "The owner of the camel will come with us so he can lead the beast back to the village when we're done. Everyone in the village who owns a camel is in the camel-renting business. It shouldn't be a problem."

Clovis moaned. He bent over the bucket and dry-heaved. When nothing came out, he leaned back and gasped for air.

"There's nothing left. I'm runnin' on fumes, boys. I'm empty. If I don't get some serious fluids soon, I'm gonna shrivel up like a prune."

Gysin said, "There is no medical clinic here, but there is in the town of Chefchaouen on the way back. We should be able to get an IV in your arm in a few hours."

"I'm too weak. I'll never make it."

Bobby said, "We'll carry you out of here. We can take turns. I told Erlene I'd look after you."

Clovis laughed, which turned into a cough. "That's funny. I told Cricket the same thing."

"You want to carry me?"

Clovis shook his head.

Suddenly, a big silver-and-gray pigeon with a band of green iridescent feathers around its neck landed in front of them. It lighted on Bobby's knapsack and looked at them. The pigeon nuzzled the knapsack and Bobby opened it to reveal a tiny wooden pigeon cage.

"Kevin's racing pigeon!" Bobby said. "He made it!"

"You mean that bird flew all the way out here to find that cage?"

"This is no ordinary pigeon. This is a champion racer. I let him go yesterday, and he's already been to Tangier and back. Racing pigeons have been clocked at over one hundred miles per hour with a tailwind. Once he leaves that cage, he'll always find his way back."

"That's unbelievable."

"Here's the unbelievable part. That bird will take a message back to the cage it came from."

Bobby gently removed a small metal canister from the bird's leg. Inside the canister was a tightly rolled-up paper. Bobby carefully rolled it out and got out his pen. He wrote:

Message from Bobby. Finished our mission. Recorded Joujouka Musicians. On our way back. Clovis is sick. Needs medical help. Leaving today for Tangier. I'll call as soon as possible. See you soon.

Gysin watched Bobby roll the message back and place it in the canister.

"How did you get the idea for that?" Gysin said.

"I read an article on the plane about Morocco's famous racing pigeons. When I saw that the president of the local racing club was an English teenager, I paid him a visit and explained the situation to him. He was only too glad to help. There's not much to break the boredom around here."

"How do you get the message across the ocean?"

"Telegram," Bobby said. "I gave the kid some cash to cover the expenditures."

"That is totally fuckin' brilliant!" Clovis rasped. "That's why Dust Bin Bob is the leader of us all."

"Hold on, let's get out of here first," Bobby said. "We still have a long way to go."

Mahmoud returned with a camel driver leading a very pissed-off camel. The filthy beast spit and farted and took an instant dislike to Clovis. The camel, which had no actual name, appeared to be generally disagreeable.

Bobby helped Clovis to his feet. He howled with pain.

"My legs! They're cramping up something fierce!"

Bobby picked him up and swung him over his shoulder. Clovis let out a howl as his legs shifted.

The camel driver and Mahmoud forced the camel to sit and held the beast steady while Mahmoud and Bobby hoisted Clovis up on the camel's back. Tears of pain streamed down Clovis's face, but he clenched his teeth and stayed quiet. He held on for dear life as the camel slowly rose to its feet. Clovis looked down and realized he was much farther off the ground than he imagined. A fall from here would be substantial. He held on tenaciously.

The effort to get aboard the camel exhausted him, and Clovis slumped forward. Mahmoud handed Clovis a bladder bag of weak mint tea, which hydrated him slightly. They started the journey back to the Land Rover on foot.

It was the first and only camel ride in Clovis's life. Every step was agony. Even the camel was miserable. Clovis's head throbbed, his cramps came and went every few minutes, and his fever spiked. But he hung on. They were on their way back. Soon he would be resting in a nice clean hospital bed sipping San Pellegrino bottled water.

They found the Land Rover just exactly as they had left it. Except for a fine cover of dust, it had not been touched.

The camel driver somehow got the unhappy camel to sit so Bobby and Mahmoud could lift Clovis off. He groaned as they moved his legs; they were still cramping terribly. Bobby gently placed him in the car and gave him some more mint tea to sip.

"Won't be long now, buddy."

Clovis moaned.

The Land Rover started up and two hours later they drove into the ancient city of Chefchaouen. Mahmoud was able to obtain directions to the medical clinic. They welcomed Clovis and immediately put him on a IV drip and started the hydration process. Clovis sunken eyes and pale face frightened Bobby. He said a silent prayer.

One of the nurse practitioners said, "A few more hours and you might have suffered kidney failure. You're lucky your friends brought you here."

"These men are my brothers." He waved at Bobby, Gysin, Mahmoud and Brian, who were all standing around Clovis's bed.

"You caught a nasty bacterial infection. It wasn't going to go away without a healthy dose of antibiotics."

"When can I leave?"

"Not so fast. We'll need to keep you here for several days for evaluation."

"I want to get back to London."

"No way. First you rest, then maybe tomorrow we'll talk about it."

Bobby asked about telephone service and was pleased to find several private long-distance operators standing by.

He called the house on Southway. Cricket answered. Bobby had no idea what time it was back in Baltimore; all he knew was that he needed to talk to Cricket.

"Bobby?" she asked. "Oh, thank God it's you!"

"Hi, honey. We just got back to civilization. Clovis got sick and we had to take him to the medical clinic. He's all right, though."

Erlene wrenched the phone from Cricket's hand. "Clovis? Clovis? Put Clovis on!"

Bobby handed the phone to Clovis. "Hon? Is that you?"

Erlene burst into tears. "Oh, baby! Are you okay?"

Clovis chuckled. "Yeah, these guys dragged my sorry ass out of there just in time."

"What happened to you?"

"I ate some goat meat and got sick as a dog. Then I got dehydrated and rode a camel."

"Serves you right for eatin' goat meat. That ain't right."

"I'm in the medical clinic, and they gave me some antibiotics and some fluids and they say I might make it after all."

"I'm coming to London to meet you. I can't stay away from you, baby."

"But . . . I still have to work for Brian."

"I know. How is Brian?"

"Why do you ask about him? I thought you hated him."

"Because Eleanor Rigby gave me a message for him."

Clovis chuckled. "Let's worry about that later. I need to rest now."

"I'm coming, too!" Cricket could be heard to shout in the background. Erlene handed the phone back to Cricket.

"Bobby? I'm coming, too. I can't be away from you. If you have to stay and take care of Brian, then I want to be with you. We'll move back to Baltimore when we can."

"It's great to hear you say that, because I can't handle it anymore myself."

"Bobby? How in the world did you get that last telegram to me? It came from somebody named Kevin Cheswick."

"Carrier pigeon."

"You're kidding, right?"

"No. Kevin Cheswick is the son of a British diplomat stationed here in Tangier. He raises racing pigeons."

"How clever. I never would have guessed."

The trip back to London was uneventful. Clovis was fully recovered, although he'd lost some weight and he was still walking unsteadily. Brian flew first class, Bobby and Clovis sat together in coach. They'd managed to keep Brian out of the news for the time being. There were no crowds waiting for Brian Jones when they landed at Heathrow Airport.

Brian paid for a car and driver to take him to a five-star hotel. Then he dropped Clovis back at his flat before dropping Bobby off at his apartment.

Bobby hadn't been there for a while and he knew that Clovis had stashed Brian there. He expected the place to be messy, but as soon as he unlocked the door, he noticed how tidy everything was.

Bobby got an odd feeling that somebody was in his apartment. He thought he heard a sound in the bedroom. It sounded like a creaking floorboard.

Bobby's paranoia got the best of him. *Is Brian rubbing off on me?* He crept through the living room and peeked into the bedroom. The lights were off.

He tiptoed into the room and felt for the light switch. The feeling that someone was in the room was overpowering. He found the switch and flicked it on.

Nothing moved. Nothing jumped. Bobby noticed that the bed wasn't made. In fact, it was quite messy. In an apartment that had obviously been professionally cleaned, why would the bed be messed up? Bobby eyed the covers. They were flat as a quesadilla. *Nobody could possibly be under them, could they?* Bobby gripped the corner of the covers. He took a deep breath and jerked them away.

At that moment, something launched itself at Bobby. A blurred shape, naked flesh, blond hair, and a shiny knife.

Time slowed down as it often does in a physical crisis. Bobby's brain pieced all the clues together in less than a heartbeat. A naked woman with a long sharp dagger came at him from the bed where she'd been hiding. Her face was distorted, but he thought he recognized it.

She was on him so fast he couldn't react. She slashed with the knife, and Bobby's arm got in the way. The dagger sunk deep into the flesh of his forearm. Blood began to ooze out of the wound at an alarming rate. In a moment, it was all over the floor, making the room slick with blood.

"Brian!" she screamed. "I love you!" She thrust the knife into his side. It cut Bobby a glancing blow, nicking a two-inch gash under his left lower rib.

Bobby saw her face. It was Renee, her pretty face in a hateful grimace. Bobby's temper flared.

She thinks I'm Brian! Bobby sure as hell wasn't going to die as a stand-in. *It's time to turn out the lights on this party.*

Renee lunged again, the knife out in front of her. Bobby slammed his fist hard into Renee's face, causing her nose to crumple and start bleeding. Grabbing the knife out of her hand he twisted her wrist counterclockwise. She yelped as Bobby pressed her into an Aikido wrist lock that Cricket's father had taught him and applied the pressure. Her little wrist snapped like a twig, and she screamed. Bobby leveraged her arm behind her back and rode her to the ground, face-first. He twisted her arm back and put a foot on her back.

"I'm not Brian!"

He reached for the bedside phone as he held her down. The cops and ambulance were there within minutes.

The medical technicians bandaged Bobby up on the spot. He only needed a few stitches as his wounds were mostly superficial. He had been lucky; Renee hadn't pierced any vital organs or arteries.

The cops asked Bobby questions for the rest of the night. "You say you know this woman?"

"I've seen her around. She's a groupie."

"And you say she's obsessed with Brian Jones of the Rolling Stones? Is he here?"

Bobby said, "No. The woman thought she was attacking Brian Jones instead of me. Even after she saw my face, she still thought I was Brian. She even called me Brian."

"So she was stalking Mr. Jones?"

"Yes, Brian stayed here once or twice to get away from the press. He was only here a few days, but Renee must have followed him. And when I came in and tiptoed to the bedroom, she assumed I was Brian coming back."

"And then she attacked you with this?"

The detective held up a WWII German SS ceremonial dagger. Bobby's eyes got big. "I didn't notice it at first."

"This is quite like the murder weapon in the case of Claudine Jillian."

"The Nazi Ripper? Do you think Renee is the Nazi Ripper? Nah, that's too far out. What would be her motive?"

"Jealousy. Brian admitted to having sex with Miss Jillian the night before she was murdered. It's possible that Renee found out. Maybe it was an act of revenge."

"That's the only link we have right now."

CHAPTER NINETEEN

ROCK AND ROLL CIRCUS

During the night of police questioning, Bobby called Clovis and told him what happened. Clovis phoned Brian and roused him and came down right away, but Brian took a few more hours to get ready. By noon, they had all gathered at a restaurant near the police station.

"I'll tell you, boys. I can't stand this town anymore. It's just one big obstacle course for me. To make matters worse, the cops just released Renee. They said they had insufficient evidence to hold her any longer."

"That's outrageous!"

"What about the knife?"

"It wasn't the same knife, just a similar one. Her trial on assault with a deadly weapon is coming up, but for now she's out free. I'm pretty sure she wants to kill me. Rather than protect me, the cops are always waiting to pounce. I'm sick of all this harassment. I'm getting out."

Clovis and Bobby stared at Brian and blinked.

"So, what are you going to do?"

Brian smiled. "I'm going to buy a country house and live outside London."

Brian seemed proud of himself. He looked at Bobby and Clovis for their reaction. They didn't know how to react.

Neither one had ever lived in a proper English country house, something along the lines of Keith's Redlands Estate. But in typical Brian Jones fashion, their friend was anxious to get started. Brian wanted Bobby to call a real estate agent and start looking at houses immediately.

"Why such a hurry?" Clovis asked.

"The cops are watching me. I'm sunk if I get busted again. From now on, no more dope in the house. I'm going back to drinking."

"What kind of place are you looking for?"

"Something magic," Brian replied. "Something with history."

Bobby purchased some newspapers and real estate magazines. Almost immediately, a property jumped out at him.

He ran back to Brian to tell him. "Cotchford Farm is for sale down in East Sussex, about one hour and twenty minutes from London. It's the home of A. A. Milne, the author of the Winnie-the-Pooh books. The place is owned by an elderly American couple who would like to sell it."

"That's fantastic! Tell me more!"

"Built in the mid-sixteenth century, it has three floors, six bedrooms, three bathrooms, exposed timbers and beams, several fireplaces, a drawing room, study, family room, and bookshelves throughout. It's got private gardens and a heated outdoor pool, plus an ornamental fishpond and several statues of Christopher Robin. It is surrounded by a five-hundred-acre wood."

"That sounds perfect!" Brian crowed. "Let's drive down and see it straightaway."

Clovis drove Brian's Rolls south of London, through Dartford, where Mick and Keith grew up, and south on the M25 to Hartfield.

They found the property without much trouble. As they drove up, Brian had his face against the windshield. He was enthralled. Most English children grow up with Winnie-the-Pooh, and here was Brian, about to return to ground zero as an adult.

As he got out of the car and breathed in the tranquil afternoon, Brian fell in love. It didn't take more than a few minutes for him to become entranced with every aspect of Cotchford Farm. He loved the quietly babbling fishpond, the heated pool, the gentle breeze through the fragrant gardens, the stone statues of Christopher Robin, and the feeling of utter safety and contentment he got from the old house. The American couple who owned the property, the Taylors, were somewhat taken aback by Brian's appearance, but once he turned on the charm, they were happy to take his money. In fact, Clovis had never seen Brian this ebullient.

The couple walked Brian through the house and pointed out everything of interest. Brian had already made up his mind. He wanted Cotchford Farm. He couldn't wait to move in. Something about the place attracted him. He felt as if he were finally going home, the place where he would spend his days.

Bobby and Brian conferred with the Taylor's real estate agent in another room, going over details of the sale. Brian left the negotiations to Bobby. He got a great price at thirty thousand English pounds (about seventy-two thousand dollars at the time) and Brian wrote a check. He had more than enough money, of course.

When it was over, Brian stood in the living room and grinned. He spread his arms. "It's mine, all mine."

"Welcome home, pardner," Clovis said.

"Let's start moving in immediately."

"Wait a minute, do you mean me and Dust Bin Bob are going to move you in?"

Brian smiled. "Well . . ."

"No way, José." Clovis replied. "You hire some professional moving men and we'll point to where they should put the furniture."

"Very well. Gentlemen, welcome to Cotchford Farm, the new lair of Brian Jones."

Brian wandered off looking at rooms and spaces. The house had three stories, but there were so many staggered levels and mezzanines, it was impossible to tell how many levels there actually were. Everywhere he looked were the unmistakable signs of A. A. Milne. He had written all the Winnie-the-Pooh classics right there in those rooms.

They drove back to London for the release party of the new

Stones album, *Beggar's Banquet.* Clovis accompanied Brian. The rest of the band treated him as if he'd just stepped in dog shit. Clovis watched how they went out of their way to alienate Brian and it made him sad. It also pissed him off. He knew Brian's worth to the band, and this just wasn't fair.

However, *Beggar's Banquet* was a masterpiece. Brian Jones had helped lead the Stones back to their R&B roots. Brian had put his imprint on the album with brilliant slide guitar on "No Expectations" and "Stray Cat Blues," harmonica on "Parachute Woman," "Dear Doctor," and "Prodigal Son," and a host of other instruments on other songs. Brian felt good about his contributions, but the Stones never seemed satisfied by his efforts.

The Rolling Stones jumped into their next project, a TV special called *The Rolling Stones Rock and Roll Circus*, a bizarre mix of midgets, jugglers, clowns, fire eaters, and of course, rock and roll. It was to promote *Beggar's Banquet.* The show featured several popular groups of the day, including Jethro Tull, The Who, Marianne Faithfull, Taj Mahal, and John Lennon fronting a supergroup made up of Eric Clapton on guitar, Keith Richards on bass, and Jimi Hendrix's drummer, Mitch Mitchell. They called themselves The Dirty Mac.

Brian wandered around zonked out of his head. It embarrassed Clovis and Bobby, who were accompanying him. Why did he feel the need to be stoned around his peers? It was as if he were subconsciously trying to fail. Determined to keep him straight, they kept pumping coffee into him and making him wash his face with cold water.

The shoot started early and ran until very late. A studio

audience was brought in to simulate a live concert. The day started brilliantly. Everybody sounded great. Everyone there, including the Stones, thought The Who stole the show. They performed their mini-rock opera *A Quick One While He's Away*.

As the afternoon turned into evening, and evening turned into late evening, and late evening turned into early morning, the Stones finally went on. But they had misjudged the situation. The audience at this point was too tired to react and the Stones seemed to force their performance. The set sounded flat compared to The Who. The band was clearly exhausted after a full day of shooting. Overall, it was not a particularly good performance, and the Stones ultimately decided to put it on the shelf.

Brian had fun hanging around with the other musicians. Most of the groups had to make do with tiny dressing cubicles, except the Stones and John Lennon. John had demanded and got a full-size star's motor home plus another room in which his supergroup could tune up.

Brian and Bobby ran into John backstage. He was with the tiny Japanese conceptual artist everybody was talking about named Yoko Ono. Bobby, as close as he was to John, had never met Yoko. In fact, John had become somewhat reclusive since he and Yoko had been together. Old friends dropped away; he stopped calling people. Such is often the case with new lovers; the rest of the world seems to fade into the background. They prefer each other's company to old friends and colleagues.

John hugged Brian. "How's it goin', mate? How's your love life?"

Brian responded with a moment of stoned confusion. "Why? What have you heard?"

John leaned in closer and lowered his voice.

"Whoa, slow down. I haven't heard anything. Why are you so paranoid? Brian, we need to talk."

John Lennon led Brian and Bobby to his motor home dressing room. Yoko followed silently by John's side. Once they got inside, Yoko surprised Bobby by locking the door. She looked at Bobby and blushed.

"So John won't be disturbed," she said in a tiny little teacup voice.

"How about the rest of us?" Bobby wisecracked, but Yoko didn't get it. "I'm here, too."

John put a hand on Brian's shoulder. "Okay, what's going on?"

Brian cast his eyes down. "The rest of the band hates me, and I'm in serious danger of getting fired from the group."

John shook his head. "You're in danger of getting fired from the group you started? Ha! Fuck them. You should quit right now, right here today. You're the star of that band. I tell you what, let's make a deal: you quit your band and I'll quit mine, and we'll start a supergroup. We can have anyone we want."

Brian smiled. "That's incredibly kind of you, John."

"I'm serious. You have your whole life in front of you, and you can do whatever you want. You're a great musician, man, act like it."

"Sometimes I feel like giving up . . ."

"Shirrup!" John spat. "That's loser talk! You're the original Rolling Stone. Don't sit around waiting for the ax to fall, quit now. You can start a new band anytime you want. I'll help you. We can play all the blues you want."

"Thanks, John. . . . I don't know what to say."

"I saw the way they treated you." John nodded toward the door. "They spit on you. I don't like that. You should see the way my guys spit on Yoko. They treated her like a dog. You have to take the bull by the horns, Brian. Fuck the Stones and the Beatles; they're yesterday's papers. Let's form our own group and get back to the roots."

John's treasonous words hung in the air like a battle cry. He didn't care. He spoke bluntly.

Brian smiled. "Yeah, that sounds good."

Bobby changed the subject. He said to John, "Brian bought a country house. Cotchford Farm in Hartfield, Sussex. The former home of A. A. Milne."

"Christopher Robin? Winnie-the-Pooh?"

"Yes," Brian said. "The place is magic; you must come visit once I'm moved in."

"We can rehearse there in complete privacy."

Someone knocked on the door. Yoko answered. It was Eric Clapton. "Sound check, lads."

In the end, BBC never aired *The Rolling Stones Rock and Roll Circus*. The Stones thought their performance was flat. The Dirty Mac never appeared again; John soon changed their name to the Plastic Ono Band.

Erlene and Cricket arrived in London with three-year-old Winston. Bobby cried when he saw them. He knew Cricket was miserable in London, but they wanted to stay together through the Brian Jones crisis as much as possible. They had decided to move back to Baltimore as soon as things calmed down for Brian. Clovis and Erlene had also changed their plans. Now they intended to live together in London during her pregnancy. Once the child was born, they would return to Baltimore. Erlene needed to stay close to her man. She was convinced that Eleanor Rigby had passed a message to her, and as long as Bobby and Clovis stayed with Brian, nothing bad would happen.

The next morning, Clovis and Bobby drove down to Cotchford Farm. Brian had already parked his Rolls-Royce there and had installed his latest girlfriend, blonde Swedish dancer Anna Wohlin. Anna was protective of Brian, and unlike Anita, they got along perfectly. Brian banned all drugs from his property. He even went so far as to search people coming in. From now on, it would be nothing stronger than alcohol. Anna busied herself in the kitchen, and Brian fussed like an old lady. The house rejuvenated him. The spirit of Christopher Robin lived in every nook and cranny. It revitalized him.

Cotchford changed Brian almost overnight.

"I feel like I'm finally home," he said. "I never want to leave this place. I'll stay here until I die."

He showed Bobby and Clovis the room that he wanted to rebuild into a recording studio. Clovis checked it out, measured a few things, and pronounced the studio absolutely doable.

He had just enough room to install a multitrack board, and an Ampex 16-track tape recorder in the control room, and still have room for the studio itself. Brian suggested Clovis steal microphones from Olympic Recording, but he refused.

"It would wreck my karma," he said. "It's taken me a long time to get it right."

"That's why I love you so much, Clovis, you are a righteous dude."

Clovis grinned. "Ain't no big deal. . . . If I steal something from the studio, before the day is over, someone will have stolen something from me. That's how flat my karma is right now."

Brian said, "Can you put together a budget for the studio? I have no idea what's it's going to cost."

"No problemo, pardner. I'll give you a price for the equipment, and a price for the construction work. Shouldn't be too bad."

"Bobby, have you had a chance to develop the pictures from Joujouka?"

"I have to take them to a lab that specializes in custom low-light exposures. It's going to take a little extra time and cost a bit more money. I haven't had a chance to drop off the film yet."

"Can you get started on that?"

"Sure, just as soon as I get back to London."

"You can all stay here at Cotchford for the time being, if you like. Tom Keylock is coming down tomorrow to hire the general contractors to carry out the renovations. The main thing is the studio; let's get started on that first."

Anna Wohlin entered the room with a bottle of champagne on ice and several glasses.

"A toast?"

Anna poured the champagne. They all held their glasses high.

Brian's voice sounded happier than it had in years. "To Cotchford!"

"To Cotchford!"

"Home of Winnie-the-Pooh!"

"Now the home of Brian Jones."

Skully met Renee at their secret rendezvous in a darkened pub in Camden Town, London. He was nursing a pint as Renee walked in wearing tight jeans and a black plastic trench coat. She was incognito tonight, dressed to travel, dressed to kill.

She sat down next to Skully in a corner booth and spoke in low tones.

"Brian just bought the A. A. Milne house in Hartford. It's a perfect setup."

"Yeah, I know."

"I have directions. We should go down there and check it out."

"Look, there's no rush right now. I say we watch and wait."

Renee nodded. "What happened to Spangler?"

Skully dropped his voice. "I don't know. He disappeared. I think the Mafia got him."

"What do you mean 'disappeared'?"

"I mean he's missing. Hasn't been to work in over a week. Nobody's heard from him since he returned from London."

"You think the families got him?"

"I wouldn't be surprised. He was always making deals with

them, they were getting sick of it. Live by the sword; die by the sword."

Renee lit a cigarette. Her smile was feline. "He was a weasel anyway."

"He had no idea who he was dealing with."

"He knew. He just thought he could get away with it." Renee changed the subject. "You know everything about me, but I know next to nothing about you."

"What's to know?"

"When are you going to tell me who you work for?"

Skully smiled. "You're a curious little bitch, aren't you? What does it matter?"

"I have to know who I'm working with."

"Believe me. You don't want to know."

"Come on, Skully. Don't you think you owe me? You made a lot of promises." She touched his face. "Don't you remember, baby?"

Skully whispered, "I'll tell you once, right now, but you'll have to swear never to bring it up again. This information must never get out. Do you swear? If it does, we're both dead."

"I work for a secret organization called The M Group. That's all I can tell you."

"The M Group? I never heard of them."

"That's why they're secret."

"Is it a government agency? Like the CIA?"

"No, it's a private group."

"And why do they want Brian dead?"

Skully frowned. "No more questions."

Mick Jagger and Keith Richards had been talking for weeks about firing Brian from the Rolling Stones, the band that he founded. Things had changed. He wasn't contributing anymore. The incident with Keith and Anita broke his heart. Life on the road was impossible. And of course, there were the drug busts. Brian felt pressure from every quarter.

The Stones had a major tour coming up. *Beggar's Banquet* had reestablished the band, and now it was time to take it to the people. Touring had never been more important. Not only did it provide a much-needed cash flow, but it stimulated record sales, and that was the kind of promotion they needed. The Rolling Stones brand had been tarnished by the weak response to *Their Satanic Majesties Request*, a train wreck of an album with only one weak hit single: the overproduced "She's a Rainbow." Brian had warned them to get back to their roots. Now *Beggar's Banquet* had righted the ship.

Brian couldn't get a visa to tour in the United States or Japan. Keith and Mick had kicked around every idea they could think of. Eric Clapton had volunteered to take a leave of absence from Cream and join the group temporarily until the tour was over. Other guitarists volunteered. Mick and Keith had their own visa problems, but their lawyers were working hard to clear the slate.

Unbeknownst to Brian, the Stones had been jamming with a hot young guitarist from John Mayall's Bluesbreakers named Mick Taylor. They could bring this guy or that guy, but neither wanted to hire a temp. The only answer was to fire Brian Jones and move on. But Brian's roots were deep. He started the band, he named the band, he chose the members, he selected the material, and he booked the early gigs. Brian's fingerprints were all over the Stones. It would not be easy to replace him.

Mick, Keith, and Charlie drove out to Cotchford Farm to confront Brian. Firing Brian would be the most difficult business decision they had ever made. They took their time driving, mulling over what they would say. They'd have to choose their words carefully because Brian was as sensitive as a bad tooth.

The Rolling Stones new manager, American publishing mogul Allen Klein, put together the parting deal for Brian. Brian would continue to receive his share of the royalties for the albums already recorded, he would also get a one-hundred-thousand-pound settlement payment and the sum of twenty thousand pounds yearly for as long as the Stones continued to exist and make money.

Allen and the rest of the Stones avoided saying that Brian had been fired. The official press release said he was quitting the group due to "musical differences." That sort of whitewash always made Brian angry. *At least let the truth come out*, he thought. Brian didn't care if he was fired or quitting, it was all the same. He just wanted the nightmare to be over.

Mick, Keith, and Charlie walked into Cotchford with the weight of the world on their shoulders. Brian knew instantly what they were up to. He'd been expecting it. One look at their faces and he could tell. What they had to do wasn't easy, but so much bullshit had built up around the Stones that it was suffocating them. They all knew what had to be done. There was a cancer growing on the band, and it had to be cut out.

Brian led them down to his parlor and listened to what they had to say.

Keith got right to the point. "Brian, you're out of the band. You're fired."

Even though Brian expected it, Keith's words still came as a shock. Brian felt numb. It was remarkably like the day Keith stole Anita and left Brian on his own in Morocco.

Brian felt his ears ring. This was the moment he'd been anticipating, and now it was here. For a few seconds, he couldn't hear them. It all sounded like gibberish. Ever the businessman, Mick went over the settlement payments with Brian. Brian couldn't concentrate. One hundred thousand pounds, twenty thousand pounds, what did these numbers mean? They had computed Brian's worth to the Stones, and there it was written down on a piece of paper? Brian felt like crying. The irony was almost too much.

Mick seemed to be the most motivated among them; he did most of the talking. In a hurry to get through the sacking, he lost a little of his compassion and started to sound cold.

Brian felt confused. Mick made it seem like Brian wanted to quit, like he was unhappy with the band and wanted to move on. But that wasn't the case at all. He was being sacked.

Brian tried to pay attention, but it was like listening to lawyers instead of musicians.

Mick and Keith claimed they owned the rights to the name *Rolling Stones*. When Brian objected, they decided to sort that detail out at a later date. First things first: Brian had to be jettisoned before anything else could happen.

They spoke for a while, Brian becoming more quiet and withdrawn with every passing moment. When at last they left, Brian said good-bye and put on a carefree face, but he was dying inside.

Brian watched them drive away. His last sight was Charlie Watts's look of discomfort as he watched out the back window.

I am no longer a Rolling Stone, Brian thought. *After all these years, the dream is over.*

The next day, the newspaper headlines read: BRIAN JONES QUITS THE STONES AS GROUP CLASHES OVER SONGS!

Brian had the London papers brought to him every day and he followed the story. He read them again and again, tears forming in his eyes.

What a load of shit, he thought.

Fans were flabbergasted. No one outside the Stones had any idea.

CHAPTER TWENTY

THE VOX TEARDROP

In the days that followed getting fired, Brian fell into a profound funk. His life had revolved around the Stones for as long as he could remember. Without the band, there seemed no reason to get up in the morning.

Brian thought about the financial settlement. The more he weighed it, the more unfair it seemed. One hundred thousand pounds didn't seem like enough money after generating millions. Bobby sat down with Brian on several occasions and tried to explain Allen Klein's memorandum of agreement as best he could, but Brian understood little. Inside him, bitter resentment grew. He was no businessman, but he knew what was fair.

Clovis and Erlene stayed at Cotchford with Brian just to keep a watchful eye on him. John Lennon called often. Dust Bin Bob commuted from London two or three times a week, splitting time between running his store and living with Cricket.

Friends called Brian every day, trying to encourage him to play some music, but now that he was out of the Stones, his inspiration had temporarily dried up. Jimi Hendrix, Denny Laine, Alexis Korner, John Mayall, Eric Burdon, John Lennon, his phone bubbled forth with the cream of the crop of London's best musicians. But Brian was nonplused. He needed some time off.

Tom Keylock hired Frank Thorogood to do the renovations on Cotchford Farm. Frank had worked on Keith's Redlands Estate and even though Keith was less than thrilled with the quality of the work, Tom hired Frank to work on Brian's house.

Frank hired a trio of unsavory day laborers, known only as Johnny, Mo, and Dave, from nearby West Withering. Clovis called them the Pep Boys after the American auto parts store: "The Pep Boys! Manny, Mo, and Jack!" There was a classic sight gag about the Pep Boys matches. The English guys never got it until Clovis showed Brian and Bobby the infamous "Pep Boys Match Book Trick."

Clovis explained that he learned it in juvenile hall after being arrested for stealing cars as a youth.

"Please, show us!" Brian begged.

"Okay, Brian. Just for you."

Clovis had a brandy snifter full of Pep Boys matchbooks from a friend who worked in one of the stores back in Baltimore. The trick required a Swiss Army knife and a standard book of cardboard matches.

The front of the matchbook showed three caricatures of the Pep Boys bowlegged with oversize heads. Clovis made tiny slits between their legs and pushed the three matches through so that it looked like each Pep Boy had a giant red-tipped penis protruding from the front of his pants. For the grand finale, Clovis lit the three matches. *The Pep Boys' dicks on fire!*

Brian watched the Pep Boys' peckers burn. For some reason, he was fascinated with the trick. Maybe, he thought, in a weird way, his own wiener was on fire.

"Bloody brilliant!" Brian said after a hearty laugh.

Johnny, Moe, and Dave, the real English Pep Boys, kept trying to see how far they could push Brian. They were lazy and their work was terrible. Brian quickly became fed up.

The initial Frank Thorogood quote of eleven thousand pounds for the work on Cotchford Farm was way off, and the new price was close to ridiculous. Brian felt sure he was being ripped off. It only got worse.

The workers' daily presence became menacing. They took over the pool area, drinking and carousing. When Brian showed his face to check on the progress of the work, they made jokes and laughed at his skinny body and long effeminate hair.

Clovis saw what was happening and gave them a piece of his mind, demanding that they get back to work or get fired.

Frank soon became a problem himself, having moved into the flat over the garage. He turned Brian's beloved Poohville into his own private party zone. Soon the workers started inviting girls over, and nothing got done.

Frank Thorogood was thuggish and domineering and didn't seem to like Brian. He disrespected him every chance he got. When Brian asked a question, he was usually given a flippant answer. Work progressed at a snail's pace. Just because Tom Keylock worked for the Stones, and he hired Frank, Frank thought he was immune to criticism.

Brian complained, but Frank laughed at him. Frank began to order Brian around. Anna Wohlin complained that the "cowboys" Frank hired were entirely unprofessional and had to go. She didn't want them around the house. Neither did a now visibly pregnant Erlene, whose apprehension about protecting Brian had reached a fever pitch.

Bobby experienced it every time he made the drive from London and saw that nothing had progressed from the time before. Bobby joined the chorus of people who feared and/or disliked Frank Thorogood and his workers.

Clovis and Bobby had both volunteered to fire Frank, acting as Brian's spokesmen. But for some reason, Brian's intimidation froze him and he did nothing. Besides, Brian knew it would mean nothing to Frank unless it came from him. Brian had to be the man. He had to grow up and face the truth.

Frank worked for Tom Keylock, who worked for the Stones. They all worked for the Stones. Even the checks for Mrs. Hallet, the housekeeper, were issued by the Rolling Stones office in London. Did Brian feel some sort of misplaced loyalty?

Tension at Cotchford Farm mounted.

Clovis worked in the studio room with Brian and seldom came out. Unlike Frank, his work progressed nicely. He'd rewired the control room and installed a patch bay so he could plug any device into any input. He brought in a beautiful Ampex 16-track recorder and several dozen of the big two-inch tape boxes.

Brian spent hours talking to Clovis. Clovis loved to hear about the old days of British blues. Brian's mood improved when he recalled those days.

Brian pontificated freely. "That was the beauty of the early Stones. We just didn't give a shit. We were so audacious. I recently saw the old video of us doing 'Little Red Rooster' on the TV show *Ready, Steady, Go!* There I am playing these time-honored slide guitar riffs, right out of Howlin' Wolf, and I'm playing them on an ultra modern-looking white Vox Phantom teardrop guitar! It's almost sacrilegious! And Keith is playing a cheesy Harmony Sovereign acoustic twelve-string! With cheap pickups! Mick is faking my harmonica parts from the record! And, to make matters worse, it's our first English number one and *it's a song about a fuckin' chicken, man! What other group could do that?*"

Clovis and Brian laughed until their sides hurt. It was times like this when Clovis thought Brian could actually be happy and content.

"When we appeared on the TV show *Shindig!* in America, we insisted that Howlin' Wolf be on the bill with us. It caused quite a ruckus because the producers wanted only young white acts. Somehow, I don't know how he did this, but Mick had lied to them saying that Howlin' Wolf was in fact a young white group from Chicago. You can imagine their consternation when in walks this six-foot-three, two-hundred-and-ninety pound black guy. By that time, it was too late to book another act. I got to introduce him."

Brian watched Clovis work, slowly and methodically. Clovis took his time and enjoyed his work. They often talked about music and the amazing things they'd seen: Reverend Julius Cheeks, Ravi Shankar, Otis Redding, Janis Joplin, Jimi Hendrix, and the Master Musicians of Joujouka. It was music he would never forget. Lifetime music. Brian's already vast musical horizons shone like a Hawaiian sunset.

Clovis instructed Brian to order an expensive twenty-four-track Neve console. They awaited its arrival. Rupert Neve had designed it himself with an eye to keeping it compact to fit in unusual spaces.

Frank wandered into the control room looking for Brian. It was Frank's style to creep into a room and listen before making his presence known. He could see Brian and Clovis talking quietly on the other side of the double glass but he couldn't hear what they were saying due to the soundproofing.

Frank watched their mouths move. Curiosity got the best of him. Frank knew enough about the studio to turn on the talk-back button so he could eavesdrop. He slid the level of the microphones up and listened through the overhead speakers.

When Clovis asked Brian how he was going to pay for the Neve console, whether it would be a Rolling Stones check or a personal one, Brian looked surprised.

"Cash, my dear boy," he said.

Clovis did a double take. "Cash? That's over twenty grand, Brian. Who keeps that kind of money around the house?"

Brian grinned. "I do."

"Are you serious?"

In the control room, Frank Thorogood stood at attention. He'd been listening to every word they said.

Cash? Did he say cash? Frank's ears pricked up. He leaned closer to the monitor speakers so he could hear every word.

Brian smiled. "Absolutely. I have over a hundred grand in cash hidden in this house: English pounds, Swiss francs, and American dollars."

Frank almost lost his cool. His heart thumped and the sound of his blood pumping in his ears nearly drowned out Brian's words. *A hundred grand? Hidden in this house, but where?*

Clovis's jaw dropped. "Come on, that's not only stupid, it's dangerous. If anybody knew about that money, they would kill you for it."

"Relax. Nobody knows."

"Relax? Jesus, Brian! How can you sleep with that much money hanging around? We need to go to the local bank and deposit it all straightaway."

Brian sighed. "Clovis, my man. Let me explain something to you. The English tax rate for millionaires is insanely harsh; eighty-three percent for earned income and ninety-eight percent for unearned income. Ninety-eight percent! That's outrageous. They'd be all over me. As cash, that money is obviously worth a whole lot more."

"But . . ."

"I'm the only one who knows where it is."

Clovis had seen Brian's bedroom. He knew Brian kept stacks of cash on a nightstand next to his bed. It looked to be thousands of pounds. Clovis had warned Brian to never leave large amounts of cash in the open. It was too much of a temptation.

If the Pep Boys ever found out about that money, Brian would have some real trouble.

Renee and Skully drove past Cotchford Farm several times. They studied the grounds. Renee got out of the car and snuck behind the house to the pool area. She saw the floodlights and where they would illuminate. She studied the sight lines. She hid in the bushes and watched some people she didn't know cavorting and drinking beer around the swimming pool.

She returned to car with her report. "There's a bunch of guys I don't know hanging out by the pool."

"It's probably the workers Frank Thorogood hired."

"There are tons of places to hide."

"Okay, let's get back to town."

Renee watched the tranquil country house slip into the hundred-acre wood as they drove away.

Renee said, "Is that really the house of the guy who wrote *Winnie-the-Pooh*?"

"Yes. A. A. Milne moved here in 1925. He owned it for a long time. That's why it's so special."

Renee snorted. "Now that we're here, it doesn't seem like such a big deal."

Smithson Photographic Developing Labs was the type of hip young darkroom technology lab Bobby was looking for. They specialized in jobs other developers wouldn't attempt.

"These are super-dark exposures," Bobby explained. "They're going to need help."

The guy in the white lab coat sniffed. "What was your light source?"

"Candles. Dozens of them."

His right eyebrow arched up. "And what exactly are you shooting?"

Bobby told the guy what kind of film and camera he used. "I was shooting Tri-X, ASA 400."

"Did you have the lens open all the way?"

"Yes, but it was only fifty millimeters."

"*Hmmm*, I see. What was the line of sight here?"

"Over a guy's shoulder into an antique mirror."

The white lab coat shook his head. "I don't know, man. What were you shooting, ghosts?"

Bobby nodded. "That's right. Can you help me?"

"Of course I can! I'm the best. I'll squeeze every available photon of light out of these exposures. I'll have to push the film a little, that means I'll leave it in the developer a little longer. Give me until Friday and I'll see what I can do."

When Bobby returned on Friday, the prints were ready. The guy in white lab coat was excited to show him. Bobby inspected the prints.

"It was a challenge, but I think I captured what you wanted to see. Most of the time, it was this face, with flickering candlelight, but at one point it wavers and other faces appear. It happens so fast that the eye doesn't catch it, but the lens does. You were shooting bursts of exposure at top speed. It caught everything. Look."

Bobby stared at the series of prints.

"Is that Brian Jones?" Bobby momentarily forgot that Brian Jones was one of the most famous icons of rock and roll and a face known to millions.

"Yes, it is."

"I thought so. Examine please."

In the first print, Brian's face was plainly visible. In the next, Brian's face appeared to waver. In the next, it became cloudy and indistinct. In the next print, another face, a girl's face was plainly visible. *A girl's face—and Bobby recognized it.*

Eleanor Rigby! The face of infinite sadness. How could it be possible? There's no connection. Her slender white fingers against the other side of the mirror as she appeared to touch her fingertips to the glass.

In the next print, Eleanor Rigby's face became cloudy and morphed into a new face, a beautiful face, a face he knew. It was clearly visible in the next print. *Claudine Jillian*, just as she appeared at Brian's party what seemed like a hundred years ago. She too seemed to reach out to touch the glass. *What did they all want to say?*

The lab guy held the next-to-last print in his white-gloved hand. He hesitated before handing it to Bobby.

"I just want to know, how did you do this?"

Bobby took it and looked at the picture. It showed Brian flying through the air like Superman with his hair blowing in the wind. *Flying like Superman?* He almost appeared to have some kind of superhero costume on. He was up in the nighttime sky, arms outstretched, with windblown hair. From the point of view of the photograph, he was suspended in the air with a canopy of stars behind him. The full moon hung over his shoulder. Rather than being shrouded in shadow, Brian was well lit against the night sky.

"It was all shot through the antique mirror."

"You mean these images are . . . supernatural?"

Bobby looked at the lab guy with a curious look on his face. "Yeah, I guess they are. Is this all of it?"

He handed Bobby a contact sheet with about twenty shots of Brian's crazed face when he turned around unexpectedly during the mirror gazing. Bobby had fired off about four shots in surprise. Brian looked absolutely mad.

"Those are the only exposures to have anything other than Brian's face. There are over thirty-six exposures exactly like it if you want me to print them all."

Some of the images were blurry and indistinct but they were there.

Proof that scrying was real. Proof of a lot of things. Proof that dead girls from different centuries could still exist on the other side of the looking glass? And why were they all trying to get in touch with Brian? Proof that Brian had so much sex appeal he could pull chicks from the other side? Bobby's mind reeled.

He wouldn't have believed any of it if he hadn't seen the pictures with his own eyes. These images were real. They existed. They reflected light. The camera doesn't lie.

"Were you shooting an album cover? You know, in 3-D, like *Satanic Majesties Request*?"

"No."

"Because that one of him flying is definitely the album cover shot."

Bobby stared at the bizarre photograph and wondered what it meant. He put the print out of sight in the envelope with the others.

Bobby paid for the prints and ordered a second set to be delivered to Cotchford.

Erlene was almost hysterical. She woke up in the middle of the night in their bedroom at Cotchford Farm howling from a nightmare.

"Tell Brian not to go near the water!" she shouted in her slumber.

Clovis, sleeping next to her, woke up. She grabbed him and shook his shoulder.

"Get up! Tell Brian to stay away from water!"

"In the morning, hon . . ."

"Now! Get up and tell him now!"

Rather than argue about it, Clovis got out of bed. He put on his robe and went to Brian's master bedroom. He tapped on the door, but there was no answer.

Clovis eased the door open and tiptoed into the room. Anna Wohlin was asleep in the bed and Brian was sitting up, surrounded by lit candles, gazing into that cursed ancient mirror.

"Brian?"

There was no response.

"Ahh, Brian. Excuse me?"

Still no response. He was in a trance.

"Brian! Wake up!"

Brian roused himself. "What? What's going on?"

"It's me, Clovis!"

"Clovis, dear boy, what could you possibly want at this hour?"

"It's my wife."

"Erlene? Is she all right?"

"Yes, well not exactly, she woke up screaming just now. She was screaming for you to stay away from the water. She insisted I get up and tell you right now."

"Water? You mean the ocean? Stay away from the ocean?"

"That's all she said."

Brian looked at Clovis without blinking for several seconds. "Thanks for delivering the message. Tell Erlene I understand."

Clovis hesitated. Was that it?

"That's it," said Brian. "Go back to your room now. Erlene knows you did your job."

"She does?"

Brian nodded. "Go back to bed, Clovis. You'll find Erlene is already asleep."

Clovis saw the Moroccan mirror and all the candles. He looked back at Brian "Have you been mirror gazing again?"

Brian just stared at Clovis without answering. His eyes seemed to glow in the dark.

"Nothing to worry about, old chap. Just a little meditation."

CHAPTER TWENTY-ONE

WHEN BLUE TURNS TO GRAY

"The rich fag," Marty the part-time day laborer said. "Fuckin' rock star, he doesn't deserve all this."

The other laborers looked on, bemused. Yes, Brian was a pain in the ass, but as long as he kept paying them, they were happy. Marty, however, seemed to have genuine animosity.

Frank had hired the extra man to assist in the heavy lifting. No one knew much about Marty. He just showed up one day. He was a hulking presence, bigger than the other workers. And rude.

Clovis took Frank aside and said, "Look, Brian doesn't like the new guy you hired. I want you to get rid of him."

"Since when do you give the orders around here?"

Clovis snapped. "Since Brian hired me."

"You're not the boss of me. I work for the Stones."

"But Brian's no longer part of the Stones."

"Piss off."

Clovis shouted. "Look, you're really starting to make me mad. I don't like your attitude, Thorogood. I've noticed the way you push Brian around. He's in a vulnerable state right now. You're taking advantage of him. And I know you've been charging everything that comes into this house to Brian's account, ripping him off left and right. You've overcharged for everything. Don't think that Brian is unaware of this."

Frank sneered, "What are you gonna do about it?"

"Fire you and all your goons."

"That'll be the day."

"Don't fuck with me, Frank," Clovis growled. "Or I'll crack your cranium."

Frank reacted with a grunt. He wasn't used to being threatened with physical harm by a smaller man. But Clovis was fearless. When Frank turned his back, Clovis smacked the back of his head with his open palm. Frank reacted by pitching forward and almost losing his balance.

"You fucker!" Frank cursed. He lunged at Clovis. Clovis stepped aside.

"Go ahead, hit me, you piece of shit! It'll be the end of your career working for the Stones. I'll tell Keylock, and you'll be gone. I'll say I discovered you were stealing Brian blind and you attacked me."

Frank unclenched his fists.

Clovis chuckled. "That's the difference between me and you, Frank. You talk about shit. I do shit. Don't ever turn your back on me. I'm from Baltimore."

"You punk!" Frank snarled. "I'll ruin you."

Clovis said, "You don't scare me, Frank. I've faced down tougher guys than you. I got your number."

Frank walked away fuming.

John Lennon arrived at Cotchford Farm early in the afternoon and went right to work. Yoko was with him as always. John had his guitar and a notebook with him. He was determined to write a song with Brian.

They went into the studio and kicked around ideas for several hours. Brian always stayed close to the blues, something he felt comfortable with.

Clovis engineered the demo. They had no recording console yet, so Clovis improvised using a six-channel monitor board. He got a kick out of working with John and Brian. Late in the day, John came up with something that sounded like a cross between the Stones and the Beatles. It was a straight-ahead Chuck Berry–style rocker with pithy lyrics, the kind John loved to write. He mixed in his social commentary and observation, and mixed up with a spicy gumbo of peppery guitar riffs. John loved the creative process, and never got tired of writing songs. His wit never deserted him.

The diminutive Yoko never said a word. She stood next to John looking as fragile as an ivory figurine.

John strummed the chords. "The working title is 'Go to the Mountains.' I got the idea for it on the drive down from London."

John and Brian bashed out a drum track, and they built on it. John laid down the rhythm guitar part, and Brian played bass. It all came together like magic, the same way it did for the Beatles and the Stones. Denny Laine from the Moody Blues showed up and played a great lead part. And then they all had tea.

"We're gonna form a supergroup," John said. "I can get Jimi Hendrix, Clapton, Steve Winwood, you name it. Bob Dylan even called. We'll be the number-one group in the world."

"That sounds like fun," Brian said. "Are you sure you want to do it?"

"Shit, yeah! We need to send a message. Everybody takes us for granted, like it's their trip and they're just letting us in on it. Well, I've got news—it's our trip. It's always been our trip.

"Think of it. We'd be a very dangerous group. Imagine the loss of revenue and jobs if I quit the Beatles, or if Jimi left the Experience, or the Stones broke up? There's a whole lot of money involved."

Brian smiled. "I just want to play something I like."

They worked on the song all day until Brian got bored and wanted to do something else.

Brian played a demo for a song he recorded with Nicky Hopkins on piano called "Travelin' Man." It rocked like the best Stones tracks, but it wasn't the Stones, it was Brian. That was the difference nobody had ever heard.

When the day was over, John and Yoko stayed over in one of the guest rooms. Brian called everyone he knew to tell them about the new song he'd written with John. They planned to finish it in the morning before John drove back to London.

There was no doubt that a new song written by John Lennon and Brian Jones would gain instant attention. Especially when the demo rocked. This little piece of tape would definitely shake 'em up in London, Brian was sure.

Brian Jones went to bed that night feeling secure about his career for the first time in a long time. *Thank God for friends like John Lennon, Dust Bin Bob, and Clovis.*

Frank Thorogood stood in the center of the house and slowly pivoted around.

Frank's mind was working overtime. *If I was going to hide that much money, where would I put it?*

He'd already pulled a few boards here and there, in places where there might be room between the walls. He knew where there might be hiding places throughout the house. He tried not to be too obvious.

Frank thought he knew about Brian's secret places, places where he hid his stash and a few hundred quid. But where was the mother lode?

Little by little, Frank dismantled the house, looking for the money to no avail. He tried to keep it secret, but keeping secrets at Cotchford Farm was damn near impossible. There were too many people around.

Brian's paranoia, never to be outdone, noticed it first. "Why is Frank taking everything apart?"

"He says he's inspecting the wiring." Clovis checked to see if anyone was listening through the windows or anywhere else. When the coast was clear, he dropped his voice. "Checking the wiring, my ass! It's like he's looking for something."

"Like what?"

Clovis gave Brian a wink. "Keep your voice down."

"You don't think . . . ?"

"Stop! Don't even say it. We don't know that."

Brian shook his head. "There's no way."

Anna Wohlin came out of the kitchen with a tray of drinks.

Clovis said, "In America, we've got an old saying. If it walks like a duck and it talks like a duck, it's a duck."

John got up and left the next day without finishing the song. He promised to come back the first chance he got to finish it with Brian. They hugged and John drove away.

A few hours later, Alexis Korner, the father of the British blues scene, drove through the garden gate. He and Brian were very old friends. He stayed all day and they played music for hours.

Brian's healing began and ended with music. He gained strength from it. Playing the blues with Alexis was therapeutic. Any time he had to himself, he spent secretly gazing into the mirror. His headaches grew each day and the gazing soothed him.

Clovis was there to witness every note. As chief engineer of Brian's home studio, he saw it all. He knew when Brian was inspired, he could tell. He could also tell when he was bored or unenthusiastic. It was all in how he played. Those last few days had been prime vintage Brian.

Clovis hadn't planned on getting this close to Brian; after all he was just a friend of Dust Bin Bob, a second stringer from East Baltimore Street. Brian could be toxic to those around him. Clovis knew he had to be careful.

Erlene was in her third trimester. Clovis's baby grew inside her like an angry bear cub in a tote sack. Her mood swings had been as discernible as barometer readings. She was due a doctor's visit in London.

Cricket motored down to Cotchford Farm to take her while Bobby was on a buying trip in Paris. He was only going to be gone for a couple of days. Cricket planned to spend the time with Erlene.

Erlene looked forward to moving back to Baltimore right after the baby was born. Cricket had only allowed Bobby time to help Brian. But now that Brian was ensconced in Cotchford Farm, he seemed to be improving.

Cotchford Farm had changed Brian. His health was returning; his skin had some color. He stopped taking drugs, at least for the time being. He ran with his gaggle of dogs every day and took long walks along the private lane alongside his house.

"I'm never gonna leave this place," he told anyone who'd care to listen. "I'm staying here the rest of my life."

CHAPTER TWENTY-TWO

MISADVENTURE

Cricket took Erlene to her doctor's appointment in London. Dust Bin Bob stayed in Paris and visited an old friend, Johnny Hallyday, who had started out as the "French Elvis" in the fifties and had grown to be an international superstar. He had first met Hallyday when the Beatles played Olympia Hall in Paris. They had become close friends over the years, and Bobby never missed an opportunity to see him whenever he was in the City of Lights. To make matters even more interesting, Johnny had a penchant for antiques and Paris was full of them. Johnny seemed to know every antique dealer in the city. They visited several shops in the Saint-Germain quarter and had lunch at an outdoor cafe.

Dust Bin Bob had suggested Jimi Hendrix as an opening act for Johnny's French tour, and even though Jimi upstaged him and stole the show, Johnny Hallyday was forever known as the man who introduced Jimi Hendrix to France. Johnny was currently riding the Paris Top Ten with a cover version of "Hey Joe" in French.

"So tell me, how is our friend, Brian?"

"Brian? He's getting better. He loves his new country house."

Johnny watched a Parisian girl, probably a fashion model, saunter past them. She pretended not to notice him.

Bobby said, "This is such a great city, but the tax rates are insane for a Frenchman. Over ninety-five percent? It's like England, according to Brian. How can you live here?"

Hallyday laughed. "How can I live in Paris you ask? Look, I am a Frenchman. I love fine food. I love fine wine. I love to fuck. Where else would I live?"

Brian and Clovis worked in the studio while Anna Wohlin prepared lunch in the kitchen. It was an absolutely beautiful day. The pollen count was a little high, but Brian only suffered slight discomfort.

Brian strummed a guitar and called out from the studio. "What a fantastic day! I feel great!"

Frank and the Pep Boys were supposed to putting up a white picket fence today. Brian had been requesting it for weeks, but Frank had ignored him. The pieces to the fence were strewn across the front lawn, but the workers were nowhere to be seen.

Brian looked out the front window at the pieces of fence scattered around.

"Can't they even put up a lousy fence? That's it! I've had it with this lot."

Erlene and Cricket drove along the pleasant country roads of Sussex. Erlene kept shifting in her seat. She couldn't get comfortable.

"I'm as fat as a lungfish," Erlene said. "You want to talk about water retention? I'm a blimp."

"It'll all be over soon," Cricket said. "And we can get back to our lives."

"Oh my God!"

"What is it?"

Erlene had a terrified look on her face.

"We left Brian all alone!"

"No we didn't. Clovis is with him in the studio. Relax, everything's fine."

"Why did I just think that?"

"I don't know. You're so jumpy lately."

"I just want to get this baby out of me."

"Don't worry, Erlene. I'm sure the baby feels the same way. We've got bigger fish to fry. Try to forget about Brian."

"I can't!"

"Honey, you are one wound-up puppy. Why are you so concerned about Brian?"

"Because . . . because . . . I don't know."

Erlene was sweating and confused.

"Let's get you checked out and get you back to Cotchford Farm where you can stare at Brian all day if you want."

"Water . . ."

"Yeah, yeah, and you can keep him out of the bathtub while you're at it."

Brian opened the telegram from Germany as soon as it reached him. He read it and howled with delight.

"It's the Neve console! It's being shipped today!"

Clovis grabbed the paper from Brian's hand and read it himself. Brian was right. Clovis skimmed the page.

"Blah, blah, blah . . . Brian Jones . . . blah, blah . . . Cotchford Farm. Should arrive by special rail delivery to Hartfield on or about the afternoon of July 3."

Clovis handed the telegram back to Brian.

"I've got to go into town and rent a truck and some helpers."

"How about the Pep Boys? Frank could no doubt spare a few."

"Very funny, Brian."

After lunch, Clovis drove into town and rented a step van and a dolly. He hired a big moving guy named Doug to help him move the freight.

They had to wait for the stationmaster to return from his break to get the necessary paperwork to release the freight.

To kill some time, they went into the local establishment known as the Haywaggon and consumed several pints of beer and handfuls of stale pretzels.

Skully and Renee drove past Cotchford. It looked quiet.

"You think he's in there?" Renee asked.

"I know he's in there. I've been watching this place for days."

Skully looked through a pair of small binoculars. He was all business.

"The key is waiting for the right moment. There's sure to be a time when he's alone outside and that's when we move."

Skully handed the binoculars to Renee. She looked though them as he explained the plan.

"As soon as it gets dark, we'll take our positions. I have a place to hide the car, so we can park and creep up on the house via the rear garden. They'll never see us coming."

Skully breathed in violently through his nose, held it, then let it out.

"I feel so alive at times like this."

"I know what you mean." Renee said, "I'm tingling all over. Brian Jones will belong to me, and only me . . . for all eternity."

"It's too bad you can't mount him on your wall like a trophy."

"I'm going to take his soul."

"But you can never tell anyone."

"*Shhhhhh!* Someone's coming!"

"Lay down on the seat and kiss me. If we act like we're making out, they won't notice us. Come on, hurry up!"

Someone walked right past the car, looked inside, saw Renee and Skully making out like mad, and just kept on going. The faces of the lovers were not visible, and the identity of the passerby was not known, either.

As soon as the coast was clear, Skully drove to the hiding place he'd found for the car. It was a place where the car could pull off the road and disappear behind some foliage. They waited.

Bobby returned to his room at the Georges V Hotel in Paris. It was the same hotel the Beatles stayed in when they first played there. In fact, Dust Bin Bob was in the very room in which John Lennon had first learned that their record had reached number one in America and they were going to play *The Ed Sullivan Show*.

The phone blinked. There were a half-dozen frantic messages from Suki Potier, Brian's former girlfriend who now lived in Paris. He called back the number on the message.

"Allo?"

"Suki? This is Robert Dingle. You know, Dust Bin Bob?"

Her voice was like music.

"Ah yes, Dust Bin Bob!"

"What is it? You sounded upset. What's the problem?"

"I'm worried about Brian. He's been calling me two or three times a day for the past few days, and last time he said he was in some kind of danger. Says he's being watched . . . followed even. I'm scared."

Bobby's voice was reassuring.

"Come on, you know how he likes to exaggerate. I was just there a few days ago and Brian was as happy as I've ever seen him."

"When are you going back?"

"I'll be flying back in the morning. I'll see him tomorrow."

"Can you check up on him for me? Find out what is wrong?"

"Of course, Suki. My friend Clovis is with him now. We've been sort of keeping an eye on Brian, but I'm telling you, there's nothing to worry about. He's fine."

"I heard he has a new girlfriend."

"Yes, Anna Wohlin. She's a Swedish dancer. Very sweet girl. She takes good care of him."

"Good. At least he's happy."

"Anna is very nice. You should come down to Cotchford Farm and see for yourself."

Suki's French accent made everyday phrases sound exotic. He could understand why Brian seemed to exclusively date foreign women. German, French, Swedish—their accents were intoxicating.

"What's all this about an ancient magic mirror? He told me he bought it in Morocco. Is it really magic?"

"Brion Gysin says it is. He says it's a thousand years old and has powers. It belonged to a long line of shamans. The last one just died, and Brian bought it from his estate. It was Brian's idea to try the esoteric art of mirror gazing. I wouldn't put too much stock in it."

"I don't like Brian playing around with magic. He tends to become obsessed with things. It scares me."

"I've been trying to get the damn thing away from him, but he hides it."

"I'll come over and help you steal it."

As soon as Suki hung up, Bobby was overcome with a desire to get back to Cocthford Farm. Something inside, maybe a premonition, maybe a wave of paranoia, sent off strong warning signals in his head. Nervous, he stood and looked out the window. It was still early in the evening. He couldn't relax. Suddenly, Bobby was sure he had to get back to Brian. He didn't know why, but the urge to leave had become overwhelming. He called the concierge and had him book a flight leaving tonight. Bobby packed and called a cab.

Some powerful force was drawing him back to Cotchford, back to Brian. He couldn't concentrate on anything else.

* * *

Brian gazed into the mirror again. He'd been doing it all afternoon. The mirror pacified him. It cooled his brow when he felt angry. He had a relationship with the mirror now. It was his portal into another world. Brian's addictive personality embraced the mirror like it was a new kind of dope, and in a way it was. The only time Brian felt content now was when he was gazing into the mirror. His head felt light. His blood pressure dropped. His heartbeat slowed. All the little aches and pains vanished like after a good stiff drink. Scrying occupied more and more of his time, but he kept it all hidden from the others. *If they knew the power of the mirror, they'd try to take it away from me, I just know it.*

The migraine headaches that he'd been developing for the past few weeks only went away while he was gazing into the mirror. In the mirror, everything was all right. He wondered if Nostradamus had headaches.

Brian couldn't wait for the photographic prints from London to arrive. Several weeks had passed since their return from Morocco. Since Brian relied on other people to do most of his work, some things took forever. Bobby dragged his feet. He disliked the mirror, and the pictures he had taken creeped him out.

Bobby had to find the right lab and the right developer to process the prints. He'd been turned down by the first four labs he approached. It took time to find the right one, and it took them extra time to customize the processing.

When they were delivered, Brian ripped open the envelope

and studied the eight-by-ten color prints with a magnifier. The technician had thoughtfully included the contact sheets as well so Brian could watch the sequence of events.

The photographic images were just as Dust Bin Bob had described them. He looked at the two women's faces and registered a chill. The face of Claudine Jillian looked back at him, so beautiful even in death. Her delicate fingertips touched the surface of the mirror from the other side, leaving ghostly fingerprints on the glass. Her lips were slightly parted as if she were about to speak. It caused a sharp pain in his heart. Was she trying to talk to him? What did she want to say?

He flipped to the ghostly image of the girl they called Eleanor Rigby. Something familiar in her face haunted him. Had they been lovers in a previous lifetime? Eleanor's face was so sad and beautiful that it was hard for Brian to look at it for more than a few seconds. What had Dust Bin Bob called it? *The face of infinite sadness?* That it was.

It reminded Brian of one of his favorite songs by the Searchers, "Needles and Pins." He remembered Jack Nitzsche telling the story of how he came to write it with Sonny Bono waiting around after a Phil Spector session in Hollywood. Jack sang along with the record when it came on the radio driving down Sunset Boulevard in Jack's Cadillac convertible. Brian looked up at the palm trees and let the lyrics wash over him.

"I saw her today, I saw her face. It was a face I loved . . ." Jack howled out the window like Wolfman Jack. "Come on Brian, give me some harmonies!"

"Needles and pins!"

The song brought back memories of when it was fun being in the Rolling Stones.

It was hard for Brian to look at Eleanor Rigby for too long, but he found himself drawn into her face. He put it in the back of the envelope and closed his eyes for a moment to clear his mind. He took a deep breath and looked at the last picture.

It showed Brian flying. He was up in the night sky with his arms outstretched. His hair was blowing magnificently in the wind. It was a dramatic image.

Bobby called from Paris. "I'm coming home tonight. I should be at the railway station by ten."

"Why? You're in Paris. Have breakfast and leave in the morning."

"No, I'm coming back tonight. Something is telling me to do it."

They talked about the mirror-gazing photographs, and Bobby corroborated what he'd seen. The two girl's faces, one was unmistakably Eleanor Rigby, the other Claudine Jillian—both dead, both desperately trying to contact Brian from the other side. There could be no doubt. The images were indistinct and otherworldly but with just enough detail to make them one-hundred-percent familiar. Like impressionism, it required you to think and respond, and if you did, you could see great detail. Otherwise it was just a grainy image.

It was the final print that excited Brian.

"It looks like me, and I'm flying under the stars with my arms outstretched over my head and my hair blowing in the wind."

Dust Bin Bob agreed and said, "That's exactly what I saw."

"Maybe I should have it framed." Brian's voice sounded upbeat. "I'm having a hell of a day, man. I just got word that the new Neve console has arrived from Germany. Clovis has been dispatched down to Hartfield to pick it up."

"Great! Maybe I can get there before Clovis leaves. My plane is boarding now." Brian could hear female announcers on the public address system in the background, announcing flights in French.

"Listen, Brian, before I ring off . . . You're not doing any more mirror gazing are you?"

"Who, me? Nah! I just use it to shave."

"Don't be so cavalier, my friend. I don't think you should be messing around with that mirror anymore. You have no idea what you're doing. Suki called me and she's very concerned."

"She worries too much."

"Tell me the truth, are you doing it?"

"Well, just a little. The meditation helps relieve my headaches. It's actually beneficial."

"I don't have a good feeling about that mirror. I don't like the hold it's got on you."

Brian snapped. "I know, you've made your feelings known. I got the message."

Brian changed the subject, saying, "Clovis should be back with the console at any time. I can't wait to start working."

"It's great to hear you're so positive, Brian."

Brian paused. "There's only one last thing to take care of now: that bastard Frank Thorogood and the Pep Boys. I'm going to sack them all today. I've already contacted the Stones office and had their pay stopped. That should freak them out."

Dust Bin Bob paused. "Maybe you should wait until I get back before you do that."

"No, I have to do it myself. No help from anyone. Just me. It's something I have to do. I've been doing a lot of soul searching lately. I have to confront my fears and break free of this horrible paranoia. It's the only way."

"Yes, but is it safe? Frank and his goons might get rough with you. Who's there with you? Why don't you wait until Clovis gets back from Hartfield? I'll be there in a few hours."

"I really don't think that's an issue."

Clovis returned to the train station, his frustration beginning to show.

"Where is my freight?"

"We can't release it until the stationmaster gets here and signs for it."

"But where is he?"

"He went home. He wasn't feeling well. His brother is coming."

"Can his brother sign the release form?"

"Yes, yes, of course. He will be here soon."

Clovis phoned Brian and informed him of the delay. He assured him that he would get it all sussed out and he'd return with the console before the day was over. Brian told Clovis that Dust Bin Bob was expected in Hartfield in a few hours. Clovis agreed to keep an eye out for him if he was still there.

But by now, the shadows had grown long and still no stationmaster or his brother.

Among other males, Brian was as nonconfrontational a fellow as you'd ever meet. He didn't like bad scenes. He hated to yell at them or be yelled at. So it was extra difficult for Brian to find the courage to fire Frank Thorogood.

Today would be different. The deed could not be put off any longer. In Brian's mind, it had reached a critical point. He had to take care of this problem himself.

"*Er*, Frank, might I have a word?"

"Sure, Brian. What's on your mind?"

Brian paused for a second, then let it all out. "Well, I'm afraid I'm going to have to let you go."

Frank laughed, "Let me go? You can't fire me."

"I already have. Tom Keylock's getting another bloke lined up. I hate to do it Frank, I really do. It was the picket fence that finally did it. When you couldn't put up a fuckin' picket fence, I figured that was it. You and your whole crew are sacked."

Frank's jaw hung lose. He looked at Brian like he didn't believe what he was hearing.

"Are you serious?"

"Absolutely."

"But I thought you liked what we were doing."

"When you ordered the furniture, you ordered two sets, one for your house and one for mine."

Frank paced the floor, acting guilty. "Oh, Brian, don't be so petty. . . . Surely, you don't begrudge me basic furniture. Besides, you can afford it."

"And overcharging me up the wazoo for work, food, booze, everything. It all winds up on my tab."

"Well, I can explain that. You see, those are business write-offs for the Stones office. I was told to bill everything through them."

Brian spat. "Write-offs? I'm afraid it's more like rip-offs."

"No, Brian, you got it all wrong. I was hired by the Stones office to take care of you."

"Frank, you're out. Call Tom Keylock if you have any questions. He's been instructed to settle up with you."

Frank sputtered. His anger rose but he said nothing.

"You can stay the night and have dinner with us, but tomorrow you have to move out. It's over, Frank."

Brian walked out of the room leaving Frank feeling dazed.

That evening, Clovis still hadn't returned from town. After watching *Rowan and Martin's Laugh-In* on TV, Brian decided to go for a swim with Anna.

In a typical Brian Jones mood swing, Brian felt guilty that he had fired Frank Thorogood earlier in the day. To show that there were no hard feelings, Frank offered to prepare their dinner, as he often did, and ate with Brian, Anna, and Frank's girlfriend, Janet Lawson. They were all convivial and Frank's sacking was never discussed.

Later, shortly before ten in the evening, Brian walked over to Frank's flat over the garage and invited Frank and Janet for a swim.

Anna changed into her bathing suit and took Brian's dogs, Emily and Luther, down to the water's edge. Luther, an Afghan hound, was high-strung and very protective of Brian. The dogs playfully ran up and down the length of the pool, barking and nipping at each other.

Brian came back with Frank and they had another drink. The vibe was not weird, which made Brian slightly suspicious. *Shouldn't Frank be upset?*

Maybe he thought Brian was just ranting and raving and didn't mean a word of it. Janet came down to the pool with her swimsuit on. Brian and Frank dove in and swam from end to end to the delight of the dogs, who ran back and forth and barked at them. Anna went into the water but after a few minutes complained that it was too warm. She got out and went into the house. Janet didn't want to go in the water. She thought it was dangerous to swim at night after drinking. She warned them to be careful, then she slipped back into the house as well.

Brian kept several of his asthma inhalers around the pool so they'd be easy to grab if he felt the need. He reached for one and took a long hit on it and put it back. His asthma had been bothering him for the past few hours. His lungs were full of fluid. He took a tranquillizer to steady his breathing.

Renee and Skully drove back the way they had come earlier in the day.

"Something's going on here," Skully whispered. "Come on, let's check it out."

As the shadows lengthened, they slipped out of the car and crept toward the house.

The insects sang in the foliage, filling the early evening with a grand symphony of natural sounds. The smell of newly cut grass mixed with the chlorine smell of the pool. Steam rose off the eighty-degree pool water. Brian kept the pool warmer than most people preferred.

The bust of Christopher Robin near the famous A. A. Milne sundial in the center of the garden seemed to keep watch over the tranquil scene. It bore more than a passing resemblance to Brian.

Renee and Skully hid together behind some rhododendrons. They settled in for the wait.

Skully whispered, "As soon as this is done, we'll get the hell out of here. What will you do next?"

"I don't know. Commit suicide, maybe."

"Why would a beautiful young girl like you throw her life away?"

"Boredom. Brian. Ennui . . ."

"Forget about Brian. He's a loser. You want to come along with me?"

"Where?"

Skully paused. "I can't tell you."

"The M Group is going to kill another rock star, aren't they?"

"Clever girl."

"Who?"

"No, not The Who. Somebody you already know. Does that excite you?"

"Yes," she whispered.

Renee thought of Brian. She had become obsessed with him. In the early days while she stalked him, she kept a professional distance, but as time went by she wanted him more. Once she slept with him, and they had fabulous sex all night, she couldn't get him off her mind. Brian was a devil all right. He became her private incubus.

Skully allowed Renee her insecurities, even helped her kill that model bitch Claudine Jillian out of sheer revenge. *That one was a freebie.* Skully hated those kinds of chicks anyway. It was good to let Renee run wild now and then. Renee was a good lover and a skilled assassin when she had to be. So was Skully.

Neither Renee nor Skully spoke for a while. Renee eventually broke the silence.

"Does it ever get to you?"

"Does what get to me?"

"This."

Skully thought for a moment. "Don't flake on me now, girl. We're just getting started. I recruited you for this, remember?"

Renee's voice became tiny, barely audible. "Did you know I'm in love with Brian?"

Skully looked at her suspiciously. *Was she losing her nerve?*

"That's okay, as long as you can kill him."

"How can you kill somebody you love?"

"You always kill the ones you love. Isn't that an old Mills Brothers song?" He sang the chorus of "You Always Hurt the Ones You Love" with the new lyrics he'd just made up.

"You always kill, the ones you love, the ones you shouldn't kill at all," he sang.

"It scares me," Renee said.

"Yeah, I'll bet. But it's your destiny, Renee. Quit worrying so much about it. When we met, you told me your life had no meaning. I told you I could fulfill all your fantasies. You stick with me and together we'll change the world."

CHAPTER TWENTY-THREE

MIRROR GAZING

Skully watched as the two women went inside the house, toweling themselves as they walked. Now it was just Frank and Brian in the pool, swimming lazily back and forth. The dogs had retreated back into the building, and it was quiet but for the water lapping against the sides of the pool and the low buzz of the nocturnal insects.

The oasis of light illuminated by the floodlights was bright, but beyond its beam it was as dark as outer space. Living in a country house meant no streetlights, no traffic, and no police sirens. It could be incredibly dark when the lights were out.

They crept closer. Frank and Brian were still swimming.

The moment was at hand.

"Watch out! Don't drop it. Easy, easy . . . there," Clovis said. The Neve console seemed to weigh a ton.

They put the huge wooden crate in the truck bed. The big guy named Doug he hired to lift the crate asked him what it was.

"It's part of a recording studio."

"You mean, like, for rock and roll?"

"Yep."

"Blimey, you'd think these yobbos would jump at the chance to move one of these. 'Oo's it for? Da 'Oo?"

"No, it's not The Who."

"Faces?"

"Not likely. Look, why don't I just tell you and—"

"No! Don't tell me! Let me guess! Led Zep? Cream?"

"Stop! It's for Brian Jones!"

The big guy scratched his head.

"Brian Jones? Never heard of him."

"From the Stones."

"Oh, THAT Brian Jones. I thought they broke up."

Clovis spat like a cowboy. "I have to get started back to Cotchford Farm. I gave you directions. Come out first thing in the morning, and help me get this thing off the truck and into the studio. I'll pay you double."

"I'll be there, mate!"

Clovis knew the Neve would make all the difference in the world when it came to Brian's music. With his home studio up to professional standards, he could literally make albums in his house. That meant anytime he had an idea, or a guest musician, he could cut a professional track on the spot.

It would only be a matter of time until Brian would have

enough for a solo album. Clovis visualized connecting the board; it seemed easy in his mind. He daydreamed about recording there with people like John Lennon and Jimi Hendrix.

As they were closing the back of the truck, the final train to Hartfield pulled out of the station. It left two people on the platform as the smoke and steam evaporated.

Dust Bin Bob stood triumphantly with his suitcase. He put his hands on his hips and surveyed the situation. He had made it back from Paris to Hartfield on the same night against all odds. The other passenger from the train disappeared into the shadows.

Bobby walked to the empty cabstands and saw Clovis and another big guy closing a truck. *What incredible timing.*

"Hey! Is that the Neve board?" Clovis looked up, surprised to hear Bobby's voice.

"It sure is. Looks like you're in the right place at the right time, pardner. Climb in."

Bobby looked around at the nearly deserted station, wondering where the other passenger had gone. He hadn't noticed the man's face because he sat in the car behind him.

"Let's roll."

On the other side of the building, hidden from view, a car and a driver were waiting with their lights off.

Bruce Spangler got into the car and nodded to the driver. Without saying a word, he started the car and drove off.

* * *

Brian Jones felt good. The warm water felt pleasant against his skin. He launched himself forward through the water with swift, strong strokes. He had always been an excellent swimmer. His asthma had been bothering him, but swimming seemed to help.

He heard splashing behind him and turned his head to see another swimmer. *Was it Frank? Who else would it be?* Brian skimmed through the water effortlessly.

His mind had been racing all night; it was as if it were a machine he couldn't turn off. He kept thinking about the mirror, the ghost girl, and Claudine. The mirror was his connection to them, and he fought the constant urge to hide away and gaze into it all the time. It was the only way to make his headaches go away.

So deep in thought was Brian that he hardly noticed when someone grabbed his foot.

He turned to confront whoever it was. Was somebody being playful?

Frank? Is that you? What the fuck are you doing? He felt something push down on his shoulders, and then a foot in the middle of his back.

Brian tried to accelerate away, but the hand still gripped his ankle. *Was this just horseplay, or something more?* Still, Brian wasn't overly concerned. He knew he could swim his way out of anything.

Then the downward pushing became more forceful. *Frank? What the fuck? Come on, let go!*

Brian fought to get away. But it seemed as if there were an extra pair of hands in the water now.

This is not funny!

Brian kicked at the hand and freed himself momentarily. He needed to surface and take a breath of air. Asthma made filling his lungs with oxygen more difficult. Still they pulled him down.

Brian's lungs burned. He held his breath even though he felt about to explode. He fought desperately to get away. He couldn't get a good look at who was pushing him down, but he assumed it was Frank. But this guy seemed heavier than Frank, and more forceful.

Distortion in the water made it difficult to see faces.

Brian was losing time. He fought to hold his breath. Something in Brian clicked. Suddenly, it all made sense.

This was what the mirror had been trying to tell him.

Suddenly, everything went black. The floodlights had gone out. He was suspended in the dark.

He fought a losing battle against the dark. He became disoriented. *Which way was up?* Finally, he opened his mouth to cough and water rushed into his lungs. At that moment, he realized his fate.

He felt his body sink slowly to the bottom of the pool. With his lungs full of water, he lost his natural buoyancy. He heard someone get out of the pool, but it seemed miles away.

The floodlights came back on. The entire pool area lit up again.

Is this how it ends? Brian looked down at the scene below. He saw himself floating lifelessly at the bottom of the pool. He watched as his last moments ticked by.

Claudine Jillian came to him. Eleanor Rigby appeared to

him. They embraced him, saying nothing, understanding everything. Looking around, he saw that he was on the other side of the mirror now, too. He saw the mirror in his room. He could see the light coming through it from the other side and looked in, there he saw himself in the pool.

Brian understood that this was his fate. It always had been. It always would be. To fight it would be to fight nature. Though Jillian and Eleanor had tried to warn him, there was no turning back. He was part of rock's tragic legacy of death. Every A side like the Stones has a B side like Brian Jones. He couldn't escape it. He wouldn't be the first and he certainly wouldn't be the last.

Brian accepted it. *This is my fate, God's will*, he surmised. *Call it what you will. I had a good run.*

He hadn't noticed, but while he was contemplating his life, everything around him had turned into a great white light. A vortex of intense brightness swirled before him, blinding him and filling him with light at the same time. He was drawn toward it. Its pull was irresistible. He felt like smoke being sucked through a fan.

Brian Jones let go of life. He let go of the Stones. He let go of his women and his constant need for affection. He let go of the booze and drugs. He let go of trying to prove himself. He let go of fame and fortune. He let go of history and history let go of him. Legend would take over from here.

You can't sing the blues unless you pay the dues.

* * *

Skully crouched down and ran along the line of deck chairs next to the pool. Somewhere behind him, Renee was running along in her black tracksuit, blending with the shadows.

Skully watched Brian, but something was not quite right. Something was different. The cadence of the swimming had changed.

The smooth steady swimming laps had ceased. There was a rush of water, and a great thrashing underneath the surface.

Abruptly, the floodlights went out. The pool, the house, and the yard were plunged into darkness. Only light from inside managed to leak out in feeble beams.

Skully, taken by surprise, looked up in the direction of the light switch, which he knew was just inside the door. He saw a backlit body silhouetted for split second before the door closed. *An accomplice in the house?*

Shit! I should have kept an eye on the lights! That's the oldest trick in the book!

Suddenly, there seemed to be more bodies in the water. Where had they come from? Skully couldn't be sure, but he thought he heard them splash as they hit the water. In total darkness, Skully had no idea what was happening in the pool. He only heard the sound of water splashing.

Was it Frank? Skully couldn't see a thing. From what he saw just before the lights went out, this guy was much more muscular than Frank.

What the hell was going on here?

It was pitch-black in the pool. For some reason, he didn't think he was looking at Frank when the lights went out. It was hard to tell. The glare of the floodlights wiped out all the details when they were on. And when they were off, they made you blind.

Whoever controlled the light switch controlled the situation. Skully couldn't tell if the figure he saw at the door was male or female.

Someone shouted something that Skully couldn't hear and the lights went back on. The floodlights illuminated the entire pool area again, blinding Skully temporarily. The lights had only been off for a few minutes, but in that few minutes, something had happened.

When his eyes adjusted, he saw Brian at the bottom of the pool. He was alone and still.

"What the fuck?" Skully said in a hoarse whisper. "Did you see that? I don't believe it."

"Somebody drowned Brian," Renee said flatly. "Who was it?"

Skully and Renee looked at each other in astonishment.

"Was that Frank?" Skully asked. "I couldn't see. They turned off the fucking lights!"

"Who else would it be?"

Skully said, "Are you kidding me? This is insane. We come all the way out here to kill this guy, and somebody else beats us to it? I've never heard of such a thing. Exactly how many people wanted him dead? What are the odds?"

Skully began to laugh, quietly at first, until it became a phlegmy cough.

"The fucking nerve of those guys!"

Renee began to cry, tears trickled down her face, hesitantly at first, then with more gusto. Skully put his arms around her and pulled her close. She was trembling like a wet cat. He handed her a tissue.

"Why are you crying? Is it because Brian is dead, or is it because you didn't get to kill him?"

"I loved him. I earned the right."

"The politics of passion never made sense to me."

Renee sniffed and said, "I was ready, I was mentally prepared to do it. It took me all this time to get this close. Now it's been wrenched away from me."

Skully heard some noises coming from the house.

"Get out of sight! They're coming back!"

Suddenly, there was shouting at the back door and several people ran out.

Anna charged out of the house screaming, "There's something wrong with Brian!"

Running right behind her was Frank Thorogood, still in his bathing suit but now smoking a cigarette. Anna dove into the water and went directly to Brian's body in the deep end of the pool and started to pull him up. Frank tossed his cigarette aside and dove in to help her. But Brian was dead weight. In the water, he weighed a ton. They struggled together to get him out of the pool. Anna and Frank rolled him over and started pumping water out of him. Anna gave him mouth-to-mouth resuscitation. Brian's hand reached out and gripped her wrist.

"He's alive!" she shouted.

But Brian's lips were cold, and try as she may she couldn't get him to breathe. The tears streamed down her face as she desperately tried to breathe life into her man.

"Come on, Brian! Don't die! Hang on!"

But Brian would not take a breath. Frank and Anna were frantically trying everything to get Brian to breathe again, but nothing worked. They kept pounding his chest and pushing lungfuls of air down into his gullet, only to watch it dissipate in his unmoving throat. The hand that had gripped Anna a moment ago now fell limp.

Janet phoned for an ambulance. Brian wasn't moving anymore. His body was pale and unresponsive.

Anna kept trying to revive him. She rolled him on this side and that side, trying to expel water from his lungs. Nothing seemed to have any effect. It was if Brian had already left his body and didn't want to come back.

Anna became more desperate. "Come on, Brian! Breathe!"

She could visualize Brian's spirit hovering above the scene, looking down as they frantically tried to resuscitate him. She threw her hands into the sky and shouted into the night.

"Brian! Come back, damn you! It's not your time yet! Please, come back!"

Somewhere Brian heard her. Her voice seemed so far away. *Come back! Come back . . . Come back . . .*

But it was too late. He didn't want to come back. He'd had it with this world. Brian's soul hovered above them, watching the drama below, and then he was gone, instantly and permanently gone.

* * *

Clovis was only a half a mile from Cotchford Farm. He couldn't wait to see the look on Brian's face when he saw the console for the first time.

He's gonna flip!

Bobby sat in the cab next to him. "I've got a bad feeling about Brian. That's why I came back tonight."

"You mean like Erlene's visions?"

"No, I don't really know how to describe it. It's just a premonition, I guess. He was going to sack Frank and the others today, I thought maybe that might cause trouble. I didn't like him being alone with Frank and those goons."

"Good point. Was he really gonna sack 'em all by himself? That doesn't sound like Brian."

"He told me he had to face up to it."

"Maybe he's beginning to see the light."

From somewhere behind him, an ambulance wailed. The flashing lights were a mile behind and coming fast. In a few racing heartbeats, the ambulance was right behind Clovis, blinding him with flashing red lights and a siren that made the hairs on the back of his neck rise.

The ambulance filled the night with lights and noise. Clovis eased the big truck over to the side of the road so the ambulance could pass. It hurried on ahead, disappearing between the trees, lights flickering on and off.

"Somebody's not having a good night," Clovis said. "I wonder who it is?"

"God bless 'em, whoever they are," Bobby whispered.

As they came around the final turn, Bobby was shocked to

see that the ambulance had turned into Cotchford Farm's driveway. Alarms began going off in his head. Somehow, someway, at that exact moment, Bobby knew who the ambulance was for. He should've known it all along. There was only one answer.

Oh no! Oh please! God no! Don't let it be that!

"Uh-oh," Bobby said. "It's Cotchford."

For a moment, Bobby thought his mind was playing crazy tricks on him. They brought the delivery truck to a halt and got out and ran to the house just as they were wheeling Brian out on a gurney. He had a sheet over his head. Bobby knew who it was without looking.

"Oh, shit!"

"Is it . . . ?" Clovis asked.

Anna nodded slowly, tears streaming down her face.

The ambulance attendants wheeled Brian across the lawn where the pieces of the white picket fence were still piled up. They slid Brian's gurney into the ambulance. The lights and siren went back on and in a moment it disappeared back up the driveway. They took Brian's body and just like that, he was gone. Gone from this earth.

Brian Jones was dead. Bobby felt numb. Clovis tried to hold back the tears.

Bobby felt wracked with guilt. *Oh God, I left him alone. We were never supposed to leave him alone. Erlene warned us.*

As Bruce Spangler passed Cotchford Farm, he saw the ambulance lights flashing in the driveway. He told the driver to keep going. A chill went down his back.

If anything happened to Brian, I'm a dead man.

Renee and Skully were back in London a few hours later, checking out of their hotel. They looked like any young couple now as they chartered a cab for the airport. They passed the newsstand, and the headlines of every paper were the same, in as big a type as possible: BRIAN JONES DEAD! they screamed the shocking banner in every language. *BRIAN JONES MORT! BRIAN JONES IST TOT! ¡BRIAN JONES MUERTOS!*

The cops called it "Death by Misadventure." No one seemed to know anything remotely close to the truth. The police made it seem like a simple drug and booze overdose. These rock stars did it all the time, didn't they? There was no mention of Frank Thorogood. According to all reports, Brian simply drowned in his pool. He took too many drugs and passed out in the water. Simple as that.

Skully said, "The lights go off, he's alive, the lights go back on, he's dead. It's like a cheap paperback murder mystery."

"Can you believe it?"

"I swear, in all my years, I never heard of anything like that. How many people do you think were trying to kill him?"

"Apparently, more than we thought."

Erlene awoke from a nightmare in her bedroom in London. She screamed and the lights went on. Cricket was beside her in a flash.

"What's wrong, hon?"

"Am I awake? Or is this a dream?"

"You're awake."

"Can I have a sip of water?"

Cricket handed her a glass and she sipped. She took a deep breath. Lately, her pregnancy had sparked vivid psychic visions, especially at night. Her dreams were haunted by disturbing images of Brian Jones. She felt linked to Brian through the mirror.

"We have to call Clovis."

"Now?"

"Yes, right now. I think something terrible has happened."

Bobby and Clovis spent a sleepless night at Cotchford Farm. In the morning, there were still police sniffing around the garden and pool area. Frank Thorogood was still around, too, making statements to the press and posing for pictures.

"Why are you still here? Get your shit and get out!" Clovis shouted. "You have no legal right to be here anymore, Frank!"

Frank glared at them. He said nothing. They went into the house. Frank continued loading moving boxes into his car.

They huddled together in the center of the room, some quietly sobbing, others brooding, some angry.

Clovis pulled Bobby aside. He dropped his voice. "If there's money in this house, we gotta get it before Frank finds it. He's probably been searching all night right under our noses."

"Shit!"

"Brian never told me where it was. Did he ever tell you?"

"No. How much do you think?"

Clovis whispered. "He told me it was over a hundred grand in cash in American dollars, English pounds, and Swiss francs."

Dust Bin Bob whistled low. "A hundred? That's a lot of jack."

They looked around and saw several places where Frank had already pried panels loose from the wall. Anywhere he thought there would be room to hide the cash he searched. He wasn't very careful about putting things back. It was obvious he'd been looking.

"I thought he was packing all night."

As Frank finished loading the last of his personal items into his car, Bobby went after him.

"See here, sir. Any money you find in this house is the property of Brian Jones's estate. You must report it to the police."

"Piss off," Frank said.

Bobby knew there were a few thousand pounds at the very least in Brian's bedroom in plain view. In true rock-star style, Brian slept with piles of money around him. If he had to pay for something, he loved to lay in bed and count out the bills in cash. That money magically disappeared after the ambulance left, and Bobby was pretty sure of where it went.

As soon as Frank drove away, Bobby called the police and suggested they search Frank's car. They stopped him within ten miles. They didn't find a huge stash of money; only a few thousand English pounds that Frank claimed were his.

Frank was the last person to see Brian alive. That officially made him a suspect in the eyes of the police. The cops treated him as such.

Bobby brought their little group into the studio to view the mirror-gazing photographs he'd shot in Morocco.

"I thought we should look at these all together."

He passed them around. Erlene stared at them all, one by

one, until she came to last picture of Brian. Tears welled up in her eyes.

"You know these visions I've been having? I don't think they're coming from me."

"What do you mean?"

Erlene pointed to her swollen belly. "I think they're coming from in here."

"You think the baby is psychic?"

She nodded. "I never had such powerful visions before I was pregnant."

"But how could the baby know anything about Brian? It hasn't been born yet."

"It knew enough to warn us to never leave him alone. Eleanor Rigby and Claudine Jillian were trying to warn him, too. Somehow they all knew Brian. Somehow they all loved him."

Cricket said, "I get the feeling that Brian has loved and been loved by lots of women going back many lifetimes."

Erlene grabbed Clovis's hand. She bent over and gasped.

"Ahh!" she screamed. Suddenly, the floor beneath her was wet.

"What is it?"

"My water just broke!"

Clovis turned a whiter shade of pale.

"Oh my God! She's having the baby!"

Cricket said, "Get in the car, and we'll drive you to the hospital!"

Erlene shook her head. Her words were coming in short phrases now, in between the bursts of breathlessness.

"No time . . . for that now. We're going to have to . . . do it right here. I can feel it coming."

For the second time in two days, an ambulance was dispatched to Cotchford Farm. Only this time it was for the opposite reason. Life, not death, was in the air tonight. Cricket called while Clovis made Erlene comfortable.

"Boil some water," Bobby told Clovis.

"They always say that in the movies when there's a baby coming; boil some water. Why?"

Bobby laughed. "To make tea, of course."

The ambulance arrived in ten minutes, and the emergency medical workers delivered the baby shortly thereafter. Clovis and Erlene were the parents of a healthy young baby boy.

Erlene held the baby in her arms and smiled.

"What should we name him?"

"How about Brian?"

"How about not Brian?"

"As in Not-Brian-Jones Hicks?"

Erlene shook her head.

"That's not what I meant and you know it. This baby's gonna have a great Hicks name like his daddy. Clovis Junior."

Clovis wanted to hold the baby. He scooped him up out of Erlene's arms every chance he got. Each time, she insisted he give him back after a few minutes. This continued until feeding time. When it was over and Clovis Junior was dozing contentedly, Erlene said, "Would you bring me the mirror-gazing pictures, hon? I want to see something."

Clovis quickly retrieved them and handed them to Erlene.

Erlene studied them carefully.

She rubbed her fingertips and touched the photo of Brian again. She closed her eyes.

“Now I understand. He wasn’t flying. He was floating. This is from the bottom of the pool looking up. See? We all thought he was flying, but he wasn’t. He was floating facedown in the pool. It was the dead man’s float.”

Erlene opened her eyes again.

“That’s what the spirits in the looking glass were trying to tell us. They were trying to warn Brian.”

Dust Bin Bob said, “You can’t save a man from himself.”

Erlene held her new baby. She spoke softly. “I think Brian knew his fate all along. I think he knew, deep in his heart, that it was inevitable.”

Clovis said, “He was right about one thing.”

“What was that?”

“Just before he died, he told me that he wanted to spend the rest of his life here at Cotchford Farm. He wanted to die here. And he did.”

EPILOGUE

Brian Jones was laid to rest in his childhood home of Cheltenham. It was the biggest funeral the town had ever seen. The only Rolling Stones in attendance were Bill and Charlie.

The Stones went ahead with their plans for a huge free concert in Hyde Park a few days after Brian's death, except now it was a memorial concert for their fallen guitarist. Twenty-year-old guitar phenomenon Mick Taylor from John Mayall's Bluesbreakers replaced Brian in the Stones. Brian had planned on attending the Hyde Park gig with Anna to show there were no hard feelings between him and the band. He wanted to wish them luck.

The next day, Mick Jagger and Marianne Faithfull left for Australia to film the movie *Ned Kelly*. During that trip, Marianne would suffer a nervous breakdown and attempt suicide.

Keith Richards and Anita Pallenberg had two children together but never married. They stayed together until 1980.

In a deathbed confession, Frank Thorogood supposedly admitted killing Brian Jones. The mystery continues to this day. I suspect we will never know what really happened at Cotchford Farm.

Ironically, Dust Bin Bob noticed the date of Brian's demise was exactly three years and a day from the date he had saved the Beatles from an assassination attempt by his brother, Clive, in Manila. This time, he wasn't there to save the day. Brian's fate had been sealed.

During the next two years, rock and roll would lose Jimi Hendrix, Janis Joplin, and Jim Morrison.

And, of course, we all know what happened to the Stones. When Brian predicted they would go on for another fifty years without him, he was prophetic. The greatest rock and roll band in the world keeps rolling on. Ronnie Wood eventually replaced Mick Taylor and the band got even bigger. They survived the loss of Brian Jones just like they survived everything else.

ACKNOWLEDGMENTS

Thanks to Judy Coppage and Michael Rose at the Coppage Company. Special thanks to my longtime manager, Joel Turtle. Thanks to Skyler Turtle for everything he does to keep my career moving forward. Thanks to Pete Heyrman, editor at Bear Press. Of course, once again, thanks to my wonderful wife, Jay, who puts up with me and whose kisses are still as sweet as honey. Thanks to Joel Harris. I also want to thank the Greg Kihn Band, and all the musicians I've had the pleasure of playing with over the years.

And thanks to you, my extraordinary fans.

CPSIA information can be obtained at www.ICGtesting.com
Printed in the USA
BVOW05s1637030515

398756BV00001B/7/P